ACROSS THE GREAT RIFT

BY
SCOTT WASHBURN

Cover image by

Winged Hussar Publishing, LLC, 1525 Hulse Road, Unit 1, Point Pleasant, NJ 08742

This edition published in 2016 Copyright ©Winged Hussar Publishing, LLC

ISBN 978-1-9454303-1-2
LOC 2016921579
Bibliographical references and index
1.Science Fiction. 2. Alien Worlds. 3. Action & Adventure

Winged Hussar Publishing, LLC All rights reserved

For more information on Winged Hussar Publishing, LLC, visit us at:
https://www.WingedHussarPublishing.com

Across the Great Rift

Chapter One

All through her training, Carlina had been amazed at how easy it was to kill a person. There were so many places where even a modest amount of force applied in just the right fashion would cause fatal damage. Now that she had actually done it, she was relieved to discover that it had been just like training—easier, really, since she had no instructor hovering close by to criticize her technique. Of course, it was fortunate that she had chosen Petty Officer Jerrin Eastman for her first victim. The man was a jackass and had rubbed her the wrong way from her first day aboard Exeter. He seemed to think because he was related—very distantly—to Lord Allendale that she should have strained a muscle hopping into his bunk. So now, when it was time to act, it had been no problem at all tempting him into this bunk—or to kill him. It was just a matter of waiting until he was in the proper position and then a quick blow had crushed his larynx. He'd choked to death in just a few moments and she'd only had to restrain his first panicked thrashings. She had found no pleasure in doing it—not really—but she'd had no real qualms, either.

She wasn't sure the rest would be quite so easy.

She carefully disentangled herself from his arms and legs and then began to get dressed. The bunk space just off the bridge was for the use of the captain or the senior watch officers, but it was still about the size of a closet. She banged against the bulkhead several times before the task was done. She turned to open the hatch and then hesitated. Fear rose up in her and she pushed it back down with some difficulty. She'd been trained—very carefully and thoroughly trained—but she had never actually done anything like this before. Her instructors were now an impossible distance away and she was utterly alone, completely surrounded by enemies. She shut her eyes, clenched her fists and breathed deeply for a moment until the panic was gone. She had a job to do and she would do it.

Carlina quickly opened the hatch, slipped through, and closed it again. She glanced around the bridge and was relieved that Sharon Detweiler was still the only one there. The ten-man caretaker crew on Exeter was divided into three three-man watches, plus Lieutenant Hadley, the officer of the watch. No one else should have come wandering in here. But occasionally, Hadley would come by at random times and any of the others might drop by to chat just out of boredom. But no one else had, and now she was alone with Detweiler.

"Well, that didn't take long," said Sharon. "Although you certainly made enough noise in there. Jerrin wear himself out in one mad rush after you put him off for so long?"

Carlina froze for an instant. Apparently Eastman's death-throes had been more noticeable than she'd thought. Fortunately, Sharon had interpreted them as an entirely different biological event.

"He's finished now."

Sharon laughed and turned back to stare at the main viewscreen. Carlina walked slowly over to her own communications station and picked the stylus off her input board. It was a featureless, pointed metal rod eighteen centimeters long and a centimeter thick. She walked back over to stand behind Sharon's chair. Her heart was pounding. She'd liked Sharon, damn it. But it should be painless this way…

As Sharon Detweiler turned her head slightly to look back at her, Carlina rammed the pointed end of the stylus into her neck just below the base of the skull. The woman jerked once convulsively and then collapsed out of her chair onto the deck. Her eyes were wide open and an expression of surprise filled her face. Carlina clutched the chair to steady herself. The bridge seemed to be spinning slightly.

Two down, seven to go. Seven, seven, seven, Lucky seven. Six-five-four, three-two-one, who's the next lucky son-of-a-gun? Carlina was breathing hard, her hands trembling and her mind running in circles. Training, she had to remember her training. This was important, incredibly important. She could not turn back or fail now. Gasping, she braced herself on the control console and looked out the viewport at the Rift Fleet.

Thirty or forty ships were plainly visible, all very close and all linked together by a rigid framework of girders. They hung, seemingly motionless, against the unchanging backdrop of hyperspace. Another fifty or sixty were not in view, but they were there with all the rest. Ninety-eight ships in total, thirty of them Protectorate warships—and at this moment, there were only eight people awake aboard the entire armada.

Shortly, there would only be one.

Carlina went to work.

* * * * *

"Shit," groaned Charles Crawford, "time to get up already? Hell, it's only been ten years. I need a solid twelve or I'm cranky for the next century." He knew that no one could hear his witticism, but he said it anyway. He lay with his eyes closed, floating gently in the zero gravity. Part of him very much wanted to go back to sleep, but the drugs coursing through him would not allow that. Besides, he was getting cold. A chilly draft was brushing his bare flesh and it was getting uncomfortable.

With considerable effort he opened his eyes and then squinted against the faint light in the cold-sleep compartment. He slowly began to flex his muscles as he had been instructed to. He'd never been in cold-sleep before and the sensations were weird. Not quite like waking up from a normal sleep, not quite like restoring circulation to an arm or a leg. Something different.

After ten minutes it seemed as though he could control his movements adequately and he was becoming pretty chilled by that time. He brought up his hands and carefully began detaching the monitoring patches, the restraints, and the IV insert. He'd spent half his adult life in one zero-G construction site or another so the free fall seemed entirely natural. Finished, he slid himself out of the capsule and opened the small locker next to it. His underwear, coveralls, socks, and shoes were all right where he had left them ten years before. He quickly dressed and tried to stop shivering. The temperature in the compartment was pretty low and it was probably that way through the whole massive bulk of the construction vessel *Neshaminy*. He'd have to go back to his cabin and get warmer clothes.

After he got some coffee in him.

He moved past the other capsules toward the exit. There were rows and rows of them, almost filling the large compartment; hundreds of capsules. He instinctively glanced at the ones he passed, looking at the faces of the people within and checking the status monitors. They were all part of his construction crew and he'd known most of them for years—they were like family. An ugly lot without their clothes, that was for sure, but damn fine men all the same. There were plenty of damn fine women working for him, too, but they were all over in their own section. He was tempted to check on them as well, but there were security cameras watching all the cold-sleep compartments and sure as shooting, someone would claim he was only there to ogle them without their clothes and file a harassment grievance with the Guild. Better leave it to the machines. Hell, he was probably going to get in trouble for waking himself up early as it was, he didn't need any more problems heaped on top of that.

He went through the hatch and floated down a corridor toward the galley. Before he went into cold-sleep he'd made sure that the coffee and the coffee maker were where he could find them when he woke up. They were exactly where they had been ten years ago and shortly he had a huge zero-G bulb of evil black brew cradled in his hands. As he sucked in both the flavor and the warmth, he let out a sigh of contentment. Just the thing to wake up to after a ten year nap. He moved out of the galley and into the crew lounge. He flipped the switch controlling the viewport shutter and watched as it slid up.

The Rift Fleet was still there. Good.

For a few minutes he just stared at the immensity of it. During the months that it had taken to assemble—literally assemble—the Rift Fleet, Crawford had been so busy making sure his construction team was ready, he'd had precious little time to stand back and really look at the marvelous thing that was being created:

An expedition to cross the Great Rift.

The audacity of it was still a bit daunting. Long ago, when Mankind had first ventured out among the stars, it was natural that the explorers would travel to the systems that were closest. The disappointing realization that only one world in a million was Earth-like and that easily terraformable worlds were only slightly more common had forced the pioneers to travel farther and farther to find places worth going. But even when the distances from Old Earth became truly enormous, it still made the most sense to stay inside the Orion Arm where the stars were densely packed. The relatively empty gaps which separated them from the Perseus and Sagittarius Arms were uninviting and remained largely unexplored. Mankind expanded along the Orion Arm in both directions, both spinward and anti-spinward as directions were reckoned, but made no attempt to cross the thousand-parsec wide rifts.

Until recently.

The story of the Orion Arm was as confused and as complicated as any similar stretch of human history. The rise and glory of the United Worlds, its decline and destruction; civil war, crusade, jihad, genocide, and chaos. They were all there and the full story was lost along with so much else. But Mankind had pulled itself up as it always had and new empires had arisen. Smaller and weaker empires than before, to be sure, but with all the old ambitions to expand. The empires near the unexplored frontiers of the Orion Arm could satisfy those ambitions peacefully if they desired, but those that grew up in the center, amidst the rubble of the former civilization, did not have that option. They could only expand at the expense of their neighbors...

...or by crossing the Rift.

Naturally, most tried the former option first. It was easier and the methods were all too well understood. Wars had raged, borders shifted, planets changed hands, empires were destroyed and created and destroyed again; but in the last few hundred years, the borders had remained nearly stable and looked to stay that way. Eyes had started turning toward the Rift and the virgin stars which lay beyond.

The Petrunans had been the first to cross. Their territory lay on the edge of the rimward rift that led to the Perseus Arm and they were completely hemmed in on the coreward side by the much larger Hebyrnan Hegemony. The Petrunans had also had the advantage of two well-placed star clusters to act as way stations across the Rift, and a few daring expeditions had finally made it across about seventy years ago. Their initial reports had been encouraging: habitable and terraformable planets in about the same proportions as in the Orion Arm, fissionables in the expected amounts, and, most importantly, no prior owners. Electromagnetic scans from across the Rift, made centuries earlier, had detected signals which *might* have been of intelligent origin and considering those signals were at least four thousand years old by the time they arrived, the prospect of running into an advanced civilization had been a major worry. But the Petrunans had found no evidence of any such thing, so either the early scans had been in error, or any mythical aliens had packed up and left.

Getting across had been a great accomplishment but would have been nothing more than an interesting stunt if it had not been for some simultaneous advances in gate technology. The transport gates, which allowed instantaneous transit between star systems, had been what allowed the ancient United Worlds to exist. They were also instrumental in the rise of the newer empires. Starships were simply too slow to bind together any large political unit, but the gates provided lines of communication, commerce, and military movement that made them possible. Unfortunately, their range had always been limited to a few hundred light years—not nearly long enough to jump the thousand parsec-wide Rift.

Petrunan scientists had solved that problem, or at least partly solved it. They had developed gates which could make the jump to those handy star clusters and then from cluster to cluster until they could reach the far side. Without the gates, the trip across the Rift was hardly worth the effort. Nothing, no matter how valuable, could be economically transported across the Rift by starship. No colony established there could ever return anything to the mother country, neither resources nor military strength. And few colonists would be interested in making such a journey in the first place.

But with a gate in place, things were different.

The gates made a journey across the Great Rift no harder than jumping from system to system within the Orion Arm. Colonists could go out and bring back fissionables and anything else of value that might be found. Colonies could be tied into the commercial and military systems of the parent easily. With gates, the Perseus Arm was there to explore and exploit. And Charles Crawford had come here to build a gate; the largest and most powerful gate ever constructed.

He had a faint memory of a dream—could you dream in cold-sleep?—that when he woke up the Rift Fleet would be gone. Everyone on *Neshaminy* was gone, too. He was alone on a huge ship drifting through hyperspace. Some people would have considered that to be a nightmare, but it was only slightly disturbing to Crawford, and only disturbing because of how much more difficult it would be to get the job done without all the ships and the people. And he *would* get the job done if he had to do it alone.

He had no trouble at all with solitude. He liked being alone. People made him nervous in any non-work situation. Give him a job to do and he could command and direct a thousand workers to get it done without any qualm. Stick him in some goddamned cocktail party and ask him to socialize and he'd be ready to dive out the nearest airlock—with or without a vac suit.

So right now he was alone. He knew that there would be a skeleton watch on one of the warships keeping an eye out in the extremely unlikely event of any trouble, but hopefully they didn't know about him. In slightly less than two weeks the computers would realize that the long journey was nearly at an end and start waking everyone up. The ships' reactors would power up, the life support systems would go to normal, the artificial gravity would come on, and Crawford would not be alone anymore. *Neshaminy*'s skipper would probably be pissed as hell that Crawford had overridden the computer commands and awakened early, but there would be nothing he could do about it then.

In truth, there was no harm in it that Crawford could see. He had calculated that if he left the hatches open, there was more than enough air in the huge ship to keep him breathing without turning on the life support systems. By leaving off the artificial gravity, the amount of battery power he'd use to cook his meals and run his computer would be trivial and he'd use the toilet and shower on one of the shuttles to avoid having to use the main recyclers. No, there was no real harm in this and he intended to savor the next two weeks to the fullest.

Two entire weeks to study the construction documents and plan out his operation. Two weeks without an endless stream of people demanding he answer their questions and fix their problems — right then and there! Of course, he knew the plans nearly by heart and the entire construction schedule was laid out in precise detail, but he still wanted to go over it again. This was the biggest job he had ever been in charge of and the most important by several orders of magnitude. It would be the crowning triumph in a long, successful career. Hell, he might even wangle a knighthood out of this — and oh, the opportunities *that* would open up! He was determined to keep the screw-ups to a minimum.

He finished the coffee, washed out the bulb, and returned it to its holder in the galley. Then he propelled himself along corridors and through hatches to his quarters. These were standard shipboard accommodations which he had done little to personalize before departure; just a place to sleep and store his modest belongings. He got out fresh (and warmer) clothes and then went to the shuttle bay. He picked one of the bigger ones, went aboard to use the toilet and shower, shave off the equivalent of three weeks of beard, and dress again. Then it was off to his office, a much larger and far more personalized space than his quarters. He fired up his computer, activated the wall-sized schematics display, and went to work.

* * * * *

A red warning light began to flash on the control panel and a piercing alarm began to shriek as the computer detected a catastrophic systems failure. With a snarl, Carlina slammed shut the visor on her vac-suit to keep out the noise. It could not keep it all out, but muffled it to a tolerable level.

Nearly tolerable.

It had seemed entirely tolerable two weeks ago when she'd started this. At first she had not bothered with the suit. The noise had been annoying, but nothing more. After a few days, however, she started wearing the suit to block it out. Now it seemed she could hear that same cursed electronic wail even when she was locked away in a quiet spot. It seemed like she could hear it in her dreams. Maybe it would never go away…

"Stop that. This is your job. Do it," she said aloud. She was talking to herself a lot now. "This is the last one. The last one! Finish this and you'll never have to do it again. Never, ever."

Killing her remaining 'comrades' on *Exeter* had been hard. Not difficult, they had suspected nothing and even without regular weapons it had not been difficult—just hard. Somehow this was even worse.

She finished her sabotage on this bank of capsules and awkwardly pushed herself on to the next. The artificial gravity was switched off to save power and she did not like free fall. Fortunately, there weren't too many more. This was a destroyer and there weren't many capsules here. She'd started with the battleships and worked her way down. She'd needed an entire day for each of the capital ships, but the destroyers only took a few hours.

Two weeks. Two weeks working twenty-hour days and she was nearly done. Of course, then she would have to start on the cargo ships and the transports, but that would be so much easier. She had the computer codes for them and she could do a whole ship in just a few minutes. It would be so much easier—in so many ways. She sincerely wished she'd had the codes for the warships, too, but she was just a communications tech and had no access to them.

She reached the next row of capsules, got out a power wrench, and took off the cover to the feeds. She used her cutter to slice through cables and tubing. Sparks flew and vapor gushed out. This was the brute force approach and she ruthlessly sliced through things until a new bank of red lights were flashing and another alarm added to the noise trying to claw its way inside her skull.

"Nearly done, nearly done."

* * * * *

It was a faint thump that alerted him. It took a few moments for the tiny sound to register, but when it did, he froze in place and listened intently. Another small noise came, partly as sound, partly as a vibration through the ship. Charles Crawford was alone. There was no one else awake; none of the major machinery was running. There was absolutely nothing which should have made a noise like that. It had been four days since he awakened from cold-sleep and he had become acutely aware of the utter silence in the huge ship. But now there was a noise.

In space, that generally meant trouble.

The problem was to find out what sort of trouble. They were coasting in hyperspace; there was no acceleration to throw off any bit of debris from another ship, which might have banged against *Neshaminy*, and the strange realm of hyperspace was utterly devoid of matter so nothing could have come from there. A few ship systems were in operation, but which ones? What might have made that thump and was it something serious? The engineer in him would not allow it to be ignored. He unstrapped from his seat and pushed himself out of his office. The best place to find answers would be the bridge.

Neshaminy was a big ship, but the bulk of her inhabited spaces were forward so it did not take long for him to reach the bridge. He had looked things over there for several hours two days ago, partly out of real interest, but mostly because the captain had been such a jerk about letting 'unauthorized personnel' aboard the bridge of *his* ship. Hah, Crawford probably knew the layout of the control panels better than the old bastard did now. He immediately went to the engineering station to see if there were any alarms showing. Nothing looked out of order. He moved to the other consoles. Communications, nothing, navigation, nothing, he checked each in turn but everything appeared to be working perfectly.

Puzzled, he floated back and looked at the large, master status board. It was a diagrammatic layout of the ship. It showed the status of each hatch and airlock and would display any unusual loss of pressure, which a hull breach would cause. It did not show a lot of detail, but it might give him a clue. When it came to diagrams and plans, Crawford had a near-photographic memory. Any change from the last time he had looked at this would jump right out at him. He quickly found four hatches which he remembered that he had opened in the last two days...wait a minute, what was that? Another hatch had been open and he was quite sure he had not done it. It was right next to the access port for the intra-ship shuttle cars. Prior to setting out on this journey, all the ships of the fleet had been locked into a huge framework of girders. They would ensure that the ships did not wander out of formation, and they would provide the main structural members for the gate itself when they arrived. A system of small personnel pods ran along the girders and allowed people to move from ship to ship without resorting to shuttles or space suits. He looked closer and saw that there was one more pod stopped at *Neshaminy* than there had been before.

Someone was on the ship.

That was odd. It could only be one of the navy-types from the ship which was on watch. The briefings they had gotten before departure had not indicated there would be any in-person inspections made during the trip. Could they have detected that something was wrong over here? A wave of pre-embarrassment coursed through him like a mild electric shock. What if they had detected *him*? Maybe the increase in power or oxygen consumption, minute though it was, had shown up on their boards and they had sent someone over to check it out. Great, he could browbeat the skipper of this ship, but those Navy bastards were a whole different story. Especially since the Protector had nationalized all the provincial fleets. Shit. They'd probably blow a gasket and it would take a week to straighten things out.

Oh well, there was nothing for it. Crawford was not one to try and evade blame. He went over to the monitor displaying the order status and scrolled back until he found the name of the ship which currently had the watch. With each ship having a three-month tour it was a pretty long list after ten years. Here it was: *Exeter*, heavy cruiser, scheduled watch officer, Lieutenant Hadley. He sighed; better contact them and have them warn their boarding party that he was here—wouldn't want to give the poor swabs a heart attack.

"Caught playing hooky, Chuck, old boy, time to face the music."

He went over to the communications console and punched in the code to contact *Exeter*. No answer. He tried it again. Nothing. Strange, there should be someone on the bridge over there—that was the whole point. No answer. He checked the code, rechecked the ship and tried again. Still nothing. Now *that* was odd—unless there was something wrong with the com circuits on *Neshaminy*. Maybe that's what caught their attention: a loss of signal.

He better go talk to them. Clearly they weren't coming to the bridge or they would have been here by now. Probably down in engineering somewhere. He went back to the status board to see if any new hatches were open. He could track them that way. He stared for a minute and then spotted a hatch which was newly opened.

It was to the control room for the cold-sleep capsules.

He grimaced. He should have guessed there would be some remote monitoring on the capsules. They had probably noticed that there was one less occupant than there was supposed to be and sent someone over to check it out. Or at least he hoped so. The only other reason would be if there was something else wrong down there. A new bit of panic hit him. Hell, those were mostly his people. He twisted around and flew off the bridge.

It only took about two minutes to get there, but that was all it took to create a dozen nightmare scenarios in his head about how he could have inadvertently screwed up the cold-sleep system with his unscheduled wake-up and killed all his people. He slowed as he reached the control room. He didn't want to come barging in on them unannounced—after all, they might be armed and twitchy.

Yes, the hatch to the control room was open. He moved forward slowly and caught sight of someone at one of the consoles: a young woman in utility coveralls, the insignia of a middle-grade enlisted person on her shoulder. She was rather cute from what he could see of her. A pleasantly shaped face with an interesting nose—he liked interesting noses on women—and a nice figure under the coveralls.

But she seemed to be alone. And she was filthy. Dirt on her clothes, face, and hands. Her short blonde hair did not drift around in the zero-G like it normally would. It was so matted with dirt and sweat it just stayed in one lump. Crawford was an engineer and in his orderly mind there had to be a reason for everything—and he could think of no reason which would explain what he was seeing. The Navy was not obsessively spit and polish but there was no way this woman's superior was going to let her wander around looking like this unless there was something seriously wrong.

The woman was working on the controls for the cold-sleep capsules, typing in commands. Why? Was something wrong with them? Hell, speculation was getting him nowhere. There was one easy way to find out. He pushed himself a little further until he had a clear line of sight with the woman, but he stayed a good five meters away in hopes of not scaring her *completely* to death.

"Uh, miss…?" he said.

He'd expected to startle her, but her reaction exceeded anything he was prepared for. She screamed like she'd seen—what? A ghost? No, more like a hundred ghosts. She gave off a piercing shriek and flung herself away from him toward the opposite end of the compartment. She bounced off the bulkhead and grabbed a handhold to keep from rebounding back at him. Her pale blue eyes were nearly swallowed by the exposed whites. A look of sheer terror was on her face and she gasped for breath.

"Hey! Hey, it's all right! I won't hurt you. Calm down!" He came a little closer and stared at the woman. What was wrong with her? There were incredibly dark circles under her eyes and her face was gaunt. He recognized the signs of someone who had been running on nothing but stimulants for far too long. What the hell was going on?

"M-Maker!" she croaked after a moment. "Who are you? What are you doing here?"

"Sorry I startled you. I'm Charles Crawford, the construction manager for the Gate Project. I'm an early riser. Now, maybe I should ask who you are and what you are doing here?" He moved toward the control console she had been working on. "Is there something wrong with the cold-sleep capsules?"

"Stay away from that!"

"I'm not going to do anything," he said soothingly. "Why are you over here? Is there something wrong with the capsules?" he asked again. "Those are my friends in there and I'm a little concerned about what's happening."

The woman, instead of calming down, was looking even more agitated. She crouched back against the bulkhead like she was preparing to...

She sprang at him.

He could scarcely believe it, but she gave a shout and flung herself across the compartment, reversed herself in mid-air, and threw a murderous kick right at his head. He flung up his left arm to block it and succeeded, but a searing pain shot up to his shoulder at the blow. The impact sent him tumbling out the hatch into the larger capsule bay.

"Hey! Stop! What the hell are you doing?" he cried. He couldn't move his left arm at all, but he grabbed a handhold with his right and steadied himself. The woman had bounced off him and was now tumbling helplessly a few meters away. Despite the effectiveness of her first attack, she didn't seem very skilled in free fall—for which Crawford was very grateful. All too soon she reached a handhold and oriented herself for another attack. Crawford was ready, but he knew he couldn't hope to fight this woman. Not with a banged up arm and probably not even with two good ones. He was from a high-gravity world and probably far stronger than his opponent, but he had not been in a real fight in twenty years, while she clearly knew some martial arts. His only hope was to avoid her.

She lunged and came flying at him. He pushed off at right angles and dodged aside. His arm screamed at him; was it broken? He sailed a dozen meters across the bay and easily slowed himself with his legs and grabbed a stanchion. The woman slammed into the spot he had just been with a satisfying grunt of pain. No, she was not skilled in zero-G combat.

"Lady, what the hell is your problem? If you do this to people who get up early, what do you do to ones who oversleep?"

She didn't answer. She just got ready to come at him again. She sprang and he dodged. She missed him but recovered quicker and lunged again almost immediately. Again he managed to avoid her attack, but it was close—and she kept after him as he bounced from spot to spot in the capsule bay. After a few minutes, the woman paused to catch her breath and Crawford did the same. His arm was in agony and he was covered in sweat. He couldn't keep this up much longer. He had to either get away—or put this madwoman out of commission. She was between him and the passage that led back to the bridge and the habitable parts of the ship. He couldn't risk going that way. The only other exit from the cold-sleep chamber led aft to where the construction equipment was stored.

The construction equipment...yeah...

Without waiting for the woman to move again, he turned and dove completely across the compartment toward the other hatch. He heard a curse from behind him but did not look back. He twisted around to come in feet first and let his legs absorb his momentum. He slapped the entry button next to the door and while it was sliding open risked taking a look behind. The woman had misjudged her jump and was just thudding to a halt on the bulkhead five or six meters away. She immediately flung herself at him. Crawford moved partway through the hatch but then turned and kicked at the woman as she flew toward him. It wasn't much of a kick, but it took her by surprise and she was knocked away from the bulkhead and floundered back out into the capsule bay. Crawford pulled himself through the hatch and shut it behind him.

He looked at the controls and cursed. There was no way to lock it from here. She'd just follow him through in a moment. He turned again and launched himself down the passageway to the next hatch. As he reached it and pushed the entry button, he heard the hatch behind him sliding open.

* * * * *

Carlina scrambled through the hatch in time to see the next one, about twenty meters away, slide shut. She swore. Damn the man! Would he never stop running? She still could not believe this was happening. What in all the hells was he doing awake? It was still over a week until the fleet was supposed to start waking up.

She hauled herself along the passage to the next hatch and waited, gasping, while it opened. She had to catch this guy. There was no telling how much trouble he might make if she just let him go. It had been stupid to attack him right off the way she had, she realized that now. But he had literally scared her out of her wits. She should have talked to him, gotten close—and then killed him. Air out the lock, now. She'd just have to catch him—and kill him.

She moved through the hatch and then froze.

"Shit!"

She was in a huge compartment filled with all manner of construction gear and the man was nowhere in sight. He could be hidden anywhere. She did not have time for this. She had another twenty ships to visit and she simply could not waste a minute searching for one lone insomniac. But she had no choice.

"Hey! Mister! Come back! I'm sorry about this. You scared me there and I acted stupidly. I don't mean you any harm. Come out and we'll talk." Her voice echoed through the large space, but when the echoes died, there was no answer. Damn. She had hurt him and now he wasn't going to trust her. So that meant she had to find him. She shut the hatch behind her, but there was no way to lock it. She had to make sure he didn't get past her again. She moved carefully forward and began her search.

It was dark, only a few lights shown around the edges of the huge space. It was cold, too. Above freezing, but not by much. As the sweat evaporated on her skin she found herself shivering. The place smelled of lubricants and synthetics. Large dark shapes loomed all around her. Carlina didn't like this at all. Where was that bastard?

A sound came to her from off to the left and she spun around. Nothing. She stopped and listened, but all she could hear was her own breathing and the blood pounding in her ears. Calm down. Damn, she wished she was armed, but the weapons locker back on *Exeter* required codes she didn't have — and she never imagined she would need a gun anyway.

She glanced around and saw a locker attached to the side of a large machine. It wasn't locked and inside she found a long metal object which might have been some sort of wrench. She hefted it and felt a little better. One good whack from this and her problems would be over. She guided herself deeper into the compartment.

Was he hiding — or waiting in ambush? It looked as though he was hurt pretty badly from her first attack, so maybe he was just trying to hide. If that was so, then all she had to do was keep looking. Otherwise...

Another noise. It sounded like a hatch closing. She quickly looked behind her and she could see the hatch she had come though. It was still closed. Another hatch, but where? It sounded like it was from up ahead. She moved carefully, but more quickly. She reached a long row of smaller machines; some sort of EVA pods, she guessed. Where was...*there!*

At the far end of the compartment was an elevated room with a large window. The glow from unseen control consoles was reflecting off her quarry's face. He was looking down, not at her. Very good, she had him. She saw the door to the room and there was no way he was going to evade her again — if she could just get a little closer without being spotted. She hugged up against the pods and started forward.

She moved ten meters and the man was still looking down. Five more and she was halfway there. Just a little farther...

He looked out the window, straight at her.

An instant later something moved on the pod right next to her. She whirled to face it, but it was too late. There was a faint whine of servos and then something big and hard slammed into her head and the lights went out.

* * * * *

"Got you!" whooped Charles Crawford. He wanted to clap his hands together, but he still couldn't move his left arm. He had awkwardly activated one of the remote work-droids, a multi-purpose device with an array of built-in tools and manipulator arms, and when the woman got close enough, he had used it to bash her. She slowly spun across the compartment and disappeared behind some machinery. The wrench she had been carrying drifted off in another direction. She had said she didn't mean any harm, but that wrench put the lie to that! He was glad he had not listened. He could not see her from the control room, but now he had friends who could go and look for him. He flipped some switches and the droid detached itself from the storage rack and jetted forward, propelled by its small thrusters. He activated its remote cameras and floodlights and tried to spot his opponent.

He did not see her immediately, but she had to be somewhere over by the heavy-duty lifters. There! He spotted a lumpy shape which did not belong there, in between two of the huge machines. Piloting the droid with only one hand was difficult, but he maneuvered it in closer. He was hoping to grab the woman with one of the droid's manipulators and keep her re-strained until he could figure out what to do with her. He moved the droid in closer but then cursed. The space between the lifters was too narrow for the droid to fit. He extended a manipulator to its maximum, but the mechanical claw was still a meter short. Maybe he could get at her from the other side. He backed the droid off and flew it around to the other end of the lifters.

"Shit!" She was gone. She had only been out of his view for a few seconds, but she had taken the opportunity to escape. Now where the hell was she? Crawford hastily looked out the window of the control room to make sure she wasn't coming after him again. He did not see her but quick-ly brought the droid back to guard the door to the control room—just in case.

Fortunately, he was quite capable of handling several droids at once, even with only one hand. He activated another, and leaving the first to block the door, sent it out in search of the woman. A few minutes went by with no luck and his arm was really starting to ache. Then a sound came to him through the droid's pickup and he spun it around in time to see the door he'd originally come through sliding shut.

"Hell!" She'd gotten away. He should have sent another droid over there to block that door. Crawford leaned back in his chair, the seat belt keeping him from floating away, and gently rubbed his arm. He couldn't find any obvious breaks just from touching, but it was still terribly painful and he could hardly move it at all. Now what was he going to do? The work droids would fit down the ship's corridors if he was careful, so that seemed like his best bet, rather than leave his stronghold and search in person. He flipped switches to activate some more of his mechanical helpers.

An hour of looking convinced him that she was no longer on the ship.

He had not searched the entire huge expanse, but the shuttle pod which had brought her to *Neshaminy* was gone and there was a bloody hand print next to the door of the airlock. He had found a few other blood spatters, too. *Okay, she's hurt and decided to get the hell out. Now what?*

He blocked open the shuttle lock door so she could not get back in the way she had before and positioned a few droids to observe the shuttle bay and the emergency air locks. Then he went back up to the galley and wearily got himself some coffee. A trip to sick bay acquired some mild painkillers, but the stronger stuff was locked away. His arm was killing him.

He tried to contact *Exeter* again, but there was still no answer. So now what? He could not just let this be. Something was clearly wrong. Seriously wrong. Action was going to be necessary and as much as he hated to admit it, he was in no shape to do it himself.

He was going to need help.

Chapter 2

"**C**huck, I'm gonna rip your arm off and beat you to death with it for talking me into this," growled Gregory VanVean from his cold-sleep capsule. "Crap, I feel like iced crap."

"You look like you feel, Greg," said Charles Crawford. "And if you want to rip my arm off, go ahead. Someone else did half the job already." The grizzled foreman cracked open a red-rimmed eye and glared at Crawford, but slowly his expression of irritation became one of curiosity.

"How come you look so good?"

"It's my superb genetics, I suppose. Mom always said I was so handsome."

VanVean growled an obscenity and began flexing his muscles. These were rather impressive, despite a substantial belly. The belly was relatively new, but VanVean's muscles were what had first caught Crawford's attention years before. Greg wasn't a heavy-worlder, like himself, and kilo-for-kilo Crawford was actually stronger, but Greg had a lot more kilos and knew how to use them. He'd taken a chance and pulled the man out of the pool of indentured workers and made him a crew chief. He'd never regretted it and now he was his senior foreman. "Looks like you've been up a while, you rat. How come? And what's with your arm?"

"Yeah, I got up a little early and it was a good thing I did. We got trouble."

"What kind?"

"The kind that breaks arms for no apparent reason. I know you could fit into that category, but it wasn't you. Wake yourself up, Greg, and I'll tell you about it. There's coffee in the galley."

"Now you're talking. Anyone else up?"

"I've got most of the other foremen defrosting now. Excuse me while I go check on Sheila."

"Check her out, you mean," snorted VanVean. "Give me a second and I'll go with you."

"Put your clothes on, Greg, you'll scare her to death. Hurry up and don't forget to get some coffee. I'll be back in a few minutes." Crawford turned and shoved himself along the rows of cold-sleep capsules. A dozen of them were in revival mode and would be opening soon. He was glad that there was a fairly simple emergency override right on each capsule. He had just opened the plastic shield and pressed the button; easy. He reached the first row of the women's capsules and pulled himself over to the only one with a reviving occupant. The closed capsules had areas on the transparent front which had been frosted to provide a little modesty (unless you looked from certain angles), but Sheila MacIntyrre's capsule had already opened. The woman was starting to breath deeply — and she was quite naked.

He took one admiring look and then carefully, and awkwardly with one hand, tucked the towel he had brought along around her. She stirred and groaned when he touched her. All the control readouts were in the green range; she would be awake very soon. She groaned again and began moving.

"Sheila? Wake up, Sheila, it's Chuck."

"Go 'way. Still night time. Scram."

"I know it's early, but I need you to wake up. We got some problems."

Her eyes popped open and wandered around in disconcerting circles before finally coming to rest on him. Her full lips were still a bit blue and her face very pale, but the sparkle in her brown eyes was there. "Problems? Already?"

"Yeah. Try to wake up, okay?"

She started to nod, but the telemetry leads restrained her. She looked puzzled for a moment and then glanced sharply at him. "What the hell's going on? Why are you already awake and why are you in Women's Country gawking at my girls—and me?"

"Never could keep my eyes off you, Sheil. But I've left your girls alone; in fact that's why I defrosted you first, so you can wake them up yourself. I've even provided you with a fetching wake-up garment."

Sheila reached a hand up and disconnected the leads on her head. She looked down at the towel, which was starting to drift loose. "How nice. But if you'll excuse me, I'd like to get dressed—alone."

"Sure thing, Sheil. Decide who else you want awake and I'll meet you in the galley. Coffee's on."

"Until you tell me about the problem, how can I know who to wake up?"

"True enough. So get dressed and come have some coffee."

"Right. Now beat it." Crawford grinned and started to leave, but then he grimaced and groaned as his arm moved. Sheila was instantly alert. "What's wrong? You hurt?"

"Yeah. My arm. I think it's broken. I think you can at least start defrosting Doctor Barringir."

"Right away. Now scoot—if you can."

"I'm going." Crawford left the ladies behind and returned to his foremen. VanVean was now dressed and helping the others out of their capsules. Shortly, he had herded them down to the galley and gotten them all coffee. Sheila arrived soon afterward and helped herself to a bulb of the hot, black brew.

"Okay, boss, what's the deal?" demanded VanVean.

"The deal is that it's still eight days until we were supposed to wake up. Sixteen days until we are scheduled to drop out of hyper. And something is seriously wrong."

"What?" demanded a dozen people all at once.

"I can't raise anyone on the cruiser that is supposed to be on watch, and there's a homicidal female wandering around assaulting innocent engineers for no reason I can see." Crawford launched into a description of what had happened, casually passing over his unauthorized awakening. "After she skedaddled, I checked out what she was doing in the cold-sleep control room. It looks like she was resetting the revival date for about five months from now. None of this makes any sense to me, but it sure doesn't seem like normal operating procedure."

"Nope," said Sheila, "but what do we do about it?"

"Shouldn't we revive some of the ship's crew?" asked Fred Kimmal, the chief scheduler. "We're going to need them, Chuck."

"Yeah, but I wanted a few friendly faces around me to talk this out, first. Y'know how snippy those sailor-boys can be—even the merchies. Too damned worried about regulations to see a problem floating in front of them."

"Well, what do you *think* is going on?" asked VanVean. "I know you well enough to know you've at least got a theory, Chuck—which is a hell of a lot more than I have right now."

Crawford frowned. He did have a theory and he did not like it one little bit. He glanced from face to face and all were looking at him anxiously. He took a deep breath and let it out.

"I think there's a saboteur loose in the fleet."

* * * * *

"Damn him, damn him, damn him," groaned Carlina as she dabbed the wet cloth to her head. She looked at herself in the mirror of the sick bay on *Exeter* and winced at the ugly bruise that was emerging as she slowly wiped off the dried blood that covered a good portion of her head. The pain that throbbed in her skull was so intense she felt like vomiting.

She finished her washing and slowly applied a bandage. She cursed when she saw blood starting to seep through. Damn, she was still bleeding. She dazedly looked around for a coagulant, but did not see it immediately. The hell with it, it would stop soon enough on its own. She wobbled out of the compartment, wishing she could reduce the artificial gravity. She reached the bridge and collapsed into her chair at the com station. She sat there for a long while, staring at nothing. It was so hard to think. After a while she began to cry.

"I'm so tired. Oh, Maker, I'm so tired," she sobbed. "I don't need this, I don't!" Her frustration turned to anger, but that produced such a blinding pain in her head she was left weeping and gasping. She dimly realized that the blow from the damn droid might have done worse than give her a bruise and a cut. She might be more seriously hurt. There was an auto-medic in sick bay and she wished she could just put herself in it, go to sleep, and let it work on her.

But she couldn't.

That bastard on *Neshaminy* was still alive and she could not just let him be. She certainly could not let herself be put unconscious for hours by the medic. Could she? She tried to think. What was the date? She looked around her control console and eventually found the time. Sixteen days until drop-out. Sixteen days until they reached Landfall. And once there, it would be anywhere between two and four months before the relief squadron arrived. So, between two-and-a-half and four-and-a-half months before she could expect any help. What could that guy do with that much time?

And it won't just be him!

The realization returned that she still needed to reset the revival settings in all the rest of the transports! "Oh, Maker, what am I going to do?" In just eight days the crew and passengers of the twenty ships she had not gotten to yet were going to start waking up. Thousands and thousands of people; Protectorate people and every one of them her enemy. The plan had called for her to visit five or six ships a day, resetting the computers — and a few other things she didn't like thinking about. She'd have them all reset before anyone woke up and then none of them would wake until the relief squadron was here and in full control.

How could she do that now? Did she dare leave *Exeter* and go to those other ships? Did she dare not to? The panic began to build in her and her head hurt so much she could scarcely think.

A beep from her com panel made her jump. She looked and saw that there was an incoming signal from *Neshaminy*. Actually, there were several other messages from earlier, which she had not noticed. The guy had been signaling here? He must have noticed that she was aboard and called here to find out why — and got no answer.

She dithered for a moment. Should she answer? Could she outwit him somehow? She couldn't think of any way to fight him directly with those bloody droids working for him. Could she trick him? Trick him into getting close enough so she could kill him? She had to do something. She reached for her controls and a moment later she was facing the man on the monitor.

"*Exeter*, here, go ahead, *Neshaminy*," she said automatically. The man seemed startled to have gotten an answer. He was probably more startled by who answered.

"Oh. Uh, hello, *Exeter*."

"Just who the hell are you, mister?"

"I'm Charles Crawford, like I told you earlier. Who are you?" Carlina licked her lips. That's right, he had told her his name, but she had forgotten. He'd said something else, too. He was a construction manager or something.

"I'm Communications Tech Carlina Citrone. Mr. Crawford, why are you out of cold-sleep? That is a serious violation of regulations."

"Really? I wasn't aware. But why did you break my arm? I'm no expert, but I'd hope that was violating some regulation, too."

"I...I'm sorry about that, Mister Crawford, but you scared me half to death. I didn't act...wisely. Sorry about that."

"It looked like you wanted to kill me, Miss Citrone. You were very persistent about it, too, as I recall."

"I just wanted to restrain you. But that's beside the point. I have to insist you return to cold-sleep. I can come back over there and put you into the capsule and set the controls..."

"Why bother? We're supposed to wake up again in just eight days — unless, of course, you're resetting *all* the controls for another five months of cold-sleep."

Carlina sucked in her breath. He'd noticed what she'd done in the control room. She had been so rattled, she could not even remember if she'd gotten that far, but she obviously had — and he'd noticed. Had he noticed what else she'd done? "I, uh, I was doing that under orders. There's been some change in plans and revival has been postponed. So you see it would be best if you went back into cold-sleep. I can come over there in a half-hour and..."

"I'd like to see those orders. Can I talk to Lieutenant Hadley?"

Oh shit. He'd checked the duty roster, too. Blast the man! "He... he can't come to the com right now. He's busy." Actually, he was very dead.

"That's all right, I can wait."

"It-it might be a while. B-but if you wanted to come over here and talk to him in person, I think that would be all right. Can you make it here?" Yes, if he wouldn't agree to her going to him, perhaps she could lure him over here. That would work even better. Just wait until he was on the ship with no easy retreat and no more Charles Crawford.

"I guess that would be okay," said Crawford slowly. Carlina smiled in as friendly a fashion as she could.

"Can we come, too, boss?" said another voice and suddenly there were several other people in the background of the monitor image.

"Who... Who's that?!" she squawked.

"Oh, I was getting lonely, so I woke a few friends. Any problem if I bring them along?"

Carlina stared in horror for several long seconds and then cut the connection. She stared at the blank screen for a lot longer. Then she leaned forward and held her aching head in her hands and began to cry again.

"Oh, Dear Maker, what am I going to do?"

Crawford looked at the blank screen for a moment and then sighed. "Okaayy... what do you make of that, folks?"

"Damn peculiar," said Sheila MacIntyrre.

"She couldn't produce the watch officer and she doesn't want a mob of us coming on her ship," said Fred Kimmal. "She's hiding something."

"But what?" asked Greg VanVean.

"Did you see how wrung-out she looked?" asked Doctor Barringir. "That woman hasn't gotten any sleep for a week at least. She's running on go-juice and not much else."

"So they are short-handed over there," mused Crawford. "Maybe very short-handed."

"Just like you, Charles," said Barringir, gesturing to his arm. "Will you please come down to sick bay so we can get you fixed up?"

"We've got some pretty serious things to deal with, Giselle. Just give me something for the pain and I'll come see you later."

"No way, Mr. Crawford," snorted Sheila. "We can all talk down there as well as we can here. Greg, help me get Chuck to sick bay."

Despite his protests, Crawford was carried down to sick bay and forced to allow Doctor Barringir to treat him. All the others went with him, making helpful suggestions that ranged from enemas to amputations.

"You have some torn ligaments in your shoulder and a fracture of your ulna, Charles," said Barringir after working for a while. "She must have hit you pretty good."

"She was aiming for my neck. I was just lucky I could get my arm up to block her, or we wouldn't be having this conversation."

"So what do you suggest we do, Chuck?" asked Sheila. "I agree that something very strange is going on, but what do we do about it?"

"Well, that woman clearly isn't happy at the thought of a bunch of us coming to visit her — so maybe that's what we ought to do."

"Board a Protectorate warship, Charles?" said Beshar Hannah, his payroll manager and part-time lawyer. "That could offend... a number of people."

"Like Admiral Maynard," growled VanVean. "He's as stuck up about his 'personal honor' as anyone I've ever seen."

"Do you think he'd rather have one of his ships — hell, maybe his whole fleet — hijacked?"

"Hijacked?" said Kimmal, raising his eyebrows. "Is that what you think is happening, Chuck?"

Crawford nodded grimly and then winced as Barringir did something to his shoulder. "I can't think of anything else that fits the facts. I'm convinced that this woman is up to no good and that the watch officer over there is either dead or incapacitated. I don't know if she's alone or has anyone else helping her, but she's clearly been working herself to death lately and that would indicate it's only her or just one or two others. If she—or they—have done away with the other people on watch in *Exeter*, then they would be the only ones awake in the whole fleet."

"Except for us."

"Right. Me being awake threw a wrench into whatever plans she had. She tried to fix things by killing me. Now that that has failed, I don't know what she'll do. But I think it would be better if we pay her a visit before she manages to do it."

"But what's the point of this?" asked Barringir. "What does she hope to accomplish? Wreck the project?"

"That could be it, Giselle. There are plenty of folks who would be happy to see us fail."

"She wasn't just sabotaging us, Chuck," said VanVean, his bushy eyebrows scrunched together in concentration. "She was resetting the cold-sleep capsules for five months from now. What do you suppose is going to happen five months from now?"

"Don't know. The Rift Fleet will automatically drop out of hyper on target whether there's anyone awake or not. Maybe she's expecting some friends of hers to show up to help her."

"Show up? From where?" demanded Barringir. "Across the Rift?"

"Why not? We made it. Others have, too."

"Either that or she's got friends already here who she hasn't thawed out yet," suggested Kimmal.

"That's another possibility," admitted Crawford, not liking the idea one bit. "All the more reason for us to get moving before she can."

"God, I hope the family transports are okay," said Beshar. "Could she have gotten over there, do you think, Chuck? Maybe we ought to send some people over to check on them."

Crawford hesitated. Recruiting the people for the expedition had not been easy. Not that many people were willing to go into cold-sleep for ten years and leave family and friends behind. Preference had been given to people like Crawford, who were willing to make that sacrifice, or to people who were married to other needed professionals who could also come. But they had not been able to fill all the slots that way. A fair number would only come if they could bring their families along, and four of the ships in the fleet were carrying them. Beshar's wife and child were on one of those ships.

"I'm sure they are okay, Besh," said Crawford. "We can send a party to check later. But right now we need to deal with this situation."

"So how do you suggest we do that, boss?" asked VanVean. "Just hop in one of the shuttle cars and zip over there?"

"She'll be expecting us to do that," said Sheila.

"Yeah, I think maybe we ought to be a little sneakier."

"Like how?"

"Not sure." Crawford sighed. "But as much as I hate to admit it, I think we'd better wake up the captain and some of his crew and see what they think. Greg, take some of the others and get on it."

"Right, boss. You just relax here and let the doc fix you up. We'll take care of it."

* * * * *

Carlina awoke with a start. The last she remembered, she was sitting at her com station, alternately cursing the fate which had put her here and crying over the fact that it had. She must have dozed off. She frantically looked at the time and sighed in relief when she saw that only about a half-hour had passed. She needed another dose of stimulants. If she let them wear off, she'd probably sleep for twenty-four hours straight. A half-hour she might be able to spare, but not a whole day. The Maker only knew what Crawford could do with a whole day.

Him and his friends.

Damn him! He'd woken up more of his people and now she was outnumbered. She could not hope to just kill him. There were too many to fight bare-handed. So what could she do? Even if she could, she did not dare destroy the ship he was on. It was vital to the gate construction project and had to be taken intact. That fact had been impressed upon her by her superiors very clearly: no damage to the fleet! If the gate could not be built then this whole operation was nearly pointless. Oh, she had been given contingency orders to destroy things if all else failed, but it had been clear that all else had better not fail. Far too much was riding on this.

On her.

She could still scarcely believe they had given her a job this important. Surely there were other agents with more experience. *Of course there were, but none of them happened to be on ships assigned to this fleet.* It was just luck of the draw—and she had hit the jackpot of all jackpots.

And it should have been so simple! Everything had been going perfectly until that bastard Crawford had spoiled it all. What was she going to do? She started crying again. She was so tired. And so scared. She had never been so scared in her life.

"Stop it! Stop it and do something! You have no time for this!" She lurched to her feet and staggered down to the galley to get some water. She took another stimulant tablet and washed it down. She glanced around and tried to remember the last time she had eaten. There were a dozen discarded rations containers littering the tables. There had been no time to cook anything for a week or more, so she'd been living on packaged field rations. Her stomach was tied in knots and she had no appetite at all, but she forced herself to munch down an energy bar. The stimulants sucked a lot out of a person, and if she did not refuel she might collapse.

The routine action calmed her slightly and she made herself think about her problem and possible actions. She could not attack them directly and there was now no point in trying to reset the cold-sleep capsules on the other ships. They could just re-reset them, or hit the emergency revival buttons far faster than she could work. So, in a few days she would be outnumbered thousands to one. It seemed pretty hopeless.

But she was on a heavy cruiser and they were all on merchant ships; that must give her some advantage. She could not blast them, but she could make it as hard as possible for them to get at her. She just had to defend herself from their attacks until help came. Once the squadron arrived it wouldn't really matter if the civilians were awake or not, would it?

It won't really matter if I'm alive or not, either.

For some reason, that thought was actually comforting. She'd accomplished her primary mission and her own survival was entirely secondary now. She had hurt The Protector! Oh, yes, she had! No matter what happened now, he was going to be hurt by this on many different levels. Even if she died now, she would take that satisfaction with her. And she was so tired, dying did not seem like such a bad idea. Just fall asleep and never wake up. What a wonderful thought.

But she could not give up yet. The harder she made it for her opponents, the less time they'd have to react to the problems she had created for them. The thought of giving that Crawford a hard time felt almost as good as the idea of sleep. Almost as good as hurting The Protector. *All right, how much trouble can I make for them?*

She went to her station and got to work.

* * * * *

Doctor Barringir had just finished on his arm when the communicator in the sick bay beeped. Sheila answered and Crawford could hear VanVean's voice, although he wasn't close enough to make out his words.

"Yeah, he's still here," said Sheila. "Just a second. Why? What's wrong? Okay, okay, he's right here." She turned and looked at him. "Chuck, Greg wants to talk to you... he seems kind of upset."

Barringir nodded and Crawford pushed himself toward the intercom. They still needed to get the artificial gravity turned on, but they'd need the ship's crew for that. "Yeah, what's up, Greg?" he said into the com.

"Chief, can you come down here? Right away?" The tone in VanVean's voice sent a chill through him. He instantly knew that something was wrong—very wrong.

"On my way. Should I bring the doctor?"

"I...uh, no...yes, yeah, bring her along." He exchanged looks with the others in the compartment and then they all moved toward the hatch.

He didn't get down to the cold-sleep compartment quite as fast as he had on that first trip, but almost. He slowed himself to a stop, the others crowding up behind him, and frantically scanned the compartment. Everything seemed normal...

"Chief! Over here!" called VanVean. Crawford looked and saw his foreman near a hatch in the far bulkhead. The hatch led to the separate cold-sleep compartment used by the ship's officers. It was open and an electronic wail came from inside. The look on VanVean's face made him shudder. "What's going on, Greg? What's wrong?" VanVean just shook his head and motioned toward the compartment. Crawford swallowed and went in.

The first thing he noticed was the flashing red lights. The second thing was the smell, a strange chemical odor. The third was that everything was wet. There were some small droplets of liquid floating about, but nearly every surface, deck, ceiling, bulkheads, equipment, was glistening with moisture. Then he saw the cold-sleep capsules. They were fogged over.

And they were a wreck.

Someone had opened up the access panels and torn the internal machinery apart. Tubing had been pulled loose or cut, power leads severed. The moisture in the compartment had spilled out from inside...

"Oh, God!" exclaimed Sheila MacIntyrre from behind him.

"Let me through!" cried the doctor when she caught sight of things. She pushed past Crawford, but he could tell that she was far too late.

Chapter Three

"**H**ell, he's just a kid," grumbled Greg VanVean.

"Yeah, but he's still an officer—and he's alive," replied Charles Crawford, looking at the very young man lying in the open cold-sleep capsule. *And he's the only one on the ship that we can say that about!* The thought formed in his mind without bidding and refused to go away. The horror they'd found in the officers' cold-sleep compartment was still gripping him like some manipulator claw that had been chilled to absolute zero. They had all been dead. Every single one of the officers of the starship *Neshaminy*. Their cold-sleep capsules had been wrecked and the men inside had died without ever waking up.

Citrone. It had been that Citrone woman. Before he had caught her in the control room for the other capsules, she had gone into the officers' section and done her deadly work. *If I'd known, I would have had that workdroid wring her neck instead of just knocking her out!* Without realizing it, his hands had clenched into fists and he was staring at nothing. He jumped when someone touched him. It was Sheila.

"Chuck, it wasn't your fault. There's no way you could have stopped her."

He bristled and then stopped and nodded his head. Good old Sheila, sometimes it seemed like she knew him better than he knew himself. "Yeah, I know, but it seems like I should have... I still can't believe she would do this. She was just resetting the rest of the capsules' revival dates, why'd she kill those men?"

"I think I have the answer to that, Chief," said Fred Kimmal. He was waving to him from the officers' compartment. Crawford moved over to him by the main control console. "Look there." Crawford looked and saw where the screen was filled, from top to bottom with: 'Enter Password', followed by 'Access Denied'. Crawford looked at Kimmal.

"She didn't have the access codes. The controls for the officers' capsules were all password protected. She couldn't reset their revival dates. So she... she..."

"Yeah," growled Crawford. "She sure did."

"Charles, he's coming round," Doctor Birringer's voice echoed through the hatch. Crawford reversed himself and headed back. The young man in the capsule was awake and looking about in confusion. Crawford grimaced, Greg was right: he was just a kid. But he was an officer. Just an ensign according to the ship's roster, but still an officer.

"What's he doing out here?" asked VanVean, echoing Crawford's thoughts. "How come he ain't dead in there with all the others?"

"All the capsules in the officers' compartment were filled," said Sheila. "I guess there just wasn't room so they put him with the petty officers out here."

"Lucky break for him."

"What...? What's going on?" said the man hesitantly. "Who... who are all of you?"

"Ensign Frichette? Petre Frichette?" asked Doctor Birringir. "How are you feeling?"

"Y-yes, I'm Petre Frichette. Who are you?"

"I'm Doctor Birringir. This is Charles Crawford, the gate construction manager."

"Oh, yes, I remember you now, sir," said Frichette, looking at him. Crawford frowned slightly. While he had a great memory for plans and diagrams, his memory for names and faces wasn't nearly so good; he did not remember ever having met this kid, but he supposed Frichette must have seen him during all the preparation for departure.

"How do you feel, Petre?" said Birringir again.

"Okay, I guess. A little strange. A little chilly, too." The boy looked down at himself and blushed, his cheeks suddenly flaring pink in sharp contrast to his pale flesh. They had tucked a towel around his waist to give him a little modesty, but it wasn't much.

"We'll get you dressed in a few minutes," soothed Birringir. "Now I want you to start flexing your muscles the way you were instructed..." The doctor continued tending to her 'patient' but Crawford turned when Sheila nudged him. She handed him a small hand-comp and he saw that it was displaying Frichette's service record. He glanced at it and frowned at how short it was. The boy was only seventeen standards and this was his first shipboard assignment. He'd gone through six months of instruction at a private merchant service academy and then he'd been sent to *Neshaminy* — reporting aboard a mere week before the expedition set off. Great.

"Take a look at the next page," said Sheila, quietly. He touched the advance key and looked at the screen more closely. This showed personal information and Crawford whistled silently.

"He's one of *those* Frichettes?" Sheila nodded. The boy came from a very important family. Admiral Avery Frichette had been one of The Protector's main allies in his struggle against the Council of Fifty, and the family itself could trace its lineage back all the way to Guillume the Great and the Yarmondi Conquest. Granted, this Petre was a second or third cousin of Lord Avery, but that still made him pretty damn important. What the hell was he doing as a junior officer on a construction ship? He could not remember the baron saying anything about him.

While he had been checking out the data, Frichette had been disconnected from his capsule and was struggling into his clothes. Crawford went over to him. "My Lord? Would you come with me? We need to talk. And we have coffee ready in the galley."

"Uh, sure. B-but I don't drink coffee. Tea would be fine, if you have any."

"I imagine we can find some."

They floated out of the compartment, but Frichette looked back at the row of capsules. "Aren't the other crewmen being revived?"

"They will be shortly, but I need to talk to you first."

A few minutes later they were all in the galley, Frichette nursing a bulb of hot tea and Crawford seated across from him with coffee. He cleared his throat and tried to figure out what the hell to say. "Uh, Lord Frichette…"

"Please call me 'ensign', sir, junior officers don't use their titles on shipboard."

"Oh, well, then, Ensign, I'm afraid I've got some bad news." The boy looked at him intently. "There's been a… a problem in the officers' cold-sleep compartment." He took a breath. "I'm afraid… I'm afraid you are the only officer left alive on the ship. The others are dead."

"D-dead?" squeaked the boy. "Captain Dumphries? The first officer…?"

"All of them. I'm sorry." Frichette turned very pale and sat there blinking. He didn't look like he was going to break down and Crawford reminded himself that the boy had only been on the ship for a week before going into cold-sleep. Likely he didn't really know any of those people very well.

"What happened? How…?"

"Now it gets ugly, Ensign. It was deliberate sabotage. They were murdered."

"Murdered?"

"Yes, there is a saboteur — possibly more than one — loose in the fleet." Crawford told his tale again and the boy's eyes got wider and wider. "So, we have a big problem," he said in conclusion. "We need to stop this woman and we are going to need your help, son."

"I'll do anything I can, sir. But… but I'm just an ensign."

"You are also the ranking officer on this ship."

"Me?"

"You're the only officer here. That puts you in command, Petre."

"But what about the other ships? Surely someone else can…"

"We don't know about the other ships," said Crawford and his throat tightened. That was the other thing that had been gnawing at him. "With ninety-eight ships in the fleet, it's unlikely that *Neshaminy* was the first ship she's visited. I'm praying it wasn't the last, either, but we have to assume that this woman may have already killed a lot of the other officers."

"On the warships, too?" The lad's eyes goggled at him.

"I-I'd have to think she'd give them priority. We have to fear the worst."

"Oh, God, that's… that's…"

"Terrible," said Greg VanVean. "Yeah, it sure is. But to make sure it doesn't get any terrible-er we need to get moving and moving right quick."

"Right, will you help us?"

"Yes, yes, of course," said Frichette, his look of anxiety gave way to one of determination. "What do you want me to do?"

"The first thing is to defrost the rest of the crew. They aren't going to like this and they sure aren't going to like taking orders from me. I need you to be the authority figure here, Ensign. Get out your best uniform and be there when the petty officers wake up. Like it or not, you are in command—at least for now. You have to make them believe and accept that."

"I-yes, sir, I'll do my best."

"Good. Greg? Would you take him to his quarters and get him fancied up? Doctor? Let's start the thawing process on the petty officers."

Twenty minutes later, Frichette and Greg arrived, just as the senior petty officer was shaking off the effects of revival. The ensign was looking quite official now in a very nicely tailored gray and black uniform. If he just didn't look so damn young!

"How are you feeling, Chief?" Crawford asked to the petty officer. His name was Duncan and he looked to have a good many years in space. He peered around at the small crowd of watchers and growled an obscenity.

"Who are you? What the hell's going on? Where's the ship's doctor?"

Crawford winced, the ship's doctor had been with the officers. "We've got a bit of an emergency, Chief. We are going to need your help in dealing with it. The other petty officers are reviving now. Once that's done you need to get the rest of the crew defrosted and get the ship fully operational. We are also going to need at least one of the shuttles and then…"

"Wait a minute! Wait just one damn minute! You're part of the construction crew. I don't take my orders from you! Where's the first officer?"

"The first officer is dead, Mr. Duncan," said Frichette, suddenly pushing himself forward. "The captain and all the other officers, as well. That leaves me in temporary command."

"*You?*" Duncan stared with his face contorted in shock and amazement. "But you're just… just…"

"I'm the ranking officer, at the moment, and you will address me as 'sir'. Is that clear?"

The man stared at the boy for a long moment, but Frichette's stare did not waver and eventually Duncan's did. "Yes…sir," he muttered at last.

"Good. Now I want you to give Mr. Crawford your full cooperation. We have a lot of work to do. Let's get cracking."

"Aye, sir. Where are my clothes?"

While the chief was getting dressed, Greg VanVean nudged Crawford and nodded toward Frichette. "The kid's not bad, huh?"

"Not bad at all," said Crawford with a smile. "But come on, we've
got work to do."

* * * * *

It took a moment for Carlina to recognize the proximity alert. She
was awkwardly using a cutting torch to burn her way into the ship's arms
locker and the noise almost drowned out the alarm tone. She did not have
the code to open the locker and she *really* wanted a weapon. She would
have preferred to get something seriously lethal from the marines' armory,
but it would have taken her a week to cut through *those* bulkheads. She'd
have to be content with a laser pistol. If she had time to even get that much.

She hastily shut down the torch and sprinted for the bridge. She
had figured out — after a few agonizing hours looking through instruction
manuals — the sensor station sufficiently to set up the proximity radar and
tie it into her com panel so it would alert her if anything was approaching
the ship.

Which, apparently, something now was.

She skidded to a halt by the sensor station and clutched the back
of the chair as a wave of dizziness washed over her. Her head did not hurt
quite as much as it had, but her fatigue was like a person hanging on her
back. She swallowed and focused her attention on the display. A small,
flashing blip was approaching and it did not surprise her a bit that it was
coming from the direction of *Neshaminy*. She punched a button and an ex-
ternal camera locked on to the bogey and transferred its image to a monitor. She sucked in her breath when she recognized a droid just like the one
which had bashed her in the head. The sensor display told her that it was
about four hundred meters away and closing.

"All right, Crawford," she snarled, "you wanted to play rough, did
you? Well, I can be rough, too!"

She dashed out of the compartment and through a maze of corridors. She reached a hatch and swung herself through and into a chair
mounted to a bulkhead. In front of her was a transparent bubble and she
could look out into space. She strapped herself into the chair, pulled a
swivel-mounted control console around in front of her, and flipped a series
of switches. Lights came on and a display lit up. There were a pair of joysticks attached to the sides of the console and she grasped them. Outside
the bubble there was a point-defense laser mount and it began to move in
response to the joysticks.

Even though she did not have the access codes to activate the ship's main weaponry from the bridge, she could at least use the smaller weapons in manual-override mode. She thought she had this laser figured out well enough to hit something. Like that stinking droid.

One of the monitors was slaved to the sensor display and she quickly located her target; it was only about two hundred meters away now. Orienting herself, she swung the weapon around and brought it to bear. There was a coaxial camera which fed to another monitor. This had crosshairs to show the aiming point. She steadied the image in the crosshairs and pressed the firing button. Nothing happened. She cursed under her breath and remembered to press the safety on the other joystick. The crosshairs turned from green to red and then she squeezed the firing button again. But in struggling with the safety, she had drifted off-target and the shot missed. She continued to curse and brought the crosshairs back and fired again.

The laser beam itself was invisible in the vacuum of hyperspace, but its effect could be clearly seen. The droid exploded into a cloud of tumbling fragments. The compressed gas cylinders, which powered its thrusters, ruptured and a fine mist engulfed the debris. One of them whooshed off crazily like a missile.

"Ha! Take that, you son of a bitch!"

* * * * *

"Oops," said Charles Crawford, staring at the suddenly blank control monitor. "That wasn't very friendly."

"Right un-neighborly," agreed Greg VanVean from beside him. "Doesn't look like this dame wants any visitors."

"Yeah, but at least we know she's there," said Crawford. That had been the major objective of the reconnaissance. A half-hour of spirited debate between his foremen, the ship's crew, and anyone else with an opinion had led to this attempt. Some people wanted to try and wake up the navy crews and dump the problem in their lap, but the difficulty of getting aboard the warships, along with the fact that all the officers were probably dead, and the nagging fear that they needed to act quickly had decided the issue: they needed to take out Citrone and do it soon. He frowned and hit another button. "Ensign? Did you see that? Looks like this could be trickier than I'd thought." Ensign Frichette answered back immediately from the bridge.

"Yes I did see, sir. It was one of the three-centimeter point-defense lasers. By the way, the first shot that missed your droid almost hit *Neshaminy*. I think it did hit one of the warships. You might want to be more careful about your approach vectors in the future, sir."

"Uh, sorry about that," said Crawford sheepishly. "I hadn't really thought about that..."

"I think the critical thing to observe here is that her first shot *did* miss, sir. If that point defense laser had been on automatic control, there's no way it would have missed an easy target like that. The laser was obviously being fired on manual control."

"Uh, so what?"

"It's important, sir," continued Frichette. "If she had managed to activate the automatic systems, there's no way we could hope to get close to that ship. But on manual, she can't possibly cover every avenue of approach. If you would be willing to risk a few more droids to keep her occupied, I'm sure I can take a shuttle around to the other side—outside her field of fire—and get aboard."

"I'm willing. From what you are telling me, Ensign, if we keep them dodging, it will be even harder for her to hit them, is that right?"

"It should be, Mr. Crawford. I can't believe this woman has much experience as a gunner, or she would not have missed that first shot."

"All right, let's give it a try. But, Ensign, I can't let you lead the boarding party."

"Why not?" Crawford could hear the disappointment in his voice.

"Because you are too valuable. You are our only officer, and if this goes wrong, there will be no one left in command. We can't risk that." There was a lengthy silence before Frichette responded.

"I can see that, sir. But this is my command and I really should..."

"Your place is on your ship, sir," said Crawford with what he hoped was the right tone of respect and determination. There was another pause and then he heard Frichette sigh.

"Very well, sir. I'll have the shuttle prepared. How soon can you be ready?"

"Oh, say a half-hour to prep the droids and get my controllers in place. Are you going to want some of my people for the boarding parties?"

"If you can provide me a couple of people who are good with a torch in case we need to do any cutting, that would be excellent."

"Right, I'll scare up some people and send them down to the shuttle bay." He cut the connection.

"Count me in on that, boss," said VanVean after the circuit was closed.

"You want to go, Greg?"

"Sure. I still remember how to use a torch and I've got a hankering to meet this crazy broad."

"Okay, get your gear and an assistant and report to the shuttle bay."

"On my way."

The big man left and Crawford began gathering the people he would need for his end of things. Several hundred of his crew had been revived by this time. From where he sat in the control room, he could see small crowds scurrying about, prepping the droids he planned to use. He looked up as Sheila came in.

"So, we're going to do this, are we?" she said, looking over the activity.

"Seems like it. I sure hope it works."

"With you pushing it, I'm sure it will, Chuck. You get things done. Lord help us if we had to depend on people like Beshar to make a decision."

"He's just being cautious, and y'know, it's just possible that he could be right on this one. We're taking a considerable risk here. Maybe we should leave it to the navy."

"He's not right and you know it. All of us have learned to trust your hunches, Chuck, maybe you should, too."

"I'm an engineer, Sheil, I don't *like* acting on hunches."

"No one does in this business. We like to have detailed plans with every weld called out and all the loads and stresses calculated to the eighteenth decimal place. But sometimes we don't have that luxury. Then we have to go on instinct, and you have the best instincts I've ever run across."

"For construction, maybe. But this isn't a construction problem. I don't know a damn thing about boarding a hostile warship."

"Which is why you are here, doing what you do know — running the droids — instead of trying to be a hero and lead the boarding party. You have sense as well as good instincts. That's why your people follow you."

He eyed her carefully and hoped she wasn't reading his mind again. "Is that why you followed me all the way here, Sheil?"

"Partly." Crawford stared at her, pondering whether he could risk asking her what the other part of her reason was. He'd known Sheila for a long time and they had flirted without resolution now and again, but he didn't know how she really felt about him — or how he felt about her, for that matter. Still, she had agreed to spend ten years in cold-sleep…

He hesitated for another few seconds; more people came bustling into the control room and the chance was lost. Sheila smiled and went over to her own control station and sat down. "All right, everyone, we ready for this show?" he asked loudly.

"Sure thing, boss, all the droids are checked out, fueled up, and ready to raise some hell," said one of his remote operators.

"This is gonna be fun," said another.

"Not too much fun," warned Crawford. "We have a job to do and I'd really prefer not to lose any more droids if we can avoid it. They'll come out of the baron's profit margin — and our bonuses. Understand?"

"Sure, sure. It's still gonna be fun." That seemed to be the consensus and Crawford doubted he was going to be able to convince them otherwise.

"All right then. Power up and shut down the gravity in the bay." For all their banter, his operators were extremely professional and he knew that they would never let their horseplay compromise safety or getting the job done. In just a few minutes, a dozen droids were threading their way through the crowded equipment bay toward airlock four, which was the largest on the ship. The inner door slid shut behind them. While they were waiting for the air to be pumped out of the lock, Ensign Frichette commed, reporting the shuttle and crew were ready.

"Okay, Ensign, we're just about ready. Outer lock door is opening now. Let's see how she reacts to this."

"Roger," said Frichette. "We'll standby until we see how this goes. I'm not going to expose the shuttle until we're sure about her fields of fire."

"Understood. Here we go."

The lock was open now and Crawford put on his goggles. These transferred the images from the droid's cameras right to his eyes and it was almost like he was actually inside the machine, instead of piloting it from a distance. His injured arm made working the controls a bit awkward, but he quickly adapted. He worked the joysticks and the machine smoothly moved out into the void. The fleet hung around him in all its splendor. Ninety-eight starships and fuel tanks, all held together in a web of girders and braces. To Crawford, it looked like a colossal bunch of grapes, although only a few of the vessels were spherical.

Only a fraction of the other ships were visible, but by luck, Exeter was one of the ships which was in view. If it was luck; a more concealed avenue of approach might have been better. Still, *we are here to draw fire, so let's draw some.*

"Fred, Juan, Glendi, spread out left. Kurtz, Yvon, Dani, you go right. Tyron, Nan, and Di, you take the high road, the rest of us will go low. Try and stay close to the other ships until we get closer. Keep moving so you don't make an easy target, but watch your fuel levels. Let's go."

His crew gave a chorus of affirmatives and the droids spread out as they moved forward. Exeter was a little over a kilometer away, and unfortunately it was going to take a while to cover the distance. Built-in safety features would not let the droids go more than about ten meters per second relative to the surrounding ships.

Crawford steered his droid 'down' and hugged one of the girders which held Neshaminy to another cargo carrier. He decided to duck under the other ship, even though it would significantly lengthen the distance he had to go. The navigational display overlaid on his vision showed that his people were taking similar evasive routes. *Good, no point in bunching up.*

As he maneuvered along the ship's hull, something darted past him. "Tag! You're it!" said Sheila from the adjacent control station. He recognized the object as a Ferret, a much smaller droid equipped only with cameras and a few sensors. They were used for tight inspections and could move faster than the work droids. Sheila and some of her people were running them.

"Go and tag Miss Citrone, Sheil."

"On the way."

A minute or so went by and Crawford came to the end of his cover. *Exeter* loomed in the distance and there was no choice but a direct approach. Well, actually, he had a few other choices. He could circle around and come in from the other side, but that was the direction they would eventually send the shuttle in from. His job was to draw Citrone's attention in this direction.

"Chuck, one of the smaller turrets is moving," said Sheila, suddenly. "Looks like she's spotted us."

"Okay, it's show time, people. Let's see what sort of teeth she's got." He twisted the joysticks and his droid jetted out into the open. The navigation display showed a cluster of other dots moving forward as his people followed his lead.

"How are we gonna know if she shoots at us?" demanded one of the operators. "You can't even see the laser beams."

"You'll know when your droid gets blasted," answered Fred Kimmal.

"Only one turret, Sheil?" asked Crawford.

"That's all I can see from here. Gonna move in closer and see it I can spot anyone inside the gunner's bubble."

"Be careful."

He heard Sheila laugh from beside him. "Chuck, you sound so serious. It's not like it's me out there!"

Crawford muttered under his breath and concentrated on moving his droid. He used its thrusters to jink it up and down and right and left in what he hoped was a random pattern to throw off attempts to target it. Meter by meter he was closing on the cruiser.

"Mr. Crawford, she's fired on you," came another voice on his headset. It was Frichette.

"Are you sure? How can you tell?"

"I can tell by the bits of debris she just blew off of *Cornwells Heights* when she missed."

"Oh. Can you tell which droid she was shooting at?"

"Er...one of the ones you sent right. Kind of hard to figure out the angles with our displays. We're not a warship, you know."

"But just one shot?" asked Crawford. "Only the one turret is firing?"

"Only one is moving," said Sheila. "I think I can see our friend in the gunner's bubble."

"Okay, gang," said Crawford. "Let's keep this woman's attention on us."

"Right, boss!"

"Oops! She's seen my Ferret," said Sheila gaily. "Wow, she's mad, too. Nya, nya! Can't catch me!"

"She's trying to fire on your Ferret?"

"Trying, but I'm only thirty meters away and she ain't near quick enough. Pooh, she's given up. Watch out, guys, she's gunning for you now."

Crawford's droid was only two hundred meters away from *Exeter*. The cameras on it could see the laser turret clearly.

"Shit!" The exclamation from close at hand almost made Crawford pull his goggles off to look.

"What happened?"

"The bitch nailed my droid!" snarled Kurtz Renni. "Damn, I was just starting to have fun, too. Can I take another one out, boss?"

"No way, Kurtz!" laughed Fred Kimmal. "You've had your shot, now watch how a master—crap!"

Crawford glanced at his display and saw that a second droid was now spinning away in pieces. Hell, this was getting expensive. "Everyone back off. Open up the range. Make yourselves harder to hit."

There were a few muttered protests, but his people obeyed. Crawford, however, flipped one particular switch on his console and angled the joysticks forward. Almost immediately, a warning light appeared in his goggles telling him he was exceeding safe limits on his velocity. But he had already overridden the interlocks and he pressed on. *Exeter* grew quickly in his vision and then he engaged the reverse thrust. More warnings flashed, telling him he was about to collide with something.

I know that, you stupid machine. He was shaving things very close, and he was well aware he was going to hit the cruiser. The impact would do no harm to the heavily armored warship, but he was hoping he could slow down enough that his droid would survive. A moment later the view in his goggles jerked around crazily as it hit.

The fact that the cameras were still working was a good sign. He quickly looked over the status readout and was relieved that almost everything was still functioning. One of the thrusters was out, but he could compensate. He used the remaining thrusters to keep the droid close to the ship's hull. He turned it around and saw that he was about fifty meters from the laser turret which had destroyed his other droids. He didn't *think* it could fire at him from this close.

"Okay, Miss Citrone, let's see how you deal with *this*," he said to himself as he deployed the droid's cutting torch.

* * * * *

Carlina flinched when she heard the faint clang of something hitting *Exeter*. She swore in rage and despair when she saw that one of the droids was right up against the hull of the cruiser. How had it closed the distance so quickly? She had noticed the one droid trying to sneak in from her right, but she thought she had time to deal with it. Not so, it was here. She swung the laser turret around as far as it would go but cursed again when she could not bring it to bear on the droid. *Damn!* What would the stinking thing do now? She wiped sweat from her forehead and made the mistake of shaking her hand. Tiny droplets sprayed away in all directions in the zero-G of the gunner's bubble.

She was breathing heavily and on the verge of panic. This wasn't supposed to be happening! After she had destroyed the first droid she had hoped Crawford would give up. When nothing more happened for a while, she had gone back to her cutting and had actually gotten into the arms locker. She had the reassuring feel of two laser pistols stuck in her waistband, but it was not nearly reassuring enough. The proximity alarm had sounded again and she scrambled back to her turret only to find a whole swarm of droids heading her way.

She destroyed two of them and the rest appeared to be running, but now this other one was on the hull. A quick glance at her display showed that the others were moving toward her again, too. Damn, damn, damn. Okay, she could not hit the one on the hull, but she could still hit the others. She swung the turret around again. She fired and missed. Her IFF monitor was making angry noises, but she had overridden that. She knew she was hitting the other ships, but the light laser couldn't do much damage even to an unarmored merchant ship. And she had no choice. She lined up a dodging target and squeezed the triggers. She shouted in triumph as the droid disintegrated.

An instant later she shrieked in alarm as something big loomed into view by her gunner's station. It was the Maker-cursed droid! From this close it looked incredibly menacing. All of its grappler arms and tools were deployed like some huge, mutant pocket knife. As she watched, frozen in shock, it moved over to the turret and grabbed the projecting laser cannon.

"Go away!" she screamed. "Leave me alone!"

The polarized armorglas of her bubble darkened suddenly as the droid's cutting torch came to life. In horror, Carlina realized it was cutting right through her laser. She tried to shake the droid off by moving the turret, but it hung on and continued to cut. A dozen warning lights began to flash on her controls.

"Stop it! Stop it, you bastard!" she sobbed.

A moment later all the readouts went to red. The weapon was wrecked. What could she do? The other lasers! There were a dozen more turrets she could use. In a flash she unbuckled herself from her chair, swung through the hatch, and closed it behind her. She stumbled along the accessway toward the next turret.

* * * * *

"Okay gang, see how it's done?" asked Crawford to his crew.

"Sure, boss! Can we go back in?"

"Yup, keep her busy." He paused for a moment and glanced at Sheila. She still had her image goggles on and did not notice that he had taken his off. He toggled a switch on the com panel. "Kurtz? You wanted another shot, didn't you? You can take over my droid for a while. I need to… take a break."

"Sure thing, boss! Thanks!" Crawford transferred control to Renni's panel and then got out of his chair and headed for the hatch. He was just slipping through when he heard Shelia shouting at him.

"Chuck! Just where do you think you're going?"

* * * * *

Carlina cursed in frustration as her laser was wrecked—again. This was the third one she'd lost, but she had managed to nail another of the droids. She was just heading for another turret when the alarm sounded again. She pulled out her hand-comp and looked.

"No!"

She came to a stop and slumped against the bulkhead, gasping. She had tied her small computer into the bridge sensor station. It now showed her that a bogey was only a few dozen meters away from the other side of the ship. It was bigger than any of the droids.

Much bigger.

She pulled out one of her pistols and sprinted for the bridge.

Chapter Four

Charles Crawford stared at the light gray wall that was the hull of the heavy cruiser *Exeter* and tried to decide if he was feeling excited or just plain scared. Scared, yeah, he was definitely scared. Annoyed, too. He glanced over to where Ensign Frichette was seated in the co-pilot's chair. He had managed to slip away from Sheila's apron-strings and get down to the shuttle—only to find Frichette already there. The lad had blushed slightly but merely said that he had promised he would not join the boarding party—he'd said nothing about coming along on the shuttle *transporting* the boarding party. Crawford, himself caught playing hooky, could hardly protest, so here they both were.

"There's one, sir," said the shuttle's pilot. He and Frichette looked where the man was pointing and saw the clearly painted outline of an emergency airlock. He was fairly certain that none of the ship's defense lasers could bear on them here. Fairly certain.

"All right, latch us on," said Frichette. Crawford had nearly given the order at the same time but caught himself. The ensign was in command, he reminded himself. Doing a good job of it, too, it seemed. The boy was certainly nervous, but he concealed it quite well.

"Yes, sir, extending docking collar now. Moving in to attach."

The shuttle slowly edged closer to the side of the cruiser while the pilot carefully aligned his vessel so the collar extending from their own airlock would exactly line up with the warship's lock. As he watched the operation, he noticed Frichette stifling a yawn and rubbing at his eyes. The regulations called for a full day of rest after revival before doing any serious activity. He glanced at the pilot; he had been revived even more recently. How was he feeling?

Well enough, apparently, because it took only a minute or so before the magnetic clamps on the docking collar grabbed hold of the cruiser's hull and locked them down tight.

"Hard dock complete, sir. I'm reading a good seal."

"Nicely done." Frichette and he unstrapped from their seats and moved back into the passenger compartment. A dozen people waited for him there. Ten were reliable crewmen and one petty officer Chief Duncan had picked out for the operation. Two were workmen that Crawford had provided—Greg VanVean and Pawli Samms.

Crawford went over to the airlock and opened the inner door. The lock itself was barely large enough for two men, but with the docking collar pressurized, they could leave the inner door open and still open the outer door. Even so, they were all wearing vac suits, just in case. He entered the lock and pressed a button. The outer door hissed open, revealing the two-meter long docking collar and the emergency airlock leading to

Exeter. There was a small control panel next to the lock door. He floated over to it and pressed the entry button.

Nothing happened.

He tried again and still nothing happened. This was not unexpected, simply annoying. On a civilian ship there would have been a manual hand-crank, but military ships were a bit touchier about security and that feature was missing. He pushed himself back into the shuttle. "All right, the door won't open, we are going to have to cut. Greg, that's your department."

"Right, boss," said the big man. "Pawli, let's get to work." The two workers unstrapped and began collecting their gear. While they were doing that, Crawford went back to the shuttle's cockpit and reported his situation back to his people on *Neshaminy*. They informed him that Citrone was no longer manning the laser turrets, so that indicated she was aware of what they were doing. Sheila chewed him out for a few minutes for his 'school boy stunt' until he told her he had to go.

To avoid fidgeting uselessly in front of the others, he stayed in the cockpit and stared out at the Rift Fleet. It was a different perspective from here than aboard *Neshaminy*. He was closer to the outside edge of the cluster and only a few cruisers and destroyers were visible against the unremitting blankness of hyperspace. He was no stranger to hyperspace, most of his jobs were gate construction and usually one end of the gate was in some system without a gate there already. That meant the only way to get there was by starship. But he'd never been on a trip like this before. When they dropped back into normal space, the stars of home would be three thousand light years away...

"Boss?" VanVean was calling to him, startling him out of his musings. "We've got the controls uncovered. You might want to see what we're doing."

Crawford moved back into the passenger compartment and then into the lock, Frichette following him like a puppy. There was a considerable cloud of smoke from all the cutting, roiling oddly in the zero-G. The shuttle's air recyclers weren't designed for this sort of load and he was glad he was breathing his suit's air. He pushed himself up to look past VanVean's broad shoulder and saw that a rather neat hole had been cut around the airlock's control panel and that the whole unit was now loose, still connected by some trailing wires.

"Pretty standard design," said VanVean without preamble. "What do you think, Pawli? Can you jimmy it?"

"Think so, boss," said the other worker. "The only thing wrong here is that there's no power. Probably cut off further inside. I just need to tie in a portable power unit directly to the motor that runs the door and it should open up. I can see the leads right over there...I think."

"Well, let's find out."

"Right." The man produced a portable power unit, uncoiled its leads, and then stuck his head into the hole they had made. He began to let off a barely audible stream of cursing which apparently was just the way he worked rather than any comment on what was happening. In surprisingly short time he moved away from the ship's hull. "Okay, let's see how this does." He activated the power feed, and to Crawford's satisfaction, the airlock door slid open. Belatedly, he realized that someone might be waiting in ambush and he fumbled out his stunner, but fortunately, the compartment which was revealed was empty.

He led the way into the airlock. He noted in relief that the control panel by the inner door had some glowing lights on it. The exterior one had seemed completely dead. "All right, everyone, on your toes." He hit the entry button and the door slid open at once. He cautiously poked his head through, stunner ready, and looked around. The corridor on the other side was deserted. He let out his breath and keyed his communicator.

"Crawford to *Neshaminy*. We're in."

* * * * *

Another alarm on the control panels made Carlina look up from what she was doing. The main status board showed that emergency airlock twelve had just been opened. She cursed. They were aboard. This was sooner than she had hoped. Things were moving too damn fast, but she was nearly done here. Once she was finished she could…what? Her breath was coming in gasps and it was terribly hard to keep her concentration focused. She had one last thing to do, one last thing before the end.

The end was coming, she was quite sure of that. Crawford and his people were coming for her and there was no way for her to stop them. Everything had begun to go wrong from the instant he had found her in the cold-sleep compartment on *Neshaminy*. Looking back, she could see a dozen different things she might have done to prevent this disaster, but it was all too late now. In a few minutes or a few hours they were going to catch her. She'd fight them, but she would lose in the end. There were just too many of them. Even if she managed to kill or drive off this first boarding party there would be more. And she could not stay awake forever. She could barely stay awake now. How long had it been since she slept? She couldn't remember.

She typed the last command into her terminal and sighed in relief. For hours she had been cursing the fact that she did not have the access codes to do the things she had wanted. She couldn't use the automatic weapons systems, hell, she could not even shut the emergency bulkheads to keep the invaders out. But this was *her* com panel and she *did* have the codes to make it do what she wanted! The bastards might beat her today, but she was quite sure she would win in the end. Yes. She checked her instructions one last time and then locked down the terminal and blanked the screen.

She stood up and began struggling into her gear.

* * * * *

Charles Crawford cautiously peered around the corner and nervously looked for any sign of their quarry. His people clustered eagerly behind him. They seemed to consider this a big adventure and were chattering away in some sort of pseudo military-speak which they probably picked up from watching the vids. He, unlike any of them, had some real idea of what a boarding action could be like. Many years before he'd been on a gate construction job when a warship had escorted in a merchant ship and the pirate it had caught trying to take the merchant. There had been a lot of casualties and the construction site's medical facilities had been pressed into service. Crawford had seen the dead and wounded being brought off those ships and looked around a bit afterward. The sights he'd seen were still fresh in his memory. The pirates had fought with a savage desperation and had neither given nor expected quarter.

The woman they were hunting might be just as desperate.

Who the hell was she? He'd been asking himself that question nearly from the moment this whole nightmare began. The obvious answer was someone who didn't want the Protectorate of Andera to succeed in establishing a foothold on the far side of the Rift. Unfortunately, there were far too many someones who fit that description. It probably wasn't the Petrunans. They had gotten across first, but the Hebyrnans, out of fear, pride, or just spite, had quickly followed and browbeat them into accepting a relatively tiny slice of territory in the new arm, while they laid claim to the rest. The Petrunans were on friendly terms with the Protectorate and if they were going to be sabotaging anyone it would be the Hebyrnans.

He supposed it could be the Hebyrnans; they had made themselves pompously obnoxious about their claims to the Perseus Arm and had warned other nations to stay clear. But the Rift Fleet was heading for a spot a long, long way from Hebyrnan territory and Andera had beaten up on them sufficiently during the *last* war that Crawford doubted they wanted to start another one so soon.

"All clear, sir?" Frichette's question from right behind him made him jump slightly. He still couldn't believe he'd let the ensign talk him into coming along. Every argument he'd raised about Frichette being too valuable to risk was instantly countered by one that he, himself, as head of gate construction, was also too valuable to risk. When it became clear that the spacers, who made up the bulk of the boarding party, were far more comfortable taking orders from Frichette, he had relented. The boy seemed nervous, but determined. He was carrying an antique, but still very deadly, force-dagger in addition to a hand stunner. They all had stunners, as *Neshaminy's* arms locker not being able to provide anything more lethal.

"Looks clear. But we're getting close to the bridge. Stay alert." He eased out around the corner and moved down the corridor to the next intersection, stunner at the ready. His team followed, making far too much noise.

"Are we sure this babe is alone?" asked one of the crew.

"No, we're not. That's why I'm not letting us split up. It's unlikely that there are more than two or three, but you guys in the rear keep a close look out behind us." There were a few mumbled acknowledgments and he could nearly hear the heads swiveling to look back. He sure hoped he was right about the numbers they faced. Everything pointed to this woman being alone or with only one or two confederates, but it was all speculation. Possibly all wishful thinking.

If it was one of the major powers behind this, then it might very well only be one person. Hebyrna would have found it difficult to smuggle in a whole team. Andera's other serious rivals, Venance, Eddan, and the Jecovan Republic, might have had more luck in that department, but it still would have been difficult. Security for the expedition had been unusually tight. No, if there was more than one saboteur, it was most likely the plot came from within the Protectorate itself. The Protector and the men who backed the expedition had made more than a few enemies over the years. No, Crawford sincerely wished—for a lot of reasons—that this woman was alone.

He checked the next corridor, the one that led to the bridge, and it seemed to be empty, too. Sheila had informed him that there was no more fire coming from the point defense lasers and that there was no sign of anyone in the gunners' bubbles. So if she wasn't manning a turret, she was probably somewhere around...

"Hey! There!"

"It's her!"

"Look out! Ahhh!"

The shouts came from behind him and he spun around to see the rear of his party under attack. A figure had emerged silently from a side corridor and was blazing away with a laser pistol in each hand. Three of his people were already down and the rest were diving for cover. Well, most of them were. VanVean stood there and took very deliberate aim with his stunner and fired into their attacker point blank.

The figure lurched back a step but did not fall. It turned one of its lasers on VanVean and fired. The beam was hard to see in the bright corridor lighting, but a faint red line momentarily linked the pistol to VanVean. There was a flash and a puff of vapor as part of the man's vac suit—and the flesh underneath—vaporized. The big man collapsed to the deck. "Greg!" shouted Crawford in dismay.

"Shoot her!" someone was screaming.

"I am! It's not stopping her!"

Combat armor!

The woman was in combat armor. It wasn't powered like real battle armor, nor did it have built-in weaponry, but it was almost completely insulated against ordinary stunner bolts. Crawford's blood went cold when he realized that their weapons would be useless.

God, she'll slaughter all of us!

"Fall back!" he shouted.

The men, the ones still on their feet, bolted past him. Another tried to scramble away on hands and knees, but the woman shot him in the back and he went down with a cry. Frichette came up beside him, brandishing his dagger — now *that* could penetrate her armor if he could get close enough to use it. Citrone came on and Crawford could see her clearly through the faceplate of her helmet now. Her eyes were like the camera lenses on some droid; cold, lifeless. He fired his stunner into her and she staggered slightly. The armor wasn't completely proof against his weapon, but it was enough. He had gotten her attention now; perhaps he could keep it long enough for his men to escape or for Frichette to get close enough to strike. She strode forward and the laser pistol in her right hand swung his way. He fired again, but she stepped over one of the bodies littering the corridor and the laser was pointing right at him now.

Suddenly, the still form of Greg VanVean moved. A huge hand closed around the woman's ankle and the man surged to his feet. The woman fell forward and for the one instant longer that Crawford could look through her faceplate, her eyes were very human and very large in utter shock. She hit the floor and one of the pistols flew out of her grip. Then VanVean grabbed her ankle in both hands and swung her around one hundred and eighty degrees, like an Olympian with a hammer, and slammed the woman, full force, against the bulkhead. Her other pistol skittered away and her armored form crashed to the deck with an impact Crawford could hear through his helmet. She didn't move.

VanVean stood there looking slightly puzzled. "Damn, they don' make saboteurs like they used to," he groaned. "One good whack an' they break."

"Greg, are you all right?"

"Jus' a scratch. Had worse 'n this a hunnert times..." But the man was swaying on his feet. The lasers didn't actually do all that much damage compared to a lot of weapons, but even when they did not hit anything vital, they tended to send the victim into shock. VanVean was clearly on his way.

Still, he was alive. Crawford moved to see if that was the case with the other casualties. Amazingly, they all were. Two were not in bad shape, but two more were unconscious and clearly in need of attention. VanVean slowly slid down the bulkhead into a sitting position, all the while insisting he was fine.

"Jameson, get over here with that medkit," commanded Frichette. The next several minutes were taken up in bandaging wounds that, fortunately, were mostly cauterized, and injecting stabilization drugs. Crawford commed *Neshaminy* to report his status and they informed him that another shuttle would be dispatched with reinforcements along with Doctor Birringir as soon as possible.

Once things were under control, Crawford looked around, half in a daze. The adrenaline rush was fading and he really wanted a nap. But there was no time for that. He collected the two laser pistols the woman had dropped, kept one and gave the other to Frichette, who'd been standing guard over Citrone with his dagger. He then pulled the helmet off the mysterious woman. She was alive, but unconscious. A bandage on her head had come loose and she was bleeding slightly. Not knowing what else to do, he had Pawli Samms use some wires from his tool kit to tie the woman's arms and legs and left her for the doctor. With a groan, he turned and headed for the bridge, Frichette and the others on his heels.

"That was wonderful the way you stood up to her, sir," said Frichette. "That was really brave."

"Not brave. I was too scared to run. But you did a good job, yourself, Ensign. You stood there, too, with just that zig-sticker of yours."

"Too scared to run," said Frichette and they both laughed.

"Careful now, the bridge is just ahead."

He was nervous, but not really expecting to encounter anyone else. Surely if the woman had allies they would have attacked at the same time she did. Still, he held the pistol at the ready as the hatch slid open.

The bridge was empty.

He sighed with relief. He supposed that there could be other enemies lurking somewhere, but it seemed even less likely now. "Pawli, take two men and go down to the cold-sleep compartment. See the status board, there? It will show you the route. Don't touch anything once you're there, but take a look around. See if there are manual revival buttons on the capsules like ours have. And stay sharp, we don't know if that woman was alone."

"Right away, boss." The man selected two others and departed with Crawford's laser pistol. Except for the two men he had left with the wounded, Crawford now only had Frichette and one other man with him. His party kept shrinking and shrinking. He slumped down in the captain's chair. It was amazingly comfortable and he forced himself to get out of it before he dozed off. He couldn't remember ever being so tired. Frichette, on the other hand, was eagerly surveying the control stations like a kid with a new toy. He'd been tempted to send Frichette to the cold-sleep compartment, but he was grimly certain that all the officers there would be dead and he wanted to spare the boy that. They could get the enlisted crew revived and let the navy take care of the rest of this mess. He sure hoped that they could.

"Tell me, Ensign, do you think the enlisted crewmen will be able to run this ship—or the others—if the… if there aren't any officers to lead them?" Frichette turned to face him and looked thoughtful.

"Not sure, sir. If they are veteran crews—and I think most of them are—they will have the necessary training and skills to handle almost any of the posts. Well, astrogation and weaponry might be a problem. B-but I'm not sure about the leadership question. Without a real officer around to give direction, I'm not certain…" he trailed off and flicked a glance at the one remaining crewman from their party.

Crawford nodded and chewed on his lower lip. Yeah, that could be a real problem. Andera—like most places—had been, for all intents and purposes, a feudal state for over a thousand years following the fall of the UW. The surviving soldiers from the Great Revolt had become a ruling class and had run things ever since. The lower classes had been beaten down and reminded of their inferiority for so long, that they instinctively looked to the nobles and officers for all their decision-making. Things had loosened up a lot in Andera since the War of the Four Families, but it was still a tradition and mindset hard to break. The enlisted crews of these ships would not be well-suited to step into the positions left by the dead officers. Well, damn it, they would just have to get…

"Mr. Crawford!" The speaker in his helmet suddenly came to life and he jumped.

"Crawford here, go ahead."

"Boss! T-this is Pawli. I-I'm in the cold-sleep compartment. C-could you come down here?" The tone of the man's voice brought him to full alert.

"What's wrong?"

"I think…I think you better see for yourself, sir."

"All right, I'm coming."

He left the bridge and walked aft, Frichette trailing him again. Half-way there he suddenly realized that perhaps there had been additional saboteurs after all. Perhaps Pawli's party had been captured and this was a ruse to draw him into an ambush. That might explain Pawli's agitation. He pulled out his stunner and advanced much more cautiously. Frichette took the cue and had the laser pistol and dagger ready as well. He heard a faint electronic wail from up ahead. But when he reached the compartment, his men were alone and uncaptured. They were also standing like statues. Not saying a word.

"All right what's the…?" Crawford stopped in mid-sentence. He looked. He looked again.

"Oh, dear God in His heaven…" he hissed.

He'd been expecting the officers' compartment to look like this, to look like the one on *Neshaminy*, but this wasn't the officers' compartment! All of them? Surely not all of them...? He splashed through the goo on the deck to inspect the other rows of capsules. Not all, surely not...

All of them. Crawford could feel the sweat on his forehead and his gasping was beginning to fog his helmet visor in spite of the recycling unit. He wrenched it open and then slammed it shut again as a sickly sweet smell assaulted his nostrils. He hadn't wanted to vomit in a vac suit since he was a trainee, but he wanted to now.

Mercifully, the capsules themselves were all fogged up from inside. He could not see any of the bodies inside clearly, but he had no doubt that each one was a corpse. His men were trailing behind him as if they were afraid to get too far away from him in this chamber of the dead.

"W-why? Why would she...why would anyone...?" Pawli gasped.

"She didn't have the access codes," said Crawford with grim certainty. "Just like on *Neshaminy*, she couldn't reset the revival dates and she couldn't allow them to wake up. But here she didn't have any of the codes. So she, so she..." *Oh God.* He hit his com button. "Crawford to *Neshaminy*! Urgent!"

Chapter Five

Dead. They were all dead. All the navy personnel in the entire fleet were dead. And all the officers on forty-eight of the civilian ships—including everyone on Governor Shiffeld's command ship! Charles Crawford still couldn't get his head around this. Nine thousand men and women on seventy-eight ships, dead in their cold-sleep capsules. Well, nine of them on *Exeter* had been killed outside their capsules, but they were just as dead. The crew of *Neshaminy,* and the crews they'd revived on the other civilian ships, had spent the last four days searching through the Rift Fleet and it had been the same hideous story everywhere they went. Nearly everywhere; Citrone had not gotten to twenty of the civilian ships. Twenty ships out of ninety-eight still had officers.

Of personal concern to him, Sir Douglas Mueir was dead. Mueir was Baron Dougherty's official representative on the expedition and Crawford's titular boss. Mueir was a businessman, not an engineer, and would not have had any involvement in the actual construction job, but Crawford still answered to him. Or did. Crawford wasn't sure who, if anyone, he answered to now.

Was there anything he could have done to prevent this? He'd asked himself the question a hundred times since this began and even though the answer was certainly and undeniably no, he still could not stop asking. At least he hadn't been with the poor bastards who'd had to search all the ships to confirm the disaster, but he'd seen some of them coming back; seen the expressions on their faces.

Stop torturing yourself. Most of them were dead before you even woke up. The rest were being killed when you could not possibly have even known about it. That was probably the worst: he'd been sitting in his office, looking at plans, for days while Citrone was busily murdering people. If he'd just looked out a window and spotted the shuttle car moving. If he's just had the nerve to check in with *Exeter* when he woke up. If, if, if…

Crawford sighed and forced himself to put it behind him. This wasn't doing anyone any good. He still had a job to do and the fact that it seemed to have become very much more complicated did not change the basic fact that he had a gate to build. The largest, most powerful and longest-range gate ever constructed. He had chosen a ten year exile, given up a reasonable shot at becoming master of his guild, left some special friends behind, all for a chance at this job. He wasn't going to let anything—not even mass murder—stop him.

He glanced at the other people in the supervisor's lounge. They all seemed as dazed as he felt. The numbers were hard to grasp. Nine thousand dead. Not much of a casualty count compared to a real war, but it was all far more immediate, far more horrible somehow. Anyone who went into a cold-sleep capsule inevitably had a nagging fear that they would never wake up again. Nine thousand people had not awakened again and everyone here could not help but feel that it might have been them instead. The only good news at all was that the family transports had not been touched. He turned as Doctor Barringir entered the compartment.

"How's Greg?" he asked immediately.

"He'll live," she said as she grabbed a mug of coffee and sat down.

"I never had any doubt of that. It would take a lot more than a laser shot to kill that ugly s.o.b. But how is he, really?"

"Not too bad. He was hit in the chest, but not near the heart. Came close to one of his lungs, but he has so much natural padding, it soaked up most of the blast. He'll need a little regeneration before he's his handsome self again, but he's not in any danger."

"What about the others?"

"Two of them are in worse shape. They will need some surgery and extended convalescence, but they will recover. The other two were even less serious injuries than Greg. I have them all well taken care of— since I appear to be the ship's doctor now, too…" Crawford nodded, nearly all the doctors in the fleet had been with the officers; they were seriously short-handed in that department, too.

"How about the bitch who did all this?" snarled Fred Kimmal. "She been spaced yet?"

"No," said Barringir, looking simultaneously annoyed and embarrassed. "She's actually in a worse way than any of the others. I've never seen anyone—not even the most overtime hungry rigger—so strung out on stimulants. If she'd kept it up for even another day or two she probably would have killed herself."

"Saved us the trouble."

"I doubt she'll be spaced anytime soon," said Crawford. "We've got a lot of questions we need answered first."

"I'd be happy to help with the questioning," growled Kimmal. He was echoed by several others. Crawford shifted uneasily. The shock from the deaths had lasted for a few days and now it seemed like the anger was about to begin. He had no love for Carlina Citrone, but he could not let her be lynched—at least not until they had gotten some answers out of her. Another thought struck him. "Doctor, is everything…secure…in your sick bay?"

Barringir looked at him over the rim of her coffee cup and he could see that she understood what he was really asking. "All ship-shape, Charles—except for that guard Mr. Frichette posted there. He has been getting in my way. He seems to think Citrone needs watching, even though she probably won't wake up for another two days."

"Good." Citrone wasn't going anywhere, but hopefully the guard could handle anyone thinking about taking justice into their own hands.

He was glad the guard was there and impressed that young Frichette had thought to provide one. Frichette was impressing him in a lot of ways.

In the past five days some semblance of organization had begun to appear in what was left of the Rift Fleet. Everyone who was still alive had been revived from cold-sleep and given a sketchy briefing on what had happened. Their reactions had varied widely. Fortunately, the bulk of the people were in the construction crews for the gate and the supporting infrastructure and there had been no casualties among them at all—except for the officers of the ships carrying them—and aside from being understandably worried, had taken the news well. The crews of the ships who had lost their officers had taken it the worst. Young Petre Frichette had been right about the problems that had arisen. The loss of lawful authority had left them dazed and barely responsive. They were simultaneously unwilling to take orders from unfamiliar faces or to take any initiative on their own. Fortunately, for the moment, the ships were following automatic controls and would be until their destination was reached. After that…

After that, he didn't know what was going to happen. They had some really serious decisions to make and right now they didn't even know who was going to be making them. No one was really in charge of the fleet anymore.

"Just about time to go, Mr. Crawford." He looked up to see Ensign Frichette standing by the hatch.

He nodded and stood up. A meeting had been called and it was being held on *Starsong*, the ship that was to have been the headquarters of this entire expedition. There had been a high concentration of nobles and other VIPs on that ship, and Citrone had slaughtered nearly all of them. Only the enlisted crew had been spared. Crawford wasn't happy about going to this ship of the dead, but it had the best conference room in the fleet and it was centrally located in the cluster.

The conference room on *Starsong* was enormous. There was a main table, which could seat about thirty, and then there were rows of raised seats overlooking the table, which could handle at least a hundred more. Visual displays of various sizes and capabilities were scattered around so that everyone would get a clear view. In Crawford's experience, rooms like this were mostly to gratify the egos of the people running the meetings. It was extremely rare for any real work to get done in one of them. Still, until a permanent base could be constructed, *Starsong* was going to be the center of government—assuming they could create one—for an entire star system. Perhaps it wasn't *all* ego—beyond the hubris that sent out the whole expedition in the first place, of course.

As the head of gate construction he had a place at the main table. To Crawford's left was Jinsup Sowell, head of manufacturing. Jin would be setting up the orbital factories which would supply those items needed for the rest of the operation—over and beyond what had been brought with the fleet. Crawford had worked with Jin before and respected his abilities. Beyond him was Lu Karrigan, in charge of mining. He and his asteroid prospectors would supply the raw materials to Jin's factories. Next along the table was Tosh Briggs. This man would be in charge of constructing the orbital habitats used by the factory workers and terraformers. Crawford knew nothing about Briggs except he was here because of his political connections rather than any construction experience. He was some pet of Lord Allendale, the future governor of Landfall. Well, no matter, Crawford's team would be working out in deep space a long, long way from the planet that was to be terraformed. None of his people would be living in whatever Briggs managed to build, so it was no concern to him.

He looked to his right and saw that he was sitting next to the head of the terraforming project. Regina Nassau would have attracted attention under almost any circumstances; she was tall, statuesque, and her blonde hair, so pale as to be almost white, was cut very short except for a long braid coming asymmetrically out of the left side of her scalp. Her face was pretty—from certain angles. From other angles it was…odd, he could not decide why. She wore colorful and very non-standard clothing as well as some amazing illuminated rings and necklaces. The whole effect was striking, but strange. Well, terraformers were notoriously eccentric—even more so than engineers. Even if her appearance had been more conventional, Nassau's presence would have still attracted attention: she was the only department head who was a woman.

She saw him looking at her and turned and smiled. "Well, Mr. Crawford, I understand you went off and had an adventure on your own. That was hardly fair to the rest of us, y'know."

"I'd gladly let someone else have that sort of adventure," he said. He raised his cast-encased left arm slightly for emphasis. "And I would have been far happier if it had not ended so badly."

Her smile vanished. "Yes, what a terrible tragedy. Life is so precious that to snuff it out so…so casually is scarcely imaginable."

"Unfortunately," he said carefully, "someone was able to imagine it—and do it." She frowned and nodded.

Most of the other seats at the table were filled by the twenty surviving captains of the transport ships. Crawford had looked over their records beforehand in hopes of finding someone with the authority to take charge, but he'd been forced to admit that none of them fit the bill. Apparently, Carlina Citrone had made her murderous visits to the ships in the order of the importance of the people commanding them. The navy ships first and then the transport ships. The twenty captains still alive were all commoners with few, or no, connections to the nobility or anyone of importance. Captain Dumphries of *Neshaminy* been the last and least of the nobility.

Except for Petre Frichette, of course.

Crawford still wasn't sure what to make of the young man. He might only have been an ensign, but socially he outranked everyone else in the room. He could be useful in establishing some sort of order out of the barely-restrained chaos that was threatening to engulf the fleet. But would the others accept someone so young and inexperienced in a role like that? Would Frichette even want it if it was offered?

"I think we're ready to start," whispered Frichette from the chair beyond Nassau.

Crawford hesitated. "So who should run this, do you think?" He asked it quietly, but most everyone heard him and turned to look his way. No one spoke.

"Well, you have seniority, sir," said Frichette after a moment.

"Seniority? How do you figure that, Ensign?"

"You've been awake the longest of anyone here, sir." The boy tried to restrain a grin, but he failed, gave in to it, and then smiled broadly. Crawford snorted and several other people laughed.

"It's as good a way as any to decide," said Lu Karrigan.

"Well, I don't know," said Tosh Briggs. "My patron is Lord Allandale, himself and…"

"And he's four thousand light years away, Tosh," said Regina Nassau. "We're talking about the here and now and Mr. Crawford is more familiar with the situation than anyone else."

Briggs scowled at her but didn't argue.

"In any case," continued Karrigan, "Chuck is in charge of building the gate. That's what this whole thing is about when you come down to it. All the rest of us are just here to support that. You run the meeting, Chuck."

"Well, as long as it's just the meeting," grumbled Briggs. There were no further objections, so Crawford took a deep breath and swiveled his chair so he could face as many people as possible.

"Okay, then. You all know what's happened. We've been handed one hell of a mess and we have to decide how to deal with it."

"I still can't understand how this could have happened," said Briggs interrupting immediately. "I mean who was in charge of security? How did this Citrone woman get into the expedition? Why wasn't anyone watching out for something like this? Someone back home is going to have to answer for this disaster!"

"Yeah, but who?" said one of the ship captains. "Half the leaders of Andera have their fingers in this project!"

"Well, she was on a navy ship," said another. "It's the navy's problem, I say!"

Several others voiced their opinions and suddenly it became quite loud in the large room. Crawford let it go for a few seconds and then stood up and called for quiet. "Gentlemen," he nodded toward Regina, "and ladies, those are certainly important questions, but I submit that they are questions which can wait until later. Right now we have to decide what we are going to do next and how."

"Absolutely right," said Jinsup Sowell. "There will be plenty of time later to place blame — and I'm sure there will be plenty to go around. But Charles is right: our main task is to figure out what we do now."

"Well, what can we do?" asked Briggs. "The expedition is wrecked! You can't expect us to try and carry on with no naval escort and all the nobles dead!" Every face turned toward Briggs and the man seemed to shrink in on himself. "How can we?" he squeaked.

"Are you seriously suggesting we abandon our mission?" asked Crawford in amazement.

"I don't see how we can do anything else! Let's turn around and go home!" Crawford winced and all the ship officers were shaking their heads and muttering. Hadn't Briggs read any of the briefing materials?

"I'm afraid that's not possible, Mr. Briggs," said one of the captains. Crawford thought it was Captain Jervis of the *Gillingham*.

"Why not?"

"Simple physics, sir. We used forty-five perent of our reaction mass accelerating to our present velocity. We'll use another forty-five percent canceling out that vector. With the ten percent we'd have left, it would take us over ninety years to get home. I don't know about you, but I don't want to spend that much time in cold-sleep."

Briggs turned pale. "No, no, of course not. But couldn't we stop and get more reaction mass?"

"We'd have to drop out of hyper to do that anyway. Might as well drop out where we planned and build our gate and get home in two years instead of ten."

"Can we do that?"

"Yes we can," said Crawford forcefully. "Our gate construction team and all the supporting crews are fully intact. We can still build the gate on schedule and link up with the one on the other side of the Rift." He paused and looked around. "The question is: will we be allowed to?"

"What do you mean, sir? Allowed by who?"

"By whoever was behind the sabotage. Citrone's attack was carefully planned and not some random terrorism. There is more to this than we know, I'm sure. She didn't simply kill everyone. In fact, she only killed those people whose cold-sleep capsules could not have the timers reset. She was resetting those that she could to a time about five months from now. What do you suppose is going to happen five months from now?"

Silence met his question. Everyone was frowning and thinking; no one liked the obvious conclusions.

"She's expecting something to happen in the next five months," said Petre Frichette. "She's expecting help."

"Help? From where?" demanded Briggs.

"There are two possibilities," said Crawford. "One is that she has allies among the fleet personnel. There could be additional saboteurs here—however, I don't think that's too likely," he added quickly, seeing the looks of dismay on the faces of the people around him.

"Why not?"

"Well, it seems to me, she would have revived them first thing to help her out. As far as we can tell, she did all of her murderous work alone. If she had allies, why not get them awake and helping her? And even if there were additional traitors, I don't see how that fits in with the five-month revival delay."

"What's the other possibility?" asked Lu Karrigan.

"She's expecting help to arrive from across the Rift."

Some of the people nodded, they'd already figured that out. As he'd expected, Tosh Briggs wasn't one of them.

"Across the Rift? But... but..."

"We made it across. Others have, too. There's no reason someone else could not send ships across."

"To do what?"

"Hijack our gate would be my guess."

"Hijack? How?"

"Well, if even a small force of warships—with a lot of soldiers aboard—were here waiting for us when we all woke up, and all our leaders were dead and they had guns pointed at our heads, they could force us to build the gate—for them. Then they hook it into a gate they've built at their end and they have a route across the Rift at a bargain price."

"My God... But who...?"

"Good question and I have no answer to that. And it's all speculation anyway, I could be completely wrong. Maybe there isn't anyone coming. Maybe this was just a plot to wreck the project. Maybe Citrone was planning to kill all of us in the end and was just resetting the timers on some to give her more time to wreck all the cold-sleep capsules. We just don't know."

"Well then maybe we should find out, Mr. Crawford," said another of the captains. "Has the traitor been questioned yet?"

"No, my doctor says she is still pretty weak and in no shape to..."

"The traitorous bitch doesn't deserve any consideration, sir!" snarled another officer. "Not after what she did! My son was a rating on *Indomitable* and she murdered him! Question her now—and don't be gentle!"

Crawford rocked back in the face of such anger. He hadn't thought of that aspect to the situation. Of course there would be survivors with close ties to some of the dead. Maybe they needed a few more guards on Citrone...

"Well, I don't know, the doctor says that..."

"Chuck, how can we make any sensible decisions unless we know what's really threatening us?" asked Lu Karrigan. More voices rose up in agreement. Crawford looked around nervously.

"If she dies under interrogation, we won't learn anything..."

"If you won't do it, then I will!" shouted the angry father. Others volunteered their help. This was getting out of hand...

"All right! All right! We'll question her!" he exclaimed. "Let's adjourn the meeting for now. I'll go talk to her and then we can meet again."

"If you need any help 'persuading' her, let me know," said someone.

"That won't be necessary, thank you. Now if you'll excuse me, I'll go talk to Miss Citrone."

* * * * *

The sound of angry voices woke Carlina. She had been drifting in and out of sleep for...how long? She didn't know. It seemed like days, but she wasn't sure. She could vaguely remember her last fight. She had been blazing away with a laser pistol in each hand and then, suddenly, she was flying through the air; there had been a heavy impact and then blackness. Since then, there were only a confusing jumble of her brushes with consciousness. People hovering over her, images of what was obviously a sick bay, medical equipment too close for comfort... And clinging like a shadow, the knowledge that she was a prisoner. She had not planned on being taken alive, but they had taken her down so quickly that she'd been unable to arrange a glorious—or even an inglorious—death. Part of her was relieved. This was never supposed to be a suicide mission, and she had not wanted to die. If things had worked, she would have been found by the relief squadron safe and sound. If it didn't work, well, it hadn't and now the enemy had her.

The voices were getting closer and angrier. It was hard to concentrate, but she forced herself to pay attention.

"Charles, I can't allow this!" snapped a woman's voice. It sounded strangely familiar. "My patient is in no condition to be questioned—and I will not release her!"

"I'm sorry, Giselle," said a male voice. "I don't have any choice. If I don't talk to her, there's going to be a lynch mob coming in here—and they won't have any mercy at all."

There was another outburst from the woman and then the argument moved into the room where Carlina was laying. The woman, the doctor, looked vaguely familiar, and she immediately recognized the man: Charles Crawford. She should have expected it.

"All right!" snapped the woman. "I can't stop you from doing whatever you are going to do, but I insist being allowed to monitor her condition."

"Fine, Giselle, I want you to stay. Now, what sort of shape is she in and do you have anything you can give her to make this any easier?"

Carlina tensed. He was going to question her. She'd had some training in resisting interrogation, but what if they used torture? She started moving her arms and legs to see if she could fight them, but they felt like lead. Heavy and clumsy, like they didn't even belong to her. The slight effort left her sweating and gasping. Damn, what was wrong with her?

"She's lightly sedated," said the doctor. "I don't really have anything here that's like an interrogation drug, but I do have stronger sedatives. Those might make her babble. But Charles, I don't want risk anything too strong."

"All right, let me just talk to her for a bit and see how cooperative she's going to be." Crawford came toward the bed and pulled up a chair. He was a broad, stocky man, obviously from some high-gravity world. A thick neck supported a large head with a dark mop of hair, starting to thin on top and graying at the temples. His face would have been almost attractive if the situation were different. He was smiling faintly and Carlina noticed the cast on his arm. If only she'd broken his neck instead!

"Well, Miss Citrone, we meet again," he said. "First time I've felt safe being within arm's reach of you."

"I wish... I wish I'd killed you when I had the chance." Her voice came out as a gravelly rasp and she had to clear her throat before she could go on.

"That certainly would have simplified your life, but I'm just as glad that you did not succeed. We need to talk."

"I have nothing to say to you."

"Really? Well, I suggest you reconsider. Your actions have made a lot of people very angry. I'm willing to forgive a broken arm, but there are people out there with dead sons and daughters, cousins and uncles who aren't in such a good mood. The only thing keeping you alive is the fact that we need some answers from you. If you don't provide some, I can't stop them from coming in here and getting a lot rougher than I intend."

Carlina hesitated. All the time she was killing those people, she'd forced herself not to think about the fact that they *were* people; that they had families and friends who would grieve for them. She'd treated them like frozen slabs of meat. It was the only way to stay sane and get the job done. But that little self-deception wasn't going to work anymore. Still, she had a duty to carry out and Crawford was still the enemy. "If I tell you what you want, then you'll just kill me anyway."

"I can't make any promises about your eventual fate — you've murdered nine thousand of our people, after all — but if you cooperate now, I'll do my best to keep the lynch mob away and see you get a fair hearing."

"Fair? From the Protector's thugs?"

"Well, less painful if not fair. Miss Citrone, if you can't give me something to appease them, then there will be no restraining them at all." The doctor stirred uneasily, but said nothing. "They'll come in here and start breaking your bones—one by one. They're *angry*, girl! Do you want that to happen?"

Carlina was quivering now and she realized she was very afraid. She had not counted on this. Dying was one thing, being tortured and slowly torn to pieces by an angry mob was something entirely different. As the seconds ticked away and Crawford continued to stare at her, she realized that she didn't want to die, either. She was only twenty-three standards and she really didn't want to die. She had hurt the Protector worse than she'd ever dreamed already. Wasn't that enough? The mission was ninty-nine percent accomplished. What could she actually tell Crawford that would affect the final outcome?

"What...? What do you want to know?"

* * * * *

"Venance? Are you sure?" demanded Tosh Briggs.

"I kept at her for nearly two days," said Crawford wearily. "I'm confident of that much at least."

The assembled captains and department heads digested this news with a great deal of head-shaking and muttering. It had been Venance. The Holy and Selected Kingdom of Venance, ruled by Her Select Majesty Izelda IV, was behind the sabotage to the Rift Fleet. Crawford still wasn't sure if he was surprised or not. Venance and Andera had fought a number of wars over the years, including a particularly protracted and nasty one a century ago, but things had been relatively quiet since then. Well, politics and grand strategy were not his fields of expertise. It might not make sense to him, but clearly it had made sense to someone.

"Citrone is pretty well used up and I think she just gave in after a while. That, and the fact that she thinks she's got us beaten. She just started talking and wouldn't stop." Crawford's quick summary did not begin to describe what he'd put the girl through. She'd railed against the Protector and broken down in tears dozens of times. He could still feel himself shaking inside at the memory. It had been wearing and embarrassing and it had left him with a smoldering anger at whoever had set that kid to this horrible task. And she was just a kid, some angry kid who had been turned into a weapon and fired off with no more compassion than a torpedoman has for the ordnance he launches.

"And did you learn how the Venanci managed to slip an agent into our fleet?" Briggs was fiddling with a stylus and tapping it against the table top in an irritating fashion.

"Well, as for that, she was a bit more tight-lipped, but I think that she may have been a home-grown malcontent that the Venanci recruited, rather than someone brought in from outside. She did say 'Maker' a few times. Now that I think on it, she said 'Maker' when I surprised her in the control room, and that might indicate she's a Creationist."

"Filthy bastards," snarled Briggs. "The Protector should have made a clean sweep of that lot!"

Some of the people around the table agreed enthusiastically, while others said nothing. It was a touchy subject. The Creationists believed that Mankind had been deliberately created by a superior race or being rather than evolving from lower forms. There was nothing especially unusual about that, of course, a great many religions favored deliberate design rather than evolution. But the Creationists, in addition to believing in some sort of 'primogenitors', also believed that the job wasn't finished yet and that the next step was in Mankind's own hands. They were genetic tinkerers and that rubbed a lot of people the wrong way. Most of their tinkering was pretty mundane, except among the ruling class, who had the means for more radical efforts. Queen Izelda, herself, was said to have some rather… startling… characteristics.

Venance was the stronghold of the movement, but there were followers in many other regions. Andera had had quite a few Creationists until about fifty years ago. Then a popular movement to drive them out had taken hold and there weren't many left now. The pogroms were officially outlawed, but the Protector only paid lip-service to the law, and those Creationists who remained were secretive. It had been an ugly period. Crawford remembered a few incidents he'd seen as a child with a mixture of revulsion and embarrassment. If Carlina Citrone had been a closet Creationist, it might have been the means by which she was recruited for this job.

"But what about this 'relief squadron' she mentions?" asked Jinsup Sowell. "Did she give any specifics on that? Arrival time or strength?"

"Not really. She was so confused she couldn't even keep her lies straight. At one point she claimed it had a dozen battleships and later she refused to give me any numbers at all. The arrival time could be anything from waiting for us when we get there to five months from now."

"Actually, sir," said Petre Frichette, "it would not make any sense for the Venanci to have given her any details at all about this squadron other than it was coming. She did not need to know any of that to accomplish her mission, and what she doesn't know she can't reveal."

"Yes. But this is the bottom line: an enemy squadron is on its way here. As we feared, the Venanci are hoping to hijack our gate and hook it to a gate of their own. What we have to decide now is what to do about it."

"Well, what can we do about it?" cried Tosh Briggs. "The navy is gone! We're defenseless!"

"We still have the ships, sir," said Frichette.

"With no crews or officers! Useless!"

"Well, sir, we could probably get some of the ships operational and put together crews for them. If we don't have too large a force to contend with, we might be able to win."

"Against a dozen battleships? We only have two battleships in the whole fleet!"

"Two battleships, four battlecruisers, four heavy cruisers, six light cruisers, and fourteen destroyers, sir. A very powerful force. And Miss Citrone's statement about a dozen battleships in the approaching squadron is clearly a lie meant to frighten us. I'm sure the enemy force is much weaker than that."

"Oh, and just how did you deduce that, *Ensign?*" Crawford didn't like Briggs's tone, but he was puzzled by Frichette's store of information and confidence. He just did not talk like a seventeen-year old.

"A force that size and a proper escort would be a significant portion of Venance's battle fleet. I find it hard to believe that they would be willing to send it off on a mission that would keep it out of action for at least twelve years, sir. This whole scheme seems like a gamble by the Venanci to grab a gate across the Rift on the cheap. It would make no sense for them to commit massive resources to it. Why not just mount their own expedition instead?"

"I'd have to agree," said Captain Jervis. "The Venanci were already engaged in another war with the Etursi princes when we left. They could not afford to divert significant strength on a gamble like this. Mr. Frichette is likely right: they'd send the least force possible for this. It could well be just a couple of cruisers and a few transports for soldiers. With a little luck, we could beat a force like that."

"Luck? You might be willing to trust all of our lives to luck, but I am not!"

"Well, then, what do *you* propose?" The question seemed to catch Briggs off-guard.

"I... I don't know! But to just go there and wait for the Venanci to come and gobble us up is crazy!"

"We have a duty to carry out," said another captain, "to Andera and the Protector. Are you suggesting we give up and run? That's cowardice, sir!"

"How dare you?" shouted Briggs, turning red. "My family...!"

"We're not talking about your family, sir! We are talking about our duty! Or have you forgotten that?"

"You miserable cur!" snarled Briggs, surging to his feet. "I'll have your head off for that!"

The captain was on his feet, too, and half the people in the room as well. Crawford looked on in shock by this sudden outburst. The captain who had spoken did not seem to be armed, but Briggs had some sort of ceremonial dagger and his hand was on the hilt.

"Gentlemen! Gentlemen! Please calm down!" he shouted. He moved to put himself between the angry men. As he did so, the door to the conference room slid open and a small group of spacers stumbled inside. Had they heard the noise? Well, in any case, he was glad to have some help if this were to get out of...

He stopped and stared. So did everyone else in the room as heads turned toward the newcomers. Five enlisted spacers stood there, but it was not them that had everyone's attention. A man stood in the middle of them, half-supported by the others. He was short, slim, and wearing utility coveralls. He had a mustache, goatee, and salt-and-pepper hair all tosseled about. But it was the eyes that caught Crawford's attention. They were wide and wild, filled with fear and bewilderment. They wandered around the room as if in search of something familiar.

Crawford blinked and looked again. He knew this man. But before he could get his mouth to say anything, Tosh Briggs and half-a-dozen other voices burst out:

"Governor Shiffeld!"

Chapter Six

"**W**hat an incredible screw-up," sighed Sheila MacIntyrre. "How the hell did they miss seeing him?"

Crawford looked at his friend from across the table as they sat in the officers' lounge aboard *Neshaminy*. He took a sip of his coffee and shook his head. "Seems His Lordship didn't like the idea of being in a cold-sleep tube wearing nothing but his birthday suit out where everyone could see him. He had his tube put in a separate compartment. The search teams didn't know that, so they missed him completely. Can hardly blame them for not looking everywhere, after having to see the rest of that horror."

"Well, it was lucky for him, since Citrone missed him, too. But he's okay now?"

"I don't know if I'd call him 'okay'. Never saw a man so completely rattled. He was raving and blubbering by the time they got him to *Starsong*'s sick bay."

"Damn. Waking up to a shipload of dead would be enough to unhinge anyone."

"Yeah, and finding out that his whole grand fleet has been gutted probably isn't helping, either. He was so proud of being named lieutenant governor. I remember at some of the pre-departure meetings he was all puffed up and preening."

"But at least there is someone in charge again—at least in theory."

"In theory. And that would certainly be a relief. Just before Shiffeld showed up, Briggs and one of the captains were getting ready to kill each other. I'm not cut out for this administrative crap. I'm an engineer, damn it, I build things."

"Well, you are probably going to have do some of the administration, Chuck. The governor's entire staff is dead, right down to his valet."

"Yeah," said Crawford grimly. "He's going to need a lot of help. But I'm not sure who's here who can help him. All the other departments already have over-filled plates as it is. To try and do the mining, manufacturing, terraforming, *and* build the gate, *and* try to get some portion of the navy ships operational is going to stretch our resources way past the breaking point." He paused as Ensign Frichette came into the compartment, got a mug of tea, and sat down with them.

"Hi, Ensign," said Sheila. "Or I suppose I should call you *captain*, now."

"Oh, please don't," he sighed. "At least let me forget about it for a few minutes."

"Rough day?"

"You could say so. I'm trying to reshuffle the watch schedule and appoint acting officers to keep Neshaminy running, and at the same time, provide our share of the scratch bridge watches we are trying to set up for the navy ships. I suppose I should be grateful that we don't have to give up any officers for that or for the merchant ships that don't have them, but it's kind of hard to feel grateful under the circumstances."

"Yeah," growled Crawford, "I guess so." Frichette, being the only officer left on the ship, could hardly be taken away and assigned elsewhere. Even if someone had the authority to order such a transfer—and no one left did—it would make no sense to do so. "How are the crew responding to you being in charge?"

"Okay so far. I think they are still in shock and it's easier for them to just follow orders and do their jobs than to start questioning whether I'm fit to give those orders. I'm wondering how long that's going to last."

"Well, I must say, Captain, that you seem to be well prepared for your job. You seem to know what to do and how to do it. If you don't mind my saying so, isn't that a little unusual for someone as young as you are?"

Frichette stared at him for a few moments with a strange expression that was half embarrassment and half suspicion. "I've always been kind of ship-crazy, I guess," he answered at last. "When I was a kid—I mean when I was a much younger kid—I had toy ships filling my room. I watched vids about ships and organized my playmates into bridge crews. When I got older, I studied ship plans and schematics and ship-board procedures. I guess I was kind of obsessed."

Crawford chuckled. "Yeah, I know how that is. Except in my case it was building things. Toy building sets followed by computer simulators."

"But I'm a little curious about why you aren't in the navy," asked Sheila. "I mean with your family background and all." Crawford had been wanting to ask the same question himself and had been unsure how to phrase it. Sheila, of course, had just gone ahead and asked.

Frichette's look of embarrassment returned. "That was my mother's doing. She's an Edenite, pacifist, you know, and she wouldn't allow me to join any of the naval squadrons. Since she's my father's second wife and I've got two older half-brothers already in the navy—neither of them with this fleet, thank goodness—the family traditions are all taken care of and my father didn't object." He shrugged. "So, I had to satisfy my ship-hunger in the merchant service—although I can still dream."

"Ah," said Crawford. "I was wondering why you seemed so knowledgeable on naval matters. Well, it may have just been a hobby before, but we are really going to need anyone with military expertise now. I'll make sure Shiffeld knows about you when we start dealing with that aspect of things."

Frichette scowled. "Not sure he'll be that interested. He'll naturally look to the 'older and wiser' heads and not worry if they are *too* old—or too fat or too stupid."

"You don't look particularly old or fat," observed Crawford.

"Still not sure about the stupid part?" asked Frichette, but he smiled as he said it.

Crawford returned the smile. The lad was less than half his age, but Crawford was coming to like him quite a lot. "I'm assuming that anyone who agreed to be part of this expedition has to be slightly stupid. But you've struck me as a competent officer—and you certainly showed you had nerve when you boarded *Exeter*."

"I was scared spitless."

"Good. Me, too. Shows you got sense, too. We're going to need a lot of sensible people to get out of this mess."

"Then we are truly in trouble," said Doctor Birringer who appeared beside their table and plunked herself down in a chair. "Idiots! We're surrounded by idiots!"

"Are you referring to us or someone else, Doctor?" asked Crawford.

She glared at him. "Shiffeld! He sent some people over and they came and hauled away my patient—on a stretcher!"

"Oh?" said Crawford, surprised that Shiffeld was coherent enough to be issuing orders already.

"Yes! They took her to the brig they have on *Starsong*. Claimed she was too dangerous to just leave in my sick bay. They want her in a cell with nice thick bars. Idiots!"

"Uh, Doctor, keep in mind that this woman killed over nine thousand people single-handed and was trying to effectively sell the rest of us into slavery. Seems to me that she is a tad on the dangerous side."

Birringer frowned even more deeply, but then her face relaxed and she sighed. "Yes, I suppose she is. I have to keep reminding myself of what she's done. She seems so helpless now that it's hard to imagine her doing what she did. Hell, she's just a kid. How could anyone have convinced her to act like that?"

"If she's a genegineered Venanci, she could be a hundred years old, Doctor," said Frichette. "And they'll have medical care available for her on *Starsong*, after all."

"True. But I take this doctoring business seriously and I don't like it when amateurs try to butt in." She sighed. "So what's going to happen now, Charles?"

"We were just talking about that before you came in."

"And?"

"Haven't got a clue."

"Great." She paused and stared at him and her face grew worried. "Wait a minute, you're not kidding are you?"

"Afraid not." His people all looked at him with frowns. "There's another meeting scheduled for tomorrow to hash things over again now that Shiffeld has turned up. As for us, we are going to pretend that none of this has even happened. We've got a gate to build and we are going to get to work and build it."

"Even with bad guys on their way?" demanded Sheila.

"Yup, the gate has to be completed on time, bad guys or no bad guys. The Rift Fleet drops out of hyper in six days and we need to be ready to start work about thirty seconds after that."

"Okay, boss, if you say so."

"I do. I want a meeting with all department heads tomorrow at 0700. Sheila, pass the word."

"Will do."

* * * * *

The cell wasn't too bad, all things considered. It was actually half-again as big as her quarters on *Exeter* and she wasn't sharing it with anyone. There was even a private shower and toilet attached. Well, private wasn't really the word. There were video pickups watching her every move, but she didn't really care. She was still so exhausted that she didn't care about much of anything at the moment.

Medical people came in and checked her out three times a day and meals were delivered regularly. There was always a pair of guards—just ship crewmen, not real police; she'd taken care of all the real police—outside the cell, but none of them ever said anything to her. The only ones who talked to her were the medics, but their questions were always short and in the line of duty. She was surrounded by people—seen and unseen—and yet she was totally alone. All the people around her were enemies, enemies who hated her.

Not that they didn't have good reason to hate her, she admitted.

This was not a situation which Carlina had anticipated. She had steeled herself to perform the grisly task that she had been assigned, but she had not expected to ever have to confront the friends of the people she had killed. It was unsettling and she found she could not look them in the eye.

There was nothing whatsoever to do in her cell. No vid or sound players, no book reader, not even a clock. She found it terribly frustrating not to know even what day it was. She had lost track while she was in the sick bay and no one would tell her. It had to be getting close to the day they would drop out of hyper at their destination. If she was awake, she'd be able to feel that happen and get her reckoning back. And after that, it would just be a matter of more waiting until the relief squadron arrived—assuming she was still alive.

That was a very big assumption.

She was starting to resign herself to the idea that she was going to die. Once her captors had gotten everything they wanted out of her they would have little reason to keep her alive; and plenty of reasons—nine thousand of them—to kill her. Even if they did not kill her right away, she could not see them allowing her to live and be rescued by her friends. No, even when they realized they could not win, they would still kill her. Probably the only reason they would want her alive was in hopes that she could lead them back to the other conspirators in the Protectorate who had worked to set up this mission. They would probably be disappointed in that, too: she knew almost nothing.

Of course, the mere fact that they had existed in the heart of the Protectorate would create a good bit of panic, she suspected. That made her smile. One last blow struck against the enemy. Well, perhaps not the last. She had one more blow planned, but the timing of it was uncertain.

She just hoped she was still alive when it fell.

* * * * *

Everyone got to their feet and applauded when Governor Sir Rikard Shiffeld entered the huge conference room on *Starsong*. The man looked a lot better than the last time Crawford had seen him. Hair, beard, and mustache were trimmed and groomed, and he was wearing a very expensive suit of clothes. He was even wearing his ceremonial governor's sash and star across his chest and over one shoulder. He'd never done that before, that Crawford could remember, except during the pre-departure ceremony with the Protector. Maybe he was trying to reassure himself that this was still his expedition. His face looked gaunt, dark circles under his eyes, and a pair of the ship's enlisted ratings stood by his sides, but he smiled at the applause and nodded to the people in the room as he took his place at the head of the conference table.

"Thank you, everyone, thank you. It's good to be here. I'm just saddened that so many other people aren't." He glanced at the rows of empty seats and then sat down and bade everyone else to do likewise. "I've read the reports you were all kind enough to send me while I was... recuperating, so I'm more or less up to date on the situation." He paused and frowned. "I won't try to deceive you, people, the situation is very serious and our task, which was already a large one, has become truly enormous. However," and now he paused and ran his gaze over the entire assembly, "our task *will* be accomplished—no matter what!" He glanced down at the folder he had brought with him and his scowl deepened. "Along with your various reports, I received an anonymous... petition, asking that the Rift Fleet be turned around and that we go home. People, I am not going to try and find out who sent me this traitorous document, but I just want all of you to know—and pass this along!—we are not going to let anything stop us! The system we are heading for *will* be colonized, the gate *will* be built and we *will* finish our mission!" There was a smattering of applause which quickly grew alongside a few *hear! hear!'s*, but Crawford noticed Tosh Briggs squirming in his seat.

"Now, please bring me fully up to date. I'm assuming the fleet has begun its deceleration, correct?" A number of the captains began nodding and glancing at each other.

"Yes, sir," said Captain Jervis, taking the lead, "we are decelerating at one half gravity; you can't feel it because the artificial gravity field compensates, but we are on schedule, despite a few minor glitches."

"Such as?"

"Uh, four of the ships have had reactor malfunctions. One navy ship and three transports. We were expecting about that rate of failure after ten years without active maintenance. But the computers have automatically adjusted the thrust from the other ships to compensate and re-routed fuel flow. We should reach our drop-out point without problem, sir."

"Good. What about the bridge crews for the… for the ships which didn't have them?"

"Well, they aren't exactly bridge 'crews', sir. We have at least one officer and a few crewmen on each ship, but all they can hope to do is keep an eye on things and yell for help if there's a problem. We have a trouble team standing by if need be. But the truth is, sir, we are stretched pretty thin right now."

"Damn thin," growled one of the other captains, "even on the ships the saboteur never reached."

"Yes," said Shiffeld, "but I'm afraid we are going to be stretched even thinner. We need more than caretakers. We need to man all our ships—especially the warships—man them so they can function and fight."

Jervis looked doubtful. The other captains shook their heads and muttered among themselves. "I-I don't know where we are going to find the people, sir…"

"We'll find them, don't worry. Mr. Crawford?" Crawford jerked when he discovered the governor now looking at him.

"Uh, yes, sir?"

"Your gate construction team is intact, correct?"

"Yes, sir, no casualties—er, well, one, actually, but he's recovering quickly."

"I'm glad to hear that, and before I forget, let me offer my thanks to you and the men who stopped the traitor."

"Oh, thank you, sir, it was…"

"But tell, me, how many people do you have working for you?"

"Um, including all the subcontractors assigned to Dougherty, Ltd, it comes to four thousand eight hundred and ninety-seven, sir," said Crawford dredging the figure up from memory. A flicker of a smile passed over Shiffeld's face.

"I appreciate precision, sir." He turned to look along the table. "Mr. Karrigan, how about your mining operation?"

"Ready to go, sir. I have about twenty-five hundred rock hounds under me."

"Mr. Sowell? Refining and manufacturing?"

"We're ready, too, sir. I have around four thousand."

"Mr. Briggs? Habitat construction?"

"I uh, I have all my people, Sir Rikard, about three thousand, I think, but…"

"Mistress Nassau? Are your terraformers ready?"

"Yes, Governor. There are eight hundred and seventy-nine people in my department and we are ready to begin operation as soon as we drop out of hyper."

"Good. Now, over the next few days I want you all to start streamlining your operations. There is redundancy in every organization, no matter how efficient. Combine your activities and squeeze out every spare person you can. I'm expecting at least twenty-five percent ladies and gentlemen. That would give us nearly four thousand extra personnel, to man the warships and fill critical administrative posts."

Crawford leaned back in surprise and exchanged glances with the other managers. "Uh, sir?"

"Yes?"

"Sir, our operations were already streamlined. We cut things to the bone to make this as cheap and efficient as possible. There's damn little fat to be cut out."

Shiffeld frowned as if reevaluating Crawford's worth. "There's always fat, Mr. Crawford. And you will simply have to ask your remaining people to work harder. Put in more hours."

"I'm sorry, sir, but we were already planning on double shifts. I can't ask much more from my people."

"You'll have to. We shall all have to do more than we had planned." He fixed his gaze on Crawford and seemed to be daring him to speak. He was tempted to continue; there were only so many hours in a day, and if you asked people to work too many of them, the results were inevitable: substandard work and accidents. They could afford neither. But Shiffeld was also correct: there really wasn't much choice.

"Yes, sir. We'll do our best," he said at last.

Shiffeld looked around with an expression to quell any further objections. "Good. Now, I've made up a list of what I'm going to need immediately to reconstitute my staff here and the civil authority. I'll want about four hundred people right away. Secretarial types and men who can perform security duty for the most part, but here, I'll put it up on the screen…"

Crawford looked at the display and started making notes. He'd have to find these people somehow…

"Well, he's certainly taken charge, hasn't he?" a voice whispered from next to him. He turned and saw Regina Nassau with grim smile on her face.

"Yes, he certainly has."

* * * * *

"Time until drop-out?" demanded Captain Frichette.

"Twenty-two minutes, sir," replied the rating sitting at the astrogation station.

"Very well, have all stations report their status."

"Aye, sir."

Charles Crawford sat in an unused seat on the bridge of *Neshaminy* and watched the activity around him. The Rift Fleet was nearing the end of its long, long journey and was preparing to drop out of hyperspace. Ten years earlier they had entered this strange, shrunken universe and slowly built up their velocity using their reaction drives to about one percent of the speed of light. Not much for an interstellar voyage, but modest distances traveled in hyper equated to much vaster lengths when you returned to normal space. The acceleration had been a ticklish proposition because instead of ninety-eight individual ships, there had been this one, monstrous conglomeration of ships bound together. The thrusts of each vessel had to be very carefully calculated and balanced to keep the stresses from tearing the whole thing apart.

Now, they were reversing the process. A week earlier the computers had fired up the drives on the ships and applied about a half-gravity of thrust to kill their velocity to allow the drop-out.

"All stations are reporting ready for drop-out, Captain," said Duncan, the acting first officer. "Velocity is six KPS and falling. Drop-out in twenty minutes. It will be good to see some stars again. I've spent a hell of a lot of hours in hyper, but I always miss the stars."

"Yes, Mr. Duncan, I know what you mean," said Frichette. "I just hope that whatever stars we see will be friendly ones."

"Amen to that, sir. A friendly star, with a nice thick Kuiper Belt and asteroids sizzling with fissionables, eh?"

"Let's hope so. And ice, don't forget the ice."

Crawford's eyes went to the read-out on the ship's store of reaction mass. It was down to eight percent. They would arrive at Landfall with nearly dry tanks. Fortunately, unless the solar system which was their goal was a complete freak, astronomically speaking, there should be plenty of ice balls floating around which could be processed for the liquid hydrogen they typically used as reaction mass. Several entire ships in the fleet would be devoted to that function exclusively. Duncan's wish for fissionables was another matter, of course. Landfall's star was a typical G3 star and the odds were that there would be fissionables, uranium and thorium primarily, in sizable amounts, but there were no guarantees. G3 star systems had been found in the Orion Arm which were almost completely devoid of those vital elements.

While they would definitely need the hydrogen for reaction mass, they could complete their mission without finding any fissionables. The Rift Fleet had been well—lavishly, in fact—supplied with fissionables, despite the tremendous cost. The gate, itself, would require an enormous set of fission reactors to power it, and the backers of this mission were not going risk failure by not having enough fuel for them already on hand.

Still, it was the hope of finding fissionables in abundance which was a major driving force behind the desire to cross the Rift. Over two thousand years of intense usage by the United Worlds and the civilizations which had followed, and a failure to find any other power source that was practical for deep-space operations, had depleted the reserves in their section of the Orion Arm and driven the price of what could still be found to great heights. It was hoped that an untouched and unexploited Perseus Arm might produce fissionables in quantity and with relative ease. The men who could stake a claim on those deposits could make huge fortunes. Several of the fleet's ships were dedicated to that purpose as well, and hundreds more were waiting back home to pour through the gate once it was finished.

"But why do we have to stop *here*?" muttered the man at the helm. Frichette halted his pacing to look at him. Heads turned all over the bridge.

"Do you have some problem with the Landfall system, Mr. Kelley?" asked Frichette.

"No, sir. I mean, well, a lot of us have been wondering, sir."

"Wondering what?" The man was blushing and looking distinctly uncomfortable now.

"Well, it's just that with those Venanci bastards on their way, why are we going to hang around for them to find us? Maybe we ought to go somewhere else instead of stayin' right where they expect us to be."

"There really isn't any other choice, Mr. Kelley," said Crawford from his chair. Heads were turned his way now. Frichette smiled thinly.

"Perhaps you'd be kind enough to explain, sir?"

"It's simple enough, really. It takes a hell of a big gate to punch the wormhole across a distance like the Rift. Big and expensive. The people paying for it did not want to have to make it any bigger than absolutely necessary. So we picked Landfall because it's the closest G-type star we could find. It's in a little cluster that sticks out in our direction and the range of the gate can't reach much beyond that. There are maybe fifty other systems within range, and if the Venanci don't find us at Landfall, it would not take much searching to find us in one of the others. Clear enough?"

"Uh, yes, sir," said the helmsman. "But what if we just hid out for a bit until the Venanci give up and go away?"

"Not a good option. First, they aren't likely to go away, because they've got nowhere to go. Our gate is their only ticket home. Second, unless we get our end of the gate done on time, we're looking at another four years before we can open it up." The man looked puzzled and Crawford continued. "I'm not a physicist, but basically, the gates project a 'carrier wave' of sorts through a different sub-spectrum of hyperspace than our ships use. Its effective true-velocity is around eight hundred cee, so it takes a little over four years to cross the Rift. If our gate isn't ready to receive the carrier wave – and it's already on its way from home – the wormhole will collapse and then we have to try to initiate it from our end, which will take another four years. That's too long to wait. So, I'm sorry, but we are sort of stuck with the Landfall system."

"Thank you, Mr. Crawford," said Frichette. "That answers a lot of questions. All stations report status."

The crewmen turned back to their posts and began reporting. "Five minutes. Velocity is at one point five KPS and falling. Thrust steady. Hyper generator is at full charge. Standing by on computer control."

The minutes ticked by and the thrust died away. He watched on the status board as the drive was secured and the final preparations for the drop-out were made. Capacitors were feeding power into all ninety-eight hyper generators and an immense bubble of Wolcott Distortion began to form. Crawford could feel nothing; the forces involved did not register on human senses. But they were there and shortly they would rip a hole between the universes and spit the Rift Fleet back into the continuum from which it came. "Wolcott Field is nominal, ten seconds."

The final seconds fled past and then it happened. This time he did feel something, a tiny shock like a jolt of static electricity after walking across a certain type of carpet. The instruments indicated that the jump had been completed and suddenly there were stars in the viewscreen. A cheer went up on the bridge of *Neshaminy*.

"Astrogation, confirm our position," ordered Frichette. The man at his station was already doing so. Or trying to, the rating looked confused and flustered and Frichette went over to help him. Crawford imagined that the same thing was happening on all the other ships – all the other ships which still had bridge crews, he reminded himself. After a moment, the man looked up with a large grin.

"Bang on target, sir. Five hundred and seventy million klicks out from the primary designated as Landfall. Right where we are supposed to be." This brought another cheer. Three thousand four hundred and sixty three light years across the Rift. Ten years in hyper and they were bang on target. Frichette gave off a long sigh of relief and then smiled at Crawford. They had made it. Made it across the Great Rift.

Frichette walked around the bridge congratulating the other people there. Crawford got up from his chair and shook Frichette's hand.

"Uh, sir? Sir?" They turned and saw that Thomas Stone, the man at the communications console, was not smiling. He was staring at his panel and frowning.

"Is there a problem, Tom?" asked Frichette.

"I-I don't know, sir."

"What's wrong?"

"This place is supposed to be uninhabited, isn't it?"

"Yes..." A shock went through Crawford and he and Frichette leaned over to look at Stone's instruments.

"Well, it ain't, sir!" said Stone.

"What do you mean?"

"Captain, I'm picking up radio communications from all over the place! Hundreds of signals!" Stone waved his hands at his control panel and then looked up at Frichette.

"Somebody is already here!"

Chapter Seven

Tadsen Farsvar set aside the small block of plastic he had been engraving, stared at the control panel, and then yawned. Another boring night watch on the free prospector, *Carlenzer*. He glanced over the instruments automatically, but there was no change since the last time he had looked, five minutes earlier. He had not expected there to be, but he knew his duty and he would not neglect it. It had not been so long since he had been confirmed as a full adult in the Hasnari sept of the Seyotah clan that he had forgotten his duty! He could still remember the fear he felt before the Trial of Worlds and the pride he felt afterward. The words of his oath were still fresh in his soul. No, he would not neglect his duty — no matter how boring it might be.

And who knew what might happen? Perhaps he would be at the controls when the great find was made. Perhaps one of these times he would glance at the sensor scope and see a faint return which could not have been made by the ubiquitous iceballs that made up the inner cloud of Refuge. No, it wouldn't be ice, it would be something else. He would adjust the controls and send out a focused pulse, and the readings he would get back would make his heart race. But he would control himself and confirm the readings and then calmly — oh so calmly — inform the Execti. They would close on the object and it would be a treasure such as they had not seen before. A chunk of iron and nickel twice the size of their ship, with veins of gold, silver, and uranium thrown in for good measure. Well, the uranium probably wouldn't be there with all the rest, but if he was going to fantasize, why not go all the way? Inferno, why not have pockets of diamonds, too? Yes, it would be a find like the Hasnari had not seen since they were driven from their ancestral space in the Belt so many years ago. And at the next Conclave, Tad Farsvar would be the hero. All the men would congratulate him and the girls would cluster in, trying to catch his attention and be promised a dance. Tad closed his eyes and savored his fantasy.

Unfortunately, when he opened his eyes and checked the scope a few minutes later, the object of his fantasy still wasn't out there. Nor was it likely to be, he was forced to admit. The inner cloud was almost entirely ice. There would be the rare, rocky asteroid tossed into an eccentric orbit by the gravity of the system's gas giant, and the even rarer metallic ones, but the vast majority of the cloud objects were just ice. Not that the ice was worthless, of course. When *Carlenzer* returned to Panmunaptra, it would be towing a full load of ice, assuming Tad's fantasy did not materialize after all and allow them to be towing something far more valuable.

A load of ice would allow the family to survive, but just barely. *Carlenzer* was very nearly self-sufficient, at least in the short term. They grew their own food, recycled their own air and water, and made most of the things they needed with their own hands. The pittance they could sell the ice for would allow them to buy those things they could not make themselves. The family had done it this way for generations, but rarely had they been in so precarious a situation. A string of bad luck had plagued *Carlenzer* for several years. Vital equipment had broken down and had to be replaced and twice—twice!—they had been caught by Clorindan raiders who had taken a heavy tithe from them. The family's assets were dangerously low and just one more mishap might leave them unable to survive on their own. A few good years would allow them to rebuild their fortunes a bit, but if they were not given those years, they might be in serious trouble.

Tad clenched his fist at the thought of what might happen then. If they were lucky, they would be allowed to indenture themselves to one of the richer families in the sept and work off the debt. But if fortune did not smile on them... *Carlenzer* would be sold and the family would have to take whatever work they could find on the ships and stations in the system. They would be scattered and it would be the end of the Farsvars.

"We can't let that happen, damn it," hissed Tad to himself. He had seen the worry in his grandfather's eyes and felt the tension in all the other older adults. He looked back at the sensor display. If he could just find something...

"What the...?"

Tad stared in amazement. A few minutes ago the display had shown nothing. Now there was a massive return! A gigantic return, as large as an asteroid, and it screamed of metal! Where had it come from? Why hadn't he spotted it earlier? He eagerly began studying the other read-outs.

"Oh..."

Energy reading. Strong energy readings from the object. A ship. His hopes, so high for a moment, fell back where they belonged. It was a ship. An enormous ship, it was true, but it clearly belonged to someone else. Tad's treasure rock was still just a fantasy.

But the ship had not been there a few minutes ago. It was only a hundred thousand klicks away and something that large would have been spotted at fifty times that distance, even by *Carlenzer*'s modest sensors. That left only one explanation.

"A starship." A ship had dropped out of hyperspace. *Carlenger*'s sensors had not missed it; it literally had not been there a few minutes ago. Some of Tad's earlier excitement returned. Starships were not unknown here, indeed Refuge was one of the very few places in which a starship could be built, but the arrival of one was still a special event. And look at the size of it! No starship built here had ever been that large. It was kilometers across. Not even the legendary *Long March*, which first brought the clans here, was as large as what he was seeing now. What was it? Where had it come from? Who was aboard?

He could not answer any of those questions, but his course of action was clear. He touched a button on the com panel. A few seconds went by with no answer. He pressed the button again.

"Yeah? What's up?" said a voice. It was his cousin, Eran.

"Get your dad."

"He's kind of busy right now."

"Get him anyway. It's important."

"All right, hang on."

There was a considerable delay, during which Tad continued to monitor the intruder. It wasn't doing anything that he could detect. Then he started checking out the other contacts on his screen. He was relieved to see that there weren't any other ships closer than about twenty million klicks, and that one had a sizable vector away from the newcomer. Whoever these folks were, *Carlenger* was going to have first crack at them. Hopefully they would want to trade—not that the family had much to offer...

"Tad? What's the problem?" His Uncle Jari's voice came over the com.

"Sir, a very large ship has dropped out of hyper only a hundred thousand klicks away." He was amazed at how calm his voice was. "I think you'll want to see this."

"Are you sure about this?" asked his uncle, who was also the execti of the ship. "How large?"

"Of course I'm sure!" said Tad, his calm evaporating like a drop of liquid hydrogen. "It's practically sitting in our laps. And it's enormous! Kilometers across!"

"Tad, if this is some practical joke of yours..."

Anger flared in him. "Sir, if you refuse to come to the bridge, I'm going to have to report this directly to the captain," he said very formally. That seemed to get through to Jari. No one would try to play a joke on the captain!

"All right, Tad, settle down. I'll be right there." The connection closed and Tad waited for his uncle to arrive, alternately fuming over the older man's initial refusal to believe his report and growing progressively more excited by the contact on his scope. Who were they? Why hadn't they broadcast any sort of greeting? Typically, on the rare occasions when a starship arrived, it would quickly start sending out messages assuring the locals of peaceful intentions and a desire to trade. This ship was completely silent. What did that mean?

A few moments later his uncle drifted onto the bridge and propelled himself over to Tad's station. Tad didn't say a word, he simply pointed to the sensor scope and tried to keep a grin of satisfaction off his face. He nearly succeeded.

"By the Lifegiver's left gonad," breathed Uncle Jari. "Sorry I doubted you, Tad. Have they sent out any messages?"

"Not a thing, Uncle. They are silent as a tomb."

"That's odd."

"I've never seen or heard of a ship like this before, sir."

"No, it certainly wasn't built here. Maybe they're from Gantarani, I've heard that they build some pretty big ships—although nothing this big."

"So, what do we do?"

"Well, we're the closest ship around. I guess it falls to us to welcome the visitors."

"Should we inform the captain?"

"Grandfather is sleeping right now. I don't want to disturb him. He hasn't been well lately, you know."

Tad nodded. The family's patriarch was in poor health and Uncle Jari had been in virtual command of the ship for months. Still, this seemed important enough to wake the Old Man...

"Fire up the communications panel," said Jari. "Let's say hello to these folks—whoever they are."

* * * * *

"What's going on?" demanded Greg VanVean. Crawford had seen him hovering near the bridge in hopes of looking over some shoulders since the drop-out was complete—despite the fact he was supposed to still be resting after his wound. The commotion had drawn him in immediately. He grabbed Crawford by the arm as he asked the question. The engineer stopped and shook his head.

"Seems like the long-range scans were wrong: this system is already inhabited."

"What? By who?" Greg looked stunned.

"That's what we are trying to find out. There's radio traffic from all over the place. It's all on odd frequencies and strangely formatted, but it is definitely human. It doesn't seem like we're dealing with aliens, at least. And it doesn't seem to be anyone from our side of the Rift, either, which is a relief. No Petrunans, Venanci, or Hebyrnans waiting for us in ambush."

"But if it's not anyone from across the Rift, how can they be humans?" asked VanVean in bewilderment.

"Well, I meant that they don't seem to be anyone we're *acquainted* with from our side of the Rift. None of the usual suspects, so to speak. Clearly they are originally from our side of the Rift if they are human—we just don't know who."

"This is going to prove rather...inconvenient, ain't it, boss?" asked Greg. "What if they object to us building a gate here?"

"Yeah, that could be a problem. To say nothing of mining their asteroids or colonizing their planet. This could get real sticky."

"So what are we going to do?"

"Good question. Every skipper in the fleet, plus Shiffeld, are all trying to talk at once over the com. So far, we haven't done anything, although we are starting to get some radio messages from the locals directed at us."

"God, what a mess. I mean we have to build the gate here, there's no other choice."

"Mr. Crawford." It was Captain Frichette; Crawford turned to face him. "Governor Shiffeld is calling for all the department heads to meet aboard *Starsong*. Please go there at once."

"Right." He nodded at VanVean and headed for the shuttle cars. During the short trip over to the headquarters ship, he tried to get a handle on what this new development was going to mean. At the shuttle lock he encountered Regina Nassau of the Terraforming Team. She was wearing another amazing costume that revealed even more of her figure than usual, but she was also looking uncharacteristically serious.

"Hello, Charles, what do you think of this?"

"Not sure what to think. What about you?"

"As soon as we dropped out of hyper, my team started doing scans on the one planet in the habitable zone — at least *that* is where they told us it would be! The initial readings say it's unlivable in its current state but well within our capability to terraform, but it's occupied! Lots of radio signals from the surface and evidence of small cities. I don't know what we're going to do."

"Me neither."

"At least you can go ahead and build your gate, Charles!" she said in exasperation. "That's going to be out in empty space. But how can I terraform a planet that's already occupied? As far as I can see it, I'm out of a job."

"Hey, don't get ahead of yourself. If there are humans down there and the place is as nasty as you say, then they must be living under domes or some such. They might welcome having you turn the place into something livable."

Regina looked thoughtful. "Maybe. Some of our methods do some pretty…violent things to the planet. Not sure I'd want to be living down there when we did them. Still, you are right, I'm jumping to conclusions. Guess we better find out the situation first, huh?"

"A good idea, yes." As he said that, they arrived back in the too-big conference room where a lively debate seemed to be underway. Half-a-dozen people were talking at once, along with a batch on various com monitors, and Shiffeld was trying to establish some order.

"Please! Settle down, everyone!" he ordered, holding up his hand. "We can worry about who's at fault for the misinformation from the scans later. Right now we have to decide what we are going to do about this new situation. Ah, Mistress Nassau, Mr. Crawford, thank you for coming so quickly. I think we're all here now."

Crawford and Nassau found seats. Shiffeld looked extremely harried, not panicked, just very stressed. Crawford could barley imagine the sort of shock this had been to the governor. He glanced around and saw the other department heads and a few aides. He noted with interest that Shiffeld now had several liveried attendants and a number of nervous-looking staff people — two of whom had used to work for him.

"I trust you've all heard the news?" said Shiffeld, looking at Crawford and Nassau.

"Yes, sir. Do we have any information on who we're dealing with?"

"Nothing definite. There is a lot of radio traffic and it's evident that these people are present all through this system; on the planet, the asteroid belt, the moons of the gas giant, and in the Kuiper Belt. Some of the traffic is coded, but a lot is in the clear. The voices are human, but the language seems pretty odd."

"But who can they be?" demanded Tosh Briggs. "There wasn't supposed to be anyone here!"

"Tosh, the scans were made from over two thousand light years away. You can't expect them to find every little detail," said Jinsup Sowell.

"This is more than a little detail!" snapped Briggs. "This could totally screw up everything!"

"As if things weren't totally screwed up already," muttered Lu Karrigan.

"I think that is the bottom line, Governor," said Crawford. "Just how badly will this upset our plans? Although, as Lu points out, our plans are already pretty badly upset."

"Sir," said Regina Nassau, "our initial sensor scans are showing a fair amount of activity in the region, but nothing like you'd expect from a heavily populated system in our own part of space. Energy output from fission reactors is modest, thermal readings from the planet and moons are low, and those ships which are close enough to get good readings on all seem small. Whoever these people are, they do not appear to have developed this system extensively."

"But that doesn't give us any evidence about their military capabilities," said Captain Jervis. "We've hardly done anything to get our warships operational, and if we have to fight them, we could be in trouble."

"Why should we even think we have to fight them?" asked Regina. "If we all keep our heads, there will be no need to fight."

"That is what we hope, Regina," said Shiffeld. "But we'd be foolish not to at least keep the possibility in mind." He looked at the others around the table. "How about it, people? If these folks do turn out to be hostile, how will that affect our operations?"

Crawford shrugged. "I can hardly build the gate while being shot at. We'd have to at least secure the construction area."

"And you can almost forget about doing any mining," added Lu Karrigan. "You know how that's done: lots of little ships scattered all over the place. No way we can protect them from attack."

"Manufacturing depends on the raw materials from Lu's miners," said Jinsup Sowell. "The actual factories would be easier to defend, but they'd still be vulnerable. And without raw materials…" he shook his head.

Shiffeld looked at Tosh Briggs who looked back with an expression of apology. "Same situation here, Sir Rikard, I'm afraid. Trying to build the habitats around the planet in the face of hostiles would be nearly impossible."

"Mistress Nassua?" Shiffeld turned to the terraformer.

"Our operations are actually less vulnerable to interference, I suppose," she said slowly with a frown on her face. "But there are people on the planet and we can't just start dropping our bombs with them down there."

"Unless there's no other choice," muttered Briggs. Nassau whipped her head around to glare at the other man.

"There had *better* be another choice," she said icily.

"Hold on, everyone," said Crawford, "I think we're letting ourselves be panicked by this. Instead of being a threat, these folks could be the stroke of luck we've been needing."

"What do you mean?" demanded Shiffeld.

"Our biggest problem is a lack of manpower. We simply don't have enough people to do the mining and manufacturing *and* build the gate and try to man the warships in the time frame we've got. Well, it seems to me that if these folks are all through the asteroids then they are probably already doing a lot of mining. And if they have ships then they have manufacturing. I'd hate to put Lu and Jin out of work, but if we can get the stuff we need from the locals instead of having to make it ourselves, then we can divert a lot of our own people to manning the warships."

Shiffeld looked thoughtful, so did the others. "Yes, I suppose that could be a possibility. But what if the locals don't want to cooperate?"

"Well let's find out!" said Nassau forcefully. "I understand there is a small ship close by which has been signally us almost from the moment we dropped out of hyper. Let's talk to them!"

The governor looked at the others and they all nodded. "What have we got to lose?" added Crawford. "They already know we're here."

"All right, let's do it." Shiffeld touched a button on the table's control panel and was quickly answered by *Starsong*'s new commander, a former transport captain lured away from his old post by the chance to command the glittering headquarters ship. "Captain, please open a communications channel with the nearest ship out there and pipe it down to us here." They all swiveled their chairs to face the main monitor and then waited. It took a few minutes, but eventually the monitor came to life and it showed a rather grainy picture of two humans sitting in what looked like a control room. They were staring out of the monitor with great interest. Crawford studied them. Two men, one older and one fairly young. Their skin was a light mahogany color and they were both quite bald. There seemed to be something odd about their faces and after a moment he realized that their noses and ears were very small; there was something strange about their eyes, too, although he couldn't decide what. Still, there was no doubt they were humans. Shiffeld stood up to address them.

"Greetings, I am Lieu…Rikard Shiffeld, commander of this expedition. Who are you?"

The older man on the screen began talking and Crawford tried to make sense of what he was saying. He recognized some of the words, but others he did not; the grammar was strange and the man was talking too fast to follow. What language was he speaking? After a moment he paused. Shiffeld repeated his greeting and the man on the screen said some more things which made no sense. Shiffeld looked around. "Any of you understand this?" he asked quietly.

"Not really, what language is that?" said Lu Karrigan.

"Sounds vaguely familiar," said Sowell, "but I can't place it."

Shiffeld frowned and tried again, speaking loudly and very slowly. The two men on the screen began talking to each other excitedly. The older one started speaking again. "Eya Jari Farsvar," he said pointing to himself. "Uya Rikurd Shitfel?" He pointed at the screen.

"Shiffeld," said the governor emphatically. "Rik-ard *Shif-feld*. And you are Jari Farsvar. Are you captain of your vessel?"

"Eya execti fa *Carlenzer*. Starship master uya?"

"I think he wants to know if you are captain of this ship, sir," said Jervis.

"Yes, I caught that, but what's a 'carlenzer'?"

"Don't know, sir."

"Mr. Farsvar, we come in peace and would like to talk with you."

"Talk! Yia, talk! Eya a uya talk! Maya swappa, tu?" The man made gestures with his hands like he was giving and taking something from Shiffeld.

"Trade? They want to trade?" asked Nassau.

"Could be," agreed Crawford. "That sounds hopeful."

Shiffeld and Farsvar continued to exchange talk for several minutes without a great deal of success. Crawford shook his head. The language of the locals seemed almost, but not quite, familiar.

"Governor," said a woman two places down from Shiffeld. This was Beatrice Innis, a coldly efficient woman who used to work for Lu Karrigan as an accountant or something. Crawford had met her a few times and knew that she was about as unfriendly as a person could get. He wasn't surprised that Lu had traded her off to Shiffeld. She had been working at her computer terminal busily almost from the moment communications had been opened.

"Yes?" Shiffeld turned to look at his new assistant.

"I think we might have better luck with written communications. I've been going through some old literary files from the library computer and I think I know what language these people are speaking."

"Really? What?"

"The same language we are, actually."

"Are you crazy?" demanded Tosh Briggs. "That's not our language!"

"Not anymore, no," said Innis stiffly, "but it was once. As you might—or might not—know, our present day language evolved from the 'basic' language used by the United Worlds. What these people are speaking is very similar to the UW basic. I think. It has changed some from the reference sources I have here, but not too much. Our written language is closer to basic than our spoken language. If theirs is, too then we might have a better chance of understanding each other."

"Well, it's worth a shot, I suppose," said Shiffeld. "Give it a try."

"Yes, sir." Innis began typing. While she worked, Crawford was thinking. His thoughts led to a conclusion which was... amazing.

"They must have jumped the Rift back during the days of the UW," he said aloud and with considerable awe in his voice.

"What's that, Crawford?" demanded Shiffeld.

"These people must have crossed the Rift a long time ago, sir. Thousands of years ago! Before the fall of the UW. That would explain the language difference. We both started with basic, but their language evolved in one direction while ours evolved in another."

"God," hissed Briggs. "They could be all through the Perseus Arm by now!"

"Not all through it," corrected Crawford. "The Petrunans and the Hebyrnans haven't reported finding any 'natives' in their areas."

"At least not that they've admitted to!" replied Briggs. "The Hebyrnans are so damn secretive about their activities, they might well not have told anyone."

"True," admitted Crawford. "But the primary concern to us is that they are here and somehow we've got to deal with them."

Innis finished her message and showed to Shiffeld. It was written in a terribly old fashioned and, to Crawford's ear, flowery language. But the message was simple enough: we are here in peace and would like to meet and talk with you people. Innis tied her computer into the communications circuit and sent it off. The two locals, who had been waiting patiently all this time, got the message and quickly read it. The older one bobbed his head enthusiastically.

"Yia! Talk! Usa vo uyen talk!" He immediately began typing something into his own controls. A few moments later it came through on Innis's computer. She frowned and typed something back. Farsvar consulted with the younger man and then sent another message. Innis looked it over.

"Well?" demanded Shiffeld.

"I think they want to know whether they should come here or if we want to go there."

"Here," said Shiffeld emphatically. "Let's start this off on the right foot."

"We are the visitors here, perhaps we should..." began Regina.

"And our ships are a thousand times the size of theirs and we are representing the Protectorate, Mistress Nassau," interrupted Shiffeld. "Once the gate is built, this system will become the focus of the Protectorate's expansion into the Perseus Arm. These people are going to become subjects of the Protectorate whether they like it or not. Best that we make it clear who's in the dominant position from the start."

"I see," said Regina, frowning.

Innis had already sent Shiffeld's insistence of meeting here and there seemed to be no objections from Mr. Farsvar. But then he typed out a rather lengthy message and Innis was several minutes puzzling it out.

"This is odd, sir. They seem to be asking for information on our life support settings: temperature, air pressure, even the gas mix. I'm not sure why they would need that..."

"Well, get it for them anyway," said Shiffeld dismissively. "The chief engineer can give you the data."

"Yes, sir."

While Innis got the reply together, the others talked quietly. Crawford noticed the expression if intense concentration on Regina Nassau's face. "What's up, Regina?"

"Oh, a totally crazy idea, Charles."

"Well, let me hear it. It can't be any crazier than the rest of this mess."

"I was just thinking that these people might want the environmental data because... no, I'm going to wait until our guests get here. We'll know for sure then."

"We'll know what?"

"Never mind."

After a considerable delay, the data was assembled and sent to the other ship. Fortunately, they still used standard measurements and they seemed satisfied with what they got. Farsvar smiled and nodded. He typed in another short message.

"They are coming over," said Innis. "They should be here in about an hour."

"And then we'll see," whispered Regina.

* * * * *

"Life!" gasped Tad. "Will you look at the size of it!" The newcomers' spaceship was swelling larger and larger on the shuttle's viewscreen, and Tad stared at it with his mouth hanging open.

"Yeah, it's pretty damned big," agreed his uncle. "But look closer: it's not one ship, but a whole batch all hooked together." Tad did as directed and he could see that his uncle was right. The enormous structure consisted of dozens of smaller ships connected together by a rigid framework.

"But even the individual ships are huge. That one must be over three hundred meters long! And why would they hook them all together like this? I've never heard about anything like this."

"Nor I. I can't imagine what the purpose is. But it sure is impressive, isn't it?"

"Yes, sir!" Tad was silent for a moment and then spoke again. "Sir? Thanks for letting me come along."

"Hey, you are the one who saw them first, you deserve to be here. Besides, you are a full-fledged crewmember now and have to take hazardous duty the same as anyone else."

Tad felt himself swelling up like there had been a sudden drop in pressure. He'd officially been an adult crewmember for nearly a year, but this was the first time he had really *felt* it. He sat there smiling for a moment until the other half of his uncle's statement registered. "You think this might be dangerous?"

"We know nothing about these people. We have to assume there is some danger."

"Surely if they were hostile there's nothing we could do anyway. We're so close we couldn't run, and we certainly can't resist something like that!" said Tad, waving his hand at the huge vessel.

"True, which is why I was so quick to agree to meeting with them. Our best hope is to make friends with them as soon as we can. Now shut up so I can concentrate on piloting."

"Yes, sir." He did as he was told and watched his uncle maneuver the tiny shuttle between several of the vessels which made up the outer layer of the amazing construct. It was even more impressive from this close. Tad looked hard at the nearest ship.

"The outer layer looks like they could be fighting vessels, Uncle," he said with a note of worry in his voice. "Those projections could be pulsers."

"Yes. Maybe."

They were being guided to one of the ships near the center of the cluster, and eventually they found it and the open docking bay waiting for them. Tad wished he could stay and study the ship for a bit longer. It was, without doubt, the most beautiful one he had ever seen. Gleaming white, sleek and powerful. But all too soon they were inside. The docking bay was oddly constructed, but not so odd that they could not understand it. Instructions kept coming over the com, but his uncle responded more by instinct and common sense than by actually understanding the words. After a few moments, their shuttle was clamped in place and the door to the hanger bay slid shut.

"No docking tube," said his uncle. "I think they are pressurizing the whole bay. Okay, let's get ready to… what the…?!" Something suddenly grabbed Tad and yanked him down into his seat. For an instant he could scarcely breathe and he gasped in panic.

"What's happening?"

"We're under gravity," said his uncle in wonder.

"How? They couldn't have spun up a structure so big this fast," protested Tad.

"No. They… they must have some sort of gravity generator."

"Life!" exclaimed Tad. "Artificial gravity! That's incredible!"

"Yes," nodded his uncle. "These folks certainly have things worth trading for! Are you all right? Yes? Okay, let's get ready and meet these people." Tad carefully stood up. He had not been under gravity in several months and it felt very strange. Slowly he got into his gear. The readings the newcomers had sent them indicated that it was pretty cold aboard their ship. Not frigid, but some insulated underwear, a thick coat, hat, and some gloves would be appropriate to wear. Fortunately, their air was thick enough, although with an unfriendly mix of gasses, that a simple bubble helmet would be all that was needed. Tad finished dressing about the same time his uncle did. They looked each other over and pronounced themselves ready.

"Okay, let's go."

* * * * *

Charles Crawford stared through the window overlooking *Starsong's* main boat bay. Shiffeld and all the other department heads were there, too, along with a considerable crowd of gawkers. The word about the coming meeting had already spread through the fleet and Shiffeld's recently recruited police were having trouble keeping the hopeful spectators under control. Fortunately, rank had its privileges and Crawford had a front row seat. The shuttle carrying the locals had just settled into a docking cradle and the bay was pressurizing. Everyone was waiting for the occupants to emerge.

The craft, itself, was about the proper size for a shuttle but was very different in appearance from the ones Crawford was used to. It had a look that he could only describe as 'hand-made'. It did not look like a vessel made on a production line. It looked more like someone had cobbled it together out of spare parts and scrap metal. That wasn't to say that it looked shoddy or poorly made. On the contrary, it appeared to have been created by a craftsman; a craftsman with an artistic appreciation as well as an eye for engineering. Crawford found the vessel charming and he hoped he would have the opportunity to speak with whoever built it. He wondered if the locals' other vessels were the same way.

"Okay, here we go," said Lu Karrigan, pointing. "The hatch is opening." A large piece of metal swung away from the hull and folded back on a very odd hinge system. A moment later, two figures emerged. They were wearing rather heavy clothing and bubble helmets, but otherwise looked like regular people. Shiffeld directed that the lock to the boat bay be opened and he led a small crowd out to meet the visitors. Crawford noticed that a group of police with holstered stunners were positioning themselves so they had a clear field of fire. Shiffeld slowly approached the waiting pair. Now that they were closer, Crawford could see that these were the same ones they had talked to over the communications screen. The older man held out both hands in a gesture of peace.

"Welcome aboard *Starsong*, Mr. Farsvar," said Shiffeld, smiling and with hands out in imitation of the man opposite him.

"Besi najor, Rikurd Shitfel," said the man, his voice muffled by the thin plastic helmet he was wearing. "Than uya va bekomin vo starship."

"Beatrice, can you tell him that he doesn't need his helmet? The air is safe to breathe."

"I'll try, sir." Innis had brought along a portable display system to send written messages. She typed for a moment and then handed the device to Farsvar. The man conversed with the younger one and then typed in his own message and handed it back.

"I think he's saying he can't take the helmet off, sir."

"Why not? This is a standard atmosphere." Innis typed again and exchanged messages with Farsvar. The man was now shaking his head emphatically.

"He says that they cannot breathe this air, sir. At least I think that's what he's saying."

"That doesn't make any sense," protested Shiffeld. "You must have gotten the message wrong."

"I don't think so, sir, but I can try…"

"Well, I'll be damned!" exclaimed Regina Nassau suddenly. Everyone turned to look at her.

"What's that, Mistress Nassau?" asked Shiffeld.

"She didn't get the message wrong! They *can't* breathe our air! I will be thoroughly and totally damned! This is incredible!" Regina was nearly dancing with excitement.

"What are you talking about? Why can't they breathe the air? They're humans just like we are, aren't they?"

"No they're not! Not like us at all! Oh, this is amazing! I didn't know any of them even still existed!"

"Any of who?" snapped Shiffeld. "Mistress Nassau, explain yourself!"

Regina Nassau had the look of a child who has just found a lost puppy. "Don't you understand? They're *terraformers*! Real terraformers!"

Chapter Eight

Regina Nassau looked at the two men standing in *Starsong*'s boat bay and tried to figure out just what she was feeling. She was excited, no doubt, but there was a swirl of other emotions which she could hardly categorize. Wonder, awe, anticipation, and yes, a bit of guilt, too. She could have scarcely been more amazed if the shuttle sitting in the bay had had 'Beagle' painted on the side and Charles Darwin had stepped out!

"Mistress Nassau, what are you talking about?" Governor Shiffeld was staring at her, along with almost everyone else.

"They're Terraformers! Don't you understand?"

"No, I'm afraid I don't. You are a terraformer and I don't see that these people are anything like you. Explain yourself."

Regina shook her head in exasperation. "Our so-called education system at work," she muttered.

"Mistress Nassau, I am a graduate of Albert & Fiona, I'll have you know," said Shiffeld icily. "I graduated with honors, too. And I have no recollection of any 'terraformers' who can't breathe our air!"

Regina got control of herself. "Sorry. I suppose it is rather esoteric knowledge at that, for anyone not in the terraforming business. But these are the original Terraformers!" She gestured at the two men, still standing there patiently. "Not these exact men, obviously, but they have to be descendants of the genetically engineered terraforming teams who were created during the first expansion out from Old Earth. That's why they can't breath the air here: they were engineered for a different environment!"

"Engineered?" said Tosh Briggs with an appalled look on his face. "You mean like the damn Venanci? Those stinking Creationists?" Several other people were muttering to each other with similar expressions. A sudden chill went through Regina. She'd just made a terrible mistake without realizing it.

"No, no, nothing like that!" she blurted. But even as she said it, she realized she was wrong. Unfortunately, this was like that. Exactly the same techniques had been used to make these men's ancestors as the Venanci used to create their 'improved humanity' and, she had to admit, exactly the same sort of hubris had been involved in the decision to do it. "Not like that at all," she ended weakly.

Shiffeld was eyeing the men—and her—coldly. "You wouldn't happen to know just what these…people are doing here, would you?"

"They must have fled here some time long ago."

"Fled?" asked Briggs. "They were driven out by the real humans?"

"No! Well, I suppose they were, but not the way you are suggesting," said Regina, regaining some of her indignation. "It was a shameful episode, absolutely shameful. When people first started exploring beyond

Old Earth, they discovered that there were hardly any planets which were readily habitable. There were a lot more which could be terraformed, but their techniques in those days took a long time, centuries. And they demanded a lot of supervision and careful attention. Someone, no one's sure who now, came up with the idea of genetically engineering groups of people who could live on the planets to be terraformed without artificial aids. These people would supervise the terraforming. The idea was that each succeeding generation would be engineered back toward standard human. By the time the terraforming was finished, the terraformers would be completely human again and would be the first colonists. It was an elegant and audacious solution to the problem."

"It sounds horrible," said Tosh Briggs. "Incredible that anyone would think of such a thing — or agree to do it."

"I guess they thought it was preferable to having generations of people living under domes and in environmental suits. In any case, they went ahead with it. A few dozen variations were created for different planetary environments and they were sent out to start their jobs."

"From the fact that I've never heard of them and that these people are here, I assume it did not work?" asked Shiffeld.

"No one will ever know if it would have worked," replied Regina. "Less than a century after the first waves of Terraformers had been placed, there was a breakthrough in planetary engineering. Much faster methods of terraforming were discovered. Where it had once taken five hundred years, it could now be done in fifty, and thus the Terraformers weren't needed anymore. Worse than that: suddenly the Terraformers were actually *in the way*. They were on planets that could be quickly terraformed with the new methods."

"They were obsolete," observed Charles Crawford.

"Yes," said Regina sadly. "And the bastards in charge wouldn't let them even finish the jobs they had started and let their descendants live on those planets. The Terraformers were uprooted and shunted aside. They were unwanted embarrassments at that point."

"Should have just spaced the lot of them," muttered Briggs. "Or at least sterilized them."

"There aren't a lot of records about what happened next," said Regina. "Apparently many of the Terraformers adapted to space travel since they could set the ships' life support for their needs and became permanent ship crews and asteroid miners and the like. A few tried to get ahead of the wave of expansion from Old Earth and find planets they could claim as their own. But they were always overtaken and driven out. All mention of them disappears about fifteen hundred years ago and I doubt any of them survived the fall of the UW. But it's obvious now that at least one group of them made the decision to jump the Rift. Oh, this is just amazing!"

"Amazing and highly irritating," muttered Shiffeld.

"Why irritating? The opportunities for cooperation are the same as before—and we have a unique historical discovery!"

"Perhaps, but you seem to be overlooking the fact if the people living on the planet are already adapted to the environment there, they will not want us to terraform it."

Regina was taken back. She hadn't thought of that. But then she glanced at their two guests, still standing there, and shook her head. "No, these people can't be living on the planet—except under domes. You can see that they are warmly dressed and that indicates they are adapted to a hotter planet. The planet here is far colder. And its atmosphere is much thinner. These men are wearing flexible plastic helmets and you can see the pressure inside them is about the same as ours."

"Doesn't prove a thing, Regina. You said yourself that these people came in a lot of different…models. The ones down on the planet could be a sort that is adapted for it."

"I suppose that could be true," she admitted.

"Uh, Sir Rikard?" said Charles Crawford. "We're speculating in a vacuum here. And we're being a bit rude with our guests. Maybe it would be best to sit down and talk with them and find out what the situation really is, instead of guessing about it."

"Yes, you are correct on all points. Beatrice, ask our guests if they will accompany us to the conference room."

* * * * *

Tad Fasvar was still gawking around him in wonder and envy when their hosts finally stopped arguing among themselves and asked them to come along. He wasn't sure what sort of customs these people had; in most clans he was familiar with the long wait would have been considered rude, but under the circumstances, Tad didn't really mind. He spent the time looking at his surroundings. The ship, even just the boat bay, was incredibly rich and luxurious. Everything was bigger than it needed to be and it was all over-designed, elaborately decorated, and spotlessly clean. The wealth these people had was staggering.

And yet, there was something odd about the ship, too. At first he wasn't sure what it was, but it slowly dawned on him: everything was exactly alike. From where he stood, he could see five pressure doors and every one was identical to all the others. The stanchions bracing the bulkheads were all alike, too. The ceiling and floor panels, even the brass trim, which was purely decorative, they were all the same. The only thing which looked at all hand-made was an elaborate crest on the bulkhead facing the main airlock from the boat bay. Even that lacked any real character. If a craftsman had made it, it had been so over-finished that any trace of the man had been extinguished. The whole ship (or as much as he'd seen of it) seemed… sterile. It was the only word he could think of. There was no life in it and the life aboard it was just a passenger — it didn't belong here. Tad found himself pitying these people, despite their obvious wealth.

He wasn't sure what they had been arguing about, but now they were finished and beckoning his uncle and him forward. They followed along and a considerable crowd surrounded them. A number of them were obviously warriors. They carried weapons and wore some sort of uniform. Tad was rather flattered by the honor. Of course, the leader who had met them claimed to be in command of this entire super-ship, so the escort was probably for him rather than for them. Although the fact that the leader, this Rikurd Shitfel, had actually come to meet them in person was honor enough.

As they walked along the over-large corridors, Tad felt that something else was wrong, and it only took a moment to realize what: the corridor was flat. There was no curve to it at all and not the slightest hint of Coriolus force as you would normally have with spin-gravity. Artificially generated gravity! He still couldn't get over it. At his side, his uncle nearly stumbled. It really was a little hard to get used to.

"If we can learn how they make this gravity, our fortune will be made, Uncle," he said quietly.

"We'd have to buy the technology, Tad, and we have nothing to buy it with."

"We have one thing: knowledge about our star system. If these strangers come from so far that they can't even speak the language properly, they can't know anything about us or this place. They won't know who to trade with for what or… or anything! We can help them a great deal and that should be worth quite a bit to them."

His uncle chuckled. "You are talking like a merchant, Tad, not a prospector! Still, I hope you are right. This could be the opportunity we've prayed for to save the family and the ship."

As he walked, he noticed that the woman who had been talking so excitedly had fallen in beside him and was looking at him with a warm smile. She was quite attractive in an exotic way. Nose and ears too large, of course, and the white fur covering the top of her head with the long rope of it down one side was a bit disconcerting. A cold-worlder, for sure. Her skin would feel like ice if he were to touch her. Still, she was pretty enough, he supposed, and she was smiling. He smiled back at her.

"Regina," she said, touching herself.

"Tad," he replied, touching his own chest.

"Tad," she repeated, then gestured between the two them. "Frenz?"

What did she…? "Oh! Friends! Yes, sure, we are friends." He smiled and nodded and she did the same.

"Got yourself a new girlfriend, Tad?" asked his uncle.

"Not my type, sir. Too old, and a real ice maiden, I'll bet."

"You can be sure of that! It's freezing in here."

After what seemed a long walk, they entered into a huge room which was nearly as large as the boat bay. It appeared to be a space designed for holding meetings. Their hosts indicated places to sit around a large table and Tad and his uncle sank into heavily upholstered seats which were very comfortable. The standing in the boat bay and the walk to the room had been tiring on his legs. He wasn't used to the gravity and he was grateful to sit down.

There was a container of water and some glasses on the table, and after considerable discussion, with a lot of gesticulations, everyone drank some of the liquid; Tad and his uncle used small bottles with drinking tubes which they had brought with them. The sharing of water, the one common need of all the clans, was an important ritual, and Tad was glad to see that these strangers honored it just as they did.

But once the formalities were out of the way, the true discussion began. It was awkward with the language difficulties, but the assistance of the computer keyboards and visual displays was a great help. Before long, everyone at the table, including Tad, was provided with one and things went faster. Each side began to absorb some of the others' language and expressions, and misunderstandings grew fewer. Tad marveled over the computer equipment. It was clearly superior to their own. Yes, these people would have a great deal to offer.

It was hard work, and from time to time, they all needed to take a break. During one of these rest sessions his uncle pulled him aside where they could talk in private. "So, what do you think of all this, Tad?"

"They want to trade, that seems pretty clear, don't you think, sir?"

"Oh yes, they want to trade. They want raw materials and finished structural members—and in enormous quantities. They even seem to understand that while we can't supply what they want ourselves, we can act as the middlemen to get it for them."

"With even a modest percentage, it could mean a fortune for us, Uncle!" said Tad excitedly.

"Yes, almost too good to be true, isn't it?"

"You're afraid they aren't telling us the truth?" asked Tad in alarm. "You think they might try to cheat us?"

"No, I'm not really worried about that. Even though our percentage would be a fortune to us, it would still be a trifle compared to what they have and what they want. No, I'm just worried that they haven't told us all that they really want."

"What do you mean?"

"We still don't know why they are here. Did you notice how they side-stepped the questions I asked about that? I suppose they might just have not understood, but somehow I doubt that. And what do they want all the materials for? Did you notice any damage on their ships that might need repairs?"

"No, everything seemed in good order—not that I could see every-thing, of course."

"That's what I thought, too. So if they don't need the materials for repairs, they must want it to build something with. But what?"

Tad glanced around nervously. A few of the strangers were looking their way, but that was to be expected. He'd been nervous when they first arrived, but during the discussions, all his uneasiness had vanished as they tried to puzzle out each others' words. Now the nervousness returned. What did these people want? They had come from a long way off and they already had more wealth than could be readily imagined. What could they possibly want from the people of Refuge? "M-maybe we ought to talk to the captain before we make any agreements, sir."

"Exactly my thoughts. This is getting too damn big for the two of us. I hate worrying Grandfather, but this time we're going to have to."

"So we are going back to the ship?"

"In a bit. The Old Man is going to want every scrap of information we can gather for him. So keep you eyes and ears open and watch what you say!"

"Yes, sir," said Tad, swallowing nervously.

* * * * *

"So what do you think?" asked Charles Crawford. Regina Nassau shook her head and shrugged, nearly spilling her coffee.

"I'm not sure. Part of me is so excited at meeting these people and the other part is furious with myself for sticking my foot in it about the ge-netic engineering. I should have known better than mention that in front of paranoids like Briggs." She looked at him more closely, her eyes as sharp as an alignment laser. "I trust that you've got more sense than him?"

"I would like to think so," snorted Crawford. "I've got no love for the Venanci, but from what you tell me, these folks have nothing to do with them. They seem nice enough—the two we've met—and I see no reason why we can't deal with them. And they seem eager to deal."

"Yes, they do. Almost too eager. You'd think they would have more doubts about us."

"True. We pop in out of nowhere with an enormous ship, which, at least to look at, is armed to the teeth. I know I'd be damned nervous if I was in their place."

"Maybe they are just naturally very trusting," ventured Regina.

"Maybe. But they seem like pretty shrewd businessmen. Maybe they are just naturally greedy and see us as a treasure ship. Or maybe they need us as much as we need them."

"What do you mean?" asked Regina, frowning.

"I don't know what I mean," admitted Crawford. "Speculating in a vacuum again. Not something I like to do, although I've been doing it a hell of a lot lately." He glanced to his side as Lu Karrigan came up to them.

"Chuck, I just wanted thank you for putting all my people out of work. I'm sure they are all gonna want to thank you personally." Crawford was startled, but there was a flicker of a smile on Karrigan's face.

"Hey, it was just a suggestion. Besides, I'll bet all your folks will love getting a chance to play navy on the warships."

"Maybe. As long as their pay stays the same, they might not mind, I suppose. A few of them will bitch just for the sake of bitching, but the majority will accept it—I hope."

"Hopefully Shiffeld will have the sense to agree about the pay—which will probably make them the highest paid navy crews in history considering the rates you rock hounds get."

"Mining is dangerous work. They earn every penny and you know it."

"Yeah, I do. You've got good people—almost as good as mine," said Crawford with a grin. "I hope Jin's people feel the same way, though. His manufacturers aren't the natural ship crews that your folks are."

"They'll have to adapt," replied Karrigan. "Honestly, Chuck, what choice is there? If we can get what we need from the locals instead of having to make it ourselves, we can divert everyone, except yours and Briggs's construction teams, to man those warships. Otherwise, we are completely screwed—despite Shiffeld's optimism about the 'fat' we can cut. It ain't there to be cut and we all know it." He paused and looked at Regina. "What about you folks? You unemployed, too, do you think?"

"I...I guess so. There's not much we can do to the planet with people down there. And it would be incredibly wrong to try and force them out—especially after what we did to their ancestors!"

"*We* didn't do anything to their ancestors," said Karrigan. "That was centuries ago and I refuse to carry any guilt for whatever was done. This is now and that's all that matters."

"Even so, I will *not* terraform those people's home out from under them!" said Regina, hotly.

"Settle down," said Crawford. "Probably not even an issue anymore. I rather doubt these folks will let us do anything to the planet, and we can hardly afford to start a new war when we can't even fight the one we've already got."

"Well, I hope you're right, Charles. Shiffeld's not the type to let things stand in his way."

"Speaking of His Lordship, what's going on there?" said Karrigan. He pointed to where the governor was speaking with someone over the com. Shiffeld's face was getting redder by the second.

"Uh, oh," said Crawford. "Looks like bad news."

"More? What else could happen at this point?"

A moment later Shiffeld snarled in a voice loud enough for everyone to hear: "What? How? Then get her up here! At once, do you understand? Get that traitorous bitch up here this instant!" He closed the connection, looked around the room, and saw that everyone was staring at him.

"What's happened, Sir Rikard?" ventured Tosh Briggs.

Shiffeld took a moment to compose himself. "It would seem that a few minutes ago a reconnaissance drone was launched — from *Exeter*."

"*Exeter!*" exclaimed half a dozen people. This was followed by a low roar as everyone started talking at once.

"God," hissed Crawford. "That's where Citrone was holed up. She must have rigged something."

"But what?" asked Regina Nassau.

"I imagine we'll find out shortly."

Shiffeld managed to get the group under control and rather unnecessarily confirmed that he had summoned the prisoner to the conference room to get some answers. Several minutes dragged by while they waited.

"Regina?" said Crawford. "It might be better if our guests didn't see this. Why don't you take them somewhere else?" He pointed to where the two guests were standing to one side in the enormous room. They looked puzzled and more than a little apprehensive.

Nassau agreed, walked over to the pair, and began talking and gesturing. They nodded and started to move off. But before they were out of the room, four newly-minted Colonial Police officers hauled in Carlina Citrone. She was wearing a prison jumpsuit and her hands were cuffed together in front of her. Crawford looked closely at his former nemesis. She looked tired and worn and very thin, but still more alive than the last time he had seen her. In fact, she was smiling with a look of triumph on her face. She was dragged over to where Shiffeld was standing, but she did not even wait for him to say anything.

"Well, Your Excellency, I imagine you are wanting to ask me about the drone that *Exeter* just launched," she stated calmly.

To Shiffeld's credit, he did not betray any surprise at all. "Yes, that's exactly why you are here. Are you going to tell us, or shall I turn you over to Captain Garrit's people again?"

"No thank you, that won't be necessary. It is far too late to stop it, so there is no harm in my telling you."

"Telling me what?"

"That drone is accelerating away from the Rift Fleet and will continue to do so until its fuel is exhausted. It will be going at quite a clip by then. Once its drive cuts out it will be almost impossible to detect. And just to make sure, it has a cold-gas thruster which will make a random vector change of a few hundred meters per second. By the time you could get anything out there after it, you would never have a hope of finding it."

"I see. And just what is this drone going to do?"

Citrone's smile grew broader and her eyes flicked to Crawford. "When I realized that I wasn't going to be able to hold out, it also occurred to me that you might be able to bluff my comrades when they arrive by cruising the warships around under manual control and looking threatening. They'd probably believe that my mission had failed. I have no clue of the size of the relief squadron—as you've found out—but if it is smaller than your force, then a bluff like that might work. So, I decided to warn them. At the proper time, that drone will start broadcasting a message telling the squadron that I did succeed in my mission and that all of your naval personnel are…dead." Citrone's smile faltered a bit, but she pushed on. "The drone will be so far away by then you won't have a hope of silencing it, but the signal will be all through this region of space. My allies will be sure to get it and then they will know the truth."

"You damned traitor!" spat Shiffeld.

"Perhaps you see me that way," said Citrone proudly. "But I am true to my own." After a moment her smile returned.

"You can't win, Governor. But there's no need for further bloodshed." She held out her cuffed hands. "Just take these off and I can accept your surrender right now."

Chapter Nine

Brannon Gillard, archpriest of the Lifegiver and Crèchemaster of the Clorinda Clan, slowly walked down the row of gestators, carefully noting the readouts with the easy assurance of long familiarity. His practiced eye checked each of a dozen different indicators and verified them satisfactory, as much by instinct as by actually reading the numerical data. Most of the indicators were configured as bar graphs and his synapses knew exactly how long each of the colored bars was supposed to be. His eyes would tell him, long before the computer controls, if any of them were out of the optimal range.

Like that one there.

Brannon stopped and stared more closely. Gestator 131 was showing a slightly elevated pH reading. That, in itself, was no cause for great concern, but the fetus inside was at the most crucial and delicate stage of development, and if trouble was going to occur it would most likely happen now. He pressed a button on the control panel and leaned forward to carefully study the more detailed display that now appeared. The frown that creased his brow grew deeper and deeper as he paged through the readings. He checked them twice and then a third time. He straightened up with a sigh. "The Lifegiver's will be done," he whispered. He stood there for a moment more and then beckoned to one of the underpriestesses. The woman scurried over to him, her robes billowing out in the low spin-gravity.

"Yes, Father?" she said, a worried expression on her face, her eyes flicking between him and the gestator.

"Attend. The life within has failed to meet the challenge set for it by the Lifegiver. It will not survive the environment that awaits it. We must give its essence back for the use of future generations."

The woman bowed her head sadly. "As you command, Father. May I ask where the failure occurred? Was it the cloreas?"

"Yes, it is only twelve percent developed and it should be nearly full-grown by this stage. The babe would never survive."

"Lifegiver's will," sighed the woman.

"Who are the parents? I will send my condolences personally."

"I will have their names and codes sent to your desk at once, Father."

"Thank you." He stood aside as the woman and several assistants disconnected the gestator from its power and nutrient supply and wheeled it away to the reclamation center. He stared sadly at the empty space left behind. Another one lost. It was like a stone chained to his soul, the extra mass tugging at him with every move. Still, it was to be expected. The Clorindans were the most complicated and sophisticated of the Lifegiver's many children. There was more to go wrong than with the other clans and he should be thankful that the numbers who failed were as low as they were. Indeed, he was thankful and he spent a moment giving his thanks and praying for the spirit of this life which might have been. Then he shook himself and continued his inspection. An hour later he reached the last of the gestators in this section and had reason for more thanks: there had been no more failures — today.

As he opened the pressure door to the next section, his spirits, which were already on the rise, rebounded completely. No one could be depressed in here! A score of crying voices, only slightly muffled by the incubators, welcomed him like music. Life! The sound of life. It was a sound which had echoed in his soul for nearly forty standards. His very first assignment in the crèche had been in this very chamber and the wails, coos, and gurgles of the infants had been his constant companion. A companion he never tired of.

The lay-nurses and acolytes greeted him warmly as he made his rounds. He returned their greetings just as warmly. There were good people here. The best. He stopped first by the dozen infants who had been removed from their gestators only this morning. They had that unnaturally pink color of newborns and their eyes were startlingly white. Still, that was perfectly normal at this stage. They all seemed healthy in their incubators. Long habit made him check the pressure seals, even though a nurse was on hand to do that. They were all in good order, of course, and the air-mix was exactly right. He nodded to the nurse who smiled and nodded in return. He paused for a moment to exchange words with Father Durienne. This was a trifle awkward because the visiting priest was in a full protective suit to protect him from an environment which would have been quickly fatal to him. Even so, Brannon was happy to have the man here. There was far too little close contact between the clans and, aside from business meetings, it seemed like only the clergy made the effort anymore to maintain the ancient ties and exchange ideas as friends.

He finished his conversation and moved along the other rows of incubators. These were filled with babes of progressively greater age and their colors were far healthier, a good solid gray on the skin and eyes, nearly like any adult. Row by row the air-mix neared normal as the infants' metabolisms made the final adjustment to their proper environment. The last row contained babies who were fully adapted. The incubators were mostly open and a gaggle of nurses stood around, preparing them for the ceremony this evening when they would be presented to their proud parents. Brannon stood aside as a very junior acolyte wheeled past a bin filled with green-stained diapers. There was nothing wrong with the cloreases of these babies!

Brannon sighed and this time it was in satisfaction. This evening, eleven new members would be added to the clan and he would have done his duty, both to the Clorindans and to the Lifegiver. His conscience suddenly reminded him of another duty, a far less pleasant duty, that he still had to perform. The names of the couple who would not be parents after all were probably waiting in his office by now and he had a letter to write. He turned and left the compartment, some of his good mood gone again.

The passage on the other side of the pressure door was mostly the bare rock of the asteroid in which Telendia Base resided. The walls had been carefully carved and polished into a frieze giving praise to the Lifegiver and the miracle of birth, as was only appropriate for the birthing crèche of an entire clan. The long-dead sculptor had been whimsical as well as skilled. This particular section showed laughing babes sliding along a DNA strand like it was a piece of playground equipment. He moved past some of the fertilization labs and into the administrative section where his office was located.

He noticed that a number of his staff were clustered around the refreshment station, talking enthusiastically about something. He was tempted to find out what, but he knew that as soon as he approached, everyone would scurry back to their work, thinking he was upset about them apparently goofing off. He was not, of course; his people worked hard and well, and he had no problem with them taking a break now and then. Oh well, he would probably hear whatever the news was eventually.

As it happened, he heard about it only a moment later when his secretary sprang up on seeing him. "Father, have you heard the news?"

"No, I can't say that I have, Kananna, although everyone else seems to."

"A starship has entered the system."

"Indeed? And why is that something to send everyone running in circles? It's hardly that rare an event. Don't several arrive every month on average?"

"Not a starship like this one, Father! No one's ever seen anything like it."

"Really? What's so different about it?" Brannon had little interest in starships, but an uneasiness he did not understand coursed through him.

"It's enormous! People are saying that it's ten kilometers across!"

Brannon snorted. "That's absurd. Someone's pulling your leg, Kananna. Where is this behemoth supposed to be, anyway?"

"The inner cloud, I think. Some of the Seyotahs are talking with the newcomers and we've intercepted their messages back to their base. And it might not be ten kilometers across, but everyone says that it's huge!"

"Do they say where they've come from?" His uneasiness was growing and he told himself he was being foolish.

"No one seems to know yet. Apparently they are from so far they can't even speak our language."

He stiffened as his uneasiness became fear. He did everything in his power to keep that fear off his face. His secretary did not seem to notice his internal struggle and she kept babbling away. "That's all very interesting, Kananna," he said slowly and carefully. "If you get any more news I'd be interested in hearing it. I'll be in my office."

"Yes, Father." She went back to her desk and he turned, went into his office, and closed the door. He stood, with his back to the door, for a full minute, locked in indecision and anxiety. This had to be some mistake. There had to be some other explanation than the one that was screaming in the back of his skull. He took several deep breaths and then went to his desk and sat down. He glanced at the picture of his wife, gone back to the Lifegiver these five standards, but could get no comfort from it. He shook himself. No, he was not going to let himself be panicked by rumor. He needed some facts. He turned on his communicator and punched in the code for Piernan Jaroo, the base controller. It took a few moments for him to be put through the several layers of underlings with which Jaroo surrounded himself, but he had sufficient status that he did not have to wait long.

"Father Brannon, what can I do for you?" came Jaroo's voice through the speaker.

"Piernan, I've been hearing some odd rumors concerning an incoming starship. I was wondering if you could tell me the truth of it?"

"Ha, the news is spreading as fast as a change in pressure! Yes, there is a whopping big ship sitting out in the inner cloud, maybe two hundred million klicks from here."

"How big? I'm hearing some very wild things."

"We don't have good figures, but it's a lot bigger than anything I've ever heard of. A couple of kilometers across at least."

"And we don't know where it came from?"

"No. Our intercepts indicate that the Seyotahs who made first contact—the lucky scum!—were having trouble making out the language. That's pretty damn odd. Must be from some group that went haring off from the original *Long March* crew and who have been out of contact ever since. If so, they're certainly making a dramatic return! If they're willing to trade—and the Seyotahs seem to think they are—this will be the biggest thing to hit here in decades."

"Yes," said Brannon, feeling worse than ever.

"If I find out anything more, I'll let you know," continued Jaroo, "although I never thought you were interested in this sort of thing."

"I've developed an interest very recently. Thank you, Piernan, I shall see you tonight at the ceremony." He cut the connection and sat there, staring at nothing, for a long time. His hands were pressed against the cold, hard ceramic of the desktop. Jaroo's enthusiasm made the dread filling him seem all the worse. Didn't the man realize what this was? No, he probably did not. Few people ever read the entire *Book of Life* anymore.

Some of the newer versions had even been abridged…

He turned in his chair and reached over to his bookcase to pull out an old, old copy of the sacred texts. In spite of reverent care, the cover was worn and cracked, the pages yellowed and creased. It had been given to him by his grandmother when he became an acolyte and he knew it had been in the family for generations. With practiced fingers he quickly found the passages he wanted. They had frightened him as a child and angered him as an adult. He was breathing hard as he read them now.

But it came to pass that the Others grew greedy and impatient. They looked upon the worlds in the care of the Lifegiver's Children with avarice. They would not wait as they had been commanded. They would not share the land with the Children as the Lifegiver had intended. The Others lied to the Children, misled them and tricked them. They stole the airs and the lands and the seas unborn, and the Children were consigned to the Void.

The Children sought new worlds to nurture, but the Others, now accursed and named World Stealers, pursued them from star to star and drove the Children out. Generations uncounted wept bitter tears and despaired of ever finding a home to call their own. Some fell into error and became the miserable slaves of the World Stealers. Those who remained true called to the Lifegiver for aid and their prayers were heard.

The Childrens' eyes were turned. Turned away from the stars close at hand; stars which the World Stealers would soon covet. Their eyes looked across the Great Rift to stars yet untouched. The Children gathered themselves and began a mighty labor. They built a great ship and it was called Long March…

Brannon's fingers flipped past the pages describing the epic journey across the Great Rift. It was a wonderful story, but he was in haste. He found the next passage he sought.

The Children rejoiced and gave thanks and cried aloud that they had at last found a home. But Harnan, the Chosen Voice of the Lifegiver, stood forth and warned the Children: All these worlds are yours. Nurture them and love them as you have been taught. But beware! The Rift is not so wide as to daunt the greed of the World Stealers. The day may come, though it be a hundred generations hence, when they shall come again. Stand ready and do not sleep, for the World Stealers may come again!

Brannon shuddered and shut the book. His small office, which had always seemed so safe and secure, was no haven now. He felt utterly vulnerable. Was this star system, the one named Refuge, just as vulnerable?

Had the World Stealers come again?

* * * * *

"Okay, that's done it," said Charles Crawford, leaning back from his control board and rubbing his eyes. "Phase I is complete. Proceed with Phase II." He was stiff after the long period of intense concentration, but this next phase could be handled by his other supervisors. He'd just spent the last six hours overseeing the first steps in dissassembling the enormous super-ship which had brought them across the Rift. It had been a very painstaking and nerve-wracking process.

The huge structure might appear immensely strong, and treated properly it was, but apply the wrong stress at the wrong point and it could come apart like a soap bubble. This was especially true when taking it apart. No matter how carefully it was done, as each piece was removed, it would impart a force vector to the remaining structure. Every action has a reaction. This would not have been a concern if the super-ship had really been a solid object, but it was not. It was made of nearly four hundred major elements and each had its own mass and moment of inertia. The structure would bend and flex and vibrate like a bell when subjected to forces like this. It had to be done very carefully, but the first batch of ships had been disconnected without a mishap and now he could relax for a while.

"Good job, Sheila," he said to his companion.

"Thanks, not that I did anything except check you figures," said Sheila MacIntyrre.

"You kept me on the straight and narrow. Nobody else I'd rather have backing me up."

Sheila nodded and then leaned back in her chair and stretched. She ran her fingers through her short hair. Crawford looked on admiringly. She really was a good-looking woman. Why hadn't he ever made a pass at her?

"So, it finally begins," said Sheila.

"Hmmm?" said Crawford, still admiring.

"The job. Building the gate. Hey, Chuck, you awake?"

"What? Oh yeah, the gate."

Sheila laughed. "Use up all your attention on Phase I?"

"Oh, I'm still paying attention." Sheila did not seem to catch what he was really saying, or she deliberately ignored it. Probably just as well, either way. Before he could think of anything else to say, his com pinged. It was a line from his office, not any of the other controllers involved in this operation. "Yeah?" he growled. He'd given orders not to be interrupted.

"Chief, the Gov wants to know how things are going?"

"Gently, Chuck," said Sheila before he could reply.

"Right," said Crawford, biting off his angry reply. "Tell *His Excellency* that we are proceeding on schedule. No problems."

"Uh, he wants to know how long this will take?"

"He's got a copy of the bloody schedule! Tell him to read it!"

"Chuck..." said Sheila.

"All right, tell him that we expect to finish disassembly in approximately ninety-two hours—per the schedule I sent him—be sure you tell him that!"

"Right, Chief," snickered the man on the other end. "Oh, he wanted me to remind you about the meeting with him at 1800."

"I'll be there." Crawford cut the connection. "That's all I need: His Grand High Muckety-Muck looking over my shoulder and asking: 'are we done yet?'"

"Guess he's a bit nervous about things, not that I can blame him."

"I suppose." Crawford looked over at Sheila. "How about you? You nervous? Are your people nervous?"

"A bit. Well, more than a bit. They're worried about the Venanci squadron and now this whole business of the system being occupied. A lot of them are asking if it is a smart move to build the gate here. Some think we should have gone somewhere else and set up shop there."

"We can't do that. I've tried to explain why to everyone. In any case," he waved at the display showing the disassembly, "it's too late now. We can't reassemble the ship and we can't go somewhere else without leaving critical structural elements behind. We're committed."

"I know," sighed Sheila, "and I think once we really get cracking on the gate, everyone will accept it. I just think that a lot of people are worried that Shiffeld is rushing this. We haven't even finalized any sort of agreement with the locals, have we?"

"No, but they are working almost non-stop on that. If I didn't have this job to do, I'd probably still be stuck in those meetings. The last I heard they were going to send a 'commission' to the base of the people we met and try to hammer out a final agreement."

"Really? That sounds like a pretty exciting assignment."

"Yeah, I almost wish I was going along."

* * * * *

"So, Mistress Nassau, what do you have for me today?" asked Rikard Shiffeld. Regina eyed the governor from across his huge desk and still could not decide if she liked the man or not. She had joined the expedition fairly late and her contact with him had been minimal. Of course, he was one of the Protector's pets, and that was a mark against him right there. Or maybe not, she admitted; viewed from outside, *she* could well be mistaken for one of the Protector's pets, too.

"Please just call me 'Regina', Sir Rikard," she replied with a faint smile. "Titles get so tiresome after a while."

"Yes, they do, don't they? That's why I settle for 'sir' rather than the more accurate unant, but you were going to report on terraforming activities... Regina."

She raised an eyebrow at his not-so-subtle reminder that his title was a hereditary one dating back centuries, while she was nothing but a successful tech with ties to the academic class. She shrugged her shoulders in answer to Shiffeld's question and her unspoken thoughts as well. "We've done just about all we can from way out here. I've had my survey teams glued to their instruments since we dropped out of hyper and we've collected all the data we can. To learn anything more, we'll need to get closer — or get the data from the locals."

"We have made contact with the locals living on the fourth planet," said Shiffeld. "As you believed, they are from a different group than the ones we met the other day. Fortunately, their language is nearly the same, so we are making progress in our communications. It will probably be some time, however, before we can make it clear what we are proposing."

"Just what are we proposing... Governor?"

Shiffeld leaned back in his leather-upholstered chair and stared at her with unwavering eyes. She stared back at him just as steadily. *Wondering just how far you can trust me, aren't you?* Well, she couldn't really blame him. Her record of accomplishments in terraforming spoke for itself, and that was why the Protector had insisted she go on this mission. But her reputation for outspokenness and opposition to government policies also spoke for itself. She wasn't a team player and Shiffeld certainly knew it.

"Our mission is to build a gate and terraform one of the planets in this system, Regina," said Shiffeld eventually. "The Protector himself laid that mission upon us and we must do everything in our power to carry it out."

"I will not terraform that planet out from under the rightful inhabitants, Governor. To do so would be a moral abomination."

Shiffeld's expression did not change, he'd clearly been expecting exactly that answer. After a moment he shrugged. "Of course not, you are quite correct. But you are assuming that the current inhabitants would object to having their environment improved. All of our readings indicate a fairly small population clustered along the equator. Clearly they don't find their world very hospitable, either. So, assuming we can get their permission to proceed, what action could we take?"

Regina had been expecting an argument, but it still took her a moment to marshal her thoughts. While she did so, she noticed Shiffeld's eyes drifting down over her sheer blouse. About time; she was beginning to think she was losing her touch. "All right, assuming we could proceed — and that's a big assumption — the primary challenges would be that the temperatures are too cold and the air is too thin, and what air there is contains too little oxygen. But there are large ice caps at both poles. These probably contain substantial amounts of frozen carbon dioxide as well as water. At the least, we can melt these, which will increase both the temperature and atmospheric pressure."

"How do you go about melting ice caps?" he asked, leaning forward.

"We start out by using nuclear devices. Carefully detonated, they can bring about melting without throwing up a lot of dust, which would counteract the heating process we are trying to start. Once we start getting an increase in the carbon dioxide levels, the heat will continue building on its own, accelerating the melting."

"I see. They must be rather large bombs, aren't they?"
"The devices are quite large, sir. Very powerful."

"I can see why you would be reluctant to use them with people down there."

"Actually, as you said, our scans indicate that nearly all the population centers are near the equator. If they stayed away from the poles the danger to them would be minimal."

"Interesting. But you said that melting the ice was 'the least' you could do. That implies that there are other methods available."

"Possibly, and that is why we need to examine the planet directly. Just melting the ice caps will only marginally improve the planet's environment. If we can find significant magma pockets we can do a great deal more."

"Magma pockets?"

"Yes. On planets of this size and age you will often find pockets of molten rock in subterrainean reservoirs. These will contain vast amounts of dissolved gasses and are under enormous pressure. If they can be tapped, the gas and the liquid rock will rush out like opening a shaken bottle of champagne. This can add billions of cubic meters of gas to the atmosphere and the outpouring of liquid magma will also increase the surface temperatures."

"Fascinating. And just how do you 'tap' such a pocket?"

"Again, we would use nuclear devices. They have special penetrator delivery vehicles to blast through the planet's crust. We can get at pockets as deep as a hundred kilometers with them. The gas released is mostly sulfur dioxide and carbon dioxide, but once things have settled down we begin introducing our special strains of bacteria. They can metabolize the sulfur and carbon and release free oxygen. Then we need to build up the nitrogen levels in the atmosphere and to do that…"
Regina was speaking faster and faster as she got into her subject, but Shiffeld gently cut her off. "That's amazing, Regina. But releasing those magma pockets sounds rather…dramatic. How would that affect the people down there?"

Regina frowned. "The release of a major magma pocket—and we would normally try to find a dozen or more of them—will make the nuclear devices used to do it look like firecrackers. There will be major seismic activity and the rain of molten rock could extend for hundreds of kilometers in every direction. I certainly would not want to be down there when it happened."

"No, of course not. Well, thank you for the update, Regina, but I actually asked you here for another reason."

For an instant she wondered if he was going to... no, his eyes weren't on the right spots. "Oh?"

"First let me ask you: how much confidence do you have in your number two?"

"Doctor Ramsey? He's good. A bit conventional for my tastes, but he knows his stuff."

"Good. So, he could look after your shop for a week or two, if necessary?"

"I suppose so, why?"

Shiffeld leaned back again and started tapping a finger on his desk. "We've taken our negotiations with the locals as far as we can go here. They are now telling us that they must go back to their base—an asteroid, apparently—to consult with their leaders. They've invited us to send a delegation there to complete the deal. Seeing how well you seem to get along with these people, I'd like you to go with our mission."

Regina's eyebrows shot up and she could not keep the look of surprise off her face. She had not expected this. At the same time, a jolt of excitement passed through her. "That's... that's very interesting, Governor. I think I'd like that very much. Count me in. Who else is going?"

"Two of them should be waiting outside right now," replied Shiffeld. He pressed a button on his comp and a moment later the door opened. She immediately recognized Charles Crawford and Petre Frichette.

"Ah, Mr. Crawford, Lord Frichette, thank you for coming. I'm glad we're finally getting a chance to meet in a less formal setting." The governor came around from behind the desk and actually offered his hand to Frichette. "I wanted to thank you personally for your gallant action against the traitor. We all owe you a large debt of gratitude."

"I wasn't acting alone, sir. And I wouldn't have even been there except for Charles Crawford."

"Yes, of course, well done to both of you. But, please, sit down, I have something I want to talk to you about." The men sat down as directed. Crawford didn't look happy, but he nodded to Regina.

"Gentlemen, I was just telling Mistress Nassau that we are sending an embassy to the locals' base to finalize the trade agreement with them. I need both of you to accompany her."

"What?" snapped Crawford. "I can't go anywhere right now!"

"Why not? I've looked over your schedule of activities and for the next three weeks, at least, and your direct supervision doesn't appear to be needed. Every action has been pre-planned in considerable detail. You've told me earlier that you have complete confidence in your subordinates, surely they can carry on."

"Well, yes, but there are always problems to be dealt with and..."

"Your subordinates can deal with routine problems, and for anything bigger you will still be in radio communications. Please, I know this is difficult, but the fact is that we are all going to have to do more than we expected, and this is particularly true for we leaders. All of us are going to have to start wearing more hats and we are also going to have to delegate a larger share of our load to our subordinates."

"I realize that, but what's so damn important about this mission that I have to go along?"

"I should hardly have to point this out to you, Charles, since you first brought it up yourself. Getting the help of the locals in the mining and manufacturing sector is going to be crucial in freeing up the manpower to crew our warships. I need someone there who will know exactly what is needed from them and make sure that we will get it. At the same time, I want an evaluation of their overall technological capabilities. There is no one in the fleet better suited than you to carry that out and see that it is done right. In fact, I want you in charge of the entire mission. Everyone else will answer to you. Is that acceptable?"

Regina watched Crawford's face as he digested this. She was coming to know him and she suspected that he would be far more moved by Shiffeld's comment about 'getting it done right' than he would be by the bribe of being put in command. She was sure Crawford was much more interested in seeing a job 'done right' than he was in titles or prestige.

"How long will we be gone?" he asked.

"A week to ten days, I would think."

"Well, I suppose I could manage to..."

"Good! That's settled then," said Shiffeld. "I'll be sending along a few clerks and such as well as my new assistant, Beatrice Innes. Remarkably able woman, I'm finding, she'll be able to handle all the fiddly details of the agreement."

"Then why not just put her in charge and let me stay here?" grumbled Crawford.

Shiffeld frowned and was tapping his desk again. "Mr. Crawford, I'm aware that you techs are an independent lot, used to making your own decisions and having your own way. But in our society you're the exception, not the rule. The vast majority of our people—probably the majority of your own people—are used to having the peerage around giving orders." Regina snorted before she could stop herself and Shiffeld's frown was turned on her. "Yes, I know that certain people look upon our system as outdated and anachronistic, but the fact remains that we've been doing things this way for over a thousand standards and it's not going to change any time soon. The common people *do* look to the peers for leadership and they get very uncomfortable when it isn't there. Lord Frichette, you know what I'm talking about, don't you?"

"Uh, yes, sir. The ratings take most of their orders from the petty officers rather than directly from a peer, but they know the PO's authority ultimately derives from a peer, so they obey. And if there isn't a peer somewhere up the chain of command..." Frichette trailed off.

"Chaos," said Shiffeld. "I don't need to remind any of you that our people have been walking around like a pack of zombies for the last two weeks. The only thing holding them together is the familiar routine of their jobs. But that will only last so long. And as soon as we start asking them to do unfamiliar things—like man the warships—it could break down completely."

"So what do you plan to do about it?" asked Regina. She didn't entirely agree with his analysis, but she could not entirely discount it, either. "We are going to need to raise up new leaders to fill the gaps. That is already happening on an informal basis, but we are going to have to formalize it to make it stick. I'm planning to start with you, Charles."

"What?" gasped Crawford. The man looked stunned. Regina felt a bit stunned herself. Was Shiffeld actually suggesting...? Apparently he was; he sat up very straight as he looked at Crawford and spoke in a formal tone:

"Charles Crawford, I'm dubbing you knight, and appointing you to the position formerly held by Sir Douglas Mueir. As Baron Dougherty's official representative, you are hereby charged with undertaking whatever tasks are deemed necessary to complete construction of the gate as ordered by the Protector. Do you understand and accept?"

"I...I..." gobbled Crawford. The man looked as completely flustered as anyone Regina had ever seen. He swallowed, jerked his head, and croaked: "Y-yes, sir." Shiffled smiled slightly and then turned to her.

"Regina Nassau..."

"Wait!" said Regina holding up a hand. "Can I assume that you are invoking the emergency powers proclaimed by the Council of Twelve following the War of the Four Families, Governor?"

Shiffeld leaned back with a look of surprise. "Well, it seems you know more history than just that of the terraforming sciences. But yes, those proclamations are still in effect, despite being two hundred standards old. They give me the power, in the absence of higher authority, to fill critical positions and grant titles as I see fit."

"But those titles don't become permanent unless confirmed by the Council, correct?"

"Well, yes…"

"Fine. Go ahead then."

Shiffled looked puzzled, but then shrugged and went ahead and made her a knight, too, charging her with undertaking terraforming operations. "Do you understand and accept?"

"I understand, but I only accept with the proviso that whatever terraforming is decided upon will be acceptable to the local inhabitants."

Shiffeld frowned. "We are obligated to follow our orders, Mistress…"

"And I'm obligated to follow my own conscience, Governor. There it is: take it or leave it." Shiffeld looked seriously tempted to leave it, but after a moment he nodded.

"Very well. Congratulations, Dame Regina." Shiffeld was still frowning, but he turned to Frichette.

"My Lord, I don't need to bestow any title on you, as you already outrank me socially. However, the table of organization for the naval part of the expedition has been totally gutted and must be restored. I am appointing you commodore and giving you operational command of all naval vessels."

"What?" cried the young man. "Sir! You can't be serious! I'm too young and I don't have any experience and…and…"

"We are not talking about experience here, My Lord, we are talking about *authority*, the right to command. I can't begin to count the number of fleets which were commanded — and successfully, I might add — by nobles with little experience. They had professional officers to advise them, of course, but the ultimate authority derived from them. That is what I need from you, sir: to provide the legal and moral anchor around which we can reconstruct the Rift Fleet. And in any case, for the task ahead of us, you have as much experience as anyone else left to us. Do you accept?"

"I… Well, I guess I don't have much choice, do I, sir?"

"Not really, no. None of us do. But don't worry, Commodore, I want to start you off on your new job a step at a time. As I've mentioned, we are sending an embassy to the locals' base. Sir Charles will command the expedition, but I want you to command the ship they will use."

"Ship, sir?"

"Yes. The locals have offered to take us there, but their ship cannot accelerate higher than about a tenth of a G and that would take well over a week to make the trip. We can't waste that much time just traveling. So, we want to use one of our own ships — which would be far more appropriate anyway. Considering all the circumstances, I want to use one of the warships. Felicity is one of poor Admiral Maynard's destroyers, and one of the very few we have the computer codes for. Time is critical and we can get her ready faster than any of the other ships."

"A destroyer…" said Frichette, frowning.

"I'd like you to depart no later than the day after tomorrow. Can you do it?" Frichette's blush turned into a blanche.

"Two days? But, sir, I don't have a crew or...or..."

"They are being selected as we speak. And I realize that it will take longer than two days to get the ship fully operational. But initially, all we require is that you can get her moving and to that base ASAP. Transport the delegation and I'll be happy. Can you do it?"

Regina looked at the young man and could see his intense interest. "Yes, sir. I can do it. We'll boost in two days."

"Excellent," said Shiffeld. "Well, I will let all of you go and begin your preparations. I have full confidence in each of you." The trio got to their feet and left Shiffeld's huge office. Once into the corridor, Regina turned to face the others. Both still looked rather stunned.

"Well, gentlemen, do you feel as completely *bought* as I do?"

* * * * *

Brannon Gillard completed his morning rounds through the crèche on automatic pilot. He did the things he needed to do, talked to the people he needed to talk to, but his mind was millions of kilometers away. Two hundred million, more or less. Somewhere on the fringes of this solar system, a monster was lurking. With each passing day, Brannon was more convinced that the newcomers represented a terrible danger to the clans. It was a feeling he could not shake.

But feelings were not proof. He needed proof and he had none.

He returned to his office and saw that there was a message for him from Jaroo. He had asked the controller to keep him abreast of developments and he had done so. The Seyotah clan was falling all over itself to conclude a trade agreement with the intruders and many of the other clans were also lining up to try and get a piece of that trade. To Brannon's mind, it was incredible that none of them seemed to be asking the basic question of what the intruders were really after? Had their greed totally blinded them to the potential danger? Even if these strangers were not the World Stealers as he feared, their immense power and wealth could still be a major disruption to the peace and security of Refuge. Death's Grip, but he needed more information! Well, perhaps Jaroo had something for him. He punched in the code and waited. A moment later the administrator appeared on his screen.

"Hello, Father, how are you today?"

"Well enough, thank you. And yourself?"

"Oh busy, as usual. Busier than normal with all the excitement. But you had asked me to tell you of any new developments and there has been a fairly major one."

"Oh?"

"Yes, it seems that the Seyotahs have invited some of the strangers back to their base at Panmunaptra to conclude their trade agreement. They will be setting out in the next day or two."

"Interesting. Will they be traveling in the Seyotahs' ship?"

"No, they will take a ship of the strangers. Apparently, that enormous vessel of theirs is really a whole lot of smaller ships all joined together. I say 'smaller' but only in comparison. They are still very large. Anyway, they are disassembling the big ship and one of the smaller ships will go to Panmunaptra."

Brannon stared at the screen for a few moments and then thanked Jaroo and broke the connection. Then he sat and stared at the blank screen for quite a while longer. Disassembling their ship? That would only make sense if they were planning to stay. And that could mean...

He typed in another code on his communicator terminal and then waited. There were several more layers of underlings to get through this time than when he contacted Jaroo, but eventually he reached the man he was seeking. Herren Caspari, the leader of all the Clorinda Clan, stared out of the monitor at him. Brannon had not spoken with him in nearly a year, but the man had not changed to look at: a stout gray face with pale gray eyes, long braided hair nearly white with the years, tied with green and yellow ribbons. The large mouth drew back in an unaccustomed grin when he saw who was calling. "Father Brannon! It is good to see you again. It has been too long."

"Yes, it has been, K'sur. I trust you are well?"

"Well, enough, and drop the *k'sur* or I'll start calling you 'archpriest'." The man's eyes twinkled.

"As you wish, Herren."

"So, what can I do for you?" Caspari's expression grew more guarded. "Don't tell me it's about the newcomers. Please don't."

"Uh, I'm afraid it is. Is there some problem?"

"You might say so!" exclaimed Caspari, throwing up his hands in exasperation. "It's all anyone is talking about. Our merchant and mining septs all want permission to trade with the newcomers—in spite of the fact they would have to acknowledge Seyotah dominance! And all the young warriors want to test their mettle against them! I've had a terrible time holding the young fools back!"

"They want to attack them?" asked Brannon carefully.

"Oh just a raid, of course. Feel them out and try to gain some glory and a bit of loot for themselves. You know how it is: youngsters trying to make a name for themselves."

"But you've held them back?"

"I'm trying to! The fact that the strangers' ship is about a million times bigger than theirs doesn't seem to phase them a bit. But I'm not going to let them start something we might end up regretting. We need more information."

"Yes, I agree with you completely, Herren. In fact, that is why I have called you. I need to ask you a favor."

"Life! I certainly owe you one," snorted Caspari. "Were it not for your surgical skills, I would not have my eldest son. Name what you want, my friend."

"I have heard of the strangers' upcoming envoy to the Seyotahs. Perhaps I can suggest a task more in balance with your warrior's capabilities…"

Chapter Ten

"All hands, standby for acceleration," commanded Petre Frichette. A chorus of acknowledgments came back to him from the personnel on the bridge. Charles Crawford watched the young man go through the procedures and was impressed with the show of confidence he was projecting to his crew. Surely he must have been very nervous, but no one would ever have suspected it.

"All stations report ready for acceleration, sir," reported Lieutenant Chapman, the executive officer. He was nearly as new at his job as Frichette, but at least looked a bit older. Most of the crew seemed to be pretty good, in fact, although it was really too early to tell for sure. Shiffeld had made efforts to get the best personnel available, but considering the natural tendency of the merchant captains to want to hang onto their best people, it was inevitable that a few less-than-best would slip through.

As if in confirmation, one of the lights on the main status board, which had just turned from red to green, now blinked back to red. Chapman looked at Frichette in chagrin. "Correction, all stations are not ready for acceleration. Magazine Two is showing red, sir."

"Very well, get it sorted out, please."

"Right away, sir."

Frichette seemed a little embarrassed and glanced at Crawford. He just smiled and nodded back. He was still slightly amazed the ship was as ready as it was after only two days. It had only been possible because they had the computer access codes for this ship—something they sadly did not have for the majority of warships in the fleet. The codes allowed them to use the main controls on the bridge, and with the computers' help, they could get under way. Assuming the problem down in the magazine could be fixed, of course.

Eventually it was and the board all showed green again. "Engineering, reactor to seventy-five percent, activate the main drive. Helm come to the plotted course and take us ahead at one-point-five gravities." The chief engineer and the helmsman acknowledged. Down in the power room, the control rods were retracted from the reactor a bit more and the uranium atoms in the fuel rods began to split more frequently. The temperature in the core built up rapidly, but the energy was siphoned off to heat the liquid hydrogen that was being pumped into the drive unit. The super-hot hydrogen, now a plasma, was seized by the drive unit and further accelerated. It shot out of the drive's exhaust at high velocity and, in turn, pushed the ship in the opposite direction.

Crawford was not a ship's engineer, but he understood what was going on well enough. The principle was ancient, and primitive people had discovered it using crude chemical propellants; even the current technology had changed little for centuries and it was unlikely that it ever would until someone finally discovered a practical controlled fusion system. But ancient or not, the drive worked and *Felicity* moved away from the fleet at a steady acceleration of fifteen meters per second per second. The one-point-five gravities of acceleration would not have bothered Crawford in any case, but, in fact, the ship's artificial gravity system was able to completely nullify the extra Gs. For the first twenty minutes, the ship headed in a direction which had been picked, not to get it to its destination, but to avoid bathing any of the other ships of the Rift Fleet with its exhaust. In spite of the disassembly of the huge super-ship, which was being completed without him, damn it, the vicinity was still very crowded and they needed to be careful. But once they had reached a safe distance, the ship's bow swung around and the journey began in earnest. This slight detour did not worry anyone, as the ship's fuel tanks were full. The fleet, as a whole, was nearly dry, but there had been no trouble collecting enough from the other ships to provide tiny *Felicity* with a full load.

After a few more minutes, Crawford got up from his chair and went over to Frichette. His own position here was a bit awkward. He was in overall charge of this expedition, but it was Frichette's ship. "How's it going?"

"Okay so far, sir. But this is all fairly routine. The computers do most of the work."

"Good thing we have them working for us. I must say I'm a little confused about why we don't have the computer codes for most of the other warships. Why didn't Shiffeld have them on file?"

Frichette gave a little snort. "Tradition, I guess. Back in the old days the ships were the actual property of the *petans* and *kadors* who ruled the individual planets and systems. Their oaths might require them to supply ships and crews to their overlords, but they weren't about to let the actual ownership of them slip out of their hands. Things are a little different today, but even with the squadrons theoretically nationalized, the old ways still persist and the captains guard their codes closely. Admiral Maynard probably had copies of all the codes, but I'm sure he guarded them just as well, and with him gone there's no hope of retrieving them."

"But we do have the ones for this ship."

"Yes, a couple of the smaller ships were provided by some relative of the governor's and he did have the access codes. *Felicity* just barely rates being called a destroyer. She's actually more like the old merchant-corvettes — armed merchant ships — that were used to beat the Hebyrnians forty years ago. Not too many like her left. Fair cargo capacity, fair speed — and unfortunately — only a fair armament."

"Hopefully we won't have any need of the armament — at least on this trip."

"I hope you are right, Sir Charles. But I'm not going to depend on wishful thinking." He turned to the first officer. "Mr. Chapman, we will clear for action in fifteen minutes. Let's see if everyone can remember where their battle stations are, shall we?"

* * * * *

Tadsen Farsvar stared at the woman sitting opposite him and tried to keep his mind on the conversation. It wasn't easy. Regina Nassau was visiting him in his quarters aboard the Newcomers' ship and the measures she'd taken to be even remotely comfortable in what was, for her, the very high heat, was making *him* very *uncomfortable*. Aside from the bubble helmet, which allowed her to breathe, she was wearing nothing but some very short shorts and a sleeveless shirt, which her sweat had plastered against her rather amazing figure. Women of the clans did not nurse their infants and were generally not this well... endowed.

"Tad? Did you understand my question?"

"What? Oh, y-yes, I did," stammered Tad, forcing his eyes back up where they belonged. "I'm nineteen standards old. I've been a confirmed adult of my sept for nearly a standard. How-how old are you, Regina?"

She smiled when she saw his question appear on her small computer screen. Communications had been refined to a great degree in just a few days. Computers with voice-recognition software and automatic conversion routines had been provided by the Newcomers. They now had to just talk to one another and they could usually understand what the other was saying.

Usually.

"You want to know how big I am?" asked Regina. "Which particular dimension were you interested in, Tad?"

Tad's people did not blush the way the Newcomers did, but a wave of embarrassment washed through him. Damn machine! He hadn't really asked that, had he...? "Uh, no, I wanted to know how old, how long you have lived! The same question you just asked me!"

"Oh," and now Regina laughed. "By your reckoning I'm thirty-seven standards."

"That old?" he asked in amazement. "Y-you don't look nearly so old. You're so...so..."

"How delicious of you to say so, Tad."

Delicious? He punched a button on the computer and got several alternate possible meanings. They all seemed to involve pleasing tastes. Well, it probably meant something good.

"Can you tell me more about this place we are going?" asked Regina. "This Panmunaptra? It sounds like an important gathering place."

"Oh, it is. Very important. At least to my clan. The elders meet there and there are merchants and builders and the birthing crèches, of course."

"Birthing crèches? That does not seem to translate very well, Tad."

"Uh, it is the place where babies are made."

"Made? You mean where they are born? Like a hospital? The place where women go to give birth to their babies?"

Tad puzzled over her questions for a few moments. She did not seem to understand what he was talking about. But surely her people had similar things…

"Not exactly," he said hesitantly. "Well, yes, in a way. The man and woman go there to donate their…genetic material. Fertilization is done there and the gestators grow the baby. When the baby is ready, the parents return to claim it. I guess I'm not being very clear. But you must know what I'm talking about. It's the place babies come from."

Regina had gotten a very odd look on her face. Tad asked awkwardly: "D-don't your people do it that way?"

"Some people do," she said, slowly. "Sometimes they don't have any choice. But most women grow their own babies…here." She pressed a hand to her abdomen.

"Inside you? L-like a-animals?" Tad clamped his mouth shut after the second question. Would she find that insulting? But was she really serious? He was somewhat relieved when she smiled and nodded.

"Yes, exactly like animals, Tad. But you say your people don't do it that way?"

"No. We can't. The Lifegiver d-designed us this way. Or so the priests say."

"Really? So all of your babies come from these crèches? They must be very large—or there must be a lot of them."

"They are not so large, but perhaps ten or twelve babies are born each day. And our clan's only birthing crèche is on Panmunaptra." Regina paused and the hair above her eyes drew close together and she seemed to be thinking.

"Ten or twelve a day. That rate could only support a population of a few hundred thousand—at most. How many clans are there here? Is yours one of the smaller ones?"

"We are not one of the bigger clans," said Tad a bit defensively. "But we are not the smallest, either. There are fourteen clans here in Refuge. Of course, we have relatives in other systems, I don't think anyone knows how many by this time. And I've heard that there are three other clans who did not leave anyone here, but who traveled elsewhere."

"I think I'm beginning to see how your society is organized, Tad. Your clans are based on the original…gifts the Lifegiver bestowed on your ancestors. All the high-temperature, high carbon dioxide breathers make up one clan, while all the low-temperature, low pressure people are in another. And so on. Am I understanding this correctly?"

Regina's words took a little puzzling out, but eventually Tad thought he had it. "Yes, that's right. All of those who were made suitable for a certain environment make up one clan. It is really the only way it could be since we can't usually tolerate another clan's air or temperature preferences."

"But you do have dealings with each other?"

"Oh yes, there is a lot of trade that goes on and then there are..." Tad trailed off. He had been about to mention the raids that went on between clans, but he suddenly realized that might not be a proper thing to talk about. His uncle was off taking a tour of the ship (which Tad had impatiently managed to get earlier) and wasn't around to advise him. Best to just keep it simple for now. "There is a lot of trade," he repeated.

Regina did not seem to notice his hesitation. With their dependence on the translating computers, there were a lot of lengthy pauses in the conversation anyway. "And within the clans you are divided into, what was the word you used? Septs? And the septs are divided into families?"

"Yes, that's right."

"And about how many people, in all the clans, live in this star system?"

"Not really sure. Twenty or thirty million, I would guess."

"That's all? I thought this was one of the first places your ancestors colonized when they arrived in... in this part of space. I would have thought there would be a lot more of you by now."

"Well, it is a lot of effort to maintain ships and space colonies."

"I can imagine, Tad. But what about the fourth planet? We know there are people living there. Haven't they increased their numbers a great deal? Are they terraforming it, or have they finished?"

"I... I don't really know a lot about what's happening there, Regina. I'm sorry. The Frecendi clan are cold-worlders—even colder than you people—and too far insystem for us to have a lot of dealings with. From what I've heard, the planet is too cold even for them and they only have a few cities along the equator. The elders on Panmunaptra can probably tell you a lot more."

"I see. Well, thank you for all you've told me."

"Can I ask a question now, Regina?"

"Of course."

"Where do you people come from? Why are you here? What do you want?"

"That's three questions, Tad."

"Uh, yes. But I'd still like to know."

Regina frowned and Tad was again fascinated by the little clumps of hair over her eyes. "We come from a long way off, Tad. It took us a very long time to get here. I'm not sure, but I suspect we come from the same general region as your ancestors did so long ago."

"But you are not like us. Your temperature and atmospheric requirements are different from any of the other clans, Regina."

"No, I guess we are different. But not too much different, I hope."

"And why did you come from so far?"

"Why to make friends with you, Tad," said Regina with a smile.
Before Tad could ask any more questions, the woman got to her feet. She
was very tall. "Whew! I think this is about all the heat I can stand for right
now. If you'll excuse me, I need to go cool off for a while. Thank you for
talking with me, Tad."

She let herself out through the tiny airlock which had been added
to the compartment, leaving Tad alone with his questions.

* * * * *

Charles Crawford groaned when the alarm on the clock went off.
He slapped it to silence and then looked at the time. He'd slept for six
hours. Not too bad, really, except for the fact that he had been awake for
nearly forty-eight hours before that, getting everything taken care of for his
unanticipated absence. He was groggy and his eyes felt like they were full
of sand. He rubbed them clear and sat up in his bunk.

His bunk. It did not feel like his bunk, the mattress was too soft and
it had formerly belonged to a man who was now dead. Granted, the former
owner had not actually slept here for over ten years, it still felt…odd. As
he sat there, trying to come fully awake, he looked around the compartment. Frichette had insisted he take the commander's stateroom and the
former captain of *Felicity*, one of Shiffeld's cousins, he believed, had had
good taste — and expensive ones. The bulkheads were covered with polished slatewood paneling with built-in shelves, cabinets, and bookcases.
The deck was thickly carpeted and the furniture very nice. Several original
paintings graced the walls.

He supposed that eventually it would all go to whoever now had
legal title to it. Crawford had no clue who that might be, nor did he care,
but he had no doubt that someone, somewhere, would be eager to take
possession. Hopefully, they would be as dutiful in taking possession of the
remains of the former crew. The question of what to do with the bodies had
been a ticklish one. Not just the ones from *Felicity*, but from all the navy
ships. They could not just leave them where they were; the cold-sleep compartments had been created out of space normally used for crew quarters
and recreation facilities. They needed to be removed and stored. *Felicity*
had been given priority, of course, and her former crewmen were now in a
refrigerated storage compartment on one of the supply ships. Moving the
nine thousand others was going to be an enormous job. Crawford was glad
it was not his.

He pushed himself out of the bunk and into the small washroom attached to his quarters. The shower advanced the waking-up process, but did not complete it. Coffee would be required for that. As he scrubbed himself, he thought about his plans for today. They had made turn-over just before he had gone to sleep and they were now decelerating toward the asteroid base that was their destination. Another eight hours would see them there. Hopefully the negotiations could be completed quickly and they could get back to the fleet so he could get back to his real job. There was nothing at all for him to do aboard this ship and even the few hours of inaction were weighing heavily on him.

He finished his body-maintenance and headed for the officers' galley to get his coffee. He ran into Frichette there. The young man was seated at one of the tables with his cup of tea and munching on some ship biscuits. "Morning," said Crawford, taking a seat opposite him.

"Good morning, Sir Charles," said Frichette. Crawford started in surprise.

"Wow, *that's* going to take some getting used to," he growled. His frown deepened as another thought, one which had been troubling him for several days, came to mind. "Tell me, *Lord* Frichette, what did you think of that little comment *Dame* Regina made as we were leaving the Governor's office? Have we really been bought?"

Frichette's eyebrows went up and he glanced about to make sure they were alone. Finally, he shrugged. "Not really sure. On the one hand, what he's been doing makes sense: we do need to fill the holes in the chain of command. On the other…"

"On the other, it makes all of us—well, all of us former commoners—indebted to him on a personal as well as a professional level."

"True, and true for me, too when you consider this 'commodore' position he's given me, but that's how our system is supposed to work, isn't it, sir? Ties of personal loyalty as well as legal ones?"

"I guess. Just never saw it from this angle before."

"And we are all on the same side, aren't we? I mean it's not like we're at odds with the governor, are we?"

"No… but at the same time we all have our own patrons back home. And while I might be a babe-in-the-woods when it comes to politics, I can see the political ramifications of this whole mess. Shiffeld's going to be on the hot-seat when we get home and he's going to do everything he can to cover his own ass."

"You think he's setting us up to take some of the blame? I don't see how any of us could be held responsible for the sabotage, but you may have a point. Not sure what we could do about it, though."

"I don't either. Bah, I'm getting paranoid. Just a bad habit of looking for the cloud around any silver lining that comes my way."

Frichette nodded and then stood up. "I'm going to the bridge, would you like to come along?"

"May as well, I don't really have anything else to do." Crawford took his coffee and followed Frichette.

"Good morning, Captain," said the officer of the watch as they came onto the bridge.

"Good morning, Mr...Dunkelberg. Anything to report?"

"No, sir. We are on course and on schedule. The drive and reactor are nominal. We've detected a good many other craft, but they all seem to be more of those prospecting ships. There certainly are a hell of a lot of them around here."

"Yes. Well, keep your sensor people tracking them, it's good practice."

"Yes, sir." Dunkelberg got up from the command chair and went over to the sensor station to look over the shoulder of the nervous technician there. Frichette took his place and busied himself looking at status reports while Crawford paced about, making everyone else nervous. At one point he found himself standing next to Frichette.

"Tell me, everyone aboard keeps calling you 'captain', but shouldn't they be calling you 'commodore'?"

"Another one of those traditions, Sir Charles," replied Frichette. "The commander of any ship is called the captain, no matter what his actual rank is. I won't be called 'commodore' until I'm actually commanding a group of ships rather than just one."

"Ah, I see. I think."

Eventually, the watch changed. Frichette's exec, Lieutenant Chapman, had this watch and once the formalities were complete, he began discussing what he wanted to do for the next drill. They were still at it when the newly arrived sensor operator spoke up.

"Uh, sir, I'm getting something odd here." Chapman immediately looked up.

"Odd, Mr. Hreni? What do you mean?"

"I've got five small energy sources at about a thousand klicks and closing. They weren't there a minute ago, so they just switched on. But I can't read anything else, sir, just the energy emissions."

Chapman and Frichette went over to sensors and Crawford tagged along. "The energy levels are increasing," said Hreni. "They're nearly stationary, sir, it's our own motion that's closing the range."

"Maybe some sort of sensor buoys?" suggested Chapman.

"Odd place for them. Mr. Hreni, are you using an active scan?"

"Yes, sir, I'm trying to paint them with radar, but there's hardly any return at all. Whatever they are, they've got almost no metal in them. I could increase the power..."

"That might damage them. We don't want to appear unfriendly."

"Range is five hundred. We are going to pass them to port at about a hundred klicks at closest approach. Energy readings are still rising... God! Look at that spike!" Frichette looked at the read-out and sucked in his breath.

"Whatever these things are, they're suddenly radiating like a runaway reactor."

"Surely, this isn't a normal..." ventured Crawford

"I don't like this, Skipper," said Chapman. "Maybe we should clear for action."

Before Frichette could even reply, Hreni cried out: "Yow!" The sensor displays flashed white and then went blank. There were other flashes and other shouts from around the bridge. Then the lights in the compartment flickered and dimmed. The artificial gravity went off momentarily and then came back on at a lower level.

And the drive stopped.

The barely-noticed rumble and vibration of the main drive was missing. It was something people ignored while it was on, but even Crawford immediately noticed its absence. Everyone on the bridge was shouting. Frichette bellowed for silence and eventually got it.

"All stations report," he commanded. "Engineering?"

"The reactor has shut down, sir! An emergency shutdown. We are operating on batteries only." Not good. He looked to the next station.

"Helm?"

"The drive is out. We still have thrusters and our attitude is stable." Not good, either, but without the reactor, the drive could not function.

"Sensors?"

"We are completely blind to port, sir. All sensors on that side are not responding. The starboard sensors are still operational."

"Weapons?"

"Uh, not sure, sir. Main fire control is out. Portside batteries are giving me mixed readings. Some aren't responding and others seem to be on manual control. The starboard batteries are online using back-up fire control. Missile tubes are...not sure, sir."

"What the hell happened?" demanded Crawford.

"I don't know," replied Frichette. "But Mr. Chapman, clear the ship for action. Shut down the artificial grav, we can't spare the power for that. And bring our two guests up here. Maybe they can explain this."

"Yes, sir!"

* * * * *

Tad was instantly alert when the lights flickered. When the gravity fluctuated and the drive shut down, he knew that something was wrong. He had heard the wail of the ship's combat alarm twice the day before, but some instinct told him that this time it was not a drill. His uncle was instantly awake, too.

"Get dressed. Get your helmet on."

"Yes, sir." Tad quickly moved to comply. An instant later the artificial gravity went off completely, but Tad was used to free fall and it did not slow him down at all. He was suited up first and was helping his uncle finish when the intercom signaled them. The person at the other end seemed very agitated and it was impossible to make out anything except for 'captain' and 'bridge'. It seemed obvious that the captain wanted them on the bridge. Uncle Jari signaled his agreement and the man broke the connection.

"What's happening, sir?" asked Tad.

"I don't know, but it sounds serious. Let's get up to the bridge." They went through the tiny airlock and found two men waiting for them in the corridor. The men tried to hurry them along, but instead retarded their progress; they were not nearly as skilled in free fall. They were also hampered by the swarms of people in the passageways. Dozens of people were scrambling about in what seemed like panic.

Things were a bit calmer on the bridge, but only by comparison. Captain Frichette was snapping out orders and receiving reports continuously, but he stopped when he spotted Tad and his uncle. He and Mr. Crawford, who was also there, immediately floated over to them but then stopped and talked and waved until they were given a pair of the translating computers. Naturally, Tad and his uncle already had theirs ready.

"My ship has been attacked," said Frichette. "Can you tell me why? And by who?"

"What has happened?" asked Uncle Jari. The reply was lengthy and complicated and it took a few moments to puzzle out. But it eventually became clear that a party of warriors had used their pulsers against the ship, disabling many of its systems. Tad and his uncle exchanged fearful glances. Raiders! And surely not from the Seyotah clan. No! Someone was trying to wrest this treasure from them! They started to speculate on who it could be, but Frichette was growing impatient.

"They are raiders, Captain," said Uncle Jari. "From another clan."

"We lost track of the five who fired at us when our sensors went down," said Frichette. "They've gone past us by now and I'm trying to locate them with our remaining sensors in case they attack again."

"No, Captain!" said Uncle Jari urgently. "The first ones are no longer a danger. They have not the fuel to catch up. But there will be a second wave waiting in ambush. Maybe a third. Look ahead, not behind!"

When Frichette saw the translation he turned away and began issuing orders again. Tad moved so that he could look at the various bridge displays. Many of them were blank. Clearly the raiders' pulsers had been very effective. Not just the ship's sensors, but probably the drive and reactor as well had been knocked out. A chill went through him. The ship, even though it was one of the smallest of the Newcomers' vessels, had seemed so large and powerful. He had assumed it could deal with any possible attack by raiders. Apparently not…

"This is a disaster, Tad," moaned his uncle. "If the raiders take this ship, we will lose everything we had been hoping for. All the trade and business will go to another clan."

"Don't give up hope yet, sir. The ship isn't completely stunned. Some of their systems are still working. You saw the size of their turrets: their pulsers must be enormous. If they can take out the next waves before they can fire, we might still win through." Uncle Jari nodded and gripped Tad's shoulder.

Frichette had rotated his ship to bring his undamaged sensors to look forward. A few tense minutes went by and then several people shouted when a new contact appeared on the screen. Tad could not be sure of the scale of the display, but the contact seemed to still be a fair distance away. A few moments later there was more excitement among the bridge personnel. Frichette turned to face them again.

"The new contact is signaling us," he said. "I can't make any sense of the message. Can you translate?"

"I will try," said Uncle Jari.

Frichette ordered the message transferred to the speakers inside their helmets. They listened—and both groaned. "Clorindans!" exclaimed Tad. One of the most powerful—and aggressive—clans in the system, and an old nemesis of the Seyotah. The news couldn't be worse.

"Well," demanded Frichette. "What do they say?"

"They… they are demanding that you surrender your ship and accompany them to their base."

"Like hell!" snarled Frichette. Crawford made a similar noise.

"They say they will attack again if you do not submit."

Frichette's reply did not translate at all, but he conferred with Crawford for a moment and then began giving more orders. There were affirmative answers back from his crew and a moment later a number of new displays began to light up. Tad was no expert on such things, but they looked to him like targeting displays for pulsers. The Newcomers were not going to give in! A thrill went through him.

"See, Uncle! We aren't finished yet!"

* * * * *

"Sir, the bogey is signaling us. It looks to be a repeat of the first message," said the com technician.

"No reply. Surrender be damned," said Frichette. Then he looked at Crawford. "Sorry, sir, you are in charge here, but I'm assuming you agree?"

"Damn right." He said it as confidently as he could, but he did not feel nearly so confident. What the hell had they stuck their hand into?

"Aye, sir, do not reply."

"Range to target is twenty-two thousand kilometers and closing," said the sensor tech. "They are not evading, sir."

"You have a solid lock?" asked Frichette.

"Yes, sir, their transmission gave us a good fix. And this one is a lot bigger and with far more metal in it than those others. They won't be able to lose us, sir."

"If they aren't evading, we might be able to hit them, even at this range, sir," said Lieutenant Chapman.

"Wait. Mr. Farsvar said there could be one or two more *waves* of attackers. Presumably ones like the first. I want to hold our fire until we see those energy build-ups again and then lock-on and fire as quick as we can—before they can hit us."

"Right, sir."

"Sensors, look sharp. I want to know at the first hint of a contact. And tie in a camera to your sensors. Maybe we can get a look at these things. Weapons, standby to lock on to any sensor contact. You will fire only on my command."

"Aye, aye, sir," said both men. Crawford was becoming more and more impressed with Frichette. The lad had certainly been doing his homework!

Several minutes went by and the bogey stopped signaling. All the while, damage reports were coming in. Whatever the enemy had hit them with had fried circuits and popped breakers all over the ship. Most of the damage seemed to be on the portside, but the reactor had gone into an automatic shutdown and the chief engineer wasn't sure how long it would take to get it back up. With no reactor and no drive, they would zip past their destination at high velocity and continue on into an unexplored—and apparently hostile—star system. Crawford was tempted to grab a wrench and go help with the repairs—at least that was something he understood! But no, his place was here.

More time passed and the bridge crew was getting edgy. Frichette was wiping his hands on his tunic and rubbing his fingers together, the only real signs that he was nervous. "Sure hope these guys are right about the first batch," said Chapman quietly. "If they *are* able to double back on us, we'll never see them coming."

"Amen to that, Lieutenant. Well, in another three minutes, if nothing else happens, I'm going to open up on the one target we do…"

"Captain!" exclaimed Hreni, the sensor tech. "New contacts. Five of them, just like before! Range about twelve hundred klicks!"

"Transfer the lock to weapons! Standby to fire!"

"Yes, sir!"

Crawford drummed his fingers on the arm of his chair and then forced himself to stop. The main bridge monitor had split itself into a dozen smaller displays. Some of these were showing the status of the weapons mounts that were still functional. The two primary turrets quickly accepted the targeting information from the sensors and achieved a lock. There were four secondary mounts that could bear, but they were slower in getting a lock. Frichette had put his most experienced crews in the main turrets and the others were having trouble handling their weapons without the help of the main fire control computer.

"Sir Charles, do I have permission to fire on these targets?"

He swallowed and his eyes flicked to another display which was showing a view from an exterior camera, slaved to one of the sensors. It was at full magnification and it showed a blurry blob that was one of the targets. He couldn't really tell anything about it from the image, but in all probability there were human beings aboard them. And Frichette was asking permission to kill them.

"Sir, the energy levels on the bogies are still climbing," said Hreni.

"Captain, we better fire before they can," said Chapman.

"Sir Charles?" Frichette looked him straight in the eyes and Crawford couldn't look away, as much as he wanted to. "We're running out of time, sir."

His head jerked convulsively. "Yes."

The exec immediately turned to give the firing order, but Frichette stopped him. "Wait. I want them all in one salvo." Two of the secondary turrets had their locks now. Four of the five were targeted, but the last one was still eluding the remaining turrets. "Damn it, what's the delay?"

"Energy levels are starting to spike!" exclaimed Hreni. Crawford tensed and gripped the arms of his chair.

"All batteries..." The last targeting icon flashed from yellow to green. "...*Fire!*"

Felicity's lasers lashed out. There was no sound or motion to indicate it, but an instant later all five targets blinked off the screens, to be replaced with a symbol for drifting debris. On the video monitor there was a sudden flash and the fuzzy blob was blown to bits.

"Got the bastards!" exclaimed Chapman. Cheers erupted from all over the bridge. Crawford had to force himself not to join them.

"Well done, people!" said Frichette. "Weapons, retarget the main batteries on the remaining bogey. Standby to fire."

"Yes, sir!" The weapons officer had a wolf-like grin on his face. The sensor tech had already aimed the camera pick-up at the new target. It was larger, but much farther away and so it was just a fuzzy speck.

Crawford was learning to read the displays. It appeared that B-turret already had its lock, but D-turret was lagging behind. The secondaries were out of range. Suddenly, there was a tug on his arm. He turned to see

Mr. Farsvar beside him. The man looked agitated and he was talking rapidly. He couldn't make out any of it.

"It's all right, sir, we're taking care of them," said Crawford, absently patting the man's hand. "No need to worry now, you're safe." The man continued to talk, but it still made no sense.

"D-turret had its lock, sir," said Chapman.

"Very good. Fire."

The remaining target flashed brightly in the video display, Farsvar's grip on his arm tightened painfully and the man shouted something. Clearly the man was excited by the battle.

"Target destroyed, sir," said Chapman with satisfaction.

"Well done. But keep a sharp lookout. There could be more."

"Hopefully not too many more, sir. The capacitors for the weapons are almost exhausted. Unless we can get the reactor back up soon we aren't going to have much to shoot with."

"Yes, well let's get on that."

Crawford took a deep breath and tried to relax. Whatever the hell was going on, they had come through it more or less intact. Then he noticed that Farsvar had released his arm. He turned and saw that the two natives had retreated to the far side of the bridge and were talking to each other. Neither one looked especially happy. What was wrong with them? With no immediate crisis to deal with, Crawford unbuckled from his chair, found the little translating computer and went over to them.

"Everything is all right now. No need to be concerned," he told them. That seemed to make no impression. Their expressions were still ones of shock and anguish.

"What...? What did you do...?" gasped Farsvar.

"We destroyed the attackers." What was the matter with the man?

"But... but, you *killed* them!"

"Of course we did. They were attacking us! What the hell did you expect us to do, surrender?"

"Oh no...oh no...Lifegiver the Merciful, how could you...?" the man was shaking his head and he looked to have tears on his cheeks. "They were Clorindans! They will never forgive this—never! It will be a blood-feud forever now. We are ruined...ruined." He suddenly looked up, straight into Crawford's eyes.

"We were your friends! How could you *do* this to us?"

Chapter Eleven

Regina Nassau paused outside the door and tried to figure out what she was going to say to Tad and Jari Farsvar. During the recent excitement, she had stayed with the other 'emissaries' in their quarters and tried to understand what was going on. A passing crewman had said something about an attack, but all attempts to get information direct from the bridge had been rebuffed by an increasingly irritated communications tech. Some of the clerks had been frantic and Beatrice Innes had been outraged at the lack of information. She had been so persistent that when the captain had finally deigned to notice his passengers it had come as a great surprise that he wanted to talk to her instead of the others. Innes had been furious, but Regina was quietly delighted that she was being snubbed. She was finding that she did not like her companion at all. Innes was insufferably smug at being Shiffeld's new right hand and was used to getting her way with anyone less lofty than her boss. Regina had little patience for her.

Her conversation with Frichette had been brief; he was constantly being interrupted by his subordinates. Apparently the ship had taken some serious damage in the attack. Regina was amazed that there had been an attack, but the evidence was irrefutable. The question of why was still unanswered. The other question of why the successful repulse of the attack had so upset the two natives was also unresolved. The captain wanted Regina to find the answer to that one—and to the first question, too, if possible. She pressed the button next to their door. A few seconds later there was an answer through the intercom. It was Tad.

"Yes? Who comes?"

"Tad, it's Regina. Can I come in and talk to you and your uncle?" There was a long pause before any reply came.

"My uncle is… resting. But I will come out and talk with you."

Regina frowned. She had shucked off most of her outer clothing in anticipation of another session in the sauna. While she enjoyed startling the crew and Tad's admiring glances, it was going to get a little chilly after a while. Where to go? Back to her quarters? No, she was sharing a stateroom with her assistant and she wanted to talk with Tad alone. The grav still wasn't back on, so she floated there in indecision until Tad came through the lock. He was dressed in warm clothes and his breathing helmet. His usually cheerful expression was replaced with one of apprehension.

They traveled in silence along the ship's corridors until they found an unused mess hall. The crew were all busy making repairs and it was deserted. Regina led Tad into one of the corners and they pulled themselves into two of the chairs. Regina stared at the young man. He stared back with fear in his eyes. She got out her translating computer.

"Tad, what's wrong?"

"You...your captain and Mr. Crawford killed them."

"Who? Who did they kill? Who attacked us and why?"

"They were Clorindan raiders. From another clan."

"But why did they attack us?"

"I don't know for certain, but they probably wanted to take you away from us and get the trade agreements for themselves. They have harassed us for generations."

"Take us away from you? You make it sound like we're some object that can be owned. Do I have the translation right, Tad?"

"No, people can't be owned, but the right to trade with you can. We contacted you first, so we had first claim. But if the Clorindans had managed to take you to their base, they could have claimed the right to trade."

"Don't we have any say in the matter?"

"Of course. You could have refused to trade with them. But then concluding an agreement with anyone else here would have been...difficult. Still, it is surprising that they would try anything this high-handed with strangers like you."

"Their actions seem pretty arrogant to me. But then I don't understand why you are so upset that we drove them off. Especially if they have been your enemies for so long."

Tad looked puzzled. "I don't understand that one word, Regina."

"Which word?"

"Enemies."

Now it was Regina's turn to be puzzled. "Enemies? Uh, an enemy is a foe, someone you fight against. Aren't the Clorindans your enemies?"

"They are rivals. They cause us trouble and sometimes we do the same to them. But...but we don't 'fight'."

"They were certainly fighting us!" insisted Regina. "They attacked this ship with some sort of weapon."

"They attacked the *ship*, Regina, not you. They would have harmed no one aboard. Their pulsers, the weapons they were using, only affected your ship's electronics. They only intended to disable you and force you to submit. They weren't going to hurt anyone—and yet you killed them!"

Regina felt like she'd been punched in the belly. Shock, embarrassment, shame, all flashed through her. "We-we didn't know, Tad!" she gasped at last. "That's not the way... that's not the way we do things," she ended awkwardly. "But you don't fight? You don't k-kill?"

"It happens sometimes. There are blood-feuds when things get out of hand. Usually just between individuals or families. Now there will be a blood-feud between my clan and the Clorindans. Because of you. My people cannot win such a... such a fight." Tad waited while Regina read the translation. Then he went on. "You kill people. You kill each other." It wasn't a question and Tad's eyes were wide—and accusing.

"Yes. I'm afraid we do, Tad," whispered Regina. "We do, indeed, and I'm sorry."

* * * * *

"Governor Shiffeld, I wish to report that the ship has been attacked…" Crawford pushed the switch to stop the recording and tried to figure out what to say next. He took a breath and continued. "The attack was a complete surprise and totally unprovoked. Our guests tell us that the attackers were from a rival clan. Apparently, they hoped to capture us and force us to conclude a trade agreement with them instead of Mr. Farsvar's people.

"The weapons that were used by the attacker were… unconventional. From what we've been able to determine, they have something which will project an extremely powerful electro-magnetic pulse, similar to what is created by a nuclear explosion, except that the effects are tightly focused. This has severely damaged many of our computers and electrical systems. As you might know, sir, and as Captain Frichette has explained to me, warships are hardened to resist the effects of EMP but not for something as strong as this. The effects had the same strength as if a very large nuke had detonated only a few meters away. Since no ship would survive such an explosion anyway, our systems are not built to resist EMP of that magnitude. The enemy's first attack knocked out our reactor and drive along with most of the sensors and weapons on the side of the ship facing the attack. I don't know if it is possible to harden our systems to withstand such an attack, but you might want to put some people to work on it. On the good side, the range of the weapon seems to be only a few hundred kilometers. I should warn you, however, that the enemy attack ships are very small and almost invisible to sensors until they begin to power up their weapons. Captain Frichette will be sending his own report with all the particulars, but I wanted to give you a basic account of what has happened.

"Fortunately, with advice from Mr. Farsvar, we were able to destroy the follow-up attack and the mother ship which had carried the attack ships. No additional attackers have appeared. We are currently expediting repairs to the ship. We hope to have the reactor and drive operational in a few hours and we should be able to reach our destination only about seven hours late—if you still wish us to proceed, of course."

Crawford's expression darkened. "There is one other problem, sir. The destruction of the attacking ships seemed to disturb the Farsvars to an extreme degree. Regina, er, that is Dame Regina, has been able to determine that combat between the locals is almost always of a non-lethal variety. They were attempting to simply disable *Felicity*, not kill us. Our killing of the attackers has violated some sort of taboo and could have negative consequences on our relations and negotiations.

"Sir, I'm a bit out of my depth here. I would greatly appreciate further instructions from you on how to proceed. Crawford, out." He re-read his message and then pressed the send key. In a few moments the communications officer would encode it and send it on its way. He could only imagine the effect this was going to have on the governor. He leaned back and took a large gulp from his coffee bulb. With the grav out, they were back to zero-G containers. Damn, they made good coffee on this ship.

Well, one task done, now to look at his incoming messages. Most were just routine, but he immediately zeroed in on the one from Sheila. He smiled as her recorded features appeared on his screen. She was smiling back. "Hi, Chuck! Oh! Excuse me! Hello, Sir Charles, I do hope your lordship is passing a pleasant day, sir. I'd grovel and scrape a bit but the camera pick-up won't tilt down far enough, but consider me abasing myself before you. There, did I lay it on thick enough?"

"Thick enough to drive across you silly bitch," muttered Crawford. "I'll get you for this, girl." But his lips quirked up; damn, he was missing Sheila already.

"I'm sure you're cursing me by now, Chuckie," continued Sheila, laughing, "but I have a gift for you. You might want to find a big display for this. I'm attaching some vids of what we did this morning." Crawford smiled and tied his comp into a larger display system he'd discovered in the former captain's cabin. One wall faded to black and he seemed to be looking out into space. Two enormous pieces of metal loomed in front of him. Sheila's voice was on the audio portion. "Three meters, look sharp. Closing speed, one centimeter per second. Alignment looks good." Second by second the gap between the pieces narrowed. "Units M-1, 2, 3, and 4, five seconds reverse thrust. Kelso, have your team get those clamps in place, but for God's sake keep your arms and legs clear!"

"Right, Sheil," came the response over the com. The camera was about thirty meters away, probably in Sheila's command pod, and he could see as his men guided the first two sections of the gate's support structure. Damn, he wished he had been there. He always made it a point to be on the scene at the official start of a job.

The gap decreased and the closing speed was reduced again until it was barely possible to see the movement with the unaided eye. The two curving girders, once used to join ships of the Rift Fleet together, massed over a thousand tons apiece and could not just be clanged together. The clamps were in place and they guided the last few centimeters.

"Contact! The sections are in contact. Good job, people. Kelso, lock it down; Panno, how's the overall motion?"

"We've got a little twist and rotation, Sheila. Only a couple of millimeters per second, though, we can get it damped out in a few minutes."

Crawford smiled and shook his head; that had gone very well. It was almost like they didn't need him...

"Okay, everyone, we're building ourselves a gate!" shouted Sheila. A hundred cheers came back to her over the com.

"Getting a little cocky, aren't you, Sheila?" said Crawford to the recording. "Two pieces connected and we got what—about a million more to go?"

She didn't answer, of course, but he was correct: this was only the start of an enormous job. The two pieces just joined were part of the structural support ring. The completed gate would be over a kilometer in diameter, so these two, fifty-meter pieces had such a gentle curve, it could scarcely be seen. Sixty-seven more pieces needed to be jockeyed into place to complete the support ring—and that was the easy part. Then the supplementary bracing and reinforcements had to be added, the mounting brackets for all the reactors and equipment; align it all, check, recheck, and realign, lay in the primary induction ring—and what a bitch that was going to be—hook in the reactors and field generators, wire the whole thing, and then... Yeah there was a hell of a lot of work still to do. Nevertheless, Crawford felt the same old thrill he always did at the start of a job. He would take an empty chunk of space and turn it into something useful; what greater satisfaction could a man ask for? *And by God I'll be there for the rest of it!*

"So, Greg, you see how it's done?" asked Sheila. "Think you can handle the next one?"

"Sure, Sheil," said VanVean's voice. "It's not like I'm a rookie, y'know."

"No, you're not, but then you know how I worry."

"Yeah, I do. You're like my mother—or like Chuck."

"Hey!" said Crawford aloud.

"Watch it, Greg, I'm sending a copy of this to Chuck."

"Well, hell, if you're doing that, be sure to tell him that for running off and leaving us all the work I think he's a real son of a..."

The recording of the construction site ended rather abruptly and it left Crawford chuckling. A few seconds later he was looking at Sheila's image again, although it was huge because he was still hooked into the big display. He quickly routed it back to his comp. "As you can tell, morale is pretty good. At least for the most part." The smile left her face and she went on. "But I have to tell you that not everyone's happy. Chuck, we've been hearing rumors that they are going to keep the families in cold-sleep. You know anything about that? That's got quite a few of the married people worried. I've been stalling about answering them, but I'm going to need something pretty soon. I'd appreciate it if you could get something back to me—before you get back from your trip. I'm also forwarding a batch of routine stuff for you to look over. Wouldn't want your vacation to be too easy now, would I? And hey, watch your ass you big lunk and get it back here ASAP, okay?" The message ended.

Crawford frowned. He'd asked Shiffeld that same question about the families still in cold-sleep before he'd left, but Shiffeld had not given him any answer. Frankly, he didn't see any good answer, himself. They'd originally planned to construct some temporary living quarters in a few of the supply ships once they were emptied out, as well as in the four family transports, but there just wasn't the manpower or time to divert to that now. And it might actually be safer to have the families still in cold-sleep and ready to make a fast getaway if things went bad…

The buzzer on his door chimed.

"Come on in," he said and hit the door-release button. The metal hatch slid aside and he was somewhat surprised to see Regina Nassau floating there. "Oh, come in, Dame Regina." She did so and expertly pulled herself into a chair. Crawford nodded in approval at her skill in zero-G.

"Stuff the 'dame' business, Charles. I ain't nobody's dame."

"You accepted the title, Regina, just like I did."

"I know," snorted the woman. She was frowning fiercely and for some reason that made her look even more attractive than her usual smile. "Stupid, stupid, stupid. I should have told Shiffeld to shove that knight-hood up his…"

"You don't seem to like our esteemed leader, Regina."

She looked at him and then shook her head. "No, no I don't."

"Any particular reason?"

She hesitated for an instant before answering. "No. At least nothing I can put my finger on." She laughed sourly. "Maybe the problem is with *me*. All my life I've had an instinctive dislike of people in authority. No, let's be even more honest: all my life I've had problems with people who have had authority over me. Parents, teachers, bosses, governors… protectors, they've all rubbed me the wrong way. I keep telling myself that if I ever encounter someone who is smarter and more talented and more worthy than I am, then I won't have any problem following that person." She stopped and grinned at him. "But that hasn't happened yet. I'm a victim of my own perfection."

"Ah, I see," said Crawford, grinning back at her. "A problem I'm familiar with myself."

Regina laughed again and it had a nice sound. "At last, a fellow demi-god who is not in my own chain of command who I can commiserate with. So, tell me: why did you accept that knighthood?"

"It's something I've thought about — something I've dreamed about for a long time."

Regina's expression changed and became more serious. "Oh dear, have I misjudged my confidant? I didn't take you for a social climber, Charles."

"It's not the title," he said defensively, "it's the opportunities. You're one of the profs, from the academic class, so you might not know what it's like being a tech. Theoretically, I'm a free man, I can just walk away from a job or a boss I don't like. In practice it's not so simple. I work for Dougherty Construction, Ltd, which is owned by Baron Dougherty. My father and my grandfather worked for Dougherty, Ltd when it was owned by the present baron's father and grandfather. I'm a 'Dougherty Man'—whether I want to be or not. If I was to walk away, the baron would feel betrayed and be hurt and angry. Word would get around and I'd have a hell of a time getting hired by any of the other big firms. And despite the supposed impartiality of the guilds, the smaller firms would be leery of incurring the wrath of the big boys if they hired me." He paused and looked at Regina. She was watching him closely, it seemed. He wasn't sure why he was telling her any of this. "For a long time now I've dreamed of starting my own company. It's not that Dougherty is a bad place to work, far from it. It's just that... I really want to be my own man."

"I understand," said Regina. "Believe me, Charles, I do understand."

"Well, then maybe you can understand that this knighthood gives me the opportunity. As a peer—even an extremely junior peer—I can walk away from Dougherty. I can form my own company, and I can get work contracts and bank loans, and the baron can't do a thing about it. For him to even act angry would be disgraceful. He has to let me go and smile about it. Even more important—at least to me—tradition dictates that I can take a number of my subordinates with me. I think that was what held me back from walking more than anything else: the fact that I'd have to leave all my friends behind."

"Friends are important to you," stated Regina.

"Yes. In my experience there's nothing more important."

"Well, for your sake and the sake of your friends, Charles Crawford, I hope Shiffeld can get your knighthood confirmed when we get back. But for the moment, I'd advise you to keep eyes in the back of your head."

"Oh?"

"Shiffeld's desperate, Charles. He puts on a brave front, but underneath he's frantic. I don't know what he's got riding on this expedition—I mean personally—but he's terrified he's going to lose it. The sabotage might not be his fault—almost certainly wasn't—but he's worried, probably with good reason, that he'll be blamed for it. His only hope is to carry out the mission anyway and he's not going to let anyone stop him."

"Well, it seems to me we need that sort of mentality if we are going to win through."

"Maybe. But I've gotten a report from a friend in my department that Shiffeld has been prowling around, talking to people, making promises. Rumor has it that it's the same in the other departments. Shiffeld lost all his own cronies to the sabotage. Seems to me he's recruiting a new batch—from our people. So don't assume that every one of your 'friends' is still working for you."

Crawford frowned. He had not really thought about this. A few dozen of his clerical people had been transferred to Shiffeld's staff, but he knew who they were. Was Shiffeld recruiting other people that he didn't know about?

"But… but we're all on the same side, Regina. We're all working for the same goal."

"Maybe, but people like you and me also have guiding principles, Charles. If you fall behind schedule on your gate, would you deliberately cut safety margins and put your people at risk just to meet Shiffeld's deadline?"

"It would depend on the situation, but in general, no."

"I'm glad to hear you say that. But do you think Shiffeld would just accept your answer?"

"What choice would he have? I'm in charge of gate construction."

"Yes, you are. For right now."

Crawford frowned. He didn't like where this conversation was going. Regina seemed to sense it and unstrapped from her chair and pushed herself toward the hatch.

"Maybe I'm wrong," she said, looking back. "But I'd advise you to think about what I've said. See you later, Charles."

The hatch slid shut behind her.

* * * * *

"I am sorry, my old friend," said Brannon Gillard. "If I had not asked, none of this would have happened. I grieve with you and your family." He looked across the room to where the leader of the Clorinda Clan sat on a chair carved literally out of the rock of the asteroid. The man might have been carved of the same substance. There was no cushion or padding on that chair, but Brannon was sure that any pain or discomfort the stone might be causing him was a distant echo to the anguish in the man's heart and brain. He had known the man for many standards, through good times and bad, but he had never seen him so distraught.

"It was not you who murdered my son, my kin, and my friends, Brannon!" snarled Herren Caspari. "It was not you! But those who did shall pay! They and the Seyotah dogs who harbor them!" The look of anger and hate on the clan chief's face made Brannon cringe. It was the face of a man ready to… kill.

And why shouldn't he want to kill? His eldest son had been blasted to atoms by the Newcomers. The boy who Brannon had helped live, the boy who had grown into a fine man who someday might have led the clan after his father, had been killed without a warning, without a chance.

Revenge was his father's right. But it still made Brannon cringe. And the terrible guilt within him made it that much worse. He was the one who had sent young Darien to his death. He had not intended to, but if he had simply done nothing, the boy — and two dozen others — would still be alive.

And yet... and yet, the sacrifice was not entirely in vain. Surely this proved, beyond a doubt, that the Newcomers were indeed the World Stealers. *Thou shalt know them by their violence, said the Book of Life. They kill what the Lifegiver has made as easily as you draw breath.*

"What will you do now, Herren?"

"I shall crush...!" Caspari shouted and then cut himself off. He took a few deep breaths and was in control again. "The Newcomers have arrived at Panmunaptra," he said in a calmer voice. "All the clans have demanded access to the Newcomers and the space around has been declared open. Delegations from everywhere will be arriving soon. I plan to go myself along with, Keelen, my... my remaining son and... and see that justice is done."

Brannon nodded his head. It was as good a plan as he could see. And with all the clans gathered, perhaps more could be accomplished than Caspari's vengeance. Yes.

"With your permission, I would like to come along."

* * * * *

Tad looked through the thick window at the enormous chunk of rock. "Panmunaptra," he sighed. "I had been really looking forward to coming here, Uncle. But now I wish I was a billion klicks away."

"You and me both, Tad. I had such high hopes for this. The opportunities seemed like a dream at first. Now it seems more like a nightmare."

"What's going to happen now, sir?"

"I don't know. But thank the Lifegiver, it will be up to the clan leaders and not me to decide!"

The ship, which seemed very much more like a warship now to Tad than it did at the start of the fateful journey, docked itself to one of the ports on the ends of the slowly rotating asteroid. The rock, which was over six kilometers long and nearly three in diameter, had originally been roughly cylindrical in shape and by cutting here, building on there, it was now sufficiently symmetrical to rotate along its long axis to provide centrifugal gravity. Because of the rotation, it was only possible to dock at the ends, where counter-rotating ports had been built. Felicity latched onto one of the access tubes, amid a flotilla of smaller vessels. The word that the Newcomers were coming here had already spread, and ships from all over the system were either coming or already here. Tad's own ship, along with the rest of his family, was on its way but would not arrive for another week. He found that he was missing his family a great deal.

Tad and his uncle packed up their meager belongings and made their way to the ship's airlock. Captain Frichette met them there, along with Regina and Charles Crawford and other members of the delegation. Tad stared at Crawford. He had not seemed like an evil man when he first met him and he still did not, despite his troll-like stature. But how could he have ordered the deaths of the Clorindan warriors the way he did? And how could Frichette have carried out that order? Regina had tried to explain the ways of her people, but it was hard to believe. How could any people survive when they were so willing to slaughter themselves? But clearly they had and now they were here and they had to be dealt with. Regina came over to them holding a clear bubble helmet.

"I guess we're ready to go," she said. "From what you've told us of the environment of Panmunaptra, these should be sufficient to allow us to breathe. The heat is going to cause us some problems after a while, though. If it becomes necessary, I suppose we could use space suits with cooling units." Tad noticed that Regina was not dressed as revealingly as she had at other meetings and he was glad.

"I've exchanged a few messages with the base administrator to set things up," said Uncle Jari. "They've lowered the temperature in most of the areas you'll be going into to something you should be able to tolerate. There will be quarters available for your use that are completely suited to you."

"Thank you, Mr. Farsvar, that's very kind of you."

"Not at all, we have visitors from other clans here all the time. We need to be flexible."

"Wonderful. Then I think we should get going."

Tad could sense the tension in his uncle. Until the slaughter of the Clorindans he had been very open and easy-going with the Newcomers, but now he was treating them like an alien life-form which had unexpectedly revealed itself to be far more dangerous than it looked—which exactly described these people, Tad supposed. But it wasn't just the Newcomers, he knew his uncle was worried about the reception they would receive on Panmunaptra. The word of the slaughter would be all through the system by now. What would the clan leaders' reaction be? Would they simply order the Newcomers to be off? They might see it as the only way to deflect the wrath of the Clorindans. And that would be the end of the trade agreement and also the end of the Farsvar family's dreams of prosperity. Tad wasn't sure how he felt himself. Darn it, he'd *liked* Regina…

The Newcomer woman and Uncle Jari rounded up the delegation, which consisted of six people, and herded them into the airlock. Tad was glad that Captain Frichette was not coming along, but he wished Crawford would have stayed behind, too. When the airlock door opened into the docking tube, everyone reminded each other that the ship's artificial gravity ended there. The transition from full gravity to zero-G was abrupt and odd, but they all managed it without problem. Two of the Newcomers' delegation seemed to be complaining about the free fall, but the more experienced ones — including Regina — helped them along.

A small escort, sent by the clan leaders, waited for them at the other end of the tube. They took them to an elevator, which lowered them over a kilometer through the asteroid's rock to the main level. The spin of the asteroid produced a little over half of a standard G at this distance from the axis of rotation. By the time the elevator reached its destination, everyone was standing comfortably on the floor; even the two who had been complaining seemed at ease. The doors opened and they moved out of the car. Almost immediately, the party of Newcomers stopped short. Tad looked back and was puzzled at the expressions of astonishment on their faces.

* * * * *

"Good heavens..." gasped Regina. Similar cries of surprise came over her helmet intercom from the five other members in the party. She had spent a lot of time on ships and space stations during her life, but she had never seen anything like this. She had been expecting the usual maze of sterile corridors and small or medium-sized compartments carved out of the rock usually found in such places, but instead, she had stepped off the elevator and found herself in... paradise.

Or the nearest thing to paradise she had seen in a long, long time. The space was enormous, a huge cavity hollowed out of the asteroid's interior. It was well over a kilometer long and nearly as wide, the floor curving upward slightly to either side. The roof could scarcely be seen overhead as it merged into a diffuse lighting system that mimicked a natural sky. Behind her, the wall was a sheer cliff that housed the elevator shafts, but the other walls stepped up in a series of terraces climbing toward the roof. And everywhere things were growing.

She stood on a paved path, but beyond its edges was a thick lawn. Trees, some of them very tall, grew here and there. She could see small woods in the distance. Bushes, flowers, and ferns were planted in neat arrangements. Thick, leafy vines tumbled down from the edges of the terraces. More trees grew on those terraces; she could see their upper branches even from where she was. All the plants had odd, but not unpleasant, streaks of yellow, purple, and rust amidst their green. Regina realized they must be genetically engineered, like their owners, to survive in the higher carbon-dioxide environment and not give off too much oxygen in return. Waterfalls spilled down from terrace to terrace. To her right, one of the falls made a final leap of over a hundred meters, its water falling slowly in the lower gravity and curving bizarrely due to the Coriolis force of the spinning asteroid. As she watched, a small flock of birds took flight and disappeared into a patch of woods. Butterflies and smaller insects flitted among the flowers. Regina had a tremendous urge to tear off her helmet and smell those flowers — even though she would have passed out in short order. It was very warm, but she scarcely noticed. "Tad! Oh, Tad, why didn't you tell me about this?"

"Tell you about what?" asked the young man who looked at her with a puzzled expression.

"This! This place! It's so beautiful!"

"You like it?"

"Like it? It's wonderful! Oh, it's been so long since I saw trees and grass and flowers. I was expecting just a... well, just another space station."

"This is Panmunaptra, the heart of my clan, Regina. We've lived here for over a thousand standards."

"It must have been an enormous amount of work," said Charles Crawford. His eyes were wide, as if his engineer's brain was calculating just how much work had been needed to create this.

"There are four other such places within this asteroid. They have been added to over the centuries. I-I'm glad you like it. Uh, we had better go on."

Regina looked and saw that their escorts were beckoning them forward along the path. She followed immediately, eager to see more of this fantastic place. The path wound through some trees and tall ferns and then entered a more formal garden setting. Tall hedges rose to either side, providing backdrops for a series of large sculptures. They were mostly abstract shapes and seemed to have been cut from the rock of the asteroid. They were skillfully done and highly polished. The dark rock glittered and shone like it was wet. Regina wished she could stop and look at them, but their guides seemed anxious — and it really was hot here. *I guess they can't lower the temperature very much for us in here without damaging the ecosystem.*

The hedges gave way and a more open space spread out before them. Regina gasped again. The water from all the falls flowed in winding streams to a lake that took up several hectares, at least. An island stood in the center of the lake. A dozen or more bridges of stone or wood spanned the streams or connected to the island, and the bridges and most of the surrounding spaces and terraces were filled with people.

They had seen almost no one on their way, and apparently that was because they had all gathered here. Thousands and thousands of people were there and it was obvious they had come to see the visitors. People pointed and children laughed and shrieked in excitement. Quite a number of the people were wearing breathing helmets and a few were in environmental suits, so they were not all natives of Panmunaptra.

Feeling suddenly very awkward and self-conscious, Regina's pace slowed, but their escorts parted the crowd in front of them and led the way to a large paved area on the shore of the lake. The paving was a black and gray mosaic of flat stones in an eye-tricking pattern. A group of people, obviously dignitaries of some sort, waited for them there. These clearly were of the same people as Tad and his uncle, they had the same hairless heads, small ears, and noses; they all wore the same style clothing, although more elaborate.

Tad and Jari Farsvar appeared to be as surprised by this public ceremony as Regina was. They glanced around uncertainly and then went to one of the dignitaries and talked quietly for a few moments. Finally, they came forward to make introductions. The leader of the clan was a sharp-eyed, rather bullet-headed man (so easy to notice with no hair) named Vanit Gorin. He smiled and shook everyone's hand. Next came the chief administrator for the Panmunaptra base, an intense woman called Pemula Rohln. A dozen lesser-ranked people followed and Regina could not hope to remember their names or positions, but fortunately, her translating computer was recording it all for later review.

They had brought ten more of the translators along with them and when they sought to give some of them out, this seemed to trigger a mass gift-giving session. Regina, Crawford, Innes, and their respective aides were nearly buried under an avalanche of flowers, carvings, and other gifts of unknown function. All they could do was nod and smile and feel the sweat trickle down their backs, and stack up the gifts beside them as a nearly endless line of people moved forward to present them.

"This is all very kind and friendly," groaned Crawford after about fifteen minutes, "but unless I get somewhere cooler, with something cold to drink, I'm going to pass out right here." Regina had to agree; it was nearing the end of her endurance as well. She managed to catch Tad's eye.

"Tad, we can't take this heat much longer. Can you do anything?" The youth seemed nearly as stunned by this outpouring as Regina had been and it took two attempts to get the message across, but once she did, he acted quickly. He went to his uncle and he went to Vanit Gorin and immediately the ceremony was concluded. They were whisked (well, none of them were in a condition to be whisked; they plodded) to an elevator concealed in a nearby clump of trees, and within a few minutes they were in a blissfully cool suite of rooms with the proper air mix and cold, cold water near at hand. They peeled off their helmets and collapsed into soft chairs.

"Well!" gasped Charles Crawford with a smile. "That went a whole lot better than I was expecting."

Regina nodded, her brows drawn together in thought. "Yes, it certainly did."

Chapter Twelve

"**K'**ser Gorin, I don't understand all this. Didn't you get the message I sent? Haven't you learned of what happened on our way here?"

Tad Farsvar scrunched down as far as he could in his seat and tried to become invisible while he watched his uncle addressing the leaders of the clan. The meeting chamber was far smaller than that enormous place on the Newcomers' ship, but it was much more familiar and seemed far more real to Tad. Only the events taking place in it seemed strange and unfamiliar.

"Yes we did, Execti Farsvar, and I can assure you we have not slept a moment since it arrived," replied Vanit Gorin from his spot at the chamber's head. There was no great table in the space, such as the Newcomers seemed to favor; just a small, low table in front of each person's seat. Refreshments had been placed on them, but Tad had not touched his. He dearly wished he was somewhere else. This was getting far too complicated.

"Then I am confused, K'ser," said Uncle Jari, spreading his hands. "I had half-expected us to be ordered off and refused permission to even dock. How can you welcome these strangers as you have done? They *slew* the Clorindan warriors!"

"Nothing less than those curs deserved!" snorted a large man at Gorin's right. This had to be Kar Regane, head of the clan's warriors. No one had bothered to introduce Tad to everyone, but he was certain that's who it was. And his words shocked him. "About time someone slapped them down hard!"

"But... but to kill them?" spluttered Uncle Jari.

Gorin reached out a hand to forestall any more words from Regane. "The loss of life is regrettable, Execti, but they surely brought it upon themselves. They blindly stick their unshielded hand into a container they are trying to steal. How can they complain if instead of gold, they find pure radium and are burned by it?"

"But the Clorindans will not think that way," protested Uncle Jari. "And they will blame us as well as the Newcomers. K'ser, my ship was raided twice by them in just one standard. They left my people impoverished. The next time, will they even leave us our lives?"

"It is a risk," admitted Gorin. "Indeed we spent many hours discussing exactly this issue. But these Newcomers are powerful and if we ally ourselves with them, the Clorindans would be fools to bother us."

"But do we dare to ally ourselves with the Newcomers? They kill without thought! I saw them do it. Do... do we want such allies?" Uncle Jari stopped suddenly and looked embarrassed. "Forgive me, K'ser, it is not my place to question you or the council on such a matter."

"Don't worry, Execti, we all asked those same questions, and they needed to be asked. But, in truth, what choice do we have? Even if we disavowed the Newcomers and drove them out—if indeed we could—then what? Would the Clorindans forgive us our role in this? I think not. They would take their revenge anyway and we would have no ally at all to protect us."

"And some other clan would be quick to secure the trade rights," said Pemula Rohln, from Gorin's left. "Not all fear the Clorindans as we do. They would reap the riches these strangers offer and we would still suffer. Better that we take the risk and win the prize that goes with it!"

"Yes, and the strength that prize can bring us!" said Regane. "We can smash the Clorindans and take back our ancestral orbits!"

"Peace!" said another voice. Tad looked and saw the Lifegiver's archpriest, an old man sitting three places to his left. Old, but not weak, he could see. The man's expression was stern and his voice strong. "Peace, Brother Kar, do not dishonor yourself or your clan."

"I ask forgiveness for my rash words," said Regane with a sour look. He did not sound the least bit sorry. "I was not suggesting we actually kill any of them, Father."

"No, you are hoping the Newcomers will do that."

"If they do, so be it."

"And you will shed no tears, yes, I know. But I serve the Lifegiver and killing is still killing. Blood spilled by the Newcomers will still stain our hands."

Regane appeared to be marshaling an angry response, but before he could loose it, Gorin broke in. "Father Darri, please! Let's not break this seal again. We argued this for hours yesterday. With the Lifegiver's blessings, no blood will be spilled at all. But the decision has been made: we will conclude an agreement with the Newcomers and, if need be, defy the Clorindans. There simply is no other vector open to us." The priest subsided and Regane leaned back with a small snort. Gorin looked around the room but no one else spoke immediately. Tad flinched when the leader's eyes flicked across him. But then, to his surprise, Uncle Jari dared to speak into the silence.

"What will the other clans think of us?"

Pemula Rohln laughed. "Don't worry about them. Six clans had already offered us subcontracts to deal with the Newcomers before the news of the battle arrived. Since then, two more have made offers—and none of the first ones have been withdrawn."

"Blinded by greed," muttered Father Darri, earning a stern look from Gorin.

"Be that as it may, the other clans are supporting us in this. There could be immense profits to be made—for all. And let me assure you, Execti," Gorin paused and nodded at Uncle Jari. "You and your family will not be forgotten. The standard finder's percentage will be yours, and even though I strongly suspect the volume of this will send it to the bottom of the scale, it will still make you rich beyond your dreams."

"Thank you, K'ser. My family is grateful." Tad could see the surprise — and relief — on his uncle's face. He suspected his own face looked the same. Instead of disgrace and disaster, the family was saved!

"You have earned it. Or, perhaps I should say: you will earn it. Right now, we are going ask for everything that you and your nephew can remember about the Newcomers. No detail is insignificant. We want everything. After that, we are going to want you to remain as their guides and escorts. They seem to trust you and you are familiar with their ways — or more familiar than anyone else. Most of their time will be taken up with trade meetings, I'm sure, but there will still be social events and I imagine they will want a tour of Panmunaptra. You will conduct those."

"We will be honored, K'ser."

"Good. You'll be provided with assistants to make sure our guests are comfortable. And with all the other clansmen arriving here, you'll have an escort to ensure their security." Gorin paused and fixed his gaze on Regane. "Kar, there will be representatives from all the clans here — including the Clorindans. We've agreed to this and I want all of your men to know that I want no trouble. Do you understand me on this? I mean no trouble!"

Kar Regane frowned, but he nodded. "Yes, K'ser, I understand: there'll be no trouble. At least none that's started by us — I can promise *no* more."

* * * * *

Regina Nassau looked over her meager wardrobe and tried to decide just how daring she wanted to be today. She certainly did not want to offend her hosts, but she wasn't entirely sure yet what they found offensive. Most of the people she'd observed on Panmunaptra the last four days had been modestly dressed — but then they found the temperatures here comfortable. How far could she peel down in the heat before it became scandalous? The only display of public nudity she'd seen so far was in that zero-G sporting contest she'd watched on the video last night. All the players, male and female, had been naked to the waist. But then the local women's breasts were non-functional and small. Her own tended to attract more attention. Topless today?

She shook her head and chided herself. There was no need to shake up hormones around here; the Seyotahs were friends. Still, it would be fun to outrage Beatrice Innes, although it was so easy to do, it was hardly a challenge. And since there was so little risk of serious consequences it would not be much of a thrill, either. *The price of success, Regina, dear.*

She had never expected success. Years ago she had convinced herself that the system stank and that she could never rise to the top anyway, so she had used her sexuality to shock and disrupt and, occasionally, advance her prospects in a manner that she fully expected to eventually self-destruct her career. Amazingly, it had not; and now, somehow, she was one of the top professionals in her field. She was good, no doubt of that, but she was the first to admit that her current success was due, in great measure, to luck as much as anything else. A looming ecological disaster on the planet of Galgan IV had, by a chance that still amazed her, exactly matched the parameters of a theoretical model she had been constructing. Her boss had been totally clueless about what to do, and desperate enough to listen to her, and the rest, as the saying went, was history. Suddenly she had been a heroine and able to write her own ticket.

So why'd I write a ticket to here?

She'd asked that question a number of times and she still did not have a satisfactory answer for herself. The stock one, the one she gave when people asked her, was the adventure and excitement of the whole thing. Across the Great Rift! Andera's first foothold in the Perseus Arm! Who would pass up the opportunity? The answer to that question, of course was lots of people. Ten years in cold-sleep and another two in isolation while the gate was built was enough to turn a great many people away from the project. And it was not like they would be the first humans across the Rift—she snickered at how upset the Petrunans were going to be when they learned that they had not been first, either. Nor would she have been the first to terraform a planet in the Perseus Arm—assuming she got to terraforming any planet here at all.

No, the secret truth, the very secret truth, was that she wanted to get away from Andera for a while. She did not like what was happening back home, and she hoped that by the time contact was reestablished, things would have changed. There was no doubt that changes would happen in twelve years, but for the better—or worse? *Hopefully someone will have found the guts to put a bullet through the Protector's head by then!* The Republic of Andera had never been a democracy, but the 'reforms' made after the Protector seized power had been disturbing setbacks for personal liberties. Regina had never been that interested in politics, but she had never let political consideration temper her actions, either. She feared that if she stayed around she would ultimately make some blunder that even wearing sexy clothing could not fix. *But maybe after twelve years…*

"Reggie? Aren't you even dressed yet?" She turned and saw Jeanine Sorvall, her assistant, standing in the doorway. "Tad will be here soon. You're not going to torment the poor boy by parading around naked in front of him, are you?"

"I'm not naked," insisted Regina, although the robe she was wearing was sheer and transparent enough that she might as well have been.

"But I was thinking that if I just wore shorts I could undo my braid and sort of let it hang down in front to cover things."

Jeanine giggled. "It's not quite long enough for *that*. But it does sound delicious. Maybe you could model it for me when we get back." Regina smiled. Jeanine was the perfect assistant, but there had never been any doubt in Regina's mind that the young woman was more than a little bit in love with her boss. She'd been tempted, at times, to see where things might go, but if she did, then Jeanine wouldn't be the perfect assistant anymore…

"All right, I will behave today." She pulled out modest underwear, shorts, and shirt and quickly put them on. She noticed that Jeanine watched every move. Well, let her have her fun. She finished and then moved back into the common room of the suite. The gifts that had been bestowed on them earlier were scattered around in piles. Regina went to one especially fascinating sculpture and picked it up. "These are all really beautiful. I'm sure people back home would pay well for them. The locals have things to trade besides ice and metals, it seems."

"They are nice," agreed Jeanine. "There are some very skilled craftsmen here. You can see it in everything they make." She waved at the room itself and Regina nodded. Everything was beautifully decorated. The walls, the doors, the furniture all had a hand-crafted look to them. The use of the native stone and the wood grown in the parks gave the place a very… organic feel. She remembered Charles Crawford's comment about the shuttle that Tad and his uncle had arrived in. No mass-produced, factory items here!

"Tad says they have been living here for over a thousand years. A thousand years, Jeanine! How many structures back home are that old?"

"A few, but I don't think anyone still lives in them anymore."

"But they do live here, and think of the effort and love they've put into this place. I like it."

"So do I… ah, here we go," said Jeanine, turning her head as the door intercom chimed. It was the door to the common room of the suite rather than the one leading to the outside corridor. She got up and went to answer it. As she expected, it was Charles Crawford.

"Morning, ladies," he said cheerfully. "Ready for some touring? Our guide is waiting outside."

"Yes, indeed. Sorry you missed the one yesterday."

Regina slipped on her shoes, picked up her helmet, and followed the other two. They checked each other's gear in the airlock and then cycled through to where Tad was waiting. He smiled when he saw them, although he gave Crawford a worried glance for an instant, and Regina thought that it was an easier and more natural smile than he'd been wearing lately. Tad had been very uneasy around her since the battle, but he seemed to be slowly getting used to her again. Regina was glad; she liked

Tad a great deal and she would hate to have their friendship ruined by recent events.

"Is it just the three of you, today?" asked Tad.

"Yes, the others all have a full day of negotiations ahead of them—and they are welcome to it. I'd much prefer seeing more of Panmunaptra."

"Are the negotiations going well? My uncle attends them, but he's too tired afterward to tell me much of anything about them."

Regina smiled. "Well, Charles and Beatrice don't tell me a whole lot either, but I gather that they are happy with how things are going. But business dealings make my head ache." She and the others looked to Crawford. He shrugged. "It's all pretty routine, really. It's taking longer because of language difficulties and unfamiliar financial systems, but we've got the main points hashed out—which is why I'm free today. Beatrice and the others are working on the details today."

"I know what we are hoping to get from the Seyotahs," said Jeanine, "but what are we going to give them in return?"

"Technology, mostly. Our artificial gravity system alone will be worth a fortune to them."

"Can we trade that away?" asked Regina. "I mean, we don't really have the right to trade away patented technology, do we?"

"Oh, I'm sure that the lawyers will get it all squared away when we get back and issue all the proper licenses. Even outfits like Technodyne aren't going to squawk too loudly when we're acting with the Protector's blessing. But enough of that, I spent all day talking about crap like that. Where are you going to take us today, Tad?"

"Where would you like to go? We saw the birthing crèches yesterday and the recycling and environmental centers the day before. I guess we could see the refineries and manufacturing workshops today, if you like."

"That would be fine, but..." Regina hesitated. She knew Tad wasn't going to like what she asked next. "Would it be all right to bring along Captain Frichette? He has asked me to get permission for him to take a look at some of your electronics factories. He wants to see how you harden your systems against those EMP weapons you use." Tad's smile vanished and his expression of uneasiness reappeared. The youth's hesitation could not be blamed on the translating computers this time. "He's not a bad person, Tad, really. I know that he feels awful about what happened—and he certainly won't be causing any trouble here. Please?" She batted her eyelashes at him and smiled.

"I-I guess it will be all right. So we should go to the docking bay first."

"Good! I'll call ahead and let him know we are coming." Regina activated the com in her helmet and told Frichette to get ready. He seemed pleased. "Okay, let's go."

Tad took them to an elevator which lifted them up to the zero-G section of the asteroid along the spin-axis. This was a different elevator than the first one they had taken, and for two hundred meters of its path the shaft was transparent and revealed one of the four great 'parks' within Panmunaptra. Regina had spent the entire first day here exploring those wonderful places. She resolved that when things settled down she was going to try and arrange tours of the parks for all the personnel in the fleet.

"Damn, that's pretty," said Crawford. "Y'know, usually I can't wait to get on to the next job, but I'm starting to wonder what it would be like to be able to keep tinkering with the same job until it was exactly right—like this place."

All too quickly the glimpse of paradise disappeared behind rock walls again. A red light flashed on in the elevator car warning them to grab a handhold as they decelerated. With the centrifugal gravity dying away, they would have been flung against the roof of the car, otherwise. The car stopped, the door opened, and they floated out into the main thoroughfare. A long corridor had been bored down the length of the asteroid, connecting the docking bays at one end with the shipyards, refineries, and zero-G factories at the other. Businesses, storerooms, and small workshops lined the corridor in between. In the center of the corridor there were a series of moving cables with handholds that towed people along at a brisk pace. Tad led them over to this and grabbed a passing handle. Regina, Crawford, and Jeanine did likewise. Suddenly being accelerated from zero to about ten kilometers an hour jolted the arm a bit, but they had tried it several times yesterday and were now used to it. They weren't that far from the docking bays, so a ten minute ride was all it took to get them there. Regina used the opportunity to study the people she saw about her.

"It looks like you have a lot of visitors here, Tad," she said, pointing with her free hand. "Lots of helmets and environmental suits."

"Yes, we usually have quite a few people from other clans who come to trade, but there has been a huge influx of merchants and other people hoping to get a piece of the business with your people."

"Is that really such a big deal?"

Tad awkwardly manipulated his translator for a moment. "I imagine the contract would be very large."

"Uh, no, I didn't really mean the size of the business contract, Tad. I meant a large event, an important occurrence. People seem very excited about us. You do have starships, you've told us, so you must have trade with people outside this system."

"We have some, but not all that much, really. Certainly nothing on a scale like you are asking for."

"Do you have much contact with people in the other systems? How far have you expanded since the original... settlers arrived in this part of the arm?"

"Contact is pretty… irregular, Regina. After the original colony ship, the Long March, was disassembled, a number of smaller starships were constructed. Some clans left here entirely, while others left some people here and sent some out to explore. The only news we get is from the trading starships. I guess there are settlements on a few hundred other systems by now. Maybe more. As you saw yesterday, our numbers don't increase very fast."

"So there is no central authority of any sort?"

Tad laughed. "No, we don't have any central authority even in this system, let alone out there."

"But you do seem to get along pretty well—except for the raids."

"It… works. And we have the Church to mediate for us if need be."

"Yes, your church. I'd like to know more about that. The Church of Life, is that correct?"

Tad nodded. "That's it. But I can't really tell you a whole lot about it. Maybe I can introduce you to one of the priests. He could explain it better, I'm sure."

"Maybe that nice one at the birthing crèche we talked to yesterday?"

"I'll see what I can do."

They reached the end of the cable run and released their grip, letting their momentum carry them to the lock leading to the docking bay. It was crowded here and quite a few of the people stopped to stare at them. Regina just smiled and they worked their way past a set of guards, who seemed to be keeping mere gawkers away, to the bay where Felicity was docked. Captain Frichette and another man were waiting for them.

"Good morning, Captain. How are things going?"

"Well enough, I suppose. Dame Regina, I don't think you had a chance to meet Don Kurk on the voyage out. He's my chief engineer." Kurk was a half-head taller than Frichette, and as broad as the other man was thin—nearly as broad as Crawford, in fact. But he smiled in a friendly fashion as they shook hands all around.

"Have you completed your repairs, Mr. Kurk?" asked Crawford.

"As many as I can manage under the circumstances. Some equipment needs to be replaced that I don't have spares for—unless the locals can supply replacements."

"Well, why don't we go and see if they can? Mr. Farsvar is willing to take us down to their shipyards and factories to see what we can find."

"That would be excellent," said Frichette. "Shall we get going?"

They went back the way they had come and were soon on the cable-pull going the other direction. A lot more people were staring at them now and Regina imagined it was because of Frichette's and Kurk's uniforms. The people here did not seem to go in for anything even vaguely resembling uniforms, not even the so-called 'warriors' who escorted them from time to time. Most of the clothing Regina had seen were trousers and shirts, pleated at waist, wrists and ankles for zero-G practicality, but the cut, colors, and decorations varied wildly. The only constant was that there was nothing that could drift free or get tangled around something, another concession to the free fall. In contrast, the black uniforms with gold trim of the spacers shouted for attention.

After they had gone a few hundred meters, Tad pointed out a second set of cables above them which was moving faster. Transferring from one to the other was a little tricky, but they all accomplished it and were soon zipping along at nearly twenty kilometers per hour. The breeze this generated on her bare arms was welcome since it was very warm. The air recyclers in their helmets had been modified to cool the air as much as practical, and while this had increased how long they could endure the heat, it was still far from comfortable. She could see Frichette sweating in his heavy uniform. *Maybe I should have warned him to dress lighter. But no, he knew how hot it was going to be, his decision; let him live with it.*

Jeanine made the mistake of inquiring more closely about the repairs to the ship and Mr. Kurk launched into a detailed explanation which took up most of the twenty minute trip. Meanwhile, Crawford kept pointing out places he wanted to check out later. The transition back to the slower moving cable was not as tricky as Regina had feared. It was elegantly simple, in fact: just let go of the fast cable and wait until air resistance slowed you enough to match speed with the slower cable. It would not have worked in a vacuum, but it worked just fine here.

The area around the entrance to the shipyard was not as crowded as the other end had been, but they were not allowed to go right in, either. Tad talked with one of the guards and then asked them to wait while someone in authority came to show them around.

"I guess they don't want us just wandering around unsupervised," said Regina.

"It is not you they would worry about. With all the strangers on the base right now, we have to be careful. Hijacking a ship from its building slip would be nearly as great a coup as taking one in space. The warriors are always trying to show off their skills." Tad's voice trailed off when he saw Frichette listening to him.

"I would greatly appreciate it if someone would explain the rules of engagement around here sometime," said the captain. Tad glanced at his computer and looked puzzled.

"I'm not sure I understand your question."

"I just don't want to make the same mis..."

Frichette was cut off by a loud shout from behind them. The guards on either side of the lock tensed and Regina spun herself about to see what was happening. A dozen men and women in environmental suits had gathered silently behind them. She looked at them closely and realized she had not seen any of this clan before. Unlike Tad, they had hair and it was done up in thick braids. It had a strange gold-green color. Their skin was a medium gray and their eyes glinted darkly inside their helmets. They all appeared to be angry. From her side Tad gasped out: "Oh, Life! Clorindans!"

"What's going on?" demanded Crawford.

"Tad says they are from the same clan as the ones who attacked us. The same as... as..."

"The same as the ones I killed," finished Frichette grimly. "What is this? Relatives out for revenge? I'm unarmed, Dame Regina."

The guards from the lock came forward to put themselves between them and the Clorindans—but there were only three of them, although a crowd of onlookers was starting to gather. One of the Clorindans came forward and began talking quickly and angrily. He was pointing right at Crawford. Tad moaned.

"What is it?" asked Regina. "Tad, what's happening?"

"The one who's speaking is the brother of one of the dead Clorindans—and he's also a son of the leader of the whole clan. He's...he's demanding justice from the leader of your group—from Mr. Crawford."

"Justice? What sort of justice?" said Crawford. Tad swallowed nervously.

"A trial by combat—t-to the death."

Chapter Thirteen

"Trial by combat?" asked Charles Crawford in a stunned voice. "You mean like a duel or something?"

"Yes, a f-fight until one of you is dead," said the young native called Tad.

"You allow such things here?" demanded Regina Nassau with a look of disbelief on her face.

"I, uh, yes, it is allowed — but very, very rare, Regina. But it is within his rights to make the challenge," he said, gesturing toward the angry Clorindan.

"Well, it damn well better be within *my* rights to refuse!" exclaimed Crawford.

"I… I'm not sure what the law says. We need to get word to K'ser Gorin and his officials."

But it seemed as though the guards by the lock had already been calling someone. More guards appeared as if from nowhere, and before long a much more comfortable cordon had been thrown up between Crawford and his challenger. Eventually someone with authority appeared and the Clorindans were taken away. Crawford and the rest of the party were conducted off in another direction. An elevator took them down and Captain Frichette sucked in his breath when the sides of the shaft proved to be transparent and revealed a spectacular park-like vista. Crawford had forgotten that the young man hadn't seen this yet. "That's… that's very impressive," he said to Regina.

"Yes, I was hoping to show this to everyone on the ship."

Sadly, the view only lasted a few seconds and then the elevator car was swallowed up by the rock again. They were conducted back to their suite of rooms. Crawford was glad to get out of the heat and take his helmet off. He collapsed into a thickly upholstered chair and tried not to shiver.

"Well, this is a hell of a mess, sir," said Frichette. "You're not actually going to fight that geek are you?"

"Of course not — and watch you language around here," he cocked an eye at Tad Farsvar and the one guard who had followed them in. The locals had put on heavy coats and now had their own breathing helmets.

"I didn't mean them, sir."

"I know, but it's a bad habit to get into. Don't want to offend anyone."

"No, sir, I'll leave that to you — you're much better at it."

"Yeah," snorted Crawford. "I guess I am."

"Not that I didn't do a pretty good job on my own. After all, I was in command of the ship, sir. Perhaps I should…"

"I gave you the go-ahead to shoot, Captain," said Crawford immediately, to head off any heroics by the kid. "It's my responsibility."

"Tad, I can't believe you actually allow duels like this," said Regina. "I mean, you don't fight, you said."

"It really is rare, Regina, and I'm very sorry this has happened. But the law recognizes that sometimes people just can't accept any other solution. It provides a final outlet to resolve disputes and it has prevented far worse things when clans are in conflict."

"There are places within the Protectorate that allow dueling, Dame Regina," said Frichette with a shrug. "It's not that unusual, really."

Regina just shook her head and moved away. It was only a few minutes later when the four remaining members of the delegation arrived with several of the locals. Eric Briggs, a nephew and assistant of Tosh Briggs, was nearly beside himself. Clearly hysteria ran in the family. He tore off his helmet and flung it aside when he saw Crawford. "Sir Charles, just what the hell is going on? We had almost completed our negotiations and then we were suddenly dragged away and everyone was shouting that you were in a fight! What did you do?"

"He didn't do anything!" said Regina angrily. "Or at least he didn't do anything new. Just calm down Eric and listen."

Briggs began an angry reply, but Beatrice Innes cut him off. "Yes, do calm down, Mr. Briggs and let's find out the facts, shall we?" Briggs subsided and Crawford sat in silence while Regina explained the mess. Meanwhile, Tad and the guard were huddled with the other locals. Outraged snorts came from Briggs periodically, but Crawford ignored them. He could scarcely believe this was happening. He looked up as the locals approached him. He slowly got to his feet.

"Mr. Crawford?" said the one he recognized as Vanit Gorin, the leader of the Seyotahs.

"Yes."

"I sincerely regret what has happened, but we are constrained by our own laws. The Clorindans are within their rights in what they demand. What will you do?" Crawford fumbled with his translator and Regina came over to help. Eventually he had it figured out.

"Do? Well, what sort of options do I have?"

"You can fight or you can flee."

"Flee!" said Crawford emphatically. He was echoed by Regina, Eric Briggs, and several of their assistants an instant later. Gorin nodded his head.

"You may do so, but by our laws you must then leave immediately and not return."

"I can live with that... uh, what exactly do you mean by 'leave'? Just from here or from the whole star system? *That* could be a bit awkward at the moment."

"In theory, you should leave the star system, but for now just returning to where you fleet is orbiting would be sufficient."

"All right, I'll be on my way." Gorin nodded again but did not look happy.

"As you wish. What is the name of your second in command?"

"Well, I suppose it would be Captain Frichette, here. Why do you ask?"

"Because the challenge now falls to him."

"*What?*"

"Since the action the Clorindans seek redress for was done by your ship rather than any one individual, if you refuse, then the challenge falls to the next in line of authority. That is the law."

"Well, he refuses, too!" He looked to Frichette. "Right?" The young man looked pale, but Gorin went on before he could say anything they might regret.

"Very well, then who is third in command?"

"He refuses! We all do!"

Gorin frowned. "I am sorry. Then I must ask you all to board your ship and depart. It saddens me that our friendship must end so abruptly." He nodded toward Briggs and Innes.

"Wait a minute! This doesn't involve us!" cried Eric Briggs. "We were just passengers!"

"You were on the ship that did the violence. Each and every person aboard is liable to the challenge."

"That's ridiculous! We're here to negotiate a trade agreement, not fight duels!"

"I'm afraid the agreement will have to be negotiated by someone else, Mr. Briggs," said Gorin. "And as angry as the Clorindans seem to be, I doubt that they will let the challenge drop at your ship only. They will follow you out to your fleet and challenge your Governor Shitfeld, since he is your leader."

"Absurd! He won't even consider it! And we don't have the time to waste on this nonsense! Tell these Clorindans to get the hell out and leave us alone!"

"I am sorry, but that is impossible. Until this is resolved one way or another, there will be no agreements — with any of the clans. None would deny the Clorindans their rights."

"I don't believe this," wailed Briggs. "My uncle and the governor will go crazy! Beatrice, do something!"

Innes had said almost nothing since arriving. The brows on her mousy face were drawn together in concentration and she kept glancing at Crawford in a fashion that made him distinctly uneasy. Finally she looked at the clan leader. "K'ser Gorin, if the challenge were to be accepted, what happens then?"

"The challengers fight until one is dead."

"Then what?"

"I don't understand."

"What are the consequences of victory or defeat?"

"One man will be dead and the issue is closed."

"Closed? So win or lose, this dispute with the Clorindans would be over and done with? No feud? No more challenges?"

"No, that is what the law was made to prevent. Once the challenge is resolved, the entire matter is finished."

Innes shrugged and turned to the others. "That's straightforward enough, and so is the solution to our problem: someone has to accept this challenge."

"What?" cried Regina. "Have you gone crazy?"

"It's the only way out that I can see, Dame Regina. We must make this agreement and we must make it now. And I'm sure Sir Charles can see that this clearly falls within his duty. He was willing to take command and fight in defense of the expedition, now he simply has to fight the Clorindan challenger."

"That's not the same thing at all!"

A chill passed through Crawford. As much as he hated to admit it, Innes was correct. Like it or not, this was his duty. He'd been willing to fight the saboteur, he'd even accepted that he might have to die in battle when the Venanci squadron arrived, if need be; this wasn't really any different. *The hell it's not! I haven't fought hand to hand since... since...* Well, only a couple of weeks ago, if he included the fight on *Neshaminy*, but he doubted that this challenge was going to be quite like that. But what other option was there? He couldn't refuse and allow anyone else on the ship to accept instead, and if *Felicity* had to leave, it could cause a long—and probably fatal—delay before the trade agreement was finalized.

"Sir Charles, I'm sure the governor would be *extremely* grateful to you," said Innes.

"Beatrice, shut *up!*" snarled Regina. "You can't ask him to do this!"

"Yes, I can. I have to. I know my duty and so does Sir Charles."

"Then why don't *you* accept this challenge? Charles, you don't need to do this!"

"But someone does, Regina. Miss Innes is correct." He heard his mouth saying the words, but it was like someone else was controlling his voice. The edges of the room seemed to blur as his focus constricted to a narrow tunnel. What the hell was he doing?

"Well, why does it have to be you?"

"I can't ask anyone else to fight for me, I... just can't."

"Then get one of those new colonial policemen the governor is recruiting! Surely some of them are better suited to this sort of thing!"

"There's no time, Dame Regina," said Innes. "It could take weeks to work it all out. We don't have weeks to waste."

"Oh, then why don't we just shoot poor Charles right now, give the body to the Clorindans, and you can go back to your negotiations!"

"Thank you, Regina," said Crawford, rolling his eyes.

"You don't seem to have much confidence in Sir Charles's abilities."

"You didn't see his challenger! Younger and a trained warrior!"

Crawford put up a hand to still the argument and turned to the local leader. "How does this challenge work? What are the weapons and what are the rules? I'm not going into this blind—this time."

"The fight is with hand weapons. A variety of knives and clubs are allowed. As the challenged, you have the choice of either the weapon or the environment."

"Environment?"

"The air mix and temperature you prefer, and it can be in zero-G or whatever gravity fields we have available here. You would have a breathing helmet if you wish, but you'd probably want your own atmosphere since the Clorindan air would be far more damaging to you than your air would be to them if you lost the helmet." Crawford nodded; as he understood it, the Clorindans didn't actually use the chlorine in their air, but they could tolerate concentrations of it that would kill a normal human in short order. Unfortunately, the reverse wasn't true and they could tolerate normal air for long periods with no ill effects.

While he was thinking, one of the other locals had called up some pictures on a computer monitor that showed a selection of the weapons available. There were about a dozen different types of knives with a variety of blade lengths and curvatures. There were also several things which looked like mining picks: a wicked point on one end and a hammer on the other. One was nearly a meter long. A couple of objects looked like spears, but he realized they were also converted prospecting tools. All of them looked to be seriously lethal in the hands of someone who knew what they were doing.

Which he very seriously did not.

Well, all I need to do is go out and die. I'm sure the Gov will get me a posthumous promotion and a big fat medal.

But dying held no particular attraction to him. Somehow he had to win this fight. But how? He was a strong man, but not especially quick, and he'd never had any hand-to-hand combat training beyond what he'd picked up in a few bar room brawls. So, the type of weapon wasn't going to help him at all.

But what about the environment?

"I can select any environment I want?" he asked Gorin.

"Yes. Or at least any we can recreate here." Crawford nodded and made his decision.

"Very well. Please let the Clorindans know that I accept their challenge. I want to choose the environment. And the environment I pick is the one I grew up in: a standard oxygen-nitrogen mix, twenty degree temperature... *and a one-point-nine gravity!*"

Gorin twitched and looked embarrassed. "I'm sorry, sir, but we don't have a gravity that high on Panmunaptra. We are limited to what our spin can produce. At the outer rim it is only zero-point-eight and we dare not increase it."

Crawford smiled. "That's all right, sir. We can generate a gravity like that with no problem at all—on the ship."

* * * * *

"This is a trick!" raged Herren Caspari. "A clear violation of the laws! I won't stand for it, do you hear?" Brannon Gillard sat quietly and watched his friend's angry face.

The Seyotah priest, who had delivered the message from the outlander captain, bowed gravely, but shook his head. "Your pardon K'ser Caspari, but the law clearly allows the challenged to choose any standard environment that he is comfortable with. This has always been assumed to include the person's native one. Granted that Charles Crawford's environment is not one that we are used to here, but it is within his right to demand it. K'ser Gorin has consulted with the representatives from the other clans who are here and they all agree that this is proper."

"The scum! They all side with the Seyotah to insult the Clorindans with impunity!"

The priest bowed again, and this time Brannon detected the flicker of a smile. "As you say, K'ser, but the conditions of the challenge stand. Do you wish to press it—or withdraw?"

"It is all right, Father," said Keelen Caspari, "I can take my brother's murderer no matter what the environment."

"One-point-nine gravities, Keelen? That's more than twice what you are used to. You'll scarcely be able to move, let alone fight!"

"I'll be able to fight. Don't worry, Darien will be avenged!" He seized the small pick-axe that was his favored weapon and went through a blindingly-fast series of movements. "Let the murderer have his gravity; I will have my weapon and he shall feel it bite!" Brannon winced at the young man's words. Keelen had never killed; there was hardly a man in the entire clan who had ever killed. They practiced their warrior skills and sometimes put them to use, but the fights were always until one side yielded, never to the death. Blood would be spilled sometimes, but more by accident than intent. Keelen was filled with anger over his brother's death, but he was not a killer.

The man he wanted to fight surely was.

Maybe not in single combat, but the man did not hesitate to kill. And he would be frightened and desperate; he would not flinch at killing Keelan...

"Herren, perhaps we need to rethink this..." said Brannon.

"Rethink? What's to rethink? We either go through with the challenge, or turn our tails and run! If we run, we give up all claim on justice — and become the laughingstock of all the clans!"

"Is our pride worth risking another life?" Brannon nearly quailed at the ferocious look this earned him from Herren. This was not going the way he had hoped. He had come here in order to see the strangers for himself and talk with the priests of the other clans to convince them that these were, indeed, the World Stealers. The challenge had been entirely secondary in his mind. He had assumed that the strangers would either refuse — or accept and be killed. But now he feared that his friend could lose his other son before this was over. He had not planned for that. But what choice was there? If they refused to accept the terms given to them, then they would have to leave and the strangers' status would climb, and his chance to make the clans see the danger would be lost.

"Please, Father, I know I can win," said Keelan.

"There is no choice but to accept," growled Herren, "But perhaps I should fight the murderer myself..."

"Father! No! This is my task! I've even thought of something that will give me an advantage."

"Herren, don't be absurd," said Brannon in alarm, "your warrior days are long past. You are too old and too slow, and forgive me my old friend, much too fat for a fight like this." The clan leader glowered, but he did not say anything. His glance drifted down to his belly, which was neither flat nor firm.

"So it is settled then," said Keelan excitedly. "I will fight this Crawford in his environment — but with my choice of weapon!" He brandished his pick.

The Seyotah priest bowed again. "I will convey your message. The challenge will be resolved tomorrow at the sixth hour."

* * * * *

"Nasty looking sucker," said Frichette. "Think you can use it?"

Charles Crawford hefted the metal pick-hammer in his hand. It massed about two kilos and either the flat end or the one with the wicked point could inflict a deadly wound. The handle was about forty centimeters long and would allow the user to transmit tremendous force when he struck. In a nearly two-G gravity field, the blows would be even harder...

"Guess I'll have to."

"Are you sure you want to go through with this, Charles?" asked

Regina Nassau.

"I can hardly back out now," he said, gesturing toward the gathering witnesses. Representatives from all the clans had come to *Felicity* to watch the fight. The scene of combat would be in the boat bay. The shuttle had been moved out along with all the movable equipment, and that left a rectangular space about twenty meters long by fifteen wide. It was nearly four meters high, but under the gravity he had asked for, no one was going to be doing any jumping. The boat bay had been a good choice for another reason since the artificial gravity generator here was separate from the rest of the ship to allow the shuttle to launch and land easily. It had taken a little tinkering to get it to produce one point nine gravs, but it had been done and everything was now ready.

Nearly everything.

He certainly wasn't. His heart was pounding, his palms were sweaty, and he was as scared as he had ever been in his life. He looked past the crowd of dignitaries, who were lining the windows looking into the bay, at his opponent. A young man, or so he guessed; it was hard to tell with that gray skin and greenish hair. Taller than he was, but much thinner. Not too heavily muscled, but wiry and fit. He moved like a dancer; Crawford knew that he moved like a bulldozer. In normal gravity the Clorindan could run rings around him, he was sure. Would the higher gravity make enough of a difference? *It had better, it's all I've got.*

One of the Seyotahs, bundled against the cold and wearing a breathing helmet, approached and bowed. "Your opponent, Keelan Caspari, son of the clan leader, says that he is ready. Are you ready to meet him, Charles Crawford?"

"As ready as I'll ever be, I guess." He turned to Regina with a lopsided smile. "Wish me luck?" To his complete surprise, the woman grabbed the back of his head and pressed her lips to his in a passionate kiss. He pulled away and looked at her in amazement.

"Good luck—and be careful," she whispered.

"Was that a good-bye kiss?"

"Consider it incentive to stay alive."

"I already had plenty of that—but I won't turn it down." He had no idea if she was serious, but she wasn't smiling. "Uh, I'll talk to you later."

He followed the local to the hatch. By good fortune, there were two hatches opening onto opposite ends of the boat bay. He could go through one while the Clorindan went through the other.

"Watch the increased gravity," he warned the Seyotah. The man nodded, but still nearly fell as he stepped through. Crawford grabbed his arm and steadied him. He stepped through himself and felt the increased drag. Back on *Neshaminy* he had exercised (not frequently enough) at higher gravities, but he had not done that since being revived, and not for the ten years before that. Other than a one hour workout in the boat bay this morning, he had not been under high-G for a long while. The pull seemed very strong and he wondered if, perhaps, he had made a very serious mistake. Still, he could move easily enough and he was in no danger of falling. His muscles and reflexes were designed for this and they remembered even if he didn't. He hefted his weapon and looked across at his opponent.

Keelan Caspari did not appear dismayed by the gravity, but he was moving slowly and carefully. There was another Clorindan with him and the two were talking intently. Caspari shook his head emphatically and pointed back toward the hatch. After a moment the other man went back out and took a spot at one of the windows. The Seyotah led him over to Caspari.

"Are you both resolved to carry through with this? Speak now or combat will be joined."

"I do not desire this fight," said Crawford. "I regret the lives lost before, but if no payment but my death will satisfy, then I am resolved to fight." The man relayed this to Caspari who barked something angry through his helmet.

"Keelan Caspari will only accept your death. I am sorry."

"So am I. One question: If I disable my opponent so he can no longer fight, do I have to kill him?"

"You may offer him mercy if you choose. If he accepts, the matter is done. If he does not—and I doubt he will, stranger—then you must kill him—or the challenge is not resolved."

Crawford stared at the man. "Let's get on with this." The Seyotah bowed and nearly overbalanced; Crawford grabbed his arm and steadied him.

"So be it. I will withdraw. On my signal you may begin." The man walked very slowly back to the hatch. Both hatches were closed and secured and the man took a position at the center window. While he did so, Crawford backed off a few paces and studied his adversary. The man was wearing a tight-fitting, single-piece suit of some black material. His breathing helmet was rigid plastic, sealed around the neck of the suit. It seemed like the heavy helmet would be an encumbrance compared to one of the light, flexible ones, but then he realized that it would also act like a piece of armor, too. Damn. Crawford had opted for ordinary coveralls and work boots. He hefted his weapon and waited. The Seyotah raised his hand on the other side of the window. Caspari nodded. So did Crawford.

The man dropped his hand and it began.

Caspari went into a crouch and started to sidle to his right. His steps were small, slow and careful, sliding his feet rather than lifting them. Unfortunately, he seemed to be adapting to the gravity quicker than Crawford had hoped. He had seen people stumble and fall under this gravity when they were not used to it. And even a simple fall could be nasty when you were being sucked down at nineteen meters per second, per second. Still, this could not be easy for the man and Crawford simply turned in place to face him. Let him wear himself out with maneuvering if he wanted.

But the circling was also a narrowing spiral. The man was getting closer, too, and Crawford held his weapon at the ready. The shaft on his hammer was thick and long enough that it could be used to block a blow as well—if you were quick. Caspari was three meters away now and Crawford went into his own crouch. He had no real idea what to do. Attack? Wait for Caspari's attack and then counterattack? Just ward off the man's blows and wait for him to exhaust himself? Ultimately he would have to attack…

Caspari struck.

The young man suddenly leapt forward with flashing speed and swung an overhand blow at him. Crawford jumped backward and the sharp end of the pick whistled past him, missing by centimeters. But while Caspari had adapted to the increased difficulty in moving, he had completely misjudged what the gravity did to balance points. He had extended himself almost completely making his strike and there was no way to recover. The one point nine Gs grabbed him and slammed him to the deck, almost at Crawford's feet.

For a moment, the Clorindan was completely vulnerable. His back was exposed and Crawford could have finished him with a blow. But he had no experience or training for this sort of action. Thinking about driving a sharp metal object into someone's body and actually doing it were two very different things. He hesitated. Just for an instant, he hesitated, but it was an instant too long before he struck. Caspari rolled away and Crawford's blow hit the deck instead of his opponent. Caspari scrambled to his feet and away, face drawn in anger and surprise. Crawford pursued for two steps and then halted.

The two men stood facing each other for a dozen long seconds and then Caspari started moving to the side again. Crawford found that he was gasping and forced himself to breathe normally. His heart was pounding and sweat ran down his face. The realization was finally breaking through: *I have to kill this guy.* There was no other way out—except to be killed, himself, of course. He stared at Caspari and tried to imagine him dead.

Suddenly the Clorindan stopped his advance and backed off. As Crawford watched in puzzlement, the man started turning and hopping from side to side and making strikes at the empty air. His first moves were clumsy and he nearly stumbled several times, but second-by-second they became smoother and more confident. *He's practicing, damn him.* Getting used to the gravity, working out… growing more dangerous.

This was no good; his one real advantage was slipping away before his eyes. He had to do something. He swallowed and started forward toward his foe. Caspari saw him coming, of course, and braced himself to meet the attack. Crawford stopped a meter and a half away and made a tentative swing with his weapon. Caspari dodged it easily. He swung again, more strongly, and again Caspari dodged. Another swing and this time the Clorindan deflected the blow with his own hammer and then made a counterblow. He was expecting it and dodged in turn. He struck again and was blocked again; Caspari's counterattack nearly struck him as he barely deflected it in time. Crawford was gasping again, but he was pressing the smaller man back, step by step. If he could just push him into a corner so he could not dodge…

During the next exchange, Caspari tricked him. The smaller man swung at him with the sharp point of the weapon as before, but immediately stopped the swing as it went past and reversed it, hitting Crawford with the blunt end in his shoulder. There wasn't much force behind the blow, but he staggered back and the Clorindan shouted in triumph.

"Okay, so you hit me first, you bastard," said Crawford. "But you're going to have to do a lot better than that!" His shoulder was tingling where he'd been struck, but there was no real pain. He'd have a hell of a bruise tomorrow though—assuming he was still alive tomorrow. Enough of this. He advanced again and swung an overhand blow with all his strength.

Now it was Caspari's turn to be surprised. He held up his hammer to block but completely misjudged just how much momentum the increased gravity was giving that blow. Crawford's hammer crashed down and knocked Caspari's weapon aside, caromed off his helmet, and tore a gash from his shoulder. Crawford yelled a savage cry.

The Clorindan stumbled backward, bounced off the bulkhead, and nearly fell. A spider's web of cracks covered one side of his helmet and dark blood dripped down the arm of his suit. A look of shock and pain twisted his face. "Touché, scumbag!" snarled Crawford, who advanced to the attack. He struck again and Caspari barely eluded it, sidestepping along the bulkhead. He pressed in, striking again and again. Suddenly the Clorindan was up against the corner with nowhere to dodge. Crawford drew back his hammer for another strike.

But before he could deliver it, Caspari sprang forward and grabbed his wrist with his free hand. Suddenly they were grappling at close quarters. He managed to capture Caspari's weapon arm in turn and then slam him back against the bulkhead with his greater weight. He stared into the younger man's hate-filled eyes from only a few centimeters away.

Caspari thrust his head forward and rammed his helmet into Crawford's face.

It hurt like hell and his eyes watered with the pain of it. He could feel blood leaking out of his nose. He snarled a curse and smashed his enemy against the bulkhead again with all his strength. The younger man was stunned but did not loosen his grip. Crawford pulled away slightly and slammed his barrel chest into him again. And again. Caspari tried to repeat the trick with his helmet, but Crawford was stronger and held him slightly to one side, just out of striking distance.

It was incredibly inelegant, but he had his advantage now. He slammed the Clorindan over and over. He was stronger and heavier and, if need be, he could eventually batter the young man into helplessness. Caspari seemed to realize that and struggled frantically. He briefly released Crawford's wrist and punched at him with his fist, but had to grab it again when the hammer threatened to strike. He kicked and tried to trip him, but Crawford was built with solid legs, a wide stance, and a low center of gravity. He slammed him again. Caspari tried to hit him with his helmet, but only succeeded in banging it against the bulkhead. The young man started to swing his head around wildly, but he held him at bay and the helmet hit nothing but the bulkhead.

Crawford had one instant to realize that that was exactly what Caspari wanted—and then the already-cracked helmet shattered.

A stinging cloud of chlorine-tainted air clawed at his eyes and throat. He couldn't see! He couldn't breathe! He let go of Caspari and staggered away, coughing and wiping at his eyes. He couldn't see! He swung out blindly with his hammer, trying to ward off any attack from his invisible foe. He kept back-peddling until he hit the opposite bulkhead. His vision was beginning to clear, but everything was just a tear-distorted blur.

Something dark loomed up to his left and he held out his weapon. A blow struck his forearm and then his side. He heard fabric rip and felt his flesh tear. He gasped and retreated, still swinging his hammer. Another impact tore at his left thigh. His eyes were still burning, but he could begin to see again. Caspari was pressing in on him. He frantically warded off more blows, but then another got through and grazed off his head.

Suddenly he was in a corner and only had the same option that Caspari had had a few moments earlier: he lunged forward and grappled with the Clorindan. He got hold of the man's weapon arm and tried to strike, but Caspari seized the haft of his weapon and hung on. They were face to face once more, but this time the younger man was grinning. Chlorine was in his eyes again and he realized that the gas cylinder attached to the helmet ring was still pumping out Caspari's favored atmosphere. Damn! He couldn't stand this long.

He let go of his own hammer and rammed his fist into his enemy's face with all his strength.

The man's teeth crunched under his fist. Caspari was knocked backward and slammed heavily to the floor. Crawford stood there gasping, trying to clear his eyes and his lungs. The Clorindan shook his head and slowly staggered to his feet. His nose was bleeding and his lips torn and mangled...

...but he had both hammers now.

Caspari shouted something and advanced, swinging both weapons. Crawford retreated as fast as he could, but there was nowhere to run in the empty bay. A blow came at him and he dodged. Another and he caught the haft of the hammer on his forearm and knocked it aside in return for an agonizing jolt.

But the Clorindan was staggering now, too. The exertion was clearly taking its toll and Crawford put some distance between them. They stood there gasping for at least a minute, and for the first time, he actually noticed the audience watching through the windows. He tried to spot Regina, but then Caspari was moving again and he could not spare the attention.

To his dismay, the man actually sprinted toward him, closing the distance in a terrifying instant. The hammers swung and he ducked and dodged. Caspari got too close and Crawford landed another heavy punch into the man's ribs, driving him back. But as he did so, a hammer clipped him and he staggered to one knee. Something sharp crunched under him and he glanced down to see the shards of Caspari's helmet scattered around him. The Clorindan stood over him with one hammer drawn back to kill. Crawford grasped a long, sharp piece of the helmet and lunged forward, his huge thighs propelling him like hydraulic pistons.

The edges of the shard sliced through his hand as he drove it into Caspari's belly, but he did not let go. He pushed the curving piece in as far as he could and ignored the hammer hafts wildly pummeling his back. He wrapped his free arm around the Clorindan and bore him to the deck, landing on him with all his weight in the terrible gravity.

He lay on top of him, looking into eyes glazed with pain and shock. But then the chlorine was assaulting him again and he rolled away, yanking one of the hammers out of Caspari's now-feeble grasp as he went. He crawled off a few meters and collapsed against the bulkhead, choking and staring at his enemy.

The young man, hell, he looked like a mere boy now, lay on his back, one hand still clutching his hammer and the other fumbling at the end of the shard protruding from his stomach. Blood dripped down his side and pooled on the deck. He tried to sit up, but fell back with a gasp, his head thumping hard.

Crawford dragged himself to his feet and staggered over to the boy. They looked at each other. Finally, Crawford spoke.

"Yield, damn you. Give up. I don't have to kill you."

The boy shook his head and said something he couldn't understand. Crawford turned slightly to look at the watchers. One of the Clorindans was pounding on the glass and howling silently. Several others were trying to restrain him. He spotted Regina with her hands over her mouth. He finally saw the Seyotah who had been officiating and waved at him.

"Get in here! Tell him he has to give up! Get in here!"

After a moment, the man made his way to the hatch and carefully walked over to him. "Tell him to yield. Tell him this is over and he doesn't have to die." The man bowed slightly, wary of the gravity this time, and spoke to Caspari. He could hear shouts coming through the open hatch. The boy listened but shook his head and said a few words.

"He will not yield. You must kill him," said the Seyotah.

"Ask him again! I don't want to do this." The man spoke to the boy, but again he shook his head.

"He says that his honor will not allow him to yield." As if in confirmation, Caspari tried to raise his hammer. The gravity sucked it back down after a moment and he gasped through clenched teeth.

"Blast his honor!" cried Crawford. He stepped forward and kicked the hammer out of the Clorindan's hand. It slid across the deck to bang against the far bulkhead. "You can't beat me now! Stop this madness!" Caspari stared at him and grated out more words he could not understand. The boy was shaking now and clutching at the shard in his stomach.

"He says that if you do not kill him, he will get well and then come again to kill you when he can. I am sorry, k'ser, but he speaks the truth. You must do what you must do if this is ever to end."

"Damn you," growled Crawford. "Damn you and your laws!" He turned to face the watchers. "Damn you! Damn you all to hell!"

Then he turned and stooped and swung his hammer. He let the gravity suck the spiked end down into the boy's chest and through his heart.

Chapter Fourteen

"**O**uch! Careful there!" Charles Crawford growled at the medic changing his bandages.

"Stop squirming, Charles, and let him do his job," said Regina Nassau from her chair beside the exam table. "This is the third time you've had this done since you were hurt, I'd think you'd be used to it by now." The medic manfully kept a straight face. Good thing for him, too, since Crawford was ready to peel a strip off of just about anyone at that moment. But then he saw Regina smiling steadily at him and a grin grew on his own lips in spite of all his efforts. He finally snorted and shook his head.

"There you are, sir, all done; see you again tomorrow," said the medic cheerfully. He packed up his gear and withdrew while Crawford carefully pulled his shirt back on. Regina was still looking at him.

"So, how are you doing?" she asked.

"Fine."

"Really?"

He stared at her for a moment before answering: "No. I hurt and I... I feel all twisted up inside. Not sure why..."

"You're not? I am. Anyone would be twisted up after a nightmare like that."

"I can still see that kid's face. Why the hell wouldn't he yield? He was going to lose his clan's challenge anyway, so why not stay alive?"

"Other cultures' mores can seem incomprehensible sometimes. Like the Amerhammi Tribes on Jerdall III; they eat the brains of their dead in hopes of preserving their memories."

"Ick."

"I don't know what was motivating that young man, Charles, but it was obviously something very important to him."

"Damn. I've never killed anyone before, at least not face-to-face, like that. I don't think I like it very much."

"Well, I'm glad of that! I... I don't think I could like anyone who enjoyed killing."

"I don't like myself very much right now as it is." He finished buttoning his coat. She was still looking at him. "So why'd you kiss me before the fight?"

Regina blushed and looked down at the deck. "I'm not really sure," she said quietly. "I was worried about you, of course. But it was just that everyone else was only looking at you as a way to get the expedition out of a jam. Briggs and Innes didn't really care if you won or lost, as long as the issue was settled and they could get their damn trade agreement. I just wanted you to know that... that someone cared about you as a person."

"Thank you, Regina. I really do appreciate that. And I guess I should have expected you to put people ahead of objectives."

"Oh dear, has my reputation as a radical preceded me?"

"Well, we did talk about that a little bit a few days ago, as you'll recall, and I talked to your assistant a little bit the other day…"

"Jeanine ratted on me? The little snake! I'm going to have to give her a spanking, I think."

"I rather imagine she'd like that—from you."

Regina's mouth dropped open and she turned red. "Just what did you two talk about?" she demanded.

"You, mostly. But it was pretty obvious that she really likes you a lot. She admires you as a professional, but she couldn't hide the fact that her feelings go deeper."

Her blush was slowly fading, but she looked away. "She's a sweet kid, but she is just a kid. She doesn't know what she wants yet."

"She was sure enough that she was willing to follow you all the way out here."

"I know. I… I feel bad about that, but she was so eager I didn't have the heart to say no. But someday she'll figure out what she really wants."

"What about you? Have you figured out what you really want yet?"

"Oh, peace, prosperity, truth, beauty, and justice for everyone, of course. I was going to take care of that this week, but your damn duel got in the way and I'm behind schedule."

"That's it: blame it on me."

"You're handy. But why all the deep questions, Sir Charles?"

Now it was his turn to blush. "Oh, I was still just trying to figure out what you meant with that kiss—and the crack about being incentive to stay alive. So, it worked and I'm still alive, what gives?"

She pursed her lips, tugged on her hair braid and shrugged. "Don't know. You seem like a nice enough guy, but I hardly know anything about you. I suppose the kiss was just some ancient instinct women get about preserving departing warriors for the gene pool."

"I'm an engineer, not a warrior, and I didn't realize you could transfer genetic materials just by kissing…"

"No, that is the flaw in the theory, isn't it? But what about you? What does the big, engineer-not-a-warrior really want? Aside from his own construction firm, I mean."

It was Crawford's turn to shrug. "I like building things. Gates are my specialty, but it doesn't really matter what I'm building. Creating something where there wasn't anything before is just so… so satisfying." He looked at Regina speculatively. "But that must all seem like pretty small stuff to a woman who creates whole new worlds."

"I don't create worlds, Charles, I just tinker with them a bit."

"Still, it must be very satisfying to take some worthless rock and turn it into a place people can live. A lot more satisfying than... killing things."

"It is satisfying, but I'm also a worse killer than... than any warrior. Life is incredibly persistent and even the nastiest worlds seem to have something living on them. When I create a new ecosystem suitable for humans, I inevitably destroy most, or all, of whatever was there before. It might just be bacteria or some alien slime mold, but it bothers me sometimes."

"But you do it anyway."

"Yes, I do. For the greater good and the glory of humanity and me, right? I guess you and I aren't all that different after all, are we Charles?"

"Well, we have more in common than we do with some alien slime mold, I suppose."

Regina laughed. For some reason that made him feel good. "That is the essence of it, isn't it? You've hit on something profound, Charles: 'Men and Women—more alike than slime mold'."

Crawford laughed now and that made him feel good, too. "Well, in most cases, anyway. I've known a few who seemed more like slime mold."

"Oh really? Men or women?"

"Not saying; it would only get me in trouble."

"You do have a knack for that, it seems. But it also seems that both of us are avoiding the real issue."

Crawford stared at the woman. She really was amazingly attractive. Her face had some odd angles to it, or seemed to; maybe it was the long braid hanging down on the side, but she was very pretty in an exotic sort of way. And her figure... whew. On a purely physical level he was very attracted to her; and she was smart and interesting and... But did he want to get involved with her? There was so damn much going on right now. On the other hand, if they were going to get blown to bits by the Venanci squadron in a few months then it didn't really matter what they did right now, did it? She was staring at him again.

"Okay, so what do you..." He stopped short as a medical orderly popped into the room. Crawford guiltily realized he had been sitting in here, alone with Regina, for nearly fifteen minutes.

"Sorry to bother you, sir, but you've got a call from the governor on the com. You can use the terminal here if you want, sir."

"Very well." He got up from the table, uncertain if he was irritated or relieved by the interruption, and stepped out of the exam room into *Felicity*'s small sick bay office. The orderly left the compartment. Regina offered to go, too, but he waved her to a chair outside the arc of the camera pickup. Now what did Shiffeld want? The trade agreement had been finalized with commendable speed once the duel was done and now Felicity was less than an hour from rendezvousing with the Rift Fleet. Shiffeld had been kept fully informed about events. Oh well, one way to find out. He hit the key to open the circuit and Shiffeld's face appeared on the screen. The transmission delay was down to only about two seconds, so he began to speak almost immediately.

"Sir Charles! I'm so glad to see that you are well! You gave us quite a scare, but you did a superb job. We're all proud of you. You've done a tremendous service to Andera and I just wanted to express my own profound gratitude."

"Thank you, sir. I was lucky."

"Not as lucky as we were to have someone with your courage and dedication in that spot. A lesser man would have turned down that challenge and left us all in the lurch."

Crawford had no clue what to say, so he said nothing. Shiffeld paused for a moment as if waiting for a response, but when he did not get one he went on. "I've been thinking of the proper way to reward you, and in my experience, the usual reward for a job well done is a tougher job. So it shall be with you, Sir Charles. You might recall our last conversation? We were talking about leadership?"

"Yes..."

"Well, while you've been gone, I've been working with some of the surviving merchant captains to try and come up with a plan of action to get the warships back in action. Assuming that the locals can deliver the materials and products we require, we can divert most of the mining and manufacturing personnel to provide at least skeleton crews for most of the ships. We are hoping that will allow us to man the engines and weapons with the minimum needed for basic operations. However, that will still leave us very short handed in places like damage control. What we hope to do is to take some of your people—yes, yes, I know you have none to spare, but hear me out, please. I'm only talking about for a few weeks of basic training and then during the actual period of the Venanci attack. Surely you can make up that small amount of time out of a two-year construction schedule?"

"Well... maybe..."

"Good! I knew I could count on you! But even that still leaves us terribly short in the leadership department, especially at the highest levels. I'm going to need men in place who our people will be willing to follow into battle. Lord Frichette will be in overall command, of course, but I need some people as squadron commanders. I want you to be one of those, Sir Charles."

"What? I don't know anything about stuff like that!" exclaimed Crawford, aghast.

"I know you don't, but you'd be amazed at how many of Andera's victorious fleets had leaders who were complete amateurs. It's not your technical skills we need, Sir Charles—although you might want to study up on this a bit if you can—it is your leadership. When the crisis comes, there will be thousands of your people on those ships, people already used to following you. They'll do for you what they might not for some stranger. Can I count on you, sir?"

Crawford was dumbstruck. Command a group of warships? How the hell could he do that?

"I might add," continued Shiffeld, "that you are quite the hero among the people of the expedition. Men will be eager to follow you into battle, I think."

"I...I suppose I could at least sit in the chair and pretend I know what I'm doing, if you think that would help..." stuttered Crawford, finding his voice.

"Excellent! You have my thanks. Oh, and if you don't mind, would you be kind enough to pass a message on to Dame Regina that I'd like to see her when you get back on a different matter?" Crawford's eyes darted to the woman close beside him. Her eyebrows were raised in speculation.

"Yes, sir, I'll pass that along."

"Good. Talk to you later. Shiffeld, out." The screen went blank. Crawford swiveled to look at Regina.

"Well, that's a bundle of news."

Her speculative expression was still there. "Yes, I wonder what he's up to now?"

* * * * *

"May the Lifegiver accept and cherish the soul of our departed brother as we cherished and loved him in life," intoned Archpriest Brannon Gillard. "May his spirit find new use and purpose in the Lifegiver's service, just as his mortal remains will do in the service of his family and clan." His fingers lightly brushed the head of Keelan Caspari. The young man looked peaceful enough, despite his broken nose, shattered teeth, and bruised lips. Far more peaceful than he looked during the last few minutes that life had remained in him. Brannon prayed that Keelan's soul was at peace now, too.

At the touch of the dead flesh, a sadness passed through Brannon, but a strange thrill of faith tingled his brain as well. For all the standards he had spent bringing new life into the universe, somehow, the death of a person was also a stirring confirmation of his beliefs. The thing floating before him was not Keelan Caspari. It was just an inert lump of organic materials, soon to be recycled in the clan's nutrient tanks. And the force that had animated this lump was far more than just an ordered series of chemical reactions. No, Keelan's body was dead because the spark which had been Keelan had fled it, the sharp metal object that had pierced the heart was almost incidental. Almost.

He glanced at Herren Caspari, clutching a handhold and staring frozenly at the body of his son. The violent deaths of his only children, mere days apart, had shaken the clan leader to his core. Brannon had tried to console his old friend, but he had been no more responsive than the lump which had once been Keelan. Even his attempts to explain his fears that the Newcomers were, indeed, the ancient World Stealers had left Caspari unmoved. The man had withdrawn into himself, into an impervious shell. Brannon had seen him in such a state only once before, when it had seemed certain his first son would not survive the incubator. Herren had emerged joyfully from his shell that time; this time Brannon did not know when or how he might emerge—if he ever did.

"We ask for the Lifegiver's blessings on Keelan Caspari and all those who knew and loved him." Brannon raised his arms and all the assembled mourners gave the ritual response: "So be it." They all bowed their heads for a long moment and then the people slowly drifted out of the compartment. Herren did not move. Brannon sighed quietly and pushed himself over next to him, but still the man made no sign that he was even aware of him. "Herren," he said gently, "the ship is due to leave for home almost immediately. I want your permission to stay behind. You remember what I told you about the Newcomers yesterday? I have to stay and talk to the other priests. I need to try and convince them of the danger." There was still no reaction. Brannon carefully reached out to touch his arm. "Herren, it is time to move on. We have work to do. This is finished."

Caspari remained frozen for a few seconds longer and then suddenly jerked his arm away. His eyes, which had been fixed on his son, were now fixed on Brannon's; a fierce intensity burned in them. "Do what you will, priest! Nothing is finished!" He turned away and launched himself out of the compartment.

Brannon stared after his friend for a long time, shocked and fearful at his parting words, but then the urgency of his mission forced him into motion. He went back to Keelan's body and began sealing it in the container which would transport it home. It was a routine and mechanical duty, and his mind was already on what he needed to accomplish on Panmunaptra. As a priest, he was free to stay, despite the fact the law required all other Clorindans to leave following the duel. There would be many other priests from other clans here and he had already contacted one who was an old acquaintance. The woman would be receptive, but Brannon was still lacking any real proof of who and what the Newcomers were. Scripture was fine, but still purely circumstantial. He needed something more solid, but what? He cursed the fact that he had not thought to bring back something—anything—from the Newcomers' ship when he was aboard for the duel. Surely, there must be something that could be used...

He stopped.

Slowly, he reopened the container. Keelan Caspari's body floated within just as he had seen it a moment before. But now his eyes strayed down from the young face to the hands folded on the chest. Those hands clutched his weapon. That weapon had not been able to kill the man who had instead killed its owner.

But it had wounded him.

There was still dried blood on the pointed end. The blood of one of the Newcomers. Was there a tale that blood could tell? With growing excitement, Brannon scraped at the blood until there was a collection under his fingernails. It was a terribly crude way to take a sample, but there was no time to go to the infirmary for a collection bottle; the ship would be leaving in minutes. And this would do.

He carefully resealed the container and then headed for the airlock.

Three hours later he sat fretting in the infirmary of Andra Roualet, aboard the vessel *Edathil's Gift*. Roualet and the crew of the ship were all Methalines, methane tolerant people, but fortunately of a similar temperature requirement as Brannon. He wore his breathing helmet, but did not need other protective clothing. He stared at the priestess as she worked the genetic analyzer.

"Anything yet, Andra? It should not be taking this long."

"Well, this wasn't exactly the best sample you gave me," she responded without looking up. "There were cells from both you and young Caspari mixed in, and a lot of the blood had been damaged by the chlorine in your air. It had been exposed for what, about three days?"

"About that, I suppose. But it should have all been dry before then."

"Yes, but it still took me a while to find cells with undisturbed genetic strings. And now I'm having trouble finding a match with anything in my files."

"Really?" said Brannon, not the least bit surprised. "It doesn't match any of the clan genomes on record?"

"Not a one, not even the ones for the clans who did not stay here. Whoever these Newcomers are, they are none of the Lifegiver's original children."

"So what are you doing now?"

"Widening my search parameters. I've tied in with the Panmunaptra medical data base and I'm searching for any match at all. There could be mutations or other samples on file that could be a match."

"That could take a while."

"Yes, but you said that you wanted to find... oh, what do we have here?" Brannon sat up straighter, pressing against the strap holding him in his chair.

"You found something?"

"I think so. A match. Not perfect, but a ninty-nine point nine eight percent match."

"With what?"

Roualet pushed herself away from her instruments and looked at Brannon. "Not with anything I ever considered real." Her eyes were wide and her voice oddly hesitant. "The match is with a DNA sequence classified here as '*baseline*'. I-I had always thought of that as a sort of statistical averaging of all the clans, not for any real people."

Brannon nodded and bowed his head slightly. "*And the Lifegiver took the best of the Others and molded their seed into what He would need for His great purpose,*" he intoned. Roualet jerked like she'd been stung.

"*And from this seed He made the first of His Children,*" whispered Roualet in awe. "Life, Brannon! It's really true!"

"Did you ever doubt it?"

Roualet blushed fiercely, her clan did that far more evidently than most others. "Not many take the *Book of Life* as history anymore, Brannon," she said defensively.

"Only a few zealots like me, you mean," replied Brannon, but he smiled as he said it. The smile quickly faded. "But surely this is proof enough to convince you what the Newcomers are? These are the World Stealers come again as we were warned!"

Now Roualet looked uneasy. "Brannon, you cannot condemn these people just based on their genetic code. True, they are descendants of the Others and it was from the Others that the World Stealers sprang. Correct me if I'm wrong, but I don't recall the *Book* claiming that all of the Others were World Stealers."

"No..."

"And that was so long ago. We know nothing of these people or what has happened across the Rift since our ancestors left. How can you ask me to believe this on such scant evidence? We need proof of their intentions now."

"We certainly saw their intentions when they slaughtered my clan's warriors!"

"True that they have different customs, Brannon. Customs we find abhorrent; but that is not proof."

Brannon sighed. So close, he had been so close to convincing her. But if she was still in doubt, others would be, too. "Where can we find such proof?"

Roualet frowned. "It will not be easy. The Newcomers have gone back to their fleet so we cannot question them directly. That only leaves those of the Seyotah who have talked with them."

"High ranking members of the clan," said Brannon shaking his head. "They have clearly been blinded by greed. They will not have even tried to determine the Newcomers' true intentions. We need someone with an undazzled eye."

"Yes, you are probably right. But perhaps..." Roualet looked thoughtful.

"Perhaps what?"

"I've heard some stories about the Seyotah's initial meeting with the Newcomers. Several prospectors were in close contact with them for some time. They may know more than anyone else. But I rather doubt we'll be allowed to question them. The Seyotah are trying to maintain every advantage they can in the trade situation. And considering the... recent unpleasantness, I don't think they'd let even a priest of the Clorindans have access to them."

Brannon unhooked his seat belt and pushed himself up. He fixed his gaze on Roualet. "Then we must be prepared to act outside normal channels."

* * * * *

"And here is to the hero of the hour: Tadsen Farsvar!" His uncle's words brought on a loud cheer and Tad lowered his eyes and tried to turn his silly grin into an expression of adult dignity. He failed miserably. Dozens of people crowded around to slap him on the back or shake his hand or, in the case of the women and girls, kiss him on the cheek. Under this assault, the silly grin quickly gained full control.

The grin froze on his face when he realized that hands were grabbing him and propelling him toward the front of the gathering where Grandfather was sitting. *Oh Life, he's not going to make a bigger fuss about this, is he?* He was. The old, old man, the ancient patriarch of the Farsvar family, waited for him with a disturbing twinkle in his eye. He seemed more alive and more animated than Tad had seen him in years. Even the half-G he was sitting in instead of his usual free fall did not seem to be troubling him. The whole family and a great many relations from the sept had all met for a grand celebration in one of the finest eating establishments in Panmunaptra. It was located on a terrace overlooking one of the four grand parks in the asteroid. Trees and flowering plants were all around and a waterfall splashed down nearby. Swarms of waiters bustled about, providing an endless stream of food and drink. A live group of players provided the music. Normally, they never would have been able to afford anything like this, but the world had changed for the Farsvars.

And a lot of people seemed to think he was the one who had changed it.

"Well, Grandson," said Grandfather in a surprisingly strong voice, "I always thought you would make good, but I wasn't expecting you to make quite *this* good, quite this soon!" Everyone around laughed and Tad bobbed his head like an idiot.

"I was just lucky enough to be the one on watch, Grandfather."

"Of course you were! And if someone else had been on watch we'd be having this celebration for him—so don't let this go to your head, boy!" More laughter and Tad joined in. "But you were the one on watch and so this celebration is for you. And for the whole family." Grandfather paused and swept his gaze over the assembled crowd. "We are beginning a new era of hope and prosperity for the Farsvars. Our debts have been paid off and our ship is being refitted and enlarged. The family will go on! Let us all give thanks—and celebrate!" Everyone cheered and Tad was mercifully released from the Old Man's attention. He went back to his table and sat down. There was a glass of wine waiting and he took a gulp.

"I'm proud of you, Son," said his mother from across the table. "Your father would have been proud, too."

"Thanks, Mother. That means a lot." His glanced strayed to one of the restaurant's busboys who was clearing a nearby table. Without the arrival of the Newcomers, that might have been him in a few years. Stripped of ship and status, relegated to a petty indenture with no future and little hope. But that wasn't going to happen now.

"Sasha was asking about you earlier, Tad. She's right over there, why don't you go and say hello?" He looked to where his mother was pointing and saw the young woman looking back at him. She was a second cousin and very marriageable. His mother had been trying to play matchmaker for him ever since he had passed his tests. "Go on," she urged.

Well, why not? He got up and awkwardly made his way over to her. "Hi, Sasha."

"Hello, Tad. I was wondering if I was ever going to get a chance to talk to the great hero." He looked closely, but he could not detect any mockery in her smile. It was a nice smile. She was quite pretty, although for some reason the thought struck him that she would look even prettier with a long white braid of hair hanging down from one side of her head. *Stop that, you idiot! Regina's twice your age and it would never work. Anyway, you saw her kiss Mr. Crawford!* But Sasha did have a very elaborate wreath of flowers sitting on her brow with trailing ribbons and her nose was very small and cute, indeed. And she smelled nice, too.

"Everyone's been keeping me pretty busy..."

"Yes, and I'm sure they'll continue if we stay here. Would you like to walk with me?"

"Uh, sure." She took his arm possessively and led him to one of the stairs going down from the terrace. The stair was close enough to one of the waterfalls that conversation was impossible until they reached the bottom and moved off among the gardens. It seemed very natural and comfortable having Sasha on his arm. The park was entering its evening cycle and the overhead lights were dimming. Hundreds of smaller lights sparkled on the terraces or along the paths. It was nearly as beautiful as the girl next to him.

"I was hoping that you would come see me after your tests, Tad. I was disappointed when you didn't."

"Well, our ship was leaving right away," he stammered. "I didn't have the chance. We had debts to pay and we had to go."

"A likely excuse. But those debts are all paid now, aren't they? Now you can pay your debt to me." Tad twitched in surprise when he realized where Sasha was leading him. A line of high hedges sectioned off a part of the gardens. Inside, the hedges created a maze with many small, enclosed spaces. Each space could be 'closed' by a colored rope that would fasten across the entrance. A few of the spaces were already closed in that fashion, but most were still open. Sasha took him to an entrance. "I passed all of my tests while you were away, too, Tad," she whispered.

He gawked back at her. Was she really suggesting…? Yes, she was! Well, why not? They were both adults now and this was a normal part of the process. It wouldn't commit him to anything…

"Come on, Hero," she pulled him through and fastened the rope behind. Once they were inside the enclosure she wrapped her arms around him and kissed him. It was a long and very intimate kiss. At first he didn't know what to do, but after a moment it seemed entirely natural. After quite a while, Sasha pulled away, smiling beautifully. She unzipped the front of her blouse and shrugged it off her shoulders, letting it fall to her waist. She wasn't wearing anything underneath. She did not have a fraction of Regina's endowment, but the sight still set Tad's head reeling.

She reached out to undo his own shirt when she suddenly jumped back and yelped. "*Ow!*"

"Sasha! What's wrong?"

She looked confused and her hand went to the back of her neck. "It felt like something stung me."

"Are you sure? They don't allow stinging insects in the—Ow!" Something nipped at his own neck and his hand automatically slapped at it.

"Tad, what… what's happening?" Sasha was swaying and before Tad could even move, her eyes rolled back up in her head and she collapsed to the thick grass. He tried to reach for her, but his arms were like lead. Blackness was creeping in from the sides of his vision and suddenly the grass was rushing up to meet him.

* * * * *

"I can't believe I let you talk me into this, Brannon!"

"It is for the greater good, Andra," said Brannon Gillard as he laid the boy out flat on the grass.

"Maybe so, but we've broken more laws than I can count, and if we get caught we'll be de-frocked and locked away forever."

"No one saw us, and we're doing no permanent harm."

"You *hope* no one saw us," said Andra Roualet, eyeing the surrounding hedges. "Seyotah warriors might be closing in on us right now. As for doing no harm, well, I don't think this boy is going to be real happy when he wakes up, considering how you interrupted him."

"Neither he nor the girl will remember anything, Andra. They can take up where they left off. And if you are so opposed to this, why did you let me talk you into it?"

Andra Roualet frowned. "I suppose it was because I think you *might* be right. And we need to know."

"Yes, we do. Hand me the interface, please." Roulet opened the equipment bag and passed over what he had asked for: a medium-sized control box with two thick cables protruding. Each cable split into a cluster of several dozen smaller ones, each ending in an adhesive patch. He began attaching the leads from one cluster to the skull of the boy, his long-practiced hands locating each one precisely. "With the rope across the entrance, no one will bother us here, and considering the circumstances, I doubt anyone will come looking for these two for hours. We'll be done and gone by then." He finished attaching the last lead and then looked to Roualet. "I'm going to need your help here, Andra."

The priestess knelt next to him and started attaching the leads from the other cable to his own skull. He wasn't wearing a breathing helmet and he had already shaved his hair. To a casual observer he might have passed for a Seyotah. He had never worn his hair long like a warrior, so shaving was no great sacrifice, but he knew he would pay for going without the helmet over the next few days. The lack of chlorine in the air and the very high carbon dioxide level here would set up a chemical imbalance which would result in cramps and nausea, but not for at least another five or six hours. More than enough time to finish. He'd been tempted to bring a breathing mask, but the seals were never perfect, and considering recent events, leaving a trail of chlorine would attract far too much attention. Roualet finished her task and Brannon switched on the interface to calibration mode.

"This equipment isn't really designed for this you know," warned Roualet.

"Yes, but it will serve."

"Have you ever done this before?"

"Not on an adult, no. But I've sat in on a few psychiatric sessions. I should be able to get what I'm looking for. And it does no harm, Andra."

"No, but it is an intrusion. I feel very… awkward participating in this, Brannon."

"No more awkward than I do, believe me. But we have to, Andra, far too much is at stake." The priestess was silent and Brannon continued to work on calibrating the interface, but her words nagged at him. This was an intrusion and a serious breach of his priestly oaths. He had no legal authority to do what he was doing, and his moral authority would surely be questioned by many others. But he did not stop or hesitate. This had to be done.

The lights on the controls all turned green for the boy's output; now to calibrate his own. The sensors attached to their skulls could detect the electrical processes in their respective brains and the equipment in the box could interpret the readings and turn them into something understandable. With two people hooked up at once, communication of a sort was possible. It wasn't telepathy, not really, but a technological approximation of it. Brannon made use of similar equipment in the birthing crèche. A newborn child or a toddler in trouble could not communicate clearly; could not tell an adult what was wrong or where it hurt. Using an interface, Brannon could look into the child's mind and find out. It was an invaluable tool during those critical early years. Psychiatrists could do the same for troubled adult minds. And on some occasions, the authorities could use the process to discover criminal action, although a person who was actively trying to resist would rarely reveal much. There were laws against the indiscriminate use of the technique—laws that Brannon was breaking.

The last light turned green and he looked at Roualet. "Okay, I'm ready." He sat down next to the boy and composed himself. Finding the information he wanted was not going to be easy. If he simply wandered around inside the boy's head uninvited, it could take days—or forever—to turn up what he was looking for. No, he needed further assistance, but fortunately it was available. Roualet had taken out an aerosol dispenser and set it on the grass between him and the boy. The drug it would give off would put both of them into what amounted to a focused trance. In that state, the level of communication would be greatly enhanced. Brannon could very nearly relive the days in the boy's life that he was interested in.

He nodded to her and she opened the dispenser. He flipped the switch on the interface to put it in active mode. A faint white mist rose from the container and he breathed it in. It had no odor he could detect. Roualet had promised that it would work equally well on Clorindans and Seyotahs; he hoped she was right. But it was surely doing something, he was feeling very light-headed and there seemed to be another sleepy voice echoing in his ears. He could dimly see Roualet in her breathing helmet dragging the girl a little farther away from the mist. He closed his eyes and tried to concentrate on his mission.

"Brannon, Brannon, snap out of it." Someone was whispering in his ear and shaking him. It was hard to concentrate, but the voice and the shaking was persistent, and he forced open his eyes and looked around. Everything was as he last remembered it, except that Roualet was right beside him. "Are you all right? We need to get out of here! Someone's looking for this pair!"

"What?"

"A group of youngsters went by a few minutes ago, calling for these two. I think they were just trying to harass them a little, but they almost came in here. I bluffed them away, but they might be back. We need to go!"

"How… how long was I…?"

"Almost three hours. Did you get what you need?"

"I-I'm not sure…"

"Well whatever you got will have to do. Come on!" Brannon shook his head, trying to clear it and saw that Roualet had already removed all the electrodes and packed the equipment away. The boy was still sleeping peacefully. "Here, help me move the girl."

He was still woozy, but he assisted Roualet as best he could. They moved the young woman over so she was halfway on top of the boy. They draped his arms around her. The priestess bent down and used a hypo-spray on both of them. "There, they'll wake up in a few minutes. Let's go." She took his arm and guided him out of the enclosure. They looked both ways but saw no one, then ducked under the rope without unfastening it. Arm-in-arm they left the gardens, trying to look completely nonchalant. Fortunately, it was quite dark and not many people were around. They found an elevator and headed back to the docking bays.

On the trip, Brannon tried to make sense of what he had learned. There were a flood of Tadsen Farsvar's recent memories floating around in his head and grabbing them and putting them into order was not easy. A number seemed particularly intense and surfaced again and again: the image of the girl reaching out for him, the duel in which Keelan Caspari lost his life, a scene on a ship's bridge which appeared to be the battle where Herren's other son died, the image of the Newcomers' fleet growing larger through a shuttle's viewport. One of the Newcomer women, the odd one with the long white hair, appeared frequently. Bit by bit he sorted them out. He knew that the boy would have strange dreams and the flashes of memories not his own for a few weeks, but nothing more.

They arrived back at *Edathil's Gift* and Brannon retrieved his helmet and then collapsed in the infirmary. Roualet hovered around for a while, running tests on him and then set herself in a chair opposite him. "Well?" she demanded.

"It worked. At least I certainly have a lot of the boy's memories here. I'm trying to make sense of them. Whether there will be anything of use…let me think for a while."

So she did. Brannon sat and thought for several hours, slowly arranging things in his head. This was a lot different from working with infants! One thing that did become apparent fairly quickly, though, was that this Tadsen Farsvar was a good lad. His hopes for the trade with the Newcomers wasn't based on greed, but on desperation for his impoverished family. And he'd been thoroughly horrified by the slaughter of the Clorindan warriors, in spite of his family's good reason to dislike them. The duel had left him shaken and sick at heart. But did he have any knowledge of the Newcomers' intentions? Try as he might, Brannon could not find anything beyond their stated desire for trade. The boy's conversations with the woman named Regina were very strong in his memories, but the woman revealed little except her body to Tadsen. Still, she had provided more information than any of the others. Brannon forced the memories into order. When had he first met her? Ah, the meeting aboard the huge, white vessel. Yes, now it was coming to the surface. A great meeting room, the leader of the Newcomers, translation problems. He and his uncle trying to communicate. And then... and then... what was this? The leader becoming very angry, shouting, but not at Tadsen or his uncle, at someone talking through a communicator. Confusion in the room. Many people talking. The Regina woman trying to take Tadsen away and then...

A woman in chains!

A prisoner is brought into the room. Many angry words between her and the leader. And then, Brannon almost howled in frustration, Tadsen was taken from the room and the woman is not seen again.

"Brannon? Are you all right?" He started and saw Roualet staring at him.

"Yes," he said breathlessly. "Yes, I think I've stumbled on something."

"Information? The Newcomers' intentions?"

"No, not exactly. But the boy saw something on the Newcomers' flagship. A prisoner, a woman in restraints. The leader was very angry with her."

"Really? Well that's interesting, but I don't see how it helps us."

"Not directly, no. But it proves that there is some sort of dissension in the Newcomers' ranks. If we could somehow talk to this woman, she might have reasons to cooperate with us."

Roualet snorted. "And just how are we going to get the Newcomers to let us talk to her?"

"I don't know, but we have to try."

"What do you mean we?"

"The Newcomers have agreed to receive embassies from all the clans out at their fleet. I can go to represent the Clorindans. But I will need transport. You are headed out there yourself, aren't you?"

"Yes, in a few weeks, but..."

"Please Andra! You can't quit on this now!" The woman stared at him for many long seconds before answering.

"I can't believe I'm letting you talk me into this!"

Chapter Fifteen

"**D**ame Regina, I know this will be difficult for you, but I desperately need your help."

Regina Nassau stared across the large polished desktop at Rikard Shiffeld and tried to keep the annoyance she was feeling off her face and out of her voice. She glanced at where her second-in-command, Doctor Kurt Ramsey, was sitting and then back at Shiffeld. "I'm a terraformer, Sir Rikard, not a diplomat."

"You underrate yourself," said Shiffeld with a grin Regina was coming to dislike. "The communications we've had from the Seyotahs has been uniformly complimentary on your performance during the embassy to Panmunaptra. They were very impressed with you and so am I. And yes, I realize that your primary task is terraforming, but we are all being asked to do double and sometimes triple duty. I know that you would prefer to accompany the terraforming ship to the fourth planet, but we need you here to handle all of the incoming delegations from the local clans. I'm sure you can see how important it is that we establish good relations with the locals, Regina."

She frowned and silently cursed the man for being so persuasive. What he said did make a certain amount of sense and a large part of her did, indeed, want to stay here and interact with the locals. So far she had been able to get frustratingly little information on their history and she was determined to discover when, how, and why they had made the great leap across the Rift. *But that's not your job, girl, you're a terraformer, not an historian or an ambassador!* But there weren't any other historians with the fleet and she shuddered at the thought of the damage that might be done with some other 'ambassador' on the job. It was very tempting…

Still, she hesitated. Shiffeld was proposing that *Bastet*, the fleet's terraforming ship, be sent on to the fourth planet to begin detailed surveys—without her. Ramsey would be in command while she was away. The local inhabitants had given permission, and the ship was due to leave in a few hours. If she accepted Shiffeld's offer, she would remain behind on *Starsong*. She did not like that idea at all. On the other hand, all the activity on *Bastet* for the next several months would be strictly data collection, a completely routine activity which the people there could easily carry out without her. Doctor Ramsey was fully qualified, indeed overqualified, to supervise the operation. Her presence would not be needed until they began to model the possible course of action they could take.

"Dame Regina?" prompted Shiffeld. "Can I count on your help?"

"Very well, I accept."

"Excellent! The first delegations will be arriving in three days. I leave all the arrangements in your hands."

"All right. But I want it understood that I'm not taking this on as a permanent assignment. When we get to the next stages of the terraforming evaluation I intend to be back on the job."

"Of course. I had assumed that."

She looked at Ramsey. "I'll be sending you a detailed set of instructions, Doctor. You will be in charge of all the surveys, but I want to be kept fully informed. Start with a chemical analysis of the soils and the ice caps, and then proceed with the seismic probes. Then..."

"I know how to conduct a planetary survey... Dame Regina," interrupted Ramsey. They stared at each other for a moment before Regina dropped her eyes.

"Yes, of course you do, Doctor. I'm sorry, but this is coming as a bit of a surprise." She and Ramsey had always had a rather awkward relationship. He was nearly twice her age but had never achieved a fraction of her fame — or notoriety — and she suspected that he resented it. Still, he was a solid professional and, like it or not, now she had to trust him.

"We both have full confidence in you, Doctor," said Shiffeld. Regina nodded and then turned her attention back to the governor.
"I also want to know just what you hope for me to accomplish with the locals."

"Oh, the same sort of thing you've already been doing: talk with them, exchange cultural information, you know, keep them happy."

"In other words: keep them out of your hair."

"Yes, quite," said Shiffeld with a smile. "Well, I'm sure you have a lot of preparations to make, Dame Regina, so I'll leave you to them."

Which really meant: 'you've given me what *I* want, so please get out of my office so I can get back to my work.' Regina just nodded and got up from her chair.

"Oh, Doctor, would you mind staying for a moment?" said Shiffeld to Ramsey. Regina glanced at the two men for a moment and then shrugged and left the office.

Jeanine was waiting for her outside. The young woman looked at her with curiosity. "So, Reggie, are we going or staying?" Regina did not answer until they were well away from the governor's headquarters.

"*I* am staying. *You are going.*" Regina winced at the look of dismay that washed over Jeanine's face.

"What? What do you mean?"

"I've agreed to stay here and play ambassador to the locals — for a while. Ramsey will be in charge until I get back. But I need someone — someone I can really trust — to go along with Bastet and keep me informed about what's going on there. I'm sorry Jeanine, but I need you to do this. It's important."

"But... but Doctor Ramsey will send you copies of all the reports..." protested her assistant.

"He'll be sending me reports. I imagine he'll be sending me mountains of reports, plus all the raw data as well. But I'm also quite sure there will be other reports coming out of *Bastet* that I won't see; reports going straight to Shiffeld. I know you won't be able to get hold of those, so don't try. But I need you to be my eyes and ears there, Jeanine. Please?"

The young woman still looked hurt to be sent away, but her expression slowly became thoughtful, and eventually she nodded. "Okay."

"Good. Now let's get over to the ship, I need to get some of my stuff before they leave."

* * * * *

"I am standing here with Sir Charles Crawford, chief engineer for the Gate Project, the man responsible for seeing that this colossal undertaking is finished on time. Mr. Crawford, it is over a month since the Rift Fleet arrived at Landfall, is the project on schedule?"

"Well, we..."

"As you know, the Gate Project has faced a number of unforeseen difficulties: the dastardly sabotage of the naval personnel's cold-sleep capsules, the threatened arrival of a Venanci squadron, the unexpected presence of natives in the Landfall system. How have you been forced to adapt your operations to these new realities, sir?"

"Well, we..."

"And what about the natives? Has the trade with them been as big a boon as was hoped? Are the materials they are delivering satisfactory? Has this help been enough to offset your other difficulties?"

Charles Crawford stared at the intense young man standing less than half a meter away and resisted the urge to grab his sound pick-up and stuff it up his nose. He was already regretting that he'd agree to give the twit 'a few moments of his time'. But he was a distant relation of one of the major backers of the expedition and determined to make a name in media circles by documenting what happened here. Shiffeld had pleaded that everyone cooperate with the man as much as they could. He glanced over to where Sheila MacIntyrre was looking on in amusement and then back at his interviewer. Crawford continued to stare until a good five seconds had gone by without any further questions.

"You done?" he asked.

The man frowned, but it passed in an instant, no doubt he realized he could edit this part out. "Uh, yes, Sir Charles, can you answer any of my questions?"

"I can try. Currently we are about one week behind our planned schedule. This is due primarily to the difficulties you just named. Fortunately, we have not been falling any farther behind schedule and during the last few weeks actually managed to pick up a day or two. All of my people are responding very well to this emergency and putting in the extra effort to meet schedule. We are all confident in our ultimate success."

"And the natives?" prompted the man.

"For the most part they have been a great help, although their primary assistance has been in providing us with raw materials—which is not my department; you should talk to Lu Karrigan and Jinsup Sowell about that. But as I understand it, they have supplied us with enough ice to crack for reaction mass that the fleet should have full fuel bunkers in another month or so. Of more importance to me, they've delivered enough of the various ores we need to begin laying the primary induction ring next month. Once Jin Sowell has his refineries online, we can get started."

"Oh yes, quite a few people who I've talked with have mentioned the induction ring. It sounds very important. Could you tell us a little more about that?"

"It's the heart of the gate," replied Crawford. "The single most important component of the entire apparatus—and the most difficult and demanding item to fabricate. It cannot be assembled in pieces, it must be cast in place in one continuous 'pour' which will take nearly eighteen months. You've probably seen the two micro-laminators that are being mounted on the support ring…"

"Yes! Enormous machines the size of apartment buildings!"

Crawford nodded, ignoring the interruption this time as he warmed to his subject. "The largest ever made. When everything is ready, these will start laying the ring. The actual material of the ring is a complex metallic crystal that is laid down literally molecule by molecule. The two laminators will start face to face and then work away from each other, moving only a couple of meters a day, building the ring until they meet again on the opposite side of the support structure. Once the process starts, it cannot be stopped until it is complete. Any interruption would ruin the inductor and we'd have to do it all over again—if we even could. The ring material is as near to indestructible as anything made by man. We'd have to replace all the supporting structure it was attached to, as well. And the tolerances! The final ring has to be perfectly circular—and I mean perfect! If it was off by as little as a micro-micron, it won't work. So we've made the support ring as nearly circular as we can, but that's still incredibly crude; we're probably off by a few centimeters in spots. So the laminators compensate for that when laying the ring, making certain sections thicker or thinner as needed. And that also means keeping all parts of the ring at an even temperature to avoid thermal distortions. We do that by…"

Fifteen minutes later the young interviewer was fidgeting noticeably and finally managed to break in. "Well! Thank you, Mr. Crawford. You've certainly given us a great deal of information and I want to thank you. I'll be sure to come by again when you start to lay this ring you've been telling us about. Thank you again, sir!" The man and his camera-holder backed away and then fled. Crawford looked over at Sheila and pouted.

"I was just getting to the interesting part."

"For a man we can't pry two consecutive sentences out of at a party, you sure can run at the mouth on engineering subjects, Chuck," snickered Sheila.

"Well, I am an engineer, Sheila."

"Yup, twenty-four hours a day, seven days a week, year in and year out."

"And what exactly does that mean?" he asked, looking hard at Sheila.

"Oh, just that I worry about you sometimes. You never seem to relax, you never join in any of the fun and games during off hours…"

"What off hours?"

"Exactly. You never even notice when I flirt with you."

"When have you ever flirted with me?"

"See?" Crawford jerked his head around and saw that she was grinning at him. For some reason the image of Regina Nassau kissing him flashed into his head and it made him feel… how? Guilty, maybe? "Well, anyway, you gave the man a nice interview, I'm sure he'll manage to edit it down to about thirty seconds."

Crawford snorted. "Yeah, probably."

"Although I doubt he'll edit out your little white lie, there."

"What lie?"

"Oh, the one about morale being high and everyone being confident of success. Surely you don't believe that, do you?"

Crawford frowned. "It's not that bad, Sheila."

"Maybe not now, but it's getting worse day by day and you should know it. You haven't been down in the trenches the way you've been on most jobs…"

"I can't! Damn it, I want to, but this job is just so bloody big I can't spend the time I want with the workers. And now this business of me commanding a naval squadron…"

"I know and I'm not criticizing, but the fact remains that you haven't been able to. I see it a lot closer and what I see is scaring me: arguments, fights, drunkenness…"

"Drunkenness? Where are they getting enough booze to get drunk? It's all strictly rationed."

"I'm not sure, but I'm suspecting that the natives may be delivering more than ice and ore, Chuck."

"Already?" he asked in surprise.

Sheila laughed. "Y'know: supply and demand. And however different these locals might be, they still have alcohol, and it wouldn't take much in the way of communication skills for our people to make it clear what they wanted."

"But what are our people trading for it? The big technology exchange deals aren't going to work with local bootleggers."

"No, but little technology exchanges probably work just fine. Music and vid players, hand-comps... tools."

"Damnation! If I catch anyone doing that I'll..."

"What? Fire them? You can't do that here and everyone knows it. The worst you can do is fine them and that isn't much of a threat under the circumstances. Chuck, discipline is getting pretty bad. My supervisors have complaint lists as long as your arm for every shift."

"Hell, I didn't realize... Why haven't I been getting reports about this?"

"You are. From me. Right now."

"I mean through normal channels!" Crawford was surprised and embarrassed by what Sheila was telling him and getting angry—at himself.

She shrugged. "Everyone knows how busy you are and how much pressure you're under. They're trying to deal with it themselves and not bother you."

"Well, you let them know that from now on I want to be bothered! I'll want full reports from every shift, every day!"

"Oh, and I suppose you'll cut your sleep from four to three hours a day so you can look at them?"

Crawford frowned at her. "How am I supposed to notice your flirtations if you keep acting like my mother?"

"You had a mother? Wow, everyone here thinks you were just assembled out of spare fabricator parts. Wait 'til I spread the news—not that anyone will believe it, of course."

"All right, Mom, just what do you suggest I do about this mess?"

Now Sheila frowned. "I'm not sure. Everyone's afraid, Chuck. They're thinking that staying here was a real bad idea. Yes, I know about the problems of relocating, but most of them don't care that much about the Gov's grand plans or schedules. The Venanci scare them—a lot."

"If we had relocated it would have been at least six years before we could open the gate—and the Venanci might have still found us. It's too late now anyway."

"They know all that. Of course, it will all be resolved in a few months—one way or another. Either the danger will be passed, or we'll all be working to build a gate for the Venanci."

"They'll have a hell of a time making this lot work for them," growled Crawford.

"Don't be so sure, Chuck. If they capture the family transports, they'll have hostages. The people with families will work—and they'll convince the others to work for their sake."

"Shit. Well, it sounds to me that our best bet, in the short term, is to be as upbeat as we can about our chances of defeating the Venanci when they arrive. Try to restore some confidence in them."

"Good luck. They have enough contact with Lu Karrigan's and Jinsup's people who have been transferred to know what a mess the navy ships are. And the fact that a lot of them will be starting damage control training in a few days is also disturbing them."

"They'll all improve. And once our folks are involved themselves..."

"I sure hope so. But I'm still worried, Chuck; the business of keeping the families in cold-sleep is really wearing on some people."

"I know, Beshar was bending my ear on that a few weeks ago."

Sheila nodded. "One of my girls, Ginny Lansdor, was sitting in the lounge just crying and crying the other day. Her little boy is in cold-sleep and she's been begging me to get him thawed out. Nothing I can do, of course, but it breaks your heart to say no."

"It will only be another few months..."

"Yes, but until what? Victory? Defeat? Will Ginny have to watch her boy used as a hostage while she slaves away for the Venanci? Or just see the family ships hyper out to escape and not know if she'll ever see her child again? The uncertainty is killing people."

"Damn it, Sheila, what am I supposed to do?"

"Fix everything and make it better, of course. I know you can't, but everyone expects you to—which is highly unfair, I know. But the gang trusts you and depends on you, Chuck. You've always done right by them in the past but now they're worried; really worried."

"Well, thanks for letting me know the real score, Sheila. There's not much I can do, but at least I won't be blindsided." Sheila reached out and gave his hand a squeeze. He looked at her. "You flirting with me?"

"Sorry, not this time. We have to get down to the boat bay for the ceremony."

"What...? Oh, that's right. I nearly forgot." He snorted. "Whose idea was this? If we are worrying about peoples' morale, this is just the thing to buck them up!"

* * * * *

Carlina Citrone sat up on her bunk at the noise outside her cell. Again? So soon? She shuddered in fear of another session in the interrogation room. She wasn't sure what was worse, being interrogated by ruthless experts or by the batch of fumble-fingered amateurs they had here. The newly recruited police had found some interrogation drugs among the gear of their predecessors and had been trying them out on her over the past weeks. She was a little amazed that they had not accidentally killed her. They'd come close a couple of times and she'd been left dangerously ill on two occasions. She had no clue how much they had found out from her. They still wanted information on the relief squadron which she didn't have. They'd also started grilling her on the people who had sent her on this mission and about any additional agents here with the Rift Fleet. She'd done her best to conceal information about her handlers and at the same time fabricate information about non-existent confederates. Let them become as paranoid as possible! When they started rooting out additional 'traitors' from among their fellows, it could only serve to further disrupt their operations. But she didn't know if she was having any success or not. The thought suddenly struck her that perhaps there really were additional agents here with the fleet. She would not have been informed about them and they might well exist. Not that it would do her the slightest bit of good. She was caught and of no further use. She would be left to her captors' attempts at interrogation.

And she didn't want to go through it again.

So far, their use of physical torture had been pretty limited. They'd cuffed her around a few times, but none of them seemed to have the ruthlessness for anything more severe. They hadn't even abused her sexually, although they'd made a few unconvincing threats of that nature. They really were amateurs and her trainers would have laughed at them. But it did not make the sessions the least bit pleasant, and the knowledge that with time they might lose their squeamishness was gnawing at her. She was being worn down bit by bit. She'd hoped to be left alone today…

Several guards appeared outside her cell, but to her surprise, they did not open the door. Instead they had a video monitor on a wheeled cart which they set up so she could see it. She almost asked them what was going on, but the looks of raw hatred on their faces stopped her cold.

"Here, traitor," said one of them, "we've got something to show you."

"I'm not…" she started to say that she wasn't a traitor, but cut herself off. She'd started that argument a dozen times, at least, and at best it had cost her a meal and at worst it had gotten her beaten. No point in it. Instead she asked: "What am I going to see?"

"The results of your handiwork, bitch!" snarled the second guard. "Take a look!" He flipped a switch and the screen came to life. Carlina edged closer on her bunk to see, but then pushed herself back against the wall. No…

The image on the monitor was divided into several sections. In the upper left corner was a small image of Governor Shiffeld, in the upper right were a group of people she did not recognize, although the image was so small she doubted she'd be able to recognize anyone anyway. Across the bottom was slowly scrolling a line of pictures showing peoples' faces, more strangers. In the center were…

Cold-sleep capsules.

Rows and rows, stacks and stacks of cold-sleep capsules. The camera pick-up was slowly panning across a large cargo hold filled with them. And right underneath the scrolling pictures was written: *P.N.S. Agamemnon.* As she watched with widening eyes, there was a short gap in the line of pictures and then another group appeared, led by a man in a navy captain's uniform. The words changed to: *P.N.S. Barbican.*

The dead. They were showing the dead naval crews…

"My friends," came the voice of Governor Shiffeld, "we have gathered at this hour to pay tribute to our departed comrades. Comrades foully struck down in their sleep by a traitor in the pay of a foreign power…"

"How much did they pay you, traitor?" asked one of the guards.

"N-nothing," she stuttered. She had not done this for pay.

"Oh, so you'll murder people for nothing at all? An altruistic butcher!" The man slammed his fist against the bars of her cell and Carlina flinched back.

"…while we rightly mourn our dead," continued Shiffeld, "we must carry on and complete the task they had committed themselves to. Finishing the gate and foiling the plot of the traitors will be the finest tribute we can give them."

The governor droned on and after a while the other group of people began to speak. They were chaplains or priests, it seemed. Unofficial ones, probably, but they went ahead and gave eulogies or benedictions for the various denominations the Anderans followed. Carlina scarcely noticed. She was staring at the faces of the dead. She'd deliberately never looked into any of the capsules when she was… when she was… She turned away and closed her eyes.

"Watch!" snarled one of the guards. "You're going to see this, you Venanci whore!" She didn't respond and the man became even angrier. "Open your eyes, damn you! Open them or we'll come in there and pin them open!"

She twitched and her eyes popped open, and for an instant she was staring at the man. His expression left not the slightest doubt that he would carry through with his threat. Slowly she turned back and looked at the screen. The dead stared back at her. She did not recognize any of them…

… but they were showing the dead crew of *P.N.S. Daring* now and *P.N.S. Exeter* would be coming up soon.

* * * * *

Brannon Gillard watched with growing anxiety as the Newcomers' ship swelled in the viewport. It was as huge as he'd been told. Part of him was glad that the monstrous super-ship they had arrived with had been disassembled. Its components were now far enough away to be merely bright specks among the stars. The sight of *that* behemoth might have unnerved him completely. On the other hand, the fact that they had disassembled their vessel meant that...

"You can just make out what they're building," said Andra Roualet from beside him. "See it over there?" Brannon looked and after a moment picked out the faint image of a nearly circular structure, surrounded by many smaller objects. There was nothing to give it any scale, but he had been told that it was over a kilometer across.

"And we still don't know what it's for?"

"No. Most people seem to think that it will be some sort of enormous space station. Being circular they can spin it for gravity, except..."

"Except they don't need spin gravity. They can make their own."

"Yes, that's true. Brannon, do you... do you think it might be some sort of weapon? I mean if you are right and these really are the World Stealers..."

"I think that I am right, Andra, but as for what that thing may be... well, it seems to me that should be one of the first things we ask these people. After all, this is our star system and I don't think anyone, not even the Seyotahs, gave them permission to build anything like this."

"Well, it is open space, Brannon. It's not like an asteroid field orbit that you can lay a claim to. Anyone can build out here."

"Any one of us. They are not one of us. You would think they would have at least asked — or told us what the thing is!"

"Yes, that does seem a bit... presumptuous of them. Arrogant, too."

"Arrogant, yes. Just as we are told the World Stealers are. Andra, we must find our proof and present it to the clans!"

The woman looked very uneasy. She glanced at the two men on the far side of the compartment and then back at Brannon. "You aren't going to cause any trouble here, are you?"

He followed her glance. The two men were wearing priestly robes just as they were, but they were not priests. They were men with very special skills who Brannon had hired. Andra had been fretting over them the whole voyage here.

"Well, I'm not planning on killing anyone or blowing anything up, if that's what you mean. But to get what I need may require going outside normal channels. Those two are supposed to be very good at that sort of thing."

Andra shook her head and turned back to the viewport. They had arrived at their destination. The Newcomers' headquarters ship loomed nearly motionless a hundred meters away. A long tube projected from the side of the vessel and ended in a large docking module which could handle a dozen ships at once. Half of the attachment points already had ships connected to them. Their own ship was gently moving to hook on to another.

"They are being polite enough now," said Andra. "Inviting us here, providing us with facilities and supplies, talking to us. Their ambassador seems very gracious from what I've heard."

Yes, their ambassador, the same woman who was so prominent in the boy's memory. He'd been amazed when he'd first seen her picture. Surely the Lifegiver's hand was guiding the events here, but to what end? "But their hospitality could all be to disguise their true purposes. We must get past this screen and find the truth."

Andra shook her head again. "I can't believe I let you talk me into this."

Chapter Sixteen

"Ladies and gentlemen, please make yourselves comfortable," said Regina Nassau. Tad Farsvar looked at his friend from across the large conference table and wondered if he should tell her that the clans did not make use of the sort of tables the Newcomers favored. Would she be embarrassed or angry? He doubted it, as Regina seemed to be very adaptable—and very hard to embarrass. He was simultaneously glad and disappointed that the 'average' temperature that had been agreed upon for the general meeting area was a bit lower than Regina found comfortable. Because of the chill she was dressed quite modestly today—at least for her. The thick white sweater she wore was still very form-fitting and displayed her remarkable curves very well. He caught her eye as he sat down and she smiled at him. In spite of the warmth of her smile, he shivered. If the compartment was cool for her, it was downright frigid for any Seyotah. He wore a heated environmental suit and helmet, but it was still cold.

But in spite of the discomfort, he was very happy to be here. He'd been surprised when the clan council had included him in the embassy to the Newcomers, but they seemed to think he had some special connections here. Well, maybe he did. His family had been thrilled; they seemed to think he was some sort of good luck charm—well, maybe he was. Naturally, the council had included a few 'older and wiser heads' to actually run the mission and he was happy enough to leave that to them. As far as he was concerned, this was just the best sight-seeing holiday he could ever ask for, and if it served to improve the clan's relations with the Newcomers, so much the better. They had been having daily meetings like this for several weeks, but the rest of the time he was free to explore.

"Is everyone comfortable?" asked Regina. The replies all seemed to be in the affirmative, although nearly all the clan representatives were wearing some sort of protective gear. Only the Meheran representatives were not, but they wore heavy clothing and periodically breathed from small gas bottles hooked to their belts. Still, this was entirely typical for a multi-clan meeting: a few people almost comfortable while everyone else was not.

"Yesterday we had a very interesting discussion concerning the respective histories of our peoples," continued Regina. "I've had some requests that we continue that today. I think it is very important that we learn these things about each other to better understand just who we all are." Tad scarcely had to look at his translating computer. He was becoming very used to Regina's language and she was steadily adapting her own speech to what the clans considered normal. "From what we've been able to determine, your ancestors left the Orion Arm about two thousand standard years ago. Obviously, a lot has happened since then! About the time your people left, the organization which eventually became the United Worlds was just forming. Because of what came later we don't have the best records for that period, but we do know that a central government was formed, based on Old Earth, and that rapid expansion out into the Orion Arm took place."

"Which drove our ancestors from their homes and across the Rift," said one of the men sitting at the table. Tad looked and saw that it was the Clorindan priest. The man had caught his attention from the moment he saw him a few days earlier. He wore his hair in a very short, very un-Clorindan fashion, but Tad was certain that he had seen him somewhere before. On Panmunaptra, perhaps?

"Uh, yes," said Regina, "the records would tend to confirm that, sir. A tragedy, to be sure. The spirit of the United Worlds seems to have been one of relentless expansion with little regard for the rights of the individuals. This philosophy, no doubt, led to the eventual destruction of the UW."

"Destruction?"

"Yes, the UW became increasing tyrannical; a central group of Core Worlds, clustered around Old Earth, enriched themselves while the outer provinces were ruthlessly exploited. Ultimately, about a thousand years ago, a great revolt broke out and the UW collapsed and was destroyed."

"You are speaking of a... of a war, then?"

"Yes, the most terrible of wars," said Regina, shaking her head sadly. "While the UW certainly deserved destruction, the ensuing war spun totally out of control. Old Earth, the Core Worlds, and thousands of other planets were left uninhabitable. The death toll can scarcely be imagined, but it was in the trillions. The war went on and on as the rebels splintered into dozens of competing factions. Finally, there was almost nothing left to fight over—or with. A dark age followed."

"I see," said the priest, scowling in thought. "So you and your government have no direct connection with the W... with the people who drove out our ancestors?"

"Direct connection? No, no trace remains of the United Worlds or whatever came before. Andera and all the other current star nations have arisen within the last few centuries from the ruins left after the revolt."

"And now you have rebuilt your civilization—and come here. To our system. Why?" Tad leaned forward eagerly. Regina had side-stepped that question a dozen times before when he had asked, but she could not evade giving an answer this time. The other clan members looked on with equal interest. Regina hesitated for a moment but then spoke.

"First, I must tell you that we did not expect to find you here. Our records give no hint that anyone had crossed the Rift in the times before the revolt. We assumed that we would arrive in an unoccupied star system. Your presence came as a great surprise. Our initial intention was to found a colony here and then begin exploring the Perseus Arm."

"Surely you realize that will no longer be possible," demanded the priest.

"Yeah," growled the Frecendi representative from where he was slouched in his chair. "We asked ya to come look at our planet to see if it could be made a little nicer, not t' settle for yerself! It's already taken!" Tad wrinkled his nose and scowled. He found the Frecendi to be crude and more than a bit embarrassing. When the clans had first arrived at Refuge, only the Frecendi had been adapted to the sole inhabitable planet. They had landed, made themselves at home, and had generally backslid ever since. They had few dealing with the other clans except to buy bits of technology they were no longer able to produce for themselves. Their customs and even their speech had grown different over the centuries.

"Uh, yes, our colonization plans are clearly obsolete," said Regina. "Still, from what we have learned of you, vast regions of this arm are still unexplored and unoccupied. And, as we've already seen, the potential for trade between our peoples is considerable."

"So far all you have wanted from us is ice to crack for fuel for your ships and raw ore for your mysterious building project, Lady Regina. What, exactly, is that thing out there?" Many of the other clan members nodded their heads, they all wanted the answer to that question. But Regina seemed a little surprised.

"Why, it is a gate, of course."

"A gate," echoed the priest. "Explain please."

Now Regina looked puzzled. "Oh, I'm sorry, our records indicate that gate technology had been around before your ancestors were... oh, well, in any case, a gate allows instantaneous travel over interstellar distances. We are building a gate which will allow us to cross the Rift."

"Instantaneously? All the way across the Rift, from the Orion Arm?"

"Yes, as you know, crossing the Rift using starships takes years. The gate will allow us to trade with you on a practical basis. No doubt your ships could use the gate, too, and visit our worlds." Tad jumped in his seat. Visit Regina's worlds? See the places where these huge ships were built? He had never even imagined the possibility of such a thing, but now that he knew it could happen, the desire to do so was nearly overwhelming. Some of the other clan members seemed to be having similar thoughts, but the priest was still frowning.

"It would also let your people come here in large numbers, would it not?"

"I suppose; there is considerable interest in exploring the Perseus Arm and there are always the prospectors looking for new ore deposits..."

The priest looked like he wanted to say more, but there was now a flurry of questions from the others about the capability of the gate, how long it would take to complete, and how much they would be charged to use it. Regina spent quite some time trying to answer all of them and finally had to call for a recess. Everyone agreed to this since they had been in their protective gear for some time. As the meeting broke up, Tad noticed the Clorindan priest still sitting in his chair and frowning.

Where have I seen him before?

* * * * *

Brannon Gillard watched as the other clan members filed out of the meeting place. He noticed the Seyotah boy staring at him and turned his face away. Clearly some of their shared memories were surfacing and that could mean trouble. He'd never considered that the boy might be here and that was careless of him. After a few moments he looked and saw that he was gone. He sighed in relief.

The relief was fleeting, however, as the recent conversation surged back to the center of his thoughts. *A gate. A way for them to swarm across the Rift in no time at all. Disaster!* All of the half-formed plans for opposing the World Stealers which he had accumulated over the past weeks were based on the presumption that the enemy would be forced to operate at the end of an absurdly long line of communications. Supplies and reinforcements would take years to reach here. If the clans could just defeat this initial vanguard, they would have the time and breathing space to prepare for any follow-up waves of invaders.

Now all those plans were in the scrap heap.

If the enemy could bring in their supplies and reinforcements instantly, with no delay, then there would be no hope of stopping them. Panic began to grip him. *No! Calm down and think!* He gripped the arms of his chair and forced himself to breath slowly and deeply, forced himself to think. As he did so, he slowly began to realize that he had been wrong—completely wrong.

Not disaster, deliverance!

The news about this gate wasn't bad, it was good beyond hope. He *had* been right about the difficulties of mounting an invasion across the Rift using starships, so right that his enemies would not even attempt it. It was impractical and impossible—without the gate. *Without the gate!* The gate was the key to this. With it, the World Stealers would pour through and there would be no stopping them. But if the gate was destroyed…

He rose from his seat and went over to a viewport. He shaded his eyes from the inside glare and stared out into the blackness. He could faintly make out the circle of the Newcomers' gate. It was enormous, and from what he'd been able to learn, immensely strong in construction. But such a sophisticated device must have delicate components. It did not have to be completely destroyed, just rendered inoperable. *It's possible, yes.*

But he could not do it by himself. He would need the warriors of his clan, possible of several clans. It probably would not be difficult to convince Herren Caspari to lead the Clorindans in such an attack; he was burning to strike at someone in revenge for his sons. But if they were going to recruit other clans—and he suddenly realized that they had to do this since wrecking the gate would then leave them facing the angry and desperate Newcomers who would be stranded here—he would need proof of the enemy's hostile intentions.

He still had no proof. And he remembered with fear and anger the reactions of the others when they learned of the gate. All the fools could see was their own greed. Didn't they realize what this meant? Men such as those would not be easy to convince. And the Newcomers would certainly conceal their true intentions until it was too late. They would speak soothing words about trade and friendship until their gate was finished and defenses were in place to protect it. And then, then their people, people capable of annihilating entire worlds and killing trillions of their fellows, would pour through. No, he could not allow that to happen.

But where could he find the proof he needed? He rather doubted that he would find any convenient files labeled: 'Plans for the Conquest of Refuge' lying about. Nor could he expect any of the Newcomers to tell him the truth. He supposed it might be possible to kidnap and question one of them, but the low-ranking people he could easily get at probably knew little or nothing of their leaders' plans. And the high-ranking ones were too hard to get at.

The woman. The woman in chains in the boy's memory. Some instinct had told him that it would come down to her. She clearly was at odds with the Newcomers' leader. She might be able to give him the proof he needed, and he had a good idea where she was being held. During a tour of the ship he had been able to study a schematic layout and he'd spotted the area called 'Security Detention'. She was probably there. If he could just get to her.

But how?

* * * * *

"And just what the hell am I supposed to do here?" demanded Charles Crawford, sweeping his arm to take in the flag bridge of the battlecruiser, *P.N.S. Indomitable*. Petre Frichette shrugged and looked sheepish.

"Uh, take command of your squadron, sir?"

Crawford snorted. "Oh, well, if all I have to do is say: 'Crawford to Squadron: attack and destroy the enemy' then that's okay. If you're expecting anything more detailed than that, then you're in trouble, Petre!"

"Well, sir, it might not come down to a whole lot more, if we are lucky. We are trying to put together some battle plans that will not require too much high level oversight."

"Great, so what the deuce do you need me here for then?"

Frichette glanced around, but they were currently alone on the bridge. The hatch to the Combat Information Center was open, but from the amount of noise coming in from there, it was unlikely that anyone could overhear them. "To provide a solid chain of command, sir. Yes, we could probably appoint some quick-witted chief petty officer to be the acting commodore and sit in that chair, and he might even do a good job, but he would not have the confidence of his subordinates because everyone would know that he had no right to be there."

"Right? Well, what right do I have to sit there?"

"The governor has made you a peer and you already command thousands of workers. You have the right to command. People will believe that and follow."

Crawford shook his head. "This is still crazy."

"A couple thousand of your people will be helping to man these ships. They'll be laying their lives on the line. *They* have the right to have you here leading them. Sir." A note of anger had crept into Frichette's voice and it stabbed through to Crawford. He suddenly realized what he'd been saying: 'let my people fight, but I want no part of it,' and he blushed.

"Sorry. Sorry, that was damn stupid of me, wasn't it? And to be saying that to you! You've got this whole bloody fleet to worry about, not just one squadron."

"Yes, sir, and it would be a lot lighter load if I had you around to carry some of it, sir."

"Okay, you got me. But why do you keep calling me 'sir'? I should be calling you 'sir'."

Now it was Frichette's turn to blush. "Just force of habit, I guess. Tell you what: I'll call you Charles if you call me Petre."

"Deal. Now that I'm done bitching, can you explain some of this to me?" He waved at the rows of displays and instruments.

"Yes, s… Charles, the big one is the main tactical display. This will show the overall situation, it will display the positions and vectors of all friendly ships as well as any enemy ships we have data on. This smaller one is your squadron display, it will show the position, formation, and status of your own ships in more detail. Most of these others are communications stations."

"Uh, where are the helm and the weapons stations and such?"

Frichette blinked and looked startled. "Oh, uh, I guess I was getting ahead of myself. You… you really don't know anything about this, do you, Charles?"

"No, that's what I've been trying to tell you!"

"All right," said Frichette, taking a deep breath. "Maybe we better start from the beginning. This is the *Flag* Bridge, Charles. You command your squadron from here. You don't command the ship, that's the captain's job and he does that on the main bridge."

"Well, *that's* a relief," said Crawford with feeling. "So I don't have to worry about driving the ship or shooting the weapons or anything?"

"No, you will give general orders to your squadron about where to go and what to shoot at—based on my orders for the whole fleet—but the ship captains are responsible for carrying out those orders. And once we get you a staff put together, they will man all these stations and take care of all the incoming and outgoing communications. Of course, you can configure the displays to allow you to look over your captain's shoulder if you want…"

"No thanks, I'll leave that all to him. Now what's this thing over here?"

Crawford could scarcely believe the time when he checked next; an hour had gone by of Frichette running him through the purpose and operation of the equipment on the flag bridge. Or at least as much as was possible; an alarming amount of it wasn't working. The computer technicians were still trying to get around the code lock-outs and it looked like they might have to purge the computers and reload everything.

"What if we can't get it working in time?" asked Crawford after yet another piece of equipment failed to respond.

"Then we are in serious trouble. If we have to rely entirely on manual controls, the enemy will be able to pound us to bits at long range and we won't even be able to fire back. Heck, without the automatics on point defense, we wouldn't even be able to stop their torpedoes. One salvo could gut the whole fleet."

"Maybe I should reconsider this job offer," growled Crawford.

Before Frichette could respond, a rating ran into compartment and shouted: "Sir Charles! Lord Frichette! The governor needs you on the com, immediately! It's an emergency!"

The man led them at a trot through the CIC, which was mostly in pieces, and through the hatch that led to the main bridge. "God, what if it's the Venanci here already," muttered Crawford. "We're not ready!"

But it wasn't the Venanci, although it was still bad enough. Governor Shiffeld stared out of the bridge communications screen. "Gentlemen, we have a problem. There's been a mutiny."

* * * * *

"Father Gillard?" Brannon looked up as one of his 'assistants' stuck his head in through the hatch of his quarters.

"Yes, what is it?"

"Something is happening aboard the Newcomers' ship."

"What?"

"There is a great deal of commotion around their boat bay. My comrade and I were... scouting, and we saw a great many of their warriors crowding into shuttles and then leaving. From their demeanor and facial expressions, we believe that this is not some drill. Clearly, some crisis has occurred."

"You say there were many of the warriors leaving? How many?"

"We would guess forty or fifty. Father, it is our business to evaluate the strength of potential opponents. During the weeks we have been here, we estimated that there were fewer than sixty warriors aboard this vessel. There can be very few left. The area of the ship you are interested in is nearly unguarded now, we would estimate."

Brannon looked sharply at the man. He had not confided any of his fears or his plans to him. "What do you know of this?" he demanded.

"Father, it is our business to notice these things. The mere fact that you hired us at all told us much. I have... observed your actions and interests since then. If you have a task for us to carry out, there might never be a better time."

Brannon sat for a moment in indecision. Could he really do this thing? He closed his eyes and prayed.

"Lifegiver's will," he whispered after a while. "Gather your comrade and let us be about this."

* * * * *

Charles Crawford nodded to Sheila MacIntyrre and Doctor Birringer as they piled into the shuttle. "Well, you were right," he said grimly to Sheila.

"I usually am," she shot back, "but what, exactly, am I right about this time? What the hell is going on?"

"Our esteemed Governor Shiffeld is calling it a 'mutiny', but what it boils down to is that a couple hundred of the workers—including a lot of our folks, apparently—have tried to seize control of the family transports."

"Oh my gods," gasped Birringir. "Anyone hurt?"

"We don't know for sure, but hopefully not many if there are. The reports are pretty sketchy, but it seems like a rather poorly organized mutiny. They grabbed the bridges of the four ships, but failed to secure the engineering sections. So, they are demanding that the captains hyper out, but the engineers won't give them the power to move. Stalemate."

"And we are going over there to try and break it up?" asked Sheila.

"Yup. Shiffeld's sending his cops and some of the warships, but he's agreed to let us try to talk to them before he resorts to force."

"Great. Do we know who we're dealing with?"

"Unfortunately, yes. Seems like Beshar is one of the ring leaders."

"Shit!" said Sheila with feeling.

"I knew he was worried and depressed, but I didn't think that he'd — hell, I just wasn't thinking at all."

"None of us were, or not much at least. Stop beating on yourself and let's go make this all better." Crawford smiled and squeezed Sheila's hand.

It took about ten minutes for the shuttles to reach the transports. Crawford could see a cluster of other shuttles and several of the smaller warships hovering nearby. Their pilot maneuvered around to one of the transports' docking bay, but the doors were closed. A few more minutes on the com finally produced Beshar Hannah on the small communications screen. The man looked very tired and seriously worried.

"Hi, Besh," said Crawford. "Can we come aboard and talk about this?"

"We can talk right now — not that there's much to say."

"Uh, I'd rather do it face to face, Besh. I've got Sheila and the doc here with me. It would be easier and… we'd have more privacy."

Hannah twitched and he suddenly seemed to realize what Crawford was saying about privacy: no records and no witnesses. "All right, but just the three of you. And I won't open the boat bay doors; come around to… to emergency airlock six. No tricks, Chuck, we've got weapons and we'll fight."

"No tricks, there's just us and the pilot of the shuttle here and we are unarmed. Okay, we'll be at the airlock in a few minutes." He cut the connection and directed the pilot where to go. Shortly, they were hooked to the airlock and cycling through. A dozen people waited to receive them. A few had stunners and most of the rest carried things which could be used as clubs. Crawford recognized at least half of them. Hannah was there and he ordered the shuttle pilot to detach and stand off. Nothing more was said by anyone until they'd been led to a small room where they could talk in private. Hannah waved away his escort and faced them alone.

"So, what the hell is this, Besh?" demanded Crawford.

"You know perfectly well what this is: we are taking our families and getting out of this death trap!"

"Doesn't look to me like you are going anywhere, Besh. The ships won't move."

"You can get the governor to order the engineers to cooperate. I want you to do that, Chuck!"

"Or else, what? There's usually an 'or else' in these sorts of situations, isn't there?"

Hannah turned red. "I don't want it to be like that! We're not traitors or lunatics. We just want to take our families and leave. We have a right!"

"To what?" demanded Sheila. "To force the ship crews to go with you? To kidnap the families of the other people who aren't here? We've done a head count, Besh, and you've got people with you who have maybe five hundred dependents here in cold-sleep. There are *four thousand* people on these ships! Were you just going to walk off with all of them?"

"I... we... we could move all of our families," said Hannah, looking very uncertain. "We could thaw them out and put all of them on just one ship and we could go."

"Where?" asked Crawford. "Where are you going to go, Besh?"

"Anywhere but here! The Venanci are coming, you damn fools! I've got kids and if you think I'm going to let those bastards run their genetic experiments on them..."

"Beshar," interrupted Doctor Birringir, "those are just wild stories. The Venanci don't really do things like that. If we are forced to surrender they'll likely send us home once they have what they want."

"You hope! If there's a war over this, it could be years for that to happen, and what if the only ones who get exchanged are big shots like the governor or... or *Sir Charles*, here?"

The way he said it was like a slap in the face. Crawford reared back and just stared, his mouth hanging open and his eyes stinging. He didn't know what to say, but Sheila was suddenly out of her chair, her face twisted in fury.

"How dare you? Besh, *how dare you?* After all Chuck has done for you and for all of us? There's not a person in the entire team he hasn't helped out at one time or another! And most of us owe him a lot more than simple favors. Do you think he would ever — *ever!* — leave us in the lurch?" Sheila took a step forward and Hannah put his hand on his stunner. "Well? Do you?"

Hannah's eyes fell and after a moment he shook his head. "No. No, I'm sorry, Chuck, I didn't mean that. It's just that I'm so scared. We're all so scared..."

"I know, Besh, I know," said Crawford, swallowing hard. "But this isn't the answer. Even if I asked the governor, there's no way he'd let you go. If he let one group go, there would be mass desertions within weeks and the whole thing would go to hell. Maybe staying here wasn't the best idea, but we're committed. Besh, he'd blast these ships out of space before he'd let you go. We have to stick together. If we do that, we've got a chance. If we don't, there's no chance at all."

Hannah looked up and there were tears in his eyes. "So, what happens now?"

"What happens now is that I tell Shiffeld that everything is under control, his cops go back where they came from, everyone else gets back to work, and we forget this ever happened. Okay?"

"O-okay, but you really think Shiffeld will let this drop?"

"If he wants his gate built, he damn well better!" snapped Sheila.

"Exactly. I can handle Shiffeld. Can you convince the rest of your... your associates to give this up, Besh?"

"I-I think so. Once we couldn't make a quick getaway most of them started having second thoughts anyway. When I explain how things stand I think the rest will give it up, too."

"Okay, so let's go do it." Crawford stood up and they left the compartment. They had left nearly a dozen people outside, but there were only two there now. Hannah seemed surprised.

"Where are the others?" he demanded.

"Uh, you told us to keep the intercom open so we could hear," shrugged one man sheepishly. "When we saw which way this was going, the others decided to go with Plan B." He jerked his head aft.

"Oh hell," hissed Hannah.

"What's Plan B?" demanded Crawford.

"Come on! This way!" exclaimed Hannah. He led them in the direction the man had indicated. They hurried along through a series of hatches until they came to the entrance of the cold-sleep compartment. It was horribly reminiscent of the last time Crawford had done something like this, right down to the high-pitch wail.

But this time the wail was not electronic, it was very, very human. They stepped through the hatch and saw a woman holding a cold, frightened infant and trying to soothe it. Further down the rows of capsules were several other children. A group of people were dashing from place to place among the capsules and each and every sealed capsule had the warning lights of a reviving occupant. The closest woman turned to them and Crawford saw that it was Ginny Lansdor. She had a look of defiance on her face as she clutched her baby.

"Maybe you can keep us from leaving, but you can't keep our children from us any longer!"

"All of them?" asked Crawford to Hannah. He nodded.

"Yes, that was Plan B. They'll be doing it on the other three ships now, too."

"There's no way we can reverse this, Doctor?" He looked to Birringir, but she shook her head.

"No, once revival is started, it has to go on to completion."

Crawford whistled. "Granny, set another place for dinner! We got company coming!"

* * * * *

Brannon Gillard walked down the corridor of the Newcomer's command vessel and tried to look confident. His two men were with him, but they walked far enough ahead and behind that at first glance they might not appear to be together. Once again, he had shaved his head and put aside his breathing helmet. The Newcomers' air would not cause quite as much trouble for him as the Seyotahs' had, but he still hoped to complete this excursion as quickly as possible. Indeed, they had to be quick if they were to have any hope of success.

The docking module for the clan ships was attached by a long tube to an airlock in their boat bay. From there, a large section of the ship was open to clan members. These were mostly recreation and entertainment areas, along with some eating areas. They had been politely asked to stay out of the other areas, but since there was a great deal of coming and going by the Newcomer crew members, many of the hatches were left unlocked and with only a few guards.

All those guards were gone now.

Brannon had no idea what emergency had pulled them away, but it presented a priceless opportunity. His two men, skilled mercenary warriors named Jak and Ulan, moved in a seemingly random pattern through the compartments and corridors, but very shortly they all neared a closed hatch. Ulan looked around quickly and then, standing on tip-toe, reached up with a small device to a spot on the ceiling. There was a momentary flash. "Camera," he whispered, "just disabled it." Immediately, Jak moved to the hatch controls and the door slid open. He urged Brannon through and then the hatch closed behind them.

"Remember, if we encounter anyone, look like you belong there. If they challenge you, just pretend to be lost." Brannon nodded.

"How many times have you done something like this?"

"Enough. And these people are incredibly sloppy with their security. With a dozen more men, we could make off with this whole ship."

"We don't need the ship, just one person."

"As you say. Let's go."

They moved off and Brannon was quickly lost in the maze of passageways and ladders he was led along. They did meet Newcomers at intervals, but the two mercenaries just smiled and pointed at things, jabbering in a baby-like speech about what was around them. The Newcomers scarcely gave them a second glance. Finally, Jak and Ulan slowed and moved more cautiously. "The security area is just ahead. Follow us and don't say anything."

Brannon nodded and they led the way around a corner. Just beyond there was an open hatch, and beyond that a control desk with two of the Newcomer warriors standing by it. They looked up in surprise.

"Hey," said the one, "what do you geeks think you're doing here?" In the weeks aboard the ship, Brannon had absorbed some of the Newcomer's language. He understood them well enough, if not perfectly. He wasn't sure if his mercenaries did, but it did not seem to matter. They just laughed and began asking inane questions about the lights and walls and the artificial gravity.

"You. Can't. Stay. Here." Said one of the guards very slowly and loudly. "Go. Back. To. Your. Ship!" He made shooing motions with his hands. Jak and Ulan ignored him and continued to babble. The guard continued to try and send them off, but finally turned to his companion. "I can't make these morons understand. Get the sarge, will you?"

The other man nodded and touched a button on the desk. "Hey, Sarge, we got a couple of the yokels up here. Looks like they're lost, but we can't get 'em to leave. Right." He looked up. "He'll be right here."

It was only a moment before the hatch behind the desk slid open. The moment it did, Jak and Ulan went into action. The soft hiss of a compressed gas gun coughed three times in rapid succession and all three of the guards jerked in surprise.

"Hey!"

"What the...!"

The one coming through the hatch actually managed to half-draw his weapon before they all slumped to the deck. Ulan leapt forward and placed himself in the hatchway before it could slide shut again. Jak quickly moved past him into the next corridor. Brannon instinctively followed. He saw that Jak now had a tiny gun in his hand. It was entirely plastic or ceramic, had no power source, and fired drug-tipped needles. It was virtually undetectable; Brannon had used a similar device to immobilize the Seyotah boy and his girlfriend. He just hoped that whatever drug the mercenaries were using would not harm the Newcomers.

The corridor was lined with jail cells, but they were all empty; the path turned just up ahead and Jak quickly went to the corner. Brannon looked back and saw that Ulan had used one of the unconscious guards to block the door open. He looked ahead just in time to see Jak move around the corner. The dart gun coughed twice more. There was one cry of surprise and then the sound of crumpling bodies.

"All right, it's secure," said Jak. "Ulan, find the door release for cell six."

Brannon looked cautiously around the corner and saw two more guards, one male and one female, lying peacefully on the floor. He walked up to the cell they had been guarding and looked in.

The woman in the boy's memory looked back at him.

"Who... who are you?" she croaked.

"We are friends," he said. "We've come to get you out."

"I don't have any friends. Who are you?" She scowled suspiciously, and then jumped as the cell door slid open. Jak was pulling the uniform off the female guard.

"We are your friends," insisted Brannon. "And if you want to get out of here, you must come with us." Jak tossed the guard's tunic at her and she instinctively caught it. "Please, put these on. We must go quickly."

The woman stared for one moment longer. "What the hell have I got to lose?" she said. Then she started pulling on the uniform. In a moment she was dressed and Jak was tugging on both of them.

"Come on, Father, we need to get out of here."

Chapter Seventeen

"**I** want her back!" snarled Governor Shiffeld. "Her and whoever helped her!" Charles Crawford shifted uneasily in his chair and looked at the others in the governor's office. Petre Frichette, Regina Nassau, and Saunder Garrit, Shiffeld's new chief of police, all looked back just as uneasily. Only Beatrice Innes looked comfortable.

After a moment, Petre Frichette got to his feet and said: "I'm afraid that's not going to be possible, sir."

"Why not? Get your ships moving and track them down! She can't have gotten that far!"

"Far enough, sir. Assuming they really are aboard that shuttle which left, they now have a three hour head start. Despite their low acceleration, they were well out of sensor range after the first hour. From their last known location, if they changed course, which they undoubtedly did, they could now be anywhere in a sphere over fifteen million kilometers in radius. If I had all my ships with their main sensors online and a full complement of recon drones, there might be a chance of finding them, but with what we actually have, there's not a chance in a million of locating them. I'm sorry, sir."

"You can at least try, damn it!"

"No, sir, I must respectfully decline."

"What?" cried Shiffeld. "I'm giving you an order!" Crawford and the others looked on in surprise at the young man standing there shaking his head.

"Sir, you have put me in command of the Rift Fleet's warships and charged me with defending it. It would take my entire force to have even the smallest chance of finding the fugitives and the search could take days. I will not leave the transports and the construction site undefended for that length of time. I'm sorry, sir, but if you insist on that course of action, I must tender my resignation immediately."

Shiffeld's mouth was hanging open and he gobbled incoherently for a moment before snapping it shut again. Before he could recover sufficiently to say anything more, Innes gently touched the sleeve of his coat.

"Governor, he does make a good point. The escape took place because our police were distracted by the mutiny. Who's to say that this isn't part of some bigger distraction to leave us defenseless here while our warships are on a wild goose chase?" He stared at her. "We can find the traitor again later, sir."

He fumed silently for a moment before nodding. "All right then! She's gotten away for now. But I want to know how the hell this happened! Garrit, how did they just waltz into your headquarters and walk off with the traitor? Why were those savages given free run of this ship?"

The police chief looked decidedly uncomfortable. As Crawford recalled, a month ago the man had just been a mining foreman with a reputation for keeping his workers in line. Like everyone else, he was probably out of his depth. "S-sir, Miss N... I mean Dame Regina instructed me to show every courtesy to the visitors. She said they were to be allowed to go where they wanted as long as it wasn't a sensitive area. My people were instructed not to bother them. And with the mutiny, you had ordered me to send every available man to suppress it. Sir."

"So you just left the prisoner unguarded."

"N-no, sir! There were five men on duty in the detention area. I-I had no way of knowing the locals had slipped a team of... of *commandos* aboard the ship! Please, sir, try to remember that all of my people—including me—are still learning our job. Whoever took the prisoner were real professionals, with first rate equipment. There's no way I could have anticipated that!" The man was sweating and clenching the arms of his chair.

"What I would like to know," said Innes, "is how these 'commandos' even knew about the prisoner." She looked at Regina.

"I certainly didn't tell them," responded the terraformer with a snort. "But you might recall that *the governor* hauled Citrone into the main conference room while the Farsvars were there. They saw her."

"Yes!" said Shiffeld suddenly leaning forward. "And one of them is here with the other natives! I want him questioned immediately!"

Regina's eyebrows shot up in surprise. "Governor, you can't do that, he's part of the Seyotah delegation and has diplomatic immunity!"

"Don't be ridiculous, Regina, we never gave these people any sort of formal recognition. We allowed them to come here as a friendly gesture, but they are not any sort of 'delegation', nor do they have any 'immunity'! If that boy was plotting against us, I want to know it and I want him punished!"

Crawford saw the alarm on Regina's face. He knew that she was quite fond of the young native. She seemed about to make an angry retort, but she bit it back and took a deep breath. "Governor, I don't think that's a wise idea. The video records from the detention center showed that the leader of those responsible was a priest from the Clorindan clan. They are mortal enemies of the Seyotahs—and probably our enemies now, too, after we killed their warriors. There is no reason why Tad or his uncle would have deliberately told them about the prisoner or have helped them to rescue her."

"Well, somebody told them!"

"Yes, but it does not mean they were working against us! The Farsvars saw Citrone and anyone could see that there was something important going on. No doubt when they got back to Panmunaptra they were thoroughly debriefed by their own leaders. They probably mentioned the incident. Hundreds of Seyotahs could have known about it and it's entirely possible that Clorindan spies picked up on it from there. As for why they would go to such lengths to get their hands on her, I can't imagine, but I can't see any reason to risk our good relations with the Seyotahs by arresting Tad."

"Our continued good relations are certainly critical, sir," said Crawford. "The materials we are receiving will be vital to completing the gate on time."

"They could be correct, sir," said Innes. "While it is certainly irritating that this has happened, we must remained focused on the primary goal. However, I would recommend that the level of... hospitality we have shown the locals be more restricted."

"Absolutely!" snapped Shiffeld. "I'm tempted to just send them all packing right now, but in the interest of *cordial relations*," he was practically sneering as he looked at Regina, "I'll allow them to stay—in a closely guarded area!"

"Governor, I must protest!" cried Regina. "The other delegates have done nothing to deserve such treatment!"

"Protest all you like, but those are my orders and Captain Garrit will see that they are carried out—to the letter!"

Regina's face had turned almost as red as the governor's during the exchange, although it seemed even redder in contrast to her pale hair. She was clutching her long braid in one hand. "Very well!" she snapped, standing up from her chair. "Then if you'll excuse me, I better go and figure out how I'll explain all this to them!" Without waiting for an answer, she turned and left the room.

Shiffled stared after her and then was silent for a minute or more, while his face slowly regained its normal color. "There is one more matter here that concerns me," he said at last. "The timing of the mutiny and the jail break. While it is true that the jail breakers might have simply taken advantage of the distraction caused by the mutiny, we can't assume that. Citrone has made assertions, during questioning, that she has confederates still loose in the fleet. It's possible that some of them arranged the mutiny specifically to allow for her escape."

"Governor, that seems very unlikely," said Crawford, who was afraid he saw exactly where this was leading. "The people involved in the... disturbance were just scared parents and spouses who made a bad decision."

"Nevertheless, I want all the ring leaders questioned. I assume you have them all in custody, Captain Garrit?"

The police chief looked really uncomfortable now. He glanced at Crawford. "Uh, no, sir, Mr. Crawford—I mean Sir Charles—wouldn't allow it."

"What! These people committed a criminal act! They should be in jail!" He looked at Crawford in astonishment.

"I promised them all immunity in return for giving up. It seemed the best thing to do and I stand by my decision, sir."

"You had no right to make such a deal and I'm canceling it right now! Captain, round up all of the mutineers!"

"Don't even think about it, Captain," said Crawford, putting out a hand. "Governor, you were smart enough to realize that you couldn't defend your fleet without Lord Frichette. I hope you'll be equally as smart and realize you can't build your gate without me and my people."

"Are you threatening me?" spluttered Shiffeld.

"Yup, I sure am. You touch just one of my people and I'll shut this operation down. I don't bluff, Governor, so I advise you to take the threat seriously."

Shiffeld was turning red again. "This is blackmail, damn you!"

"Yes, I guess it is. You can have the Protector slap me in irons when this is all over, but for now, you don't have much choice."

"I could arrest you right now!"

"Governor...!" said Innes, touching his sleeve again.

"You could," said Crawford, "but my people know what to do if I don't come back from this meeting."

"Governor, please calm down," said Innes. "There are better ways to handle this." He looked at her and they locked eyes for a long moment. Finally, Shiffeld let out a long breath and twitched his shoulders.

"All right! We'll forget about it—this time! But you damn well better keep your people in line from now on, Crawford."

"I'll do what I can. But now, with all the families thawed out, the likelihood of this happening again is pretty small. But that brings up the topic of quarters for all the revived dependents."

"Let your mutineers figure out what to do," snorted Shiffeld.

"Actually, sir," said Frichette, breaking in, "this incident might have a bit of a silver lining."

"Really? Could you explain how?"

"Well, there's no shortage of living space on the Rift Fleet. We lost nine thousand people to the traitor and there are only four thousand on the transports. With all the people we've been transferring to the warships, there will be plenty of space on the work vessels."

"True, but that's a pretty thin silver lining."

"Yes, but there's more, sir. I was looking at the statistics on the people actually on the family transports. Over two thousand are children, but the rest are adults. Some of them were skilled or semi-skilled workers in their own right back home. It seems to me that for the extent of this crisis, we could put a few hundred of the least skilled adults to work providing day-care for the children. The rest, say twelve hundred or so, could be put to useful work with the fleet or the construction teams."

"That's a possibility, sir," said Crawford. "You've 'borrowed' over half of my clerical staff. I could certainly use the help there and I'd bet I could find work for some of the others. Hell, just preparing meals and doing laundry would free up some of my people for other work."

Shiffeld looked at Innes who raised an eyebrow and shrugged. "It's certainly a possibility, sir. At the least, it's better than them all sitting around taking up space and doing nothing."

"Very well, put some proposals together for me."

"Yes, sir." Innes stood up. "And on that positive note, may I suggest we adjourn the meeting, sir?"

"Yes. My blood pressure is high enough as it is. That's all, gentlemen." Crawford took this dismissal with relief. He, Frichette, and Garrit popped up out of their chairs and were out before Shiffeld could change his mind. Once the door shut, he let out a long sigh and exchanged glances with the others. Garrit looked away, excused himself, and hurried off.

"Shiffeld has got him by the short hairs, that's for sure," he said quietly.

"Yes, but I'm rather amazed at how easily Ms. Innes handles our governor. You should take a few pointers from her, I think, Charles." He looked at Frichette and saw the young man was smiling.

"What? You mean use finesse instead of charging straight in like a runaway ore-crusher? What fun would that be?"

"Who was the ore-crusher?" asked Regina Nassau, who had been waiting outside the office suite. She got up from where she was sitting and came over to them, the anger still plain on her face. "And who got crushed? Shiffeld, I hope!"

"Oh. Yes, he's been thoroughly crushed—at least for now. You and I knocked him down and then Charles jumped up and down on him. Sorry you missed the climax."

"Really? What happened?"

"Bastard wanted to arrest my people and set Garrit to work finding the traitors among them," growled Crawford.

"With the unspoken understanding that traitors would be found whether there were really any or not?" asked Regina.

"Exactly."

"What did you do? Although I think I can guess, my big, hulking ore-crusher." Regina was smiling now.

"Told him to keep his paws off my people or he can build the gate himself."

"And he gave in?"

"Completely," said Frichette failing to hold in his smile.

"At least so far—as you said. I'm sure he'll find some way to get back at us, but for now we're safe."

Frichette's smile vanished in an instant. "Safe? From our own leader? I'm not sure I like the way this is going…"

"Oh, we're all just on edge," said Crawford. "It's been a bad day. Things will get better." He wasn't sure who he was trying to convince.

"I sure hope so," said Frichette, "Especially considering what's coming up."

"Oh? What's coming up?" asked Regina.

"We're starting all-out fleet training in two days. We've really been pushing our luck, in my opinion, by assuming that the Venanci would not be showing up for three or four months, but we can't do that any longer. They could show up literally any minute now and we have got to try and get ourselves ready. Charles and a lot of his people will be transferring to the warships and we have a lot of work to do."

"Well, at least we won't have to try to fit in a search for Citrone with all the rest," said Crawford. "I mean, I want her to pay for what she did as much as the next person, but we have to stay focused on priorities."

"Yes, but I really wish we had her back for other reasons," said Frichette.

"Oh?"

"Yes, I'm worried about what she can tell the people who rescued her. So far, we've managed to keep our precarious situation a secret from the locals. They see our huge, gleaming warships and are properly awed. I'm not sure what they will think if they learn that they are just empty shells for the most part."

"Well, it's up to us to put some stuffing in those empty shells, eh?"

"And you are just the people to do the stuffing," said Regina. She was smiling, but then her smile faded a bit. "I guess I won't be seeing much of you for a while." She didn't say which 'you' she meant, but she was looking at Crawford. It sent a strange thrill through him. "If you do get any free time, come and say hello. I'll buy you a drink."

"Uh, sure, I'll try and do that."

"Good. So, I'll leave you two to your tasks. As for me, I have some diplomatic fences to mend. See you later."

* * * * *

"I thought I would talk to you first, Tad, since we are friends," said Regina. "Do you understand my explanation for these new restrictions? Do you think the other delegates will mind?"

"Yes, I understand," said the young man. "I am very sorry that this has happened. I cannot understand why a priest, even a Clorindan priest, would do such a thing. Perhaps, if you asked the other clans for assistance, they could help you track down your missing prisoner."

Regina blinked in surprise. She had not thought of that possibility. Would Shiffeld agree to that? If they succeeded would it change his opinion of the natives? "I, uh, I will have to discuss that with the governor, Tad, but thank you for the offer. In the meantime, I hope you and the others won't object to these new restrictions on your movements."

"I don't think there will be any objections once you explain why you are doing them. Frankly, I think everyone was a little surprised at how much freedom you were giving us here."

"Well, that's a relief, I was worried that you would be offended at everyone being punished for the actions of a few." Regina hesitated for a moment before continuing. "Tad, do you have any idea why this priest would want to take our prisoner? Or how they knew she even existed? We are trying to make sense of this."

Tad frowned and seemed to be thinking hard. "I don't know why they would want her, Regina. You have never told us anything about who she is or why she is a prisoner. As for how they knew about her... My uncle and I did see her when we were first aboard. We told our own leaders about the incident, but I have no idea who else they might have mentioned it to." He looked up at her and appeared to be very uneasy. "But, Regina, I have never spoken to the Clorindan priest, but somehow I feel I've met him before coming here. I can't explain it, but somehow I know him!"

* * * * *

Brannon Gillard looked at the woman sitting across from him in the cramped shuttle's cabin. He wasn't sure exactly what the Newcomers were supposed to look like when healthy, although he'd seen a good number of them recently, but he was fairly certain that this one was not in the best of health. She seemed very thin, the skin on her face was tight against her bones and her eyes were sunken and ringed with dark flesh. Her body, under the too-large uniform, was thin and wiry, and her blonde hair was cut close to the scalp, which somehow made her seem even more sickly. She was also clearly not comfortable in free fall, which added to her pallor.

But her eyes were sharp and attentive. They were looking back at him now.

"Brannon Gillard," he said, touching himself on the chest.

"Carlina Citrone," she replied, mimicking the gesture. They were both wearing breathing helmets since the mercenaries' shuttle held an atmosphere that neither of them could handle well. The temperature wasn't too bad, fortunately. Brannon wished they had a more comfortable transport, but the small vessel was designed to avoid detection, and had it been any larger, it would not have fit in the bay of the ship which had brought them to the Newcomers' gathering. He'd had a hard enough time to convince Andra Roualet to bring it as it was. Well, at least he would not have to talk Andra into anything else that she did not really want to do! He'd have to do something nice for Andra to repay her for all this — if he ever got the chance.

The woman was talking again, but he could not quite make out her words. She wasn't as fluent as Lady Regina had been. He held up a hand and then got out one of the translating computers the Newcomers had handed out. He guiltily realized that he had stolen this — stolen this, too, he corrected. He showed her how the device worked (which seemed strange, since it was made by her people, not his) and then used it to tell her she was safe and among friends. She seemed skeptical.

"Who are you? Where do you come from? What do you want with me?" she asked when he gave her the translator. It took a while to get across the idea that he came from this star system. Apparently, she had been kept completely in the dark about recent goings-on. Once that fact was accepted, it took more time to explain how they had gotten here, which led to more question about the clans' history. Brannon tried to answer the woman's questions to put her at ease, but she seemed to have an endless string of them and he was burning to ask his own questions. Finally, he was forced to break in.

"Why were you a prisoner?"

It took her quite a while to type in an answer. She thought and then typed, erased it, thought some more, and then typed again. Finally she handed the device over to him and he read: "I am an enemy of the Anderans. I am here to sabotage their attempts to establish a colony beyond the Rift. I was successful in my mission, but I was caught and imprisoned." The term *Anderans* puzzled him for a moment until he remembered that was the name of the political entity the Newcomers belonged to, a sort of super-clan, if he understood correctly. *Sabotage* took even longer to figure out, but when he finally had it, things were suddenly much clearer. And she said the Anderans were here to colonize — just as he'd feared!

"So, you come from a different… clan than these people? You infiltrated them to strike a blow for your own clan?"

"Yes!"

"What is your clan? Are they at… at war with the Anderans?"

Her reply took a long time again, with several erasures. "I work for the Venanci, who are a rival of the Anderans. They were not openly at war when we left on this journey, but that might have changed." Brannon considered her words. She said she worked for the Venanci, but did not claim to be one of them. Was that just a quirk of the translator, or was she a mercenary?

"What was the nature of your sabotage? No damage has been observed on the Anderan vessels." The question seemed to upset the woman and once again she was a long time answering.

"I disabled their warships."

"How so? At least one of their warships was functional when it destroyed some of my clan's warriors."

This unleashed another stream of questions from the woman. She was keen to know if Brannon's people were at war with the Anderans, if she could count on their help, what sort of military strength the clan possessed. With the language difficulties it took hours, and Brannon was growing frustrated. While it was true that they had plenty of time, the evasive course the mercenaries had chosen would take over a week to get them back to the Clorindan base, he was still anxious to get the full story — and be sure it was true. Finally, he called a halt and insisted the woman eat something and then rest. The food was a bland survival ration guaranteed to be compatible with any body chemistry. The woman seemed to tolerate it with no problems. After that, she went to sleep. Brannon tried to do the same, but sleep was a long time coming.

* * * * *

Carlina awoke with a start, the unfamiliar surroundings combined with a half-remembered nightmare to put her in a near-panic. She looked around in wild confusion and fought with the restraining strap across her middle for an instant before spotting the strange man who had rescued her coming out of the shuttle's tiny head.

"You all right?" he asked when he saw her.

"Yes," she said breathlessly. "This strap it… it reminded me when I was being interrogated, I guess." The man called Brannon shook his head and got out the translating machine. She sighed and typed in her statement; this was so tedious. She finished and handed the machine back to him. He read it carefully and then gave her a reply:

"Did your captors abuse you?"

"No actual physical torture, but they were not gentle, either," was her reply. His expression was of mixed sympathy and revulsion. Or at least it seemed to be. The man's face was different enough from a normal human's that it wasn't that easy to read. Carlina was still trying to digest all that she had learned the previous day. Her rescuers were descended from a group of genetically engineered humans who crossed the Rift so long ago that there was no record of their existence! It seemed incredible, but there was no denying that they were here. She wasn't sure how they fit into her mission, but at the very least they seemed to be at odds with the Anderans. She doubted that the old saying 'my enemy's enemy is my friend' was ever truer than it was for her right now. She might not exactly be free, but she was a million times better off than she had been yesterday!

But what was she going to do now? What was her duty under these new conditions? She had carried out her primary mission as far as she could: the Anderans were crippled and she had sent out her message drone to ensure that the relief squadron knew what she had done. But she had heard enough during her imprisonment to know that her enemies were not just going to give up. They would fight, and if the relief squadron was very small, it was conceivable that they might even win. Could she enlist the aid of her rescuers in the coming battle? Despite the many questions she had asked, she had no real information on the numbers or military potential of these people. Well, she had to try. She took the translator again.

"Are you the enemies of my captors? Do you fight them? My friends, the Venanci, are coming soon. Will you help them fight the Anderans?" Brannon took a long time to reply.

"You ask us to take sides in your war? You both are invaders to our system, why should we aid either? Perhaps you will destroy each other and we will be left in peace."

Carlina frantically typed her reply. "The Venanci will be your friends! They are not invaders, they are like you. They believe in the same process which created your ancestors! The Anderans are murderers and thieves! They will steal your worlds and slaughter your people. Help us and we shall be your friends."

Brannon read her message and was silent for a long time. Finally, he wrote out another message. "You ask me to trust your word, but you have as many reasons to lie to me as the Anderans. But there is a way for me to be sure. Will you cooperate?"

It took a great deal of back and forth before Carlina understood what he was asking. He showed her some very strange equipment and some vials which apparently contained drugs. She shuddered at the thought of being drugged again. But apparently this was some sort of truth-telling device. She thought furiously: *will the whole truth serve here? Is there anything I could tell him that would hurt rather than help?* She could not think of a single thing that might hurt her cause. She hated the Anderans and the Protector and had good reasons to do so. If these people wanted to be left alone, they would have a far better chance with the Venanci. No, in this case the truth would do.

"All right, I will do what you want."

Brannon seemed pleased and immediately went to work. They both had to trade their breathing helmets for far less comfortable masks that covered mouth, nose, and eyes, held in place with a strap. Then Brannon attached a series of leads to each of their heads, all the wires running into a small box with a control pad. While he was working, one of the other men on the shuttle came in from the control room and Brannon talked to him for a while before he left again. Then more time was spent while he adjusted his device. Carlina could not feel anything happening; what did this do?

Finally, all seemed ready and Brannon slipped the drug capsules into two aerosol projectors and attached them to the air supply of their breathing masks. She was surprised and a bit relived at this. He had not made it clear that he was going to take the drug, too, but somehow it made her feel better. A faint mist filled both of their masks and after a moment, she breathed it in.

There was no immediate effect that she could notice, but Brannon made her sit comfortably and lean back against some cushions. He made a final few adjustments to his box and then took a similar position on the opposite bulkhead. She sat and waited.

Very quickly her arms and legs were tingling and feeling terribly heavy despite the zero-G. Her eyelids were drooping and she struggled to keep them open. She locked her eyes on Brannon's and tried to remain awake. His eyes were very dark, with large black pupils. She stared and stared. His eyes seemed to be getting larger and larger. Then she was falling into those huge black pools and was gone.

* * * * *

Brannon came to his senses with a groan of pain. He hurt. He ached all over and the pain in his head throbbed and throbbed. He realized that he had dislodged his breathing mask and he quickly put it back on and breathed deeply. He was glad to see that Carlina's mask was still in place and she seemed to be sleeping peacefully. Slowly the pain in his head subsided, at least the physical pain did. There was another pain there and he slowly came to realize it was coming from the flood of strange memories he had absorbed from Carlina. Carlina, she was no longer the 'Newcomer woman', she was Carlina. He had been forced to delve far deeper into her mind and memories than he had with the boy, Tad, and a large part of the woman was now a part of him. It had been a dangerous, even a foolish thing to do, but the need had been too great to turn back. He sat against the cushions, exhausted, and tried to sort out what he had learned.

Too much. He had learned far more than he ever would have wanted. Pain, despair, anger, and a burning hatred filled the woman; it colored her every thought and every desire. The image of a man floated near the top of it all, like some bigger bit of flotsam in a recycling sludge tank.

The Protector.

There seemed to be no other name than that title. He knew the man had a real name, but Carlina never thought of him that way. This Protector was the leader of the Anderans, it seemed, and Carlina Citrone hated him as she hated nothing else in her hate-filled life.

No, not entirely hate-filled. There were some good memories there, too, though deeply submerged under an ocean of rage. Images of a woman and a man and a child drifted up in Brannon's mind. Mother, father, brother, yes. And they were dead, he had not the slightest doubt of that. The Protector had killed them. Not personally, no, there was no memory of that man standing over her family's bodies with a bloody dagger, but in Carlina's mind he was responsible. But why, what was the story behind this? He looked deeper, batting aside drifting tendril of rage like overgrown vines in an untended arboretum. Deeper and back in time he delved until he arrived at the image of a place. At first it was disorienting until he divined it was on the surface of a planet and not inside a space station. A building with many seats; a church he realized suddenly, a church with a congregation. A man speaking at the front of the room, but scarcely noticed by Carlina. Her younger brother was trying to take one of her toys and her mother was telling them both to be quiet. Another memory, from a much older Carlina, briefly intruded and informed him that this was The Church of the Creator, but the explanation of just what that meant skittered away under a wave of new images. Confusion and noise in the church, people screaming. Her parents surging to their feet and grabbing Carlina and her brother. A desperate rush to get outside. A mob with weapons and fire. The person carrying Carlina falls and someone else grabs her up. One last image of her father trying to help her mother to her feet with one hand while he held her brother with his other. Then the mob obscures the scene and all goes black.

Brannon shook his head. So, an unpopular religious sect attacked by others? Somehow this Protector was behind it? Carlina's thoughts were in no logical order and explanations were usually lacking. Still, there could not be much doubt of this, as bizarre as it seemed. There was no conflict between the churches of the Lifegiver, but somehow it did not truly surprise him that these violent Newcomers would have such things.

More of her memories fell into order. A succession of places and people taking care of her, hiding her, too, apparently, all draped with an overwhelming mantle of loss, grief, and loneliness. Brannon looked over at the woman and he was filled with pity for her. He gently reached out and stroked her arm. She moaned and moved slightly, but she did not wake up. Asleep, she looked more peaceful and far healthier. She was really quite beautiful in her sad, strange way.

So, she had suffered a terrible personal loss because of this Protector, but it seemed strange to him that she would still be so consumed with hatred over something which had happened so long ago. Was there more to this? As if in response to his question, more memories surfaced and aligned themselves. Several temporary foster homes and then a permanent one with a strangely intense couple who showed little love for the troubled girl. Images of secret meetings where adults railed against the Protector, her foster parents telling her again and again that the Protector was the enemy who murdered her parents. And then... what was this? A small group of buildings surrounded by trees, far, far from any habitation. A camp of instruction for warriors? So it seemed, and Carlina was taken there a half-dozen times during her teenage years. She was trained to kill with weapons and to kill without them. Trained to use all manner of devices and trained to follow orders. Through it all, she was told again and again about the evil of the Protector and how the Venanci were the friends of this Church of the Creator. The indoctrination was so intense, Brannon suddenly found himself clenching his fists and cursing the Protector under his breath.

With a jerk of his head, he wrenched himself away from the woman's memories. He sat there gasping. Too much, he had absorbed too much from Carlina. He had to be careful, or her memories would become indistinguishable from his own, a self-induced schizophrenia. He sat there for several minutes, pushing away the woman's memories and thinking about his own. Yes, that was better. His breathing eased and the bizarre feeling of murderous rage slowly dissolved.

He regarded the sleeping Carlina and a bit of anger flared up in him again. But this anger wasn't turned against the Protector, no it was directed against the people who had trained Carlina. They had taken a young girl and turned her into a weapon. Instead of soothing her hurts, they had deliberately inflamed them to insure her cooperation and obedience. What they had done to her was as great a crime as what had been done to her parents. If these Venanci were behind it, then they were no better than the Anderans.

But what had they done with this weapon they had created? What was the sabotage of which she had spoken? He needed to know if he was to have a grasp on the Newcomers' real military strength. Reluctantly, he began to probe his stolen memories again. Strangely, at first he found nothing. Something so important and so recent should have been fresh and prominent, but there was little except memories of sitting in her cell after her capture, mixed with unpleasant images of being questioned. He pushed deeper, following a disjointed trail of linked memories that led toward a... what? It was like some dark, cancerous cyst on a medical scan, some region of her past she wanted to wall-off and forget. He came to the edge of it and then hesitated, teetering between the need to know and some instinctive fear of what he might find.

He steeled himself and pushed ahead. The dark knot unraveled and a wave of images, sensations, and emotions washed over him like a splash of acid on bare flesh. Anger, fear, pain, and exhaustion, combined with guilt and sorrow and a seemingly endless stream of dead faces to stun Brannon like a physical blow. A dead man in a bed, a woman she counted as a friend sprawled on the deck, a shower stall crimson with blood, people killed unawares with clubs and knives and her hands. And row after row of plastic cylinders spewing vapor and fluid... As the truth of what Carlina had done became clear, it was more than he could bear, he desperately tried to push the memories back into that dark place they had been in. He tore off the strap holding him and shoved himself into the small washroom. Cold water on his face could not quell the nausea that surged up in him. He choked and gasped as he tried to keep from vomiting in his breathing mask. He succeeded, but just barely. He was a long time cleaning up.

When he opened the hatch and returned to the main compartment, he was still shaking badly. He started when he saw that Carlina was awake. She stared at him and he could not meet her eyes. She had the translating computer in her hands and she gave it to him immediately.

"What did you do? I had the strangest dreams about you."

He regained his spot and looked at her. Before, she had seemed weak and sick and very helpless. He had pitied her. Now he realized, just as the Anderans had apparently found out too late, that she was the most dangerous creature imaginable. The clan's warriors, the two expert mercenaries piloting this ship, were as babes when it came to dealing death. He shivered in her presence.

But he still pitied her.

"It is a method for exchanging some thoughts," he told her eventually. He did not add that, like he had done with the boy, the device was adjusted to give him far more from her than she received from him. "I have seen… I have seen what you did aboard the Anderan vessels, Carlina."

Her face went very white and for a moment he thought she might faint. Tears began to leak out of her eyes and fog her mask. But after a moment she took the translator. "I did not want to kill all of them, but I had no choice. And now you see how helpless they are with their warriors dead. Will you help me?"

"It is not my decision. I will have to discuss all of this with my leaders."

"When will that be?"

"Perhaps a week. We are heading for my home."

She seemed to accept that and shortly excused herself and went into the washroom.

The following week seemed interminable. He would talk with Carlina for hours, and after a few days, the translator was hardly needed. They talked about their respective backgrounds and Carlina seemed especially fascinated with his description of the birthing crèche. She said that she wanted children of her own someday and they compared how differently their two peoples achieved that goal. She frequently pressed him for help in her cause and he repeatedly deflected her requests. Neither mentioned what she had done again, but Brannon could not stop thinking about it. Bit by bit, he either 'remembered' or got from Carlina details of the history of Andera and Venance. What he learned frightened him.

They were two of a group of competing empires, warring with each other on and off for centuries. They slew each other by the millions to grab pieces of the rubble left from an even more horrific conflict. Their actions almost made the legendary World Stealers look like saints.

And now their contest was spilling across the Rift.

Despite Carlina's assurances that the Venanci would look upon the clan as brethren and kin, Brannon knew it was not true. The Refuge system would just be another battlefield in an endless contest, and the clans would be little more than pawns. No, there was no hope or help to be had from either side. The only hope he could see was to let the two enemies fight and then perhaps the united clans could drive off the survivors. At the very least, they must destroy this gate they were constructing. Now if he could only convince his people!

The dreary journey at last came to an end and the mercenaries deposited him and Carlina in the docking bay of Telendia Base. He had worried that he would be accosted by warriors and others before he could contact Herren Caspari, but the bay seemed strangely deserted. He entered with only a glance given to him by the single very young warrior on guard. His initial plan had been to go directly to Caspari's headquarters, but instead, he decided to go to his office first.

His staff greeted him excitedly and his secretary, Kananna, hugged him and cried a bit. "The Newcomers are looking for you, Father!" she exclaimed. "They say you took…" she trailed off when she saw Carlina.

"This is Carlina. She's a… a friend. I'd be grateful if you could find her some guest quarters, I'll give you her environmental requirements. And she'll need food and some fresh clothing. But first I need to talk with Herren Caspari. Get through to him and I'll take it in my office."

Kananna looked uneasy. "But, Father, K'ser Caspari isn't here on Telendia."

"Oh, well get me his second, then."

"He's gone, too, nearly all of the clan leaders are gone, Father."

"Gone? Gone where?"

"We don't know. About a week ago most of the leaders and nearly all the warriors took their ships and left."

A chill went through Brannon. This couldn't be, surely Herren wouldn't…

Yes he would.

"Who is left in charge?" he demanded.

"Uh, Administrator Jaroo is…"

"Get him for me at once!" he snapped in a tone that made poor Kananna jump.

"Yes, F-father, right away," she stuttered. Brannon took Carlina's arm and nearly dragged her into his office.

"What is happening?" she asked after the door was closed.

"I don't know," he said, collapsing into his chair. "But I fear the worst." Carlina didn't ask what the worst was, and for that he was grateful. They sat in silence, Brannon wringing his hands, until the communicator chimed. He snapped on the screen and was relieved to see Jaroo's face.

"Father Brannon!" he exclaimed. "I didn't know you had returned. Where have you been? We thought the Newcomers had arrested you."

"There is no time for stories right now. Where is Caspari? Where has he taken the warriors?"

Jaroo looked very uneasy. "I-I'm not really at liberty to say…"

"Where are they, Jaroo!?!" roared Brannon, fear snapping his patience. Jaroo's eyes were very wide. Brannon never yelled at people. He forced himself to calm down. "I wouldn't ask if it wasn't important, old friend," he said quietly. "I've gotten some very critical information and I need to talk to Caspari. Please, Jaroo, on the Lifegiver's oath, I need to know."

Jaroo stared at him for a moment and then slowly nodded. "He's gone, Brannon. He's taken all the warriors he could gather and he's gone."

"Life! He's gone to attack the Newcomers?"

"No, no, he seemed like a man possessed, but he hasn't fully lost his reason. He knows the Newcomers are too strong to attack directly. So, he goes to attack their allies."

"The Seyotah?"

"Yes. You weren't here to see it Brannon, but after you had left, Caspari spent weeks whipping up the warriors—and a good many of the other people—into a frenzy of anger over the slaughter of our people and his sons. I'd never seen him like this, but you know how persuasive he can be when he speaks in front of a crowd."

"Yes."

"Well, anyway, he got them to agree and they left a week ago."

Brannon sighed. This was bad, but not as bad as he'd feared. A direct attack on the Newcomers right now would have been catastrophic. They needed time, time to present what he had discovered and rally more clans to their side. An attack on the Seyotah still wasn't good, but at least it wasn't the disaster he'd feared. But what did Caspari hope to…?

"I'm no warrior, Jaroo, but I'm puzzled over what this will accomplish. Yes, we can overcome the Seyotah warriors, seize some of their ships, gather some loot, and probably interrupt their trade with the Newcomers, but the other clans will just take up the slack. As maddened as you say Caspari was, this hardly seems like sufficient… revenge for him."

Now Jaroo's face became truly twisted with pain. "It's not, old friend, it's not. May the Lifegiver forgive all of us, but Caspari does not go to attack the Seyotah shipping, he goes to attack their home on Panmunaptra."

"What? But how? He doesn't have enough warriors to occupy a base that size!"

"H-he doesn't plan to occupy it. It was all done in great secret, but I learned of what he plans to do."

"What?"

Jaroo shook his head and looked down. "He's redirected a small asteroid. It's now on a collision course with Panmunaptra. His warriors will escort it all the way in so the Seyotahs cannot stop it. I'm sorry, Father, but he plans to kill them all!"

"Lifegiver the Merciful," whispered Brannon.

Chapter Eighteen

Carlina Citrone sat and watched Brannon's face grow grimmer and grimmer. Finally, he switched off the com screen and rested his head in his hands. He was clearly in pain and she was astounded to see tears on his cheeks.

"Brannon, what's wrong?" She found that she was genuinely worried about him, even though she had only known the man for a little over a week. Somehow, that 'thought transfer' device he had used made it feel like she'd known him for years.

"Lifegiver forgive me, what have I done," he moaned.

"What *have* you done? Brannon, talk to me!"

"This is all my fault. If I'd just left it alone, none of this would have happened!" He scrubbed the tears away and took a deep breath. "Caspari, the leader of my clan, is taking the warriors to attack the Seyotahs."

"But I thought you said they were your enemy. Aren't they the ones who have allied with the Anderans? I would think this is a good thing."

"You don't understand. He means to kill them! Kill them all!"

Carlina was about to say that no, she didn't understand, when suddenly those strange, dreamlike impressions of Brannon which had been floating around in her mind for days seemed to snap into place and suddenly she *did* understand. "Oh, Maker," she moaned. In a flash, she saw Brannon for what he really was: a gentle, gentle man, who helped make babies and loved life above all else. In spite of what he had told her on the trip here, she had been assuming that he was like the two warriors who had helped him rescue her, and now she saw that wasn't true at all. And even the 'warriors' were not what she had assumed. They were gentle men from a gentle race which had almost forgotten how to kill.

Until her kind had reminded them how.

"Oh, Brannon, I'm sorry!" She came over and tried to put her arms around him, despite the clumsy suit which protected her from his lethal air. "I'm sorry, I'm sorry..." Suddenly she was crying. She felt one of his arms go around her and they clung to each other for quite some time. Eventually, he gently pushed her away and they looked at each other. "I'm sorry," she whispered again. "What... what are you going to do?"

"I don't know. I'm not sure there's anything I can do. Caspari and the warriors will be making a silent approach to Panmunaptra, they would never respond to any message I sent them."

"Surely some of the Seyotahs will escape?"

"Some, quite a few, I suppose. But their *birthing crèche* will be destroyed! With that gone, along with nearly all their industry, it will be the end of their clan. The Seyotahs will be finished as an independent people — at least here at Refuge." He shook his head. "Some might see the destruction of a rival as a good thing, but I... I cannot."

"C-could you warn them? Warn the Seyotahs, I mean. Maybe they could save something, the birthing crèche, perhaps." She could scarcely believe she was suggesting this. These Seyotahs were allies of the Anderans which automatically made them her enemy. She should celebrate their destruction as a blow against the Protector.

But somehow she couldn't.

Somehow the thought of so many deaths, the deaths of the babies, made her physically ill. She clutched Brannon's arm hard enough to make him wince as she swallowed the bile rising in her throat. "Could you warn them?" she said again.

"You want me to betray my own warriors?" He seemed dazed by the notion.

"From what I have learned of you and your people, isn't this attack a betrayal of everything you believe in, Brannon?"

"Yes."

"And warning them wouldn't stop the attack, they would still be crippled as an ally of the Anderans, b-but maybe they could save the children if they had time."

Brannon stared off into space for a long time before he finally nodded. "Perhaps. Perhaps it could be done. I've had some professional dealings with the priest in charge of their birthing crèche. I might be able to get through to him."

"Then let's try!"

He looked down to where she was still clutching his arm and gently patted her hand with his. He looked up and smiled at her.

"Yes. Let's."

* * * * *

As you can see from the main reports, the data collection and analysis is proceeding on schedule. The planet is a normal Type F-938-B to about three decimal places, no surprises at all so far. We could melt the ice caps using standard procedures with no problem and there are no native settlements within fifteen hundred clicks.

Regina paused the display of the message from Jeanine and sighed. She really wished she was there, on *Bastet*, to oversee things personally. While she had enjoyed acting as host to the locals — even after Shiffeld's idiotic restrictions were put in place — at heart she was a terraformer and that was what she ought to be doing. She activated the message player again.

Geologic scans have located a number of magma pockets which could be tapped. Unfortunately, nearly all have local settlements inside the danger zone. There are two near the poles which might possibly be safe to tap, but that will be a judgment call — your call, Reggie. Really wish you were here to make it.

On other matters, I've kept my eyes and ears open, but I've not really discovered anything out of the ordinary. Still, there seems to be a subtle division of loyalties taking place here. Some still consider you the boss but there is a definite faction shaping up who consider Doctor Ramsey to be the one really in charge. I don't know if that's simply because he's here and you are not, or because of other factors I'm not aware of. Still, I think it would be better if you did not stay away too much longer. I look forward to seeing you. Jeanine.

Regina sighed again. She did miss Jeanine and she resolved that she would travel out to *Bastet* soon, even if it was just for a visit. But then she got back to what she'd been working on before the message had interrupted her. She was putting together a summary of what she had found out about the history of the locals. No one had asked her to do this, it was something she wanted to do.

What she had learned was fascinating—and frustrating. There were a lot of gaps in the locals' records and the farther back history went, the more 'fact' seemed to merge with legend. Their earliest, pre-exodus, records were found in the '*Book of Life*' of their religion. Regina really didn't know how much she could trust that. At first it had seemed strange that the records would be so incomplete. Granted it had all happened a very long time ago, but these people, unlike her own, had not had a horrific war tear their universe apart. She would have expected their records to have been far more complete.

But it seemed that the first, ancient, crossing of the Great Rift had been a shoestring operation at best. Nothing at all like the current expedition, it had consisted of just a single ship and one without cold-sleep capsules. The entire crew had been awake for a trip which had taken twenty years. They had used up nearly all of their resources during that journey and record-keeping had not been a priority. Regina was amazed that they had made it at all and the *Book of Life* seemed to consider it a miracle.

And when they arrived here they had little to work with. They had had to start almost from scratch in their new home. And that fact explained another thing Regina had been wondering about. The technology of the old United Worlds was a legendary thing. Before the Great Revolt, it had been far more sophisticated than what was currently available. Granted that these people had left long before the UW reached its height, but she still wondered at their relatively low tech level. Apparently, the original colonists had been reduced to what amounted to a subsistence level (if a spacefaring culture could really be termed subsistence) and had not had the means to advance much beyond it in the time since. Still, this struck her as odd; surely they must have some sort of research scientists? Or did they? She'd have to ask…

The buzzer on her door sounded and kept on sounding as though someone was leaning on the button. "All right, all right, I'm coming," she said as she got up from her chair and went to the door. It slid open and she was surprised to see Tad and several other members of the Seyotah delegation outside. The expressions on their faces told her instantly that all was not well.

"Tad! What's wrong?"

"Regina! Oh, Regina, something terrible is happening! Please, we must have your help!"

* * * * *

"So how is it going?" asked Charles Crawford to the sweating group of technicians. The looks of frustration and anger which met his question told him what the answer was without a word needed — although plenty of words were forthcoming, most of them curses.

"It's a mess, sir," said the one in charge, after the others had voiced their opinions. "This software is all crap. No way we're going to get it to work." Crawford glanced at Petre Frichette, but the young man just shrugged slightly.

"It's all we've got, Ernst," said Crawford to the foreman. "The software from *Felicity* was the only stuff we could access and you'll just have to adapt it for *Indomitable*. It can't be all that much different, can it?"

"Begging your pardon, sir, but yes, it can. *Felicity* is about thirty years older than this ship and built by an entirely different shipyard. The software might serve similar functions, but there are about a million little details which are different, and until we fix *all* of them, the damn thing isn't going to work!"

"We're having the same problem through most of the fleet," said Frichette very quietly in Crawford's ear. He nodded.

"Well, do the best you can, people," he said to the work crew. Their muttered replies were, thankfully, unintelligible. Crawford and Frichette moved off. "So, you're saying the whole fleet is in this sort of mess?"

"Unfortunately. There's no standardization at all from ship to ship. They were built in a dozen different yards over a span of nearly fifty years and there's no reason to expect software from one ship to work in another."

"There weren't any copies or backups of the proper software?"

"Oh, there were, but they were all locked into computers we didn't have the access codes for, either. We ultimately had to purge all those computers and start fresh."

"Damn, it couldn't be much worse if they had been deliberately set up to cause us trouble."

"Well, in a way, they were."

"What do you mean?"

"The code lock-outs are there to prevent unauthorized people from taking control of the ships. While that includes hijackers and such, it is primarily meant to prevent someone capturing the ship from using it against its former owners without going to a lot of effort. As far as the computers know, we could be pirates or Venanci. Nothing personal, just damned inconvenient."

"So the whole fleet is still out of action?" Crawford did not like what he was hearing.

"Not entirely. *Felicity* is entirely operational and the light cruiser, *New Umbria*, is nearly so. On that one, the captain had actually written down the security codes and we managed to find them. A serious breech of regulations, that, but lucky for us—even though *New Umbria* is just about as old as *Felicity*. Sadly, we weren't as lucky on any of the other ships. But even the other ships are not entirely immobilized. Critical ship systems like the reactor, drive, and life support all have extensive manual override controls. They are not quite as good as the main computer controls, but good enough."

"So we can move, but not fight?"

"Right now, that's pretty much the case, I'm afraid. Sensors are out and the weapons are on manual control. Not a good situation. If we are given a couple more weeks, I'm hoping we will at least have a few of the ships' point defense systems operating. They could provide torpedo defense for the rest of us. A few more weeks and we might have the main weapons operational on a couple more ships. We just have to pray that the Venanci are late."

Frichette paused and they both had to step aside as one of the new damage control teams trotted past, the leader calling out various ship systems to his members as they went. "At least those people should be able to do their jobs," he observed.

"Right now, they're all just learning where things are," replied Crawford. "Of course, since half the things on the ship don't work anyway, that makes their repair responsibilities a lot lighter. But unless we can get the weapons operational, I don't…" He stopped as both of their communicators pinged simultaneously. They stared at each other. "Uh oh."

"Sir Charles, there is an urgent call for you from Dame Regina," said the person on the other end. "She insists on talking to you right away." He looked over at Frichette, who nodded.

"Me, too."

"Okay, let's see what she wants." Into the com he said, "Very well, we'll take it in my cabin in three minutes." They hurried back to the rather palatial cabin reserved for flag officers, which had been given to him, and activated the com-screen. Regina's face appeared immediately and he was alarmed by the expression on it. "Regina, what's…?"

"Charles! Petre! We've got a real emergency. The Clorindans are launching an all-out attack on Panmunaptra! We have to stop them!"

"What?! Are you sure?"

"Yes, I'm sure! Tad was just telling me!"

"Wait a second," said Frichette. "Those EMP weapons of theirs are detectable at a huge distance when they fire, even with standard merchant sensors. We haven't picked up a thing."

"The attack hasn't started yet," she sputtered. "But it's on its way! The Clorindans have diverted an asteroid to destroy the base. We have to get moving, dammit!"

"Good God," said Crawford.

"If it hasn't started, how do you know about it?" demanded Frichette. Regina snarled in exasperation and looked like she was about to explode.

"Regina, calm down!" said Crawford. "Tell us what's happening." Regina stopped and with a visible effort, she got herself under control.

"All right, all right. Tad and the other Seyotahs have gotten word that this attack is coming. They can't stop it themselves, but they have asked us for help. They've started evacuating Panmunaptra, but they can't possibly complete it in time—and anyway, it's their home!"

"You say they got word of this attack?" asked Frichette. "Word from whom?"

"Uh, well, as unlikely as it seems, it was from that Clorindan priest who stole Citrone away from us."

"What?" cried Crawford and Frichette in unison. "Why would he warn them?" added Frichette.

"I'm not entirely sure, except that he strongly opposes what the Clorindan leaders are doing and he wants the Seyotahs to save themselves if they can. But with our help, we can save the base! Charles! Petre! You've been there yourself and you know what they'll be losing!"

His thoughts went back to that wondrous place. The thought of the gardens and all the rest being reduced to dust made him feel sick. "Yes, yes, we must help. How much time do we have?"

"The Seyotah aren't sure, but probably less than a day."

"We could get there sooner than that if we pushed it," said Frichette. "We have two ships ready for action, but..."

"But what?" demanded Regina. "We must help them!"

"What if this is a trap, Regina? All we have to go on is hearsay—hearsay from someone who is nominally our enemy. We have no hard data at all. What if they are just trying to pull our combat-ready ships away so they can attack us here instead? That Clorindan priest must know from Citrone just how vulnerable we are."

"But what if this is for real?" persisted Regina. "We can't just ignore this!"

"No, but we're going to have to talk to the governor before we do anything."

"Shiffeld?" spat Regina. "He doesn't give a damn about the locals!"

He could care less if they're all killed—in fact he would probably welcome it!" She looked beseechingly at Crawford. "Charles, please, we have a duty to help them."

"Dame Regina, we also have a duty to our own people. We cannot just go haring off and leave them naked," said Frichette with a note of sternness in his voice that was not like him. "Now, I agree we should do something, but I'm going to bring Governor Shiffeld into this conversation before we make any spontaneous decisions we might regret." Regina frowned ferociously, but she did not protest further as Frichette connected with Shiffeld. There was an exasperating delay in actually getting through to him, but finally, the screen split and all four of them were in communications.

"Lord Frichette, Sir Charles, Dame Regina, is there a problem?"

"Yes, Governor, there is," said Frichette, taking the lead. He quickly outlined the situation and concluded: "My recommendation is that we send *Felicity* to deal with this situation and keep *New Umbria* here to watch over the rest of the fleet."

"One ship!" exclaimed Regina. "Surely we can send more than that!"

"*Felicity* is the best ship for the job, Dame Regina," said Frichette. "She has the most experienced crew and some of the replacement gear we've put in her has been hardened to resist the locals' EMP weapons. Now that we know what we are up against, we should be able to handle this attack. Any other ships we might send would not even be able to defend themselves, let alone protect the Seyotahs."

"I fully agree with your analysis, Lord Frichette," said Shiffeld. "And I agree that we must send aid. For us to abandon our trade partners could have the most serious consequences for our relations with all of these people. I'm authorizing you to proceed to their assistance at once."

"You are?" said Regina in surprise. Then she blushed. "Thank you, sir, I'm very grateful."

"I'm not entirely unreasonable all the time, Dame Regina. Especially when someone presents me with a well-reasoned argument." Regina muttered something under her breath, but nodded.

"Now, sir," said Frichette, "if you'll excuse me, I need to get moving."

"You intend to command in person?"

"Yes, sir, I have more experience with this sort of thing than anyone else—besides, it will be good for morale."

"Very well. Good luck."

"Thank you, sir." Frichette closed the connection with the governor and stepped away. "Well," he said to Crawford, "better get going."

"Just a minute! Don't think you're going alone!" cried Crawford.

"Damn right!" said Regina. "We are coming, too!"

* * * * *

Tad Farsvar sat nervously in an unused chair on the bridge of the Newcomer warship. He remembered the last time he had been here and how horrified he had been when this ship killed the Clorindan warriors. He was just as nervous now as then, maybe more, but his other feelings were entirely different. This time, he was looking forward to seeing this fine ship cut a swath through the damn Clorindans! He knew he should be ashamed of such thoughts, but could anyone really blame him? The Clorindans were coming to destroy the home of his people — his home! It was still almost unbelievable. The custom of non-lethal raids between the clans had evolved over the course of centuries and it had been used successfully for over a thousand years. Nothing like this had ever happened before. Of course, nothing like the initial slaughter of the Clorindan raiders had happened before, either, but that had been an accident, a misunderstanding. Anyone could see that!

Couldn't they?

Apparently not. Rumor had it that the Clorindan leader had lost both his sons, one in the initial battle and the other in the duel to avenge the death of the first. It would seem that the loss had driven the man mad. It was the only explanation Tad could see. But whatever the reason, the Clorindans had to be stopped! Panmunaptra had to be saved and if people had to die to save it, then so be it. He could scarcely believe how angry he was.

"How are you doing, Tad?" He jumped when Regina appeared beside him. The woman slowly and carefully lowered herself into another chair. The ship was decelerating at a, to him, rather incredible three-and-a-half Gs and the artificial gravity system could only nullify a little over half of that. They were all feeling very heavy. "You look worried."

"Yes, I guess I am, a bit."

"Were you able to contact your family?"

He shook his head. "No, things are too confused at Panmunaptra right now and I couldn't get through."

"I'm sure they are out of harm's way, Tad."

"I hope so, but our ship was undergoing a major refit. If it was still all in pieces in one of the repair bays, they might be stuck there. And my cousin, Dara, and her husband's baby is due to be released from the crèche any day now. If they can't move the crèche in time, they would never leave the baby."

"Well, with any luck it won't matter. We're nearly there and everything will be all right." Regina gave him a warm smile, but he could sense that she was nervous, too.

"Thank you, Regina, thank you for helping us."

"It's the least we could do. After all, we're friends, aren't we?" She reached over and squeezed his hand through the glove he was wearing to stay warm. He nodded and squeezed back. They both looked up and let go when Charles Crawford lumbered over to them. The increased gravity did not bother him at all. Commodore Frichette was right behind, although he was moving with far more care.

"Okay, we're almost there," said Crawford. "The attack hasn't materialized yet, so it looks like we are in time."

"Potentially in time," corrected Frichette. "We only have educated guesses on the likely approach vectors the enemy will take. If they come in from some unexpected direction, we might not be in a position to intercept. Mr. Farsvar, we are going to be very dependent on your own warriors to be our advanced scouts. We've made arrangements with your leaders for them to relay sensor information to us, but so far they haven't found anything."

Tad nodded. The news that the Newcomers would provide help had started a flurry of activity among his people. The evacuation was going ahead, but all of the warriors, instead of providing escort for the refugees, were all fanning out to try and find where the Clorindan attackers were coming from. If these scouts could provide enough warning then the enemy could be engaged far enough away to possibly save Panmunaptra. Communications links had been set up between the Newcomers and the commander of the Seyotah warriors. If anything was detected, the information would be sent straight through.

Tad was still a little surprised that he was here on the bridge. There were three older members of the official delegation aboard, but they had all opted to observe remotely from their quarters. So when Regina had invited him here, there had been no problem in accepting. He just hoped they wouldn't be asking him for any official decisions!

But for the next hour nothing happened and little was said to him. The warship finished its deceleration and the increased gravity dropped away as it came to a near-halt a few hundred kilometers from Panmunaptra. More time passed; Regina excused herself and Tad was seriously thinking about returning to his cabin. He was tired, and in spite of his heavy clothing, he was chilled to the bone and dearly wanted to take off his breathing helmet…

Suddenly there was commotion on the bridge and several people were talking at once:

"Sensor contact! One of those EMP discharges! Range about three million klicks, bearing oh-four-nine by oh-one-eight!"

"Incoming message, sir! From the Seyotah commander, he reports that contact has been made."

Frichette and Crawford consulted with their people for a short time before Frichette began issuing orders. Crawford came over to him, his face set in an expression of grim satisfaction.

"We've found them. Looks like it's show time."

* * * * *

Charles Crawford stood on the bridge of *P.N.S. Felicity* and watched every move Petre Frichette made. He was acutely aware that sometime in the coming weeks or months he was going to have to do the very same job aboard the battle cruiser *Indomitable.* With each passing hour he was more and more impressed with the young man. He may have looked about sixteen standards, but he spoke and acted with the confidence of a man three times that age. And Crawford was learning a lot.

On the one hand, the job was simpler than he had feared. Frichette only issued generalized orders: go there, do that, let me know what happens. The ship's captain, Frichette's former exec, Tymmon Chapman, did all the mechanical work of carrying out those orders. But on the other hand, while Chapman's tasks were technically more complicated, they were also routine and by-the-book. The orders Frichette gave took real thought and decision-making which could only be based on knowledge and experience. For instance, Frichette had just ordered Chapman to move the ship on a certain vector at a certain acceleration. The order itself was very simple, but how had he arrived at that decision? He had just stared at the main tactical display for a while, watching it update as information on the enemy forces was added and then he had issued his orders. *Felicity* was heading almost, but not quite, directly toward the enemy position, but at only a little over one gravity of acceleration. How had Frichette known to do that? Or did he really know? Was the young man just guessing and acting confident to cover up his uncertainty?

"The readings we are getting back from the Seyotah scouts indicate that this is the main enemy attack," said Frichette coming over to stand next to him. "They lost three scouts penetrating close enough to confirm that, but they were able to spot the asteroid and that's the main thing. It is definitely on a collision course with Panmunaptra."

"Is that the red diamond there on the screen?"

"Yes. We don't have it on our own sensors yet—it doesn't appear to have much metal content and they've painted or shrouded it in black somehow, so its albedo is almost nothing—but they can't alter its course now without missing the target. We won't lose track of it. It's closing at about eighty-five KPS, so we have almost ten hours before it hits Panmunaptra."

"What about enemy ships?"

"There is a screen about fifty thousand klicks out in front and then a second group closer to the asteroid. No real info on numbers or types yet, but the Seyotah tell us there could be as many as a thousand of those small attack ships like we encountered, and fifty or sixty of the larger carrier ships."

Crawford whistled. "Can we handle that many?"

"I'll let you know in a few hours."

"What about the Seyotah warriors?"

"You can see some of them on the display, the yellow dots. Their attack ships are almost impossible to spot beyond about ten thousand klicks, even when you know exactly where to look, so most of those positions are only approximate, based on data sent from the Seyotah commander. They have over two hundred attack ships, but over half are out patrolling in other directions and probably won't be able to get back here in time for the fight. The rest are forming up and heading out. The idea is for them to go in ahead of us and force the enemy to commit their forces and reveal their positions. We'll be right behind, ready to engage."

"A hundred of them against a thousand Clorindans? They'll be slaughtered, won't they?"

Frichette quirked an odd smile at him. "They'd be slaughtered if the enemy had anything to slaughter them with. We are assuming the enemy ships are still armed only with the EMP cannons. So, the Seyotah ships will get wrecked, but I'm told they have life support for a week or more. With any luck they'll get picked up by someone in time." Frichette's expression changed. "No, if there's any slaughtering to be done, we'll be the ones to do it."

"Hardly seems fair, does it?"

"Normally I'd agree with you, but considering what the Clorindans are trying to do here, I'm not feeling terribly sympathetic."

"No, that's true. Will we be able to stop that asteroid?"

"I'm hoping we can. It doesn't look all that large and a couple of concentrated torpedo salvos ought to be able to divert it. Just in case, though, I think you should get your toys moving."

Crawford looked to the two green icons on the tactical display. They were a pair of heavy-duty lifters he'd had fitted with extra fuel tanks. They were unmanned and could only do about one G, but he'd had them follow along under remote control and they were just catching up now. "Will we have time to make a rendezvous and push the asteroid aside?"

Frichette, shook his head. "No, the asteroid is already too close. If we'd had more time then maybe, but not now. If we need them at all, I'm afraid it will be a bit messy."

"The baron isn't going to like that, but he'll just have to bill the Protector."

"Yes."

"But you say the enemy is still ten hours away?"

"No, it's ten hours until the asteroid hits Panmunaptra. We will engage long before then. Say about two hours from now. I'll be sending the crew to battle stations in an hour or so. That will let them have a meal before we engage. You might want to do the same."

"Good idea. What about you?"

"Oh, I'll grab a sandwich here."

"See that you do, Commodore," said Crawford with a smile. "I'll be back in a while."

In fact, he was back in forty-five minutes. Regina and Tad were just arriving as he did. They all had their vac suits with them as regulations required. "If the Clorindans only use those pulse weapons I don't see what we need these for," said Regina. "After all, they don't have anything to knock a hole in us with."

"Things can happen in a battle, Dame Regina," said Frichette coming over to them. "Better safe than sorry."

"Right," said Crawford. "So, what's happening?"

"Nothing new, really. Both sides are massing their forces. The Seyotah spearhead should be making contact in less than an hour."

"And then we go in?" asked Regina. "That should come as quite a surprise for the Clorindans."

Frichette chuckled and shook his head. "I'm afraid not. They've known we were coming for the last twelve hours, at least."

"Really? How?"

"Our exhaust flare. Pushing this ship at three point five Gs produces a flare visible to the naked eye for a hundred million klicks. Big ships moving at high accelerations are very hard to miss."

"So they know we are here, but they are still coming on?"

"Yes. Either they can't change their course enough to disengage, or... or..."

"Or they're mad enough not to care," said Crawford. He looked from face to face and saw that no one liked what that implied.

"We might need these vac suits after all."

That put a stop to all conversation and Crawford and the others simply observed until fifteen minutes later Frichette said to Chapman: "I think it's about time, don't you?"

"Yes, sir. Mr. Kirby, sound general quarters. Clear the ship for action." An alarm began to sound and the crew went to work. The only thing to happen on the bridge was that everyone put on their vac suits, leaving the helmets off, and every loose object was locked away in cabinets. Crawford knew that throughout the rest of the ship, however, much more extensive activity was taking place to bring *Felicity* to full combat readiness. Weapons were manned and their capacitors charged, bulkheads were sealed, certain unused compartments had the air evacuated, medical teams and damage repair parties got out their gear and took their places. It was a painstaking process, but it was less than five minutes before all the lights on the status board were green. "All decks report ready, sir," said Chapman. "The ship is cleared for action."

"Very good. Please start running target tracks on the enemy ships we have data for."

"Yes, sir." Chapman began issuing orders and his crew got to work. Frichette walked over to where the observers were seated.

"Just for practice, and to keep them occupied," he explained. "They are still far out of range."

"Great," said Regina after he stepped away. "What's to keep us occupied?"

"Nervous?" Crawford cocked an eyebrow and smiled.

"Damn right I am. I just wish this was all over."

"Will we be able to stop them?" asked Tad Farsvar. Crawford studied the young man. He had far more at stake than any of them—beyond the fact of their lives being in danger, of course—but seemed to be holding up well.

"I think we can, Tad," he said. "But... but you do realize that we are going to be forced to destroy some of the Clorindans? We don't have any weapons which can just disable them. If we have to shoot, we will be shooting to kill."

"Yes, I understand. But the Clorindans have brought this on themselves. We have no choice, do we?"

"No, none that I can see. If we just tried to go after the asteroid and ignore the attack ships, they'd disable us before we could. Your people have been trying to contact the enemy for hours now to warn them off, but they haven't replied to any of the messages."

"Then they shall have to pay the price for their folly."

Conversation died while they watched the bridge crew go through their exercises. The minutes seemed to drag for ages, but the icons on the tactical display slowly drew closer and closer together. Finally, the cloud of yellow icons was very close to the leading group of red ones. The red ones had just been 'estimations' of the enemy positions based on the initial scouting reports, but now the small white icons which Crawford knew meant EMP discharges began to appear and slowly fade on the screen and the small red dots of estimated enemies became the slightly larger and brighter icons for confirmed ones.

"So, it begins," whispered Regina.

The Seyotah warriors, in a tight clump, merged with the bigger, but less densely packed, mass of the Clorindan vanguard. The EMP discharges flickered more and more rapidly on the display and then they were past each other.

"What do the little blinking lights inside the larger icons mean?" asked Regina.

"Distress beacons, I think," answered Crawford. "The attack ships which have been damaged can't maneuver anymore and have to be rescued. They are so difficult to pick up on sensors as it is, they need those to make sure they aren't stranded."

"Uh, it looks like a lot more of the Seyotahs are blinking than the Clorindans."

"Yes," said Frichette from his command chair, swiveling to face them for a moment. "They were outnumbered two-to-one, so it's not surprising. They lost about seventy-five and took out fifty of the Clorindans. Not too bad, actually."

"And the remaining twenty-five are still going on to attack the enemy main body?" asked Regina in amazement. "They're outnumbered thirty or forty to one!"

"Well, no disrespect to the Seyotahs, but it's not that hard to be brave when the enemy isn't using lethal weapons. That's why our combat troopers rarely use stunners—there's not near as much incentive for the enemy to run—or even keep his head down." He glanced back at the display. "But excuse me, it's time for us to do our part."

Felicity was nearing the maximum range for its main battery. The Seyotah sacrifice had accomplished one thing, anyway: most of the enemy vanguard had revealed itself during the exchange of fire. Their positions were noted and the ship's sensors focused on them.

"We have good locks, sir," said Chapman.

"Very well, commence firing."

Like during the first battle, there was no physical sensation to tell them that the lasers were firing, but almost immediately some of the icons denoting the enemy attack craft began to wink out. "Three hits," reported Chapman, and then a few moments later: "Two more, sir." Minute by minute the number of remaining enemy grew less. Ten, twenty-five, forty enemy ships were blasted out of space. But the range kept getting shorter and shorter.

"Uh, are we going to be able to handle these before they are all over us, Petre?" asked Crawford nervously.

"It's looking good. So far we've only been using long range fire with the main battery. But we're just about to open up with the secondaries in point-defense mode."

"We're picking up a few new targets, sir," said Chapman. "Some of them didn't fire on the first pass with the Seyotahs, but we're starting to pick them up now."

"Your active sensors are on maximum?"

"Yes, sir. We're probably taking ten years off the service life of the emitters, but we're putting out so much energy we can spot these suckers at a pretty good range."

"Good. Commence fire with your secondaries, Captain."

The destroyer's smaller weapons joined in and the rate of destruction increased noticeably. Sixty, eighty, a hundred Clorindan ships were blasted to wreckage. "About seventy left and it will still be another five minutes before their own weapons can fire back," said Frichette with a small sigh. "We should be in the clear, folks."

"Are you okay, Tad?" Regina asked the young native and Crawford dragged his attention away from the tactical display to look at him, too.

"I am fine, Regina. But... but it is hard to believe that people are dying out there. Watching it this way—just blips of light on a screen—is so... so impersonal."

"Yeah," growled Crawford, suddenly remembering a far, far more personal combat not so long ago. "Maybe that's why we find it so easy: we don't have to look our victim in the eye before we kill them." He twitched when Regina grabbed his hand and squeezed.

He glanced at her face for a moment, but then, reluctantly, turned back to the display. As Petre had promised, the added fire of the secondary batteries was chewing away the enemy far more rapidly. The secondary batteries were designed to take out incoming torpedoes, which were smaller, faster, and more agile targets than the Clorindan attack ships. After another two minutes, the last one winked out. There was a palpable lowering of the tension on the bridge as people who had been hunched over their controls leaned back and relaxed. The only things close to them now were the Clorindans who had been disabled during the first fight with the Seyotahs, and their respective momentums would whisk them by and away very shortly.

"Well," said Crawford, "looks like we..."

"Sir!" shouted one of the crewmen suddenly. "I'm reading power spikes on two of the disabled bogies!"

"Weapons! Target them immediately!" snapped Captain Chapman.

"What's happening?" cried Regina. An instant later the lights flickered slightly.

"We've been hit, sir," said another crewman. His was nearly lost in a rapid sequence of other voices:

"Target solution complete."

"Fire!"

"Targets destroyed, sir."

"Are there any more power readings?" demanded Frichette.

"No, sir, not right now."

"Well, look sharp! Captain Chapman be ready to fire if there's even a flicker."

"Yes, sir. Uh, that hit was from maximum range and doesn't appear to have done much. One sensor is burned out and a few minor systems are disabled. Damage control is on it."

"What happened?" asked Regina again.

"Looks like two of the Clorindans were playing possum. They weren't damaged at all in the initial encounter, but deployed their rescue beacons anyway in hope we wouldn't fire at them. Worked, too, damn them." Frichette looked shaken.

"What about the rest of them?" asked Crawford. "Their course will take them very close to my lifters. If there are more fakers they might be able to knock them out. Maybe..." he glanced at Tad and then swallowed. "Maybe we should blast the rest, too."

Frichette gritted his teeth for a moment at that suggestion but then shook his head. "I don't think we need to worry about that. If there were any more, they certainly would have taken the opportunity to fire at us. In any case, there are a few of the other

Seyotah attack ships beginning to gather from their patrol zones back there. They can provide an escort for your lifters. We don't need... we don't need to kill these people."

"But we may need to kill any disabled ships in the next wave, sir," said Chapman, indicating the tactical display. The surviving Seyotahs were about to hit the Clorindan main body. "We can't afford to take any chances."

"Right. Well, I doubt there will be many disabled ships to worry about this time." Crawford sucked on his teeth at the sight of the tiny handful of warriors about to collide with the huge red cloud of enemies. The flashes of the EMP cannons flickered for a moment and then it was over. All the rest of the Seyotahs had blinking distress beacons. Only a half-dozen of the Clorindans were so marked.

"Didn't do so well this time," said Chapman.

"No, and more importantly, not very many of the Clorindans had to fire. The bulk of them are still unverified contacts. This is not good."

"They'll be in extreme range in about eight minutes, sir."

"Yes. Well, I think it's time to expend our recon drones. Set them for maximum acceleration and maximum evasive action."

"Right away, sir."

"And set their course to collide with the asteroid. With any luck, the enemy will think they're some sort of weapon and go all-out to stop them."

"Yes, sir." Chapman turned to one of the crewmen and began issuing orders. A few moments later two tiny, but distinct, shudders ran through the ship as the drones were launched. Crawford saw that two new icons had appeared on the tactical display. They pulled ahead of *Felicity* quickly and streaked toward the enemy. Less than a minute later, EMP cannons started firing. More and more of them went off as the wildly gyrating drones evaded the fire, and each time one did, another enemy ship's location was pinpointed. At the same time, the drones' sensors were operating at full power, and as the range dropped they spotted even more targets.

There were an awful lot of them.

"Hell, looks like they brought everything they had," muttered Crawford.

The first drone vanished from the display as it neared the edge of the enemy formation, but the second corkscrewed its way right through and was not disabled until it was nearly past. The picture it had painted was not a pleasant one. A huge mass of enemy vessels was clustering together, directly in *Felicity's* path. Over seven hundred confirmed contacts and at least another hundred probables.

"Uh, sir, we still have time to veer off a bit," said Chapman, looking a bit pale. "We don't have to take them all, head-on."

"No good," said Frichette shaking his head. "We need to take out all of these or they'll stop the lifters from deflecting the asteroid—which is our primary mission, Captain."

"Yes, sir, but if they take out us, it won't make any difference about the lifters."

"True. But look how close together those contacts are. Practically elbow to elbow, as it were. I think we may have a way to pare down the odds a bit. Captain Chapman, standby on the torpedoes."

"Aye, sir! Ensign McDermott! Prepare for salvo fire on all tubes." Chapman looked back at Frichette. "I-I think we may need all of them, sir."

"Indeed, I think you are correct. Carry on."

"Prepare for rapid fire. Mr. McDermott, you may empty the magazines on this one."

"Yes, sir!" said the man at the torpedo station. "I'm targeting the greatest concentrations of enemy ships sir." He flipped a few more switches. "Ready, sir."

Chapman looked to Frichette, who nodded. "Torpedoes... *Fire!*"

The ship twitched again as four torpedoes were launched from her tubes. Ten seconds later another salvo was launched. And another, and another... Once clear of the ship, the torpedoes' drives ignited and they leapt away at one hundred gravities.

"What are we doing?" whispered Regina.

"Using our torpedoes to whittle them down, I think," replied Crawford, unable to take his eyes off the screen. The torpedoes were closing on the enemy rapidly—very rapidly.

"How many torpedoes do we have?"

"I think we carry about forty."

"But there are hundreds of the Clorindans! That's hardly going to make a dent in..."

The first torpedoes detonated.

The tactical display showed the explosions in a similar manner as the EMP cannons—except the icons were much bigger.

"Oh, God, they're carrying nukes, aren't they?" gasped Regina in sudden understanding.

"Yeah. Pretty big ones, too."

"Actually, nuclear explosions in space don't usually do all that much damage," said Frichette, his voice toned like he was lecturing students. "With no air to transmit any blast effects, you need to be within a kilometer or so to be hurt by the thermal radiation. Or at least a normal warship does; the Clorindan attack ships are much more lightly built. We… we can kill them at much greater distances. And they're making it easy for us, bunching up like that."

The torpedoes continued to flare on the display. And since each blast lasted for several seconds, the relative motions of the explosions and the targets meant that the kill zones were not simple spheres, but rather long tunnels of destruction, punching through the enemy formation. Dozens, hundreds, of Clorindan ships vanished from the display as they were hammered to junk by heat and radiation.

Even before the last torpedo detonated, *Felicity*'s main batteries were firing, adding their energies to those already flaying the enemy fleet. "Looks like the torps got about half of them, sir," reported Chapman.

"We didn't use torpedoes in the first battle," said Frichette. "They weren't expecting the nukes. Maintain fire, Captain."

"Aye, sir, maintaining fire." The main batteries continued to pick off enemy ships and a few minutes later the secondaries joined in, and the rate of slaughter increased. About four hundred ships had survived the torpedoes. This quickly became three hundred and then two. But they kept coming.

"Going to be close, sir," said Chapman.

"Concentrate your fire on the ones which will come nearest to us. They're the most dangerous. Save the others until last."

"Yes, sir."

The Clorindans continued to die and Crawford could see that a few of them, around the edges of the gutted formation, were trying to peel off, to get away from the ravenous monster bearing down on them. With their pitifully weak thrusters, they had no hope of escape, all they could do was postpone the inevitable. A handful of their stouter-hearted fellows survived long enough to get off a few shots at extreme range before they died, and *Felicity* lost a few more sensors and one of the secondary turrets. If that had happened earlier, it might have been disastrous, but by this time it made no difference. The last of the targets blinked off the screen and everyone let out their breath.

"We made it," gasped someone, Crawford wasn't sure who.

"So we did," said Frichette. "Well done. But we still have those support ships near the asteroid to deal with." He swiveled his chair to face Tad. "Mr. Farsvar, those larger ships are the carriers and service ships for the attack craft, correct?"

"Yes, sir."

"Are they armed?"

"Uh, they usually are," said Tad, looking rather uncomfortable. "At least Seyotah ones are. I'd guess these would be the same."

"Damn, I was afraid of that. Captain Chapman, please set up a track on those ships. You can open fire when we are in range."

"Do you have to?" asked Regina. "I mean, they must see how hopeless their position is. Can't you demand that they surrender or something?"

"I'd like to, Dame Regina, believe me that I really would. But physics is against us here. Our vector will carry us right on past them and before we could stop and turn around they would be on top of our two lifters. If they did surrender and then reneged on it, they could disable the lifters and we'd have no way of diverting the asteroid short of ramming it ourselves. Do you want to take a chance on Panmunaptra being destroyed?"

"N-no..." Frichette turned away before she could say anything else. Now it was Crawford's turn to squeeze Regina's hand. "I hate this," she hissed.

"I know, I know. But we haven't got any choice at all that I can see." They watched in silence as the last Clorindan ships were destroyed. He felt slightly sick, despite his relief. A few minutes later, Felicity flashed past the asteroid. The ship's lasers gouged out a few chunks as they went by, but Frichette shook his head.

"Sorry, Charles, but I think we'll need your lifters. With no torpedoes left, we won't be able to deflect it enough just with the lasers."

"Right." Crawford relayed the necessary commands through the ship's communications officer to put the two heavy machines on a collision course with the asteroid. It did not really matter what direction they hit from, any significant change of the rock's course or speed would prevent the destruction of Panmunaptra. Meanwhile, Chapman had reversed the ship's course, or to be more accurate, he had turned the ship around and its drive was working to null out its previous vector and get them headed back the way they had come. By the time that was done, the icons for the lifters had nearly merged with the asteroid.

"The baron's gonna have a fit," said Crawford. "Those things cost over fifty million apiece."

"A bargain at a hundred times the price, Charles," said Regina.

"Yeah, I know that, but he might not be so easy to convince." But then he laughed and shrugged. "So screw 'im. But see if you can tie into the lifter's forward cameras. We might be able to see something."

"Right, sir," said the communications tech. "Shouldn't be too hard to... there, on screen." One part of the display split off and showed an empty starfield. No, not quite empty, there was a gray speck in the center. "I'll increase the magnification, sir." The gray speck grew and grew until it nearly filled the screen. At his side, Regina gasped.

"God!"

Crawford told himself that it was just a trick of the light and random chance, but his primal instincts weren't listening. The ship's lasers had torn through the black fabric the Clorindans had wrapped around the asteroid and blasted off portions of the dark dust-covered surface to expose the white ice underneath. The result was a slowly spinning banshee-headed monster coming right at them. A ghastly lopsided face with a ragged mane of hair streaming out grinned at them from the screen.

And it was getting bigger—fast.

The relative velocity of the asteroid and lifter was well over a hundred kilometers per second, so the image grew rapidly. The tech backed off the magnification to keep it a steady size on the screen. After a minute, the rotation of the asteroid caused the hideous face-like appearance to disappear, but it was etched in Crawford's mind now and the menace of the object did not diminish one bit.

"Can we... can we stop that thing from destroying my home?" asked Tad. Crawford glanced at the boy and he could see that he was thoroughly shaken at the sight of the Clorindans' death-weapon. He mentally kicked himself for wanting it on visual.

"Yes we can, Tad. In fact we are going to stop it just about...now." The first lifter's icon merged with the asteroid's and the image on the screen vanished. "Direct hit," said the sensor operator. He studied his instruments. "That was probably enough, Sir Charles, if you want to abort the other..."

"Nah, let's make sure. Might as well get our—I mean the baron's—money's worth."

Without being asked, the communications tech had tied into the camera on the second lifter. This time the image wasn't nearly so threatening. The asteroid was now spinning rapidly, surrounded by a cloud of smaller fragments. The fabric covering was nowhere to be seen. It just looked like a hunk of ice now. The image grew and the icons got closer, and then they hit.

"Okay, that did it," said the sensor operator. "It's in about a dozen main pieces and none of them will come within a hundred klicks of Panmunaptra. Some of the smaller stuff might still hit, but it's too small to do any real damage." The man grinned. "We did it!"

That produced a cheer from the bridge crew and Regina hugged both Crawford and Tad. They were still congratulating themselves when a message came in from Panmunaptra. Crawford was not at all surprised to see the face of Vanit Gorin, the Seyotah clan leader, appear on the screen.

"Thank you, my friends," he said. "We owe you more than I can possibly calculate. Thank you."

"Glad we could help out, sir," said Frichette. "There are quite a few disabled attack ships floating around out there. Will you be able to pick them up?"

"Ships are already on their way. But I'm hoping that you will return to Panmunaptra so that we can properly show our thanks."

"No choice, sir. Our tanks are nearly dry. Can you provide us with reaction mass?"

"Anything we have is yours. All of our people are waiting to welcome you."

"Excellent! We should make rendezvous in about four hours. I will talk to you again then." The connection was broken and Frichette got out of his chair and stretched. "Well done, everyone. Captain Chapman, my compliments to you and please pass them on to your crew."

"Thank you, sir, and I'll certainly do that. Mr. Kirby, stand the ship down from general quarters."

People began to talk quietly and take off their vac suits. Crawford did the same and had the enjoyable experience of helping Regina out of hers. Damn she was a good looking woman! "I'll treat you to a coffee," he offered.

"After this I want something stronger than coffee! I need a good stiff drink! Several of them, in fact."

"Hmmm, I'll see what I can…"

"Captain!" A sudden exclamation from the communications tech froze everyone in place.

"What is it Mr. Kirby?" said Chapman.

"Uh, I'm picking up a broadcast in the clear. It's using our frequencies. Pretty faint and it's…You better hear this yourself, sir."

"Put it on the speaker." Kirby flipped a switch and a voice came over the speakers. It sounded vaguely familiar to Crawford and then he suddenly felt his stomach drop when he heard the speaker's name.

…I repeat, this is Carlina Citrone, welcoming my bothers and sisters of the Venanci squadron. Where the roots are deep, the seed is strong. I regret that I cannot welcome you in person, but my capture is imminent. However, you must know that I have completed the majority of my mission. The crews of the Anderan warships are all dead. Do not be deceived by any show of strength you might see! The crews, the officers, and the captains of those vessels are all dead! The crews manning them now are all civilians and they will not have the access codes to operate those ships. They cannot beat you! Go my friends! Go to victory! Death to the Protector!

The message started over again, but Kirby cut it off. Frichette came over to Crawford. "The drone Citrone dispatched."

"Yes, I'd almost forgotten about it. But she didn't know for sure when the Venanci squadron was coming. We must still have a few weeks to prepare."

Frichette frowned. "Perhaps. But right now I'm more concerned with what the locals will make of this."

Chapter Nineteen

"**W**ell, they certainly know how to throw a party!"

Charles Crawford smiled as Regina spun around with her arms wide, taking in the whole wonderful canyon-park inside the asteroid of Panmunaptra. Despite all the other people, the flowers, the music, and the enthusiastic celebrations going on, his eyes were on Regina. She was wearing the most daring costume he'd yet seen her in: a halter top and a sarong-like skirt split all the way to her hip. He'd been trying to figure out for an hour if she had anything on underneath it. While he had to admit that her clothes were entirely appropriate to the heat, they were also stirring things in him which had not been stirred for a long time. He plucked at the fabric of his shirt, which sweat had plastered to his torso, and shifted in his chair.

"Yes, they do. And I must say you certainly know how to enjoy a party, Regina." She had been drinking and eating and dancing for hours. He wasn't sure where she found the energy. As he spoke, a slight wave of dizziness passed over him. Cursing silently he forced himself to inhale through his nose and exhale through his mouth. The Seyotah had provided tiny respirators which only covered their noses, so they could eat and drink without the bother of a full bubble helmet. But that still meant they had to remember to breathe the right way! At least the heat wasn't as bad as the first time they had been here. Their hosts had lowered the overall temperature as far as they dared and then set up cooling units in a number of areas to blow cold air on their guests.

"Seize the moment, Charles! God knows when we'll have another chance to have any fun." She spun over to him, put her hands on his broad shoulders, puckered her lips, leaned forward, and... clacked her respirator into his.

"Ow!" they both exclaimed simultaneously. Then they laughed.

"Seize it, but seize it carefully."

"Yes, let's try that again." She sat down on his broad lap and put her hands behind his head and slowly leaned forward, tilting her head so their respirators did not collide, and carefully kissed him on the lips.

"Mmm, that's better," he said when it ended. "But I'm not heading out into mortal combat this time, what was that for?"

"To celebrate, of course. And just because I wanted to. And because I like you, Charles Crawford." She kissed him again and this one lasted longer than the first. He tentatively put a hand on her bare ribs. He remembered thinking months earlier that Regina's face looked a bit odd from certain angles. He decided that from this angle, her face, and all the rest of her, looked just fine. They sat that way for quite a while, alternately kissing and sipping drinks and eating dainties which were provided by an attentive crew of smiling, but more warmly dressed, Seyotahs. Tad Farsvar came by with his cousins and proudly showed off the new baby. Crawford had never had much interest in babies, but it was incredibly cute. Regina never left his lap.

"You know," she said after the Farsvars moved on, "Tad was telling me about a very interesting part of the gardens here. It's like a maze with a lot of very private nooks and crannies. I think I want you to show them to me, Charles."

He felt slightly dizzy and he wasn't sure if it was because of how much he had drunk, or because of the totally intoxicating woman on his lap—or maybe he had just forgotten to breathe the right way again. Whatever, it seemed like a wonderful idea.

"Okay." He carefully set her on her feet and got up from his chair. "Think they'll mind their guests of honor slipping away?" He indicated the Seyotahs with a nod.

"They've been honoring us and praising us for two days, now. Besides, half the crew is probably already in the gardens."

"Oh? With who? Three-quarters of the ship's crew is male—not that I've inquired about their tastes."

"Well, I don't know for sure, of course, but I'm guessing that the Seyotahs aren't all that different from us," said Regina, giggling.

Crawford's eyebrows shot up. "Oh. I must admit I hadn't given any thought to that sort of fraternization."

"Well, then think about this kind." She kissed him again as they wobbled down a set of stairs from the terrace they'd been on. "Besides, a lot of the Seyotah girls are very pretty."

"Not as pretty as the one I've got right here."

"Why thank you, Charles, I was starting to wonder if you'd even noticed."

"I've noticed," he pulled her a bit closer. The steps wandered down from terrace to terrace toward the main level the gardens were on. They passed many of the locals who all greeted them warmly. Just as they reached the bottom, a voice from behind called their names and they turned, still entwined. Crawford blinked and then detached himself slightly when he saw that it was Petre Frichette.

"Petre, what are you doing here?" said Regina in a slightly peeved voice. "And how can you stand this heat in that uniform?"

"Sorry to intrude, but we may have some trouble brewing."

"Nothing new," said Regina, swaying and leaning against him. "We've had trouble brewing from the moment we got here."

"What's up?" asked Crawford, not sure he really wanted to know.

"The locals have stopped celebrating long enough to listen to Citrone's message. They've asked us what it all means. In fact, all the clans are sending delegations here to discuss the recent battle and ask us for an explanation. Governor Shiffeld is dispatching Beatrice Innes here to take part, but I'd still like you two involved. It might get a little sticky."

"Yeah, it might…"

"When is this meeting?" demanded Regina.

"In two days, I'm guessing."

"Good. Plenty of time. Now go away, Petre."

Frichette frowned and then suddenly seemed to notice how close they were standing. His eyebrows shot up and then he smiled. "Oh. Sure. Talk to you later." He walked away blushing an interesting shade. Crawford pulled Regina closer again.

"Okay, where are these nooks and crannies?"

* * * * *

"I'm sorry, Brannon, I really am," said Carlina Citrone. "Did… did the Anderans kill all of your people?" She stood next to him at his desk and touched his shoulder, cursing the clumsy environmental suit which cut her off from him. It seemed as though she could feel his anguish inside her. With each passing day it was becoming apparent that the 'thought transfer' he had performed on them had had far more effect than either had anticipated. She felt a real sense of loss and hurt over the death of Herren Caspari, even though she had never met the man.

"Nearly all of the warriors," he whispered, looking up at her. "A few dozen were captured by the Seyotahs, but that was all. Oh, Life! Everything I touch turns to death! I had just wanted them to save the birthing crèche!"

"And they did, Brannon, they saved the babies. You had no way to know they would call on the Anderans for help or that they would slaughter your warriors the way they did. But you saved the babies! Cling to that thought!" He nodded but then bowed his head again over his clasped hands. Praying? Yes, probably. He was a devout man; Carlina could feel the depth of his faith.

She stepped back and let him be, unsure what else to say. For lack of anything else, she quietly looked around his office. She had been here several times in the days since she arrived, but that could not account for the sense of familiarity she felt. More of Brannon's memories? She went over to a set of shelves filled with small sculptures. A sense of happiness filled her when she realized that these were all gifts from grateful parents who Brannon had helped over the years. She picked up a delightful one of a baby, done in some hard, shiny stone. She'd noticed that sculpture seemed to be in the blood of these people. Their asteroid base was filled with statues and carvings, and nearly every square centimeter of rock had been decorated in some fashion. They took the harsh material of their unforgiving environment and turned it into something beautiful.

She sighed and put the carving back. She continued her tour until she came to a photograph of a woman. A flood of warmth, followed by a stab of pain, instantly revealed just who she was—who she had been. "Your wife," she whispered.

"What?" She turned and saw Brannon looking at her. She hadn't thought she'd spoken so loudly.

She stood aside and pointed. "This was your wife? How did she die?" Her borrowed memories were mostly feelings and impressions, rather than hard facts.

"Yes, my wife. Her name was Felitta." He paused and sighed. "She died a few standards ago of a genetic defect. They're common among my people. We were the last and the most complex of the Lifegiver's creations. Sometimes… sometimes I wonder if the Lifegiver was not quite finished with us before turning us loose."

"I'm sorry," said Carlina. "She was very beautiful. And to die so young…"

"Oh, that photo was taken a long time ago. Felitta was actually fifteen standards older than me when we wed. Our lives together were very rich, though not as long as either of us wished. You know, it's odd, but in some ways you remind me of her."

"And no children?"

"No. The defect in her would have made it very difficult and… and we had so much to do with our work here."

Carlina nodded. A lifetime of making children for others, but none for themselves. She shook herself. "So what happens now?"

"What? What do you mean?"

"This whole situation: the clans, the Anderans, the Venanci. Me. You."

"I don't know," he said with a long exhalation. "All of the other clans, even our traditional allies, have condemned the attack on Panmunaptra. And they've heard your broadcast. Delegates from all the clans are gathering at Panmunaptra to discuss what should be done."

"What do you think they will do?"

"I haven't the faintest idea—and at this point I hardly care. I'm through trying to meddle in things too big for me."

"No. No you are not, Brannon!"

He stared at her in confusion. "What are you talking about?"

"You must finish what you've started! The World Stealers are still coming and you must warn your people!" Even as she said the words, it seemed like someone else was using her mouth. What was she saying?

"But… but how?"

"Go to Panmunaptra! Tell them what you know!"

He shook his head. "Who would believe me? What proof do I have?"

"You have me! The Anderans will be there, won't they? Spreading their lies? I will come and tell them the truth!"

His expression turned from despair to worry. "That would be very dangerous, Carlina. A truce has been declared which would cover me, but not you. If we went there, you might be taken and turned back over to your enemies."

"I'm willing to take the risk."

"But I'm not. I… I care about what happens to you, Carlina." His words sent a thrill through her that made her gasp, briefly fogging her helmet.

"I will not stay behind, Brannon. If you go—and you will—I am going with you!"

"Life!" he muttered. "You do remind me of Felitta. There was no stopping her."

"Well, there's no stopping me, either."

"Wait, wait, there might be a way to do this. Do it safely, I mean."

"How?"

A tiny smile crossed his face. "You'll think me crazy, but hear me out…"

* * * * *

"Regina? Charles? We need to talk." Regina turned her head and saw that Petre Frichette was following them down the path in the gardens. They were in one of the other open gardens today, one of the ones they had not seen yet. A few days earlier she would have been irritated by the intrusion, but today she was feeling sufficiently mellow not to mind. She and Charles turned to face him, still holding hands.

"Yes, Petre?" she said with a dazzling smile. "What about?"

"The conference," he said patiently. "I could really use your help there—or at least your attendance."

"Why? I thought things were going pretty well," said Charles. "They've condemned the Clorindan attack, praised us for our assistance, and confirmed the trade agreement. What more do we need right now?"

"And we did sit in for the first six hours. About as much as I could take," added Regina. "Besides, you've got Beatrice to help you out."

"It's not as simple as that," insisted Frichette. "Citrone's broadcast has got a lot of them spooked. A minority right now, but they are gaining strength. They are worried that we are bringing our war into their system—which we are, I guess. And a Clorindan delegation is coming today."

"Here?"

"Yes, it's that same priest who was on Starsong—the same one who warned the Seyotahs of the attack—he's been granted immunity and he claims he has new information to present to the conference. Frankly, I'm a little worried about this. They could have whatever lies Citrone may have fed them. And while Beatrice is a help, her views are a bit... rigid. I'm going to need both of your help to defuse this."

"Okay," sighed Regina. "I was hoping to take a little nap this afternoon, but we'll be there. When?"

"About three hours from now. But there is something else, something more important I needed to talk to you about."

"What?"

Frichette glanced around, but they appeared to be alone. The great celebrations were over and most of the locals were back at their jobs. "I've just gotten the latest report from the fleet and it is not good. We've managed to get the point defense systems operating on my flagship and one of the cruisers, but that's all. None of the main weapons on any ships aside from *Felicity* and *New Umbria*, nor any of the torpedoes, except what are left on *New Umbria*. There's an outside chance we might get one or two of the ships fully operational if we have two or three more weeks, but I'm worried that we won't have the time. And it might not be enough even if we do."

"We knew this might happen," said Charles. "What else can we do?"

"If we try a conventional, stand-up fight with even a modest Venanci force, we are going to lose. I hate to have to be so blunt, but with our weapons on manual control, their maximum range will only be a few thousand kilometers and the enemy will just stand off and pound us to bits."

"You've explained all this before. So what do we do?"

"We've got to even the odds."

"How?"

Frichette pursed his lips and looked around again. "We need the help of the clans," he said softly, "to fight for us."

"What?" exclaimed Regina. "You can't be serious! They'd be slaughtered against a Venanci squadron! You saw what we did with one little ship!"

"Only because we knew they were there, Regina. Remember how only a handful of attack ships almost completely disabled Felicity when they took us by surprise? If there had been even a few more of them in that first strike, they would have won. With luck, we might be able to do the same thing to the Venanci. With their sensors and most of their computers disabled, we could fight them on even terms."

"I still don't like it. So many of them could be killed."

"A hell of a lot of us are going to be killed without their help, Regina. And then the Venanci are going to be in charge."

"Damn it! They don't fight wars of their own, it's not fair to involve them in ours!"

"They are involved," said Charles suddenly. "Like it or not, they are already involved. And while I don't like it either, I'm afraid Petre is right: we need their help."

"And it will be their decision, Regina, we can't force them to fight," said Frichette. "If you won't help Charles and I convince them, then at least don't work against us."

"All... all right." Regina hesitated, not quite sure what she'd do when the time came. If the locals decided to help on their own it would be one thing, but if Frichette made any extravagant promises that she knew wouldn't be kept, there could be trouble. "All right. Three hours, you say? Then I better get back to our quarters and change."

"Why?" asked Frichette. "You look fine as you are."

"Oh really?" said Regina. She grinned and stepped away from Charles and slowly turned around. The long gown she was wearing may have looked modest enough—until you really looked. The sheer material was designed to run through a random cycle from one hundred percent opacity down to about thirty—and she wasn't wearing anything underneath.

"Oh. Ah, yes, change by all means," stammered Frichette. "I'll meet you in the conference area later."

"Come on, Charles," she said. "Just time for a shower, too—and I need someone to scrub my back."

Six hours later, despite a really exceptional round of back-scrubbing, Regina's mellow had all but vanished. The conference was going on and on with no sign that anything was going to be resolved. Petre had made his plea for assistance against the Venanci and made it well, but the reception had been decidedly mixed. A few had been strongly in favor, a few had been even more strongly opposed, but the vast majority of the people were undecided. Confused and undecided, Regina suspected. This whole situation must have been very difficult for the locals to grasp. And without understanding the consequences, how could they be expected to make a decision? And the Clorindan delegation was late. It was clear that no one was going to decide anything until they heard what they had to say. But that didn't stop them from talking.

"Why don't they just shut up and adjourn until the Clorindans arrive?" whispered Charles from beside her. While she wholeheartedly agreed with the notion, all she could do was shake her head and give his hand a squeeze. He had very nice hands; large, strong, and skilled. She liked his hands, and all the rest of him, too. Even discounting the ten years in cold-sleep, it had been too long since she'd had a lover. She suspected that it had been much longer for Charles. He was older than her, but not that much older, and his high-gravity physique was actually very appealing once she got used to it. And after she got past several thick layers of psychic defenses, the Engineer, the Shy Man, he was interesting, witty, and fun. She liked him. The fact that his career area was totally different from hers was nice, too: no feelings of competition. They could just accept each other as they were. And if something didn't happen here in the next five minutes, she was going to drag him back to their quarters so they could accept each other some more...

"Uh oh, what's happening now?" said Charles suddenly. She looked to the entrance of the conference area and saw a small crowd gathering there. The man who had been droning on and on about something stopped talking and looked that way, too. No one said anything as the crowd opened up and two figures moved through toward the front of the room. Regina had become adept and recognizing the different clans, so she instantly saw that one was a Clorindan, and it was indeed the priest who had been on *Starsong*. "He's got a lot of gall to come here," muttered Charles.

"There's a truce in place, and he did try to stop the attack, so don't get any ideas, Hon." She patted his hand.

With the priest was a smaller figure, a woman clearly, but she had a hooded cloak over her breathing helmet and Regina could not see her face. The pair came to the speaking rostrum and paused.

"I am Brannon Gillard," said the man, "Archpriest of the Lifegiver and administrator of my clan's birthing crèche. I come here to make certain facts about the Newcomers known to you. And to present a plea to you. And this..." He paused and gestured to the woman at his side. She reached up and pulled back the hood, revealing her face.

"Citrone!" exclaimed Charles. Regina gasped and grabbed his arm. It was true, it was Carlina Citrone.

"This," said Gillard, "is Carlina — my wife."

* * * * *

Carlina stood as rigid as a statue and stared back at the throng of people staring at her. She spotted several of the Anderans, including her old nemesis, Charles Crawford, but she did not quail. They dared not raise a hand against her now. She was no longer just some despised saboteur, now she was a member of the Clorindan clan — her husband's clan.

Her husband.

She could still hardly believe it, but Brannon Gillard was her husband, and she was his wife. It was entirely legal and entirely binding, and almost entirely crazy. When he'd first suggested it, she'd told him he was crazy, but the more she thought about it, the more sense it made. As things stood, she was a fugitive with no one to defend her. But as a member of the Clorinda clan, she had rights and legal status. As a Clorindan, she could attend this conference with full diplomatic immunity. And the quickest and easiest way to become a Clorindan…

It wasn't even unprecedented, Brannon had explained that diplomatic marriages between members of different clans happened from time to time and were completely legal. It had only taken a few hours to fill out the forms, a few minutes in front of some local magistrate, and it had been done. Married. Naturally, they would divorce or have it annulled or whatever they did here once the crisis was past, but it would serve very well for the moment.

"Have that woman arrested at once!" shouted someone in the crowd. She saw that it was one of the Anderans, although she did not recognize the woman. "And the man, too! He helped her escape!" The clan members looked uneasy and whispered among themselves. Brannon did not budge.

"This assembly has declared a truce and granted immunity to my clan to attend," he said loudly. "I claim that immunity for myself and my wife, who is legally married to me under our laws."

"That's absurd!" snarled the woman. "She's not one of you! She's a mass murderer and we demand she be turned over to us!"

"Will the clans break their own laws at the word of these strangers?" demanded Brannon. The clan representatives went into a huddle, but it broke up almost immediately. One of them, she thought it was one of the Seyotahs, although she still had trouble telling the different clans apart, went over to the Anderans.

"I am sorry, but under the truce, neither of these persons can be touched," he said. "Your grievance can be heard at another time, but not now."

The woman tried to sputter out a protest, but the other Anderans, Crawford, a woman Carlina was sure she had seen before somewhere, and a man who also looked familiar, grabbed her and silenced her. After a moment, the Seyotah turned back to Brannon. In spite of his backing up the immunity claim, he did not look the least bit friendly. Not surprising, she supposed, considering recent events. "Very well, Brannon Gillard, you have asked to speak before the assembled clans. You are here. Speak."

Brannon's expression became a bit less confident, but he had rehearsed what he planned to say the whole voyage here. He took a deep breath and began. "My brothers and sisters, Children of the Lifegiver, I ask you: why are we here? I do not mean here at this conference, but rather here in the Refuge star system? We all know that our ancestors' ancestors, going back a hundred generations were born of Old Earth in the Orion Arm, five thousand light years from this spot. How did we come to be here, so far from our ancient home?" Looks of confusion met him. "Come, my friends, has it been so long since you attended church? Surely you told the story yourselves to your children. It is a story we all know, but seldom think about. Once we had whole worlds of our own. Worlds given to us by the Lifegiver which we were to nurture and help grow and make homes for our great-grandchildren. Worlds suited to our needs, worlds we could walk upon and whose air we could breathe.

"And yet now we are here. In a system where we and our children live their lives in metal cans or stony prisons. Even the one clan with a planet to live upon is shut up inside metal domes. We have lived in these conditions so long they seem normal, but they are not! This is not what the Lifegiver intended for us, so why are we here?" Brannon paused and drew himself up. Suddenly he pointed at the Anderans. "We are here because of them! Because of what their ancestors did! We are the Children of the Lifegiver, they are the children of the World Stealers!"

There was a moment of shocked silence, followed by an uproar among the delegates. All of them began talking and shouting. Some talked to each other, but many shouted things at Brannon. He stood there rigidly and let the shouts patter off him like rain. In spite of her growing familiarity with the local dialect, Carlina could follow very little of this, but she suspected that Brannon's accusations had the same force as calling one of her own people a cannibal or a child molester or a... a murderer. She flinched as that comparison materialized in her head. Eventually, quiet was restored and Brannon was permitted to continue.

"Yes, I was there aboard their vessel and heard their explanations. They claim to have had nothing to do with the World Stealers. The World Stealers were all destroyed long ago and they should not be condemned because of the actions of distant ancestors. Well, their actions speak louder than their words! They had only been here a few weeks before they slaughtered two dozen of my clan's warriors. Yes, they did not know our ways, but they have clearly shown us theirs—to kill!

"And killing begets killing. The loss of his sons and so many of his people drove the leader of my clan mad with hatred. I will not try to excuse his actions, in fact I come to beg forgiveness for what he attempted to do. But I ask you: has anything like this ever happened here before? No, of course not. And yet it has happened now. Why? The only answer is the Newcomers! *'Thou shalt know them by their violence'*, says the *Book of Life* and surely we know them! They bring their ways of violence and death to us from across the Rift. Already it threatens to corrupt us. And just a few minutes ago I learned that they have now asked you for help in their wars. Can you not see what is happening?

"My wife was once one of them and she can tell you of the society they come from: war and more war across the centuries. This 'Protectorate of Andera' the Newcomers claim to be part of was built on conquest. Hundreds of worlds which were once independent have been ruthlessly incorporated into an empire ruled by an iron dictator. In the last generation they completed the conquest of a cluster of stars on the edge of the Rift—and they've now used it as a springboard to cross the Rift and bring their empire and their violence here. To our home."

Carlina held back a smile when she saw the effect Brannon's words were having on the clan delegates. At first they had been totally against him, but now some were starting to consider just what they were being told. And if asked, she would be happy to confirm his claims about Andera. Of course, Andera was certainly not unique. In the long, painful process of hauling themselves up from the wreckage of the United Worlds, all of the present star-nations had followed a similar course. Venance's history was just as bloody, just as full of conquest as Andera's. No need to tell them that, of course...

"So they are here," continued Brannon. "They bring their wars and their violent ways to our doorstep. And they build their gate to link our system with one of theirs. What will happen when it is done? They beguile you with promises of trade and the dazzling prospect of visiting their side of the Rift. Don't believe them! Once they have what they need from you, once the gate is operational, their fleets and their merchants and their colonists will swarm through and overwhelm you. You gape in awe at the mighty starships they have come in, but these are only one small squadron of the armadas at their command. Once they are secure, their promises and treaties will matter no more than the promises made to our distant ancestors — before their worlds were stolen!"

"Then what would you have us do?" demanded one of the men. "The Newcomers tell us that their enemy, these Venanci, are fast approaching. They come here to hijack the gate they are building, aided by the woman and mass murderer you now call wife. Are you telling us to trust them, instead? It seems to me that the Newcomers came here to carry out a mighty endeavor by their own sweat and labor. These Venanci seek to steal the fruits of that labor for their own. You call the Newcomers evil, but surely they are the lesser evil of the two!"

Carlina gritted her teeth and cursed the man, whoever he was, for seeing through to the weakness of Brannon's argument so quickly — and exposing it so bluntly. For that was the crux of the matter: the Anderans came here for an honest purpose with no knowledge of the locals' existence, while the Venanci were coming with pre-planned murder and theft. Damn. But they had discussed this, too, on the way here. She watched as Brannon marshaled his counter-thrust.

"What should we do? We should defend our home! We should have no dealings with either evil, lesser or greater. Stop the trade with the Anderans, deny them the materials they need to build their accursed gate. Give them no aid. Let them fight their enemies when they come, and if they destroy each other, then give praise to the Lifegiver for our deliverance. And if one should triumph, then let us let the victor know that they are our enemies. Fight them! Harry them! Destroy the gate! If we are true, they will see the hopelessness of their situation and they will go back the way they came and leave us in peace."

An uneasy silence followed as the people pondered Brannon's words. But would they listen? Did Carlina even want them to listen? She wasn't quite sure anymore. Clearly it was vital to prevent the clans from actively aiding the Anderans against the relief squadron. The mere fact that they had asked for aid showed how desperate they were. Carlina wasn't sure if the clans' aid would really help that much, but she could not take that chance. At the very least, the slaughter of their warriors by the Venanci would make any future cooperation unlikely. So she had to keep them out of the coming fight. But assuming that was done and assuming the Venanci won the coming battle, what then? At that point, Brannon's plan for non-cooperation and guerrilla war would be catastrophic. But first things first: keep the clans neutral. Later, when things had calmed down, new plans could be made.

Or at least that's what one part of her wanted. Another part, a part which seemed to be growing stronger daily, wanted all of Brannon's plan to succeed. Drive out the Anderans and the Venanci alike. Leave these people alone. What was wrong with her?

The silence gave way to low murmurs and then louder talking. She saw the Anderans in animated discussion with several of the locals. The sound quickly grew to a dull roar punctuated by sharper outbursts. Finally, the Seyotahs shouted for order and eventually got it.

"You have given us a great deal to think about, Brannon Gillard of the Clorindans," said the man who had addressed him earlier. "I suggest that a recess is in order so that we may all weigh your words carefully." There were several dissenting voices, but the majority approved and the meeting slowly broke up. Carlina went to stand next to Brannon and took his hand.

"You did very well, my husband."

* * * * *

"Well, this is a fine kettle of swamp eels," snorted Charles Crawford. "Citrone somehow is *still* making trouble for us. I wish I'd let Greg slam her clear *through* that bulkhead!"

"It's not that bad," insisted Regina. "The clans haven't made up their minds yet."

"Bad enough," grumbled Frichette. "The only ones I think we can really count on are the Seyotahs and they hardly have any attack ships left. And if they all keep wasting time, it won't make any difference. We need to get their ships in position and make some plans."

"You can't expect them to make a decision this important instantly," said Regina.

"Well, they must make it soon!" said Beatrice Innes, walking up to join them outside the conference chamber. "They've had three days to make up their minds and we must push them to decide today."

"Or else what?" said Regina. "Like it or not, we're the supplicants here. We've got absolutely nothing to bargain with—and any threats would be totally counterproductive." She fixed her stare on Innes to make her point clear.

"Commodore Frichette has his warship only a few kilometers away," said Innes, ignoring Regina's implications.

"Don't even think about it, Beatrice," said Frichette sternly. "We cannot afford to start another war! We have more than enough already."

"Amen to that," growled Crawford.

"Well, here come the other delegates," said Regina, pointing. "We may as well get in there and see what we can do." They slowly merged with the locals and moved through the door. Regina greeted them all courteously and Crawford did his best to be friendly. The responses varied greatly, some smiled, others frowned, many just pretended not to hear. Inside they found their spot, a pile of cushions next to a low table with a bottle of water sitting on it. Crawford decided he liked this arrangement far better than a traditional conference room. He could shift and stretch and even doze off without appearing rude. Regina nudged him when Citrone and Gillard entered. They now had their own spot in the conference.

"I can't believe he actually agreed to marry her."

"It was just a political move, apparently, but it does make you wonder," said Regina quietly. "Look how close they stay to each other."

"Close is nice," said Crawford, reaching a hand around her waist. She put her hand on his. He glanced to the side and saw Innes's expression of annoyance. It was clear that Shiffeld's assistant strongly disapproved of their relationship, but Crawford truly didn't give a damn what anyone thought. For the first time in longer than he could remember, he was actually having fun, actually happy. Regina had ruthlessly smashed through or slipped around all of his habit-hardened defenses and forced him to be happy. He wasn't sure if he was in love with her, he guiltily thought of the strong affection he still had for Sheila, but Sheila had always respected his defenses and he now realized that wasn't what he really needed. And yes, he fully admitted that it was insane to be starting something like this under the circumstances, but perhaps he needed more insanity in his life. Whatever, he was going to seize the moment and the rest of the universe could go scratch.

He sat there watching the proceedings, and despite Regina's presence, he grew uneasy. Gillard's argument seemed to be gaining converts among the clans, especially from those who had not done so well with the trade agreements. Few seemed willing to agree to active hostilities against the Anderans or the Venanci, as Gillard wanted, but even fewer wanted to join the battle on the Anderans' side. Beatrice and Petre made impassioned arguments, but they seemed to make little impression. This was not good.

"Is there anything we can say?" he whispered to Regina.

"I can't think of a thing that hasn't already been said. We're asking them to take a big risk with only our promises of good intentions. In their place, I'm not sure I would believe us either."

Time wore on and things got worse. Beatrice made the mistake of pointing out that with the Seyotahs promising to help, the Venanci would automatically assume any of the locals were hostile, so that their hopes to stay neutral would founder. But instead of bringing the others around, it only made them apply pressure on the Seyotahs to remain neutral, too.

"Shall one clan put all of us in peril?" demanded Gillard. "We must put our greed aside and act in unity or we shall all suffer!"

"Hell, we're losing this," growled Crawford. Innes glared and Petre looked increasingly worried. The Seyotah leaders appeared on the verge of crumbling. "What are we going to do?"

"I don't know, I..."

The doors to the conference chamber slid open and every head turned to look at this interruption. Regina gasped and Crawford twitched in surprise when he saw Tad Farsvar standing at the head of a crowd of people. He, and most of the rest were carrying babies in their arms.

"What is the meaning of this?" exclaimed the chief moderator.

"We demand to be heard!" shouted Tad. Without waiting for permission, he marched forward, followed by the others. Crawford noted with interest that the Seyotah warriors standing guard outside made no move to stop them. Nearly a hundred people crowded into the chamber, dozens of babies, too, some crying, but most quiet. All the delegates were on their feet, most visibly angry at this breach of protocol.

"We have learned that the Newcomers have asked the clans to aid them," said Tad, his voice rising above the babble around him. "We have also heard that the opinions of most of the leaders is against granting them aid. Cowards! The Newcomers aided us when we called on them. They saved these babies from death!" He held up the child and the others did as well. Crawford thought that the baby Tad held was his cousin's, but he wasn't sure.

"The Archpriest Gillard has said that the Newcomers' actions speak louder than words. In this one thing he was right! When their friends were in need, when innocent lives were at risk, they acted! They saved our babies!" A shout went up from the intruders and now quite a few more babies were crying.

"We are in their debt and we will not forget that," cried Tad when the noise subsided a bit. "There are members of every Seyotah sept here and we come to pledge our aid to the Newcomers. No matter what you may decide here, when the enemy arrives there will be clan ships at the sides of our friends!" Another roar from Tad's group and cries of alarm from the delegates. The moderator gesticulated for order, his voice lost in the uproar. A number of the warriors had crowded into the room, but they were chanting with Tad's people rather than trying to stop them. More people had gathered outside the chamber, Crawford could see them thronged by the entrance.

The noise went on for a long time and there was a great deal of wild gesticulating among the delegates. The Seyotah delegates clustered around Tad, but the boy looked as unmoving as the stone of the asteroid. After a while, Vanit Gorin, the Seyotah clan chief, and his head warrior forced their way through to Tad and there was more talk. Finally, after nearly half an hour, the noise subsided, probably more from exhaustion than any other factor. Gorin demanded the floor and got it.

"The Seyotah will aid the Newcomers," he stated and this brought another cheer. "Honor demands it and we shall pay our debts to them. You others might owe no debt, but I ask you to join us. War is coming here as we have all heard. There is no stopping it or hiding from it. War is coming and I will face it at the side of proven friends!" More cries drowned out anything else Gorin might have said, but he had clearly said enough. After a long time, order was restored and most of the intruders ushered out, although Tad and a few others were allowed to stay.

The debate resumed, but the character had changed. Two other clans, stung perhaps by Tad's charge of cowardice, pledged their aid. Then another. After long communications delays while leaders were consulted, three more joined the coalition. Gillard argued and blustered, but he was visibly losing ground. Finally, after the meeting had gone on for nearly nine hours, agreements were finalized. Eight clans would provide warriors and the rest would remain strictly neutral. The Clorindans, despite Gillard's pleas, also agreed to remain neutral. The fact that they had virtually no warriors remaining left them little choice.

"Secrecy is vital to our success," said Petre Frichette, addressing the assembly. "If any word of our plans were leak to the Venanci, it will lead to disaster. All here must do their utmost to prevent any communications with the invader when they come." The assembly agreed to this at once.

"Surely there are two who cannot be trusted!" cried Beatrice Innes. She pointed to Gillard and Citrone. "They must be kept under confinement until this is all over!"

Gillard protested that he had been guaranteed safe passage, but the others saw the necessity. Still protesting, Gillard and Citrone were led away under guard. "Well, I'll sleep easier tonight," said Crawford.

"I think we all will," said Frichette.

"Just so long as we can sleep at all!" said Regina. "I'm exhausted." Fortunately, the meeting adjourned soon after. Regina led them over to where Tad was standing. "Thank you for the help, Tad. We would have

been sunk without you." Surprisingly the boy did not look happy.
"I did what had to be done, Regina. This war of yours horrifies me. But debts must be paid."

Chapter Twenty

"**W**elcome, gentlemen, ladies, please sit down," said Petre Frichette. "We have quite a bit to discuss, but for the sake of everyone's comfort, I'll try to be as brief as possible." Charles Crawford found a seat around the conference table and wished it was a pile of cushions like the locals used. His flag captain, Harold Speirs, took a seat next to him and shivered.

"I hope he makes it brief," he whispered, "it's freezing in here."

"Just trying to be polite to our allies," replied Crawford. But Speirs was right: it was cold. The 'average' temperature used by the clans did not really suit anyone, but Frichette had insisted they use it aboard his flagship when they had meetings like this. They'd used the same temperature during the conferences on Panmunaptra, but having Regina to snuggle up to had made it entirely tolerable. He wished she was here now, because he certainly wasn't going to snuggle up to Speirs! His flag captain was an elderly merchant skipper from one of the transports and while competent enough, he was definitely not the snuggling type—and he was old enough to be Regina's grandfather.

The conference room on *Agamemnon* wasn't quite as large as the one on Starsong, but almost. There weren't as many seats, but that was made up for by the additional display devices. The commanders of the eight clan contingents huddled together in a group at one end of the table, in a wide range of environmental gear, while the Anderan squadron commanders and flag captains took the other. Crawford noted with interest that three of the clan commanders were women. He supposed that with the women not actually bearing any children, there would be less practical reasons for the old role restrictions. He'd read that before the collapse of the UW, sexual stereotypes had all but vanished, but had returned full-force with the chaos that had followed. Andera was slowly doing away with them, but many still existed; all of the Anderans present were male.

"I want to thank you all for coming and also to welcome our friends among the clans," said Frichette. "We are grateful for the help you are giving us. But now we need to plan out just how we shall make use of your help and how we shall meet the coming attack." He activated a holographic display and a representation of the star system appeared above the table. The central star, the planets, and the more prominent asteroids were picked out. A cluster of icons showed the location of the Rift Fleet and the gate, out beyond the orbit of the system's single gas giant.

"Some time in the coming weeks, the Venanci squadron is going to arrive. They have no way of detecting where we are from in hyperspace, so their emergence point is going to be more or less random, although it will obviously be outside the gravity-well boundary and probably on the side of the system facing the Rift. If we are very unlucky, they could materialize right in our laps, but the odds against that are so enormous I think we can safely discount it. In all probability, they will arrive anywhere from one hundred to five hundred million kilometers away from us. We will detect their emergence, so we should have considerable warning." He pressed a button and a large volume of the display became shaded, showing the likely emergence areas.

"It is dangerous to make assumptions about the enemy's intentions, but I think we can make a few here. They will arrive expecting to find the fleet still in cold-sleep and themselves masters of this system. Instead, they will find us awake and expecting them, and a system full of unidentified contacts."

Crawford nodded his head at this. The locals were going to try and cut down on their radio broadcasts and be as inconspicuous as possible, but there was no hope of completely eliminating them. The Venanci were going to pick up a lot of strange contacts. They just had to hope they would not realize exactly what they meant.

"Unfortunately, the Venanci will also detect Citrone's broadcast. They will learn that she was partially successful in her sabotage and that the fleet is crippled. So, what will they do?" Frichette paused for a moment and sipped from a glass by his chair. The young man was doing remarkably well. Crawford also thought it was a shame they could not have tracked down and destroyed Citrone's message drone, but it was now so far away and moving so fast that any ship sent after it would not catch up for months—and could only catch up at all by using so much fuel it could never make it back.

"The enemy will have several options open to him, but there is one factor which will have an overriding impact on their plans: lack of reaction mass. When we arrived here, our own tanks were at less than ten percent capacity, it is very likely the enemy will be in the same situation. Once again, they are expecting to find us asleep and helpless. They do not expect to have to fight a battle. Had their plan gone perfectly, they would have had access to our own cracking and refining facilities, and reaction mass would not have been a major consideration. Now, however, it will be a major factor shaping their plans. While it is possible that they might elect to find ice balls and try cracking fuel with the limited facilities they might have aboard ship, I think this unlikely. Such a course of action could take months and they will realize that we will grow more ready with each passing day.

"Therefore, I believe they will attack at once. And with their very limited supply of reaction mass, once they start heading our way, they will be committed; they will not have the ability to break off and try again, nor make any fancy approach maneuvers. They will come straight at us.

"Which is extremely fortunate since our ability to maneuver will also be strictly limited. The clan strike ships have relatively low accelerations and limited endurance and must strike from ambush. Once we are satisfied as to the enemy's approach vector, we must deploy the strike ships into their path and wait for the enemy to come close enough to attack. If the enemy should choose some other vector after we are deployed, we will not be able to shift quickly enough to meet them. At least not without giving away our positions, and that would be disastrous."

The clan members shifted in their unfamiliar chairs and muttered among themselves. Detection would mean a slaughter even worse than what happened to the Clorindans. The eight clans had provided nearly four thousand strike ships and an alerted Venanci squadron could blast every one of them to dust.

"At the time the enemy emerges from hyper," continued Frichette, "our forces will all be collected here, near the fleet anchorage and the gate construction site. I am proposing that once the enemy's vector is established that we deploy the clan ships in their path approximately a hundred thousand kilometers out from here and then place the rest of our warships about thirty thousand kilometers behind them." He touched another button and the display zoomed into a much smaller region of space showing the construction site. A red line came in from the edge of the display, right to the icon marking the gate. A cloud of green dots appeared a good distance out along the red line and a cluster of blue icons about half as far.

"Excuse me, Lord Frichette," said Lu Karrigan's flag captain, interrupting. Oops, make that *Sir Louis's* flag captain. Crawford still had trouble accepting that his old colleagues, and himself, were peers. "Why so far out, sir? The enemy can't risk damaging the gate or the construction ships. If we stayed close, they would not dare use torpedoes for fear of collateral damage. And considering how thin we are on torpedo defense..."

"An excellent point, Captain, and I had originally thought to do it that way. But then it occurred to me that to do so was to assume that we are going to lose. We are *not* going to lose, sir! If we allow the enemy to get that close, what will they do once they realize they can't win?"

The captain nodded in understanding. "They'll deliberately try to destroy the gate."

"Exactly. If they were in among the construction ships and realized they were going to lose the battle, they would surely expend their last attacks to wreck our own efforts—and there would be nothing we could do to stop them. We have to defeat them at a safe distance." Crawford was impressed. Damn this kid was good! If the Protector didn't make him an admiral once this was over, he was an idiot.

"Even so, we will be leaving Sir Tosh's squadron and the clan support vessels back with the construction ships as a final defense. The rest of us, Sir Charles, Sir Louis, Sir Jinsup, and myself will take our squadrons out to meet the enemy." Crawford glanced over at Tosh Briggs. Initially the man had protested at being given the Rift Fleet's oldest or most badly crippled ships, until he'd learned he would not be in the forefront of battle. Crawford was just as glad not to have him along.

"Each squadron has at least one ship with operational point defense for torpedo protection, and three of the four have a ship with operational long-range weapons. Given the time, we may have more ships operational as well. But the primary one will be, of course, *Agamemnon*. We have three of the main turrets operational and that will give us weapons with a range to match anything the enemy is likely to have. I'm hoping that long-range fire from *Agamemnon* will induce the enemy to try and close with us, at least to ranges where the weapons on their lighter ships will be effective. If all goes well, that will draw them right into the clan strike ships." A cluster of red icons moved in along the red line on the display and into the swarm of green dots.

"Since we can't exactly predict the enemy's course, we will have to deploy the strike ships in a fairly broad arc, to make sure that at least some of them will have a chance to attack. I'm hoping that at least a few hundred will get good shots." He paused and looked very uncomfortably at the clan warriors. "Unless we are extremely lucky and completely disable all the enemy ships with the first attack, I'm afraid that those clan ships who do reveal themselves may take heavy casualties from return fire. But those beyond attack range should be safe if they do nothing to attract attention to themselves. Our forces will immediately accelerate to close the range and distract the enemy from you so you can withdraw safely."

There was a stir among the clan warriors and then one stood up; Crawford saw that it was Kar Regane of the Seyotahs. "My warriors will not withdraw, K'ser Frichette! Our debt to you is deep. We shall lie in wait as you suggest, for this is our way, but once the trap is sprung, any of my warriors who have not been able to attack will advance on the enemy. Not all of our ships are so slow and they may still get close enough to strike!" He glanced at the others. "Let those withdraw who wish to, but the Seyotah shall not!"

This produced an immediate outburst from the others. None wished to be outdone in a show of courage. Within a minute, every clan had pledged to press their attack to the utmost. Crawford could see that Petre was not happy about this turn of events. "My lords, I truly appreciate your offers and I am in awe of your bravery, but I am not sure this is a wise course. It could lead to very heavy casualties for little advantage..."

"You will close with the enemy and fight knife to knife," said one in defiance, "we are not afraid to do the same!" Several others voiced similar sentiments, and after a moment, Petre seemed to bow to the inevitable. To continue to argue would only damage the fragile alliance.

"Very well," he said. "We shall all close on the enemy together and destroy them." This produced a healthy cheer and Petre smiled and shook his head ever so slightly.

"All right, let's look at the details of our deployment..."

Three hours later, Crawford was thoroughly chilled and was grateful when the meeting broke up. His head was whirling with battle plans. He glanced at his flag captain and wondered if he was as overwhelmed as he was. But all the plans were on his computer and if he studied them for the rest of the day, perhaps he would have a better grasp...

"Back to the ship, sir?" asked Speirs.

"Yes, let's get..."

"Hey there sailor, got a minute?" said a sultry voice. Crawford stopped in surprise. Regina was there, leaning against the bulkhead and smiling. He glanced at Speirs and blushed.

"Uh, I'll meet you back at the ship, Captain."

"Right, sir," said Speirs with an infuriating grin. The older man walked away and Regina came up close.

"Hi."

"Hi."

She kissed him lightly on the lips. "So, plans all made?"

"For now. There will still be a lot of refinements—if we have the time. What brings you over here?" He idly wondered how she had managed to get aboard the flagship...

"You, of course. I just came to say good-bye."

He twitched and took her hand. "So soon? I knew you'd be going off to Bastet eventually, but right now?"

"Yes, things are getting to a critical stage where real decisions need to be made. And Ramsey's last message said that my presence was not imperative..."

"...which made it *absolutely* imperative that you go right now," quipped Crawford.

Regina laughed. "Yes. You're getting to know me pretty well, aren't you?"

"Starting to."

"Ramsey could not have said anything *more* likely to get me out there. So, I'll be leaving tomorrow."

"Tomorrow, huh?"

"Yeah, but I guess you'll be studying this stuff all night, huh?" She pulled the computer pad from his grasp and held it up.

"Well... not *all* night..."

"Come on, if you're lucky I'll help you study." She slipped her arm around his waist and steered him toward the shuttle bay.

* * * * *

Brannon Gillard stared at the woman across from him. She was sitting cross-legged on a cushion and studying a reader, a water bottle forgotten at her side. She was wearing a simple set of coveralls. Except for her too-pink complexion, her too-yellow hair, and the oddly blue eyes, she might have been any young woman of the clan.

"What are you reading?" he asked.

She looked up, startled out of her concentration. "It's something on the history of your people."

"By Higgansen?"

She looked down and paged the reader back to the beginning and then nodded. "Yes, that's the name."

"He's the standard on the subject. A little dated now and not exactly unbiased, but still a classic. You are able to understand the writing?"

"Yes. Most of it. It takes some getting used to, but it's not that different from our own. That's not to say I understand all of what it's saying here. A lot of this is completely outside of anything I learned in school."

"Understandable. Our societies have been separated for so long."

"The year numbers on the dates don't even make sense to me. What does this suffix 'AD' stand for?"

Brannon laughed, being careful not to dislodge his respirator mask. "There's quite a bit of debate on that. Some argue that it stands for 'After Departure', referring to when the first starships left Old Earth. Others think it is after some other, more ancient, date of importance."

"What do you think?"

"It's not something I have any strong opinion on, but I suppose I'd support the latter argument. The numbers are too high to agree with how long Mankind has been out among the stars—assuming, of course that the length of a standard year hasn't changed. What is your calendar based on?"

Carlina looked uncomfortable. "It varies a bit from place to place, but most of them start with the date of the destruction of Earth during the Great Revolt."

Brannon shuddered. "I still find it hard to believe that Mankind's birthplace no longer exists. The planet was completely destroyed?"

"So the books say. Earth and all of the Core Worlds. There's still an uninhabited region two hundred parsecs across known as 'The Burned District'."

"So much death. So much hatred to do such a thing. Was this 'United Worlds' truly so evil?"

"Probably not," admitted Carlina with a shrug. "It's as much legend now as history. But the date of destruction is still a holiday and many families trace their line back to the original rebels with great pride." She paused and looked at him. "We are a violent people, Brannon. I'm truly sorry we have brought our violence to your home."

He sighed. "The events of the past weeks have shown that we are not, perhaps, so different from you. We managed to keep our violence under control through custom and ritual, but clearly the potential was always still there, just waiting for the spark to let it loose. It is not your fault, my wife." He jerked in alarm. He'd not meant to add that honorific, it had just popped out. Fortunately, Carlina seemed more amused than anything else.

"That still takes some getting used to. I... I, uh, presume that once this mess is over and once we are out of here—assuming we do get out of here—that we'll dissolve this partnership of convenience?"

Brannon glanced around at the quarters they had been confined to on Panmunaptra since the conference. They were very comfortable and his adjoining room, beyond the airlock, fully suited his needs. But it was still a prison. "I am certain we will be released once this battle is done. It was stretching the law to the breaking point just to confine us, I cannot imagine they would dare keep us prisoner once the need is past."

"I hope you are right. But you did not answer my question—husband."

"No, I didn't, did I? Well, naturally, if you wish to dissolve our marriage that is what we shall do. But..."

"But what?"

He hesitated, not sure how best to word the thoughts which had been growing in him for days. "It... it occurs to me that if the Venanci who are coming here are destroyed or forced to flee then you will be... isolated. If they are victorious, then I can understand that you will go with them. But if that choice is not open to you, what will you do then?"

"Die, probably."

"I would not wish for that."

"Well, me neither, but it seems a very likely outcome. The Anderans will not rest until they have me—one way or another."

"Alone and friendless you would have little hope, it is true. But in spite of my clan's recent disaster, I do have many friends and many who owe me favors among the other clans. They could give us refuge, or at least help hide us. It would be much easier to arrange that if you were still my wife."

"Once the Anderans are secure here, their influence will grow enormously. I doubt any refuge would remain safe for long against the pressure or bribes they could produce. Better you distance yourself from me, Brannon. You could survive this even if I don't."

The thought of her dead was like some sharp object wedged next to his heart. "Then we can flee this system. Starships do call here regularly. With word of the Newcomers spreading, more ships than ever will come. The Clorindans have other settlements in the Perseus Arm. We could travel far away, beyond the reach of your enemies."

She looked surprised. "You would do that? Leave your home and your people, everything you've made for yourself here, to save me? Why?"

"I'm not entirely sure. But I have spent much of my adult life bringing new people into the universe and I always make sure each new person has a place and a family. It is not good to be alone and surely few people have been as alone as you are. Your plight... makes my heart ache."

Carlina was silent for a long time, but her eyes never left him. "I've always been alone," she said, at last. "Ever since my family was killed. Other people saw to my needs, but they were never family. And they told me again and again that the others, the people on the street, the children in the schools, were not my friends. I was different and I must remain apart and stay secret and trust no one. Don't talk to people, don't laugh or play with them, for fear of giving yourself away. Oh yes, I've always been alone." She was talking faster and faster as if she'd open the stopper on a compressed gas canister and the contents were gushing out. Tears glistened in her eyes and one dripped down her cheek. "The people in the camps, the ones where I was trained—the students, I mean—they were almost friends. We had to endure the same things and we did not need to be secret with each other. But the camps only lasted for a month each year and the same people weren't there the next time. And then I had to go back and be alone again. When I was ordered to join the navy, it was even worse. I was surrounded by dangerous enemies and yet I could never get away from them. I think that was the worst..."

She trailed off and hung her head, as if ashamed of her confession, and wiped away the tears. "So I'm used to being alone," she said, suddenly jerking up her head and staring at him. "Don't let your soft-hearted pity lead you astray, Brannon Gillard. You've looked into my head with that damn machine of yours. You know what I am and what I've done. Trust me: I'm trouble and you should have nothing more to do with me."

"I have looked into your head," he answered slowly. "But I've looked into your heart, too, Carlina. Ruthless men trained you to commit a terrible act, and even though it was your hands which did the deed, it was their hands guiding your every action. I don't think that in your heart you are a murderer."

"So, you would absolve me of my sins, priest?" she cried, a note of anger and hysteria in her voice. "I don't think even your Lifegiver has strength enough for that!"

"The Lifegiver's strength can be found in each of us, Carlina. It is for you to find your own absolution from inside yourself. I cannot forgive you since you have done me no harm. But I am willing to stand by you and lend you what small strength I have. There is no need for you to face this alone. If you will have me, I am yours."

Carlina's lip was quivering and new tears dripped down her face. "It would be nice to not be alone," she whispered. He got up from his cushion and sat beside her. They looked at each other for a moment and then she buried her face against his chest. "I'll have you, I'll have you!" He put his arms around her and held her tight, rocking her like he would a baby. Her sobs did not go on long, but she clung to him for some time. Finally, she pulled away and smiled. "You are a good man, Brannon. Far better than an evil bitch like me could ever deserve."

"I'll thank you not to talk that way about my wife."

She laughed the first true laugh he'd heard from her, and it was nicely musical. "Uh, naturally," he said awkwardly, "in spite of being man and wife I'll not force myself on you physically—not that I could, you are a far more accomplished warrior than I."

She smiled and then frowned and then smiled again. The smile faded and she looked very thoughtful. "Is that…? Is that even possible?"

"With the proper precautions, I suppose it could be done. Some of my bodily fluids would be quite irritating to you, but with precautions… but, heh, I don't think we're quite at that stage yet…" He trailed off into an awkward mumble.

"Perhaps not," she said, but she was still looking very thoughtful as she snuggled up against him.

They were still sitting there like that when the door to the room suddenly slid open. The buzzer had not sounded and he was sure the door had been locked. They both shot to their feet and saw a half-dozen Seyotah warriors and two other men wearing Anderan uniforms.

"What's the meaning of this?" he demanded. "What are you doing here?"

"You are being relocated," said one of the warriors.

"To where?"

But they gave no answer as they seized them, clapped a respirator over Carlina's face, and hustled them out of the room.

* * * * *

"So, whadaya think, Hon? Kin ya do anything wid this iceball?" Regina stepped away from the sonic probe she had been studying and smiled at the speaker. This was Galgrin, her Frecendi guide. The man reminded her a bit of an aquatic mammal she'd seen pictures of in school. She couldn't remember the species or even what planet the creatures lived on, but Galgrin definitely looked like one. He was large, with thick layers of fat for insulation against the cold, and a huge rib cage for expanded lungs to deal with very thin atmospheres. His legs were of normal size, but looked tiny because of the larger torso. Regina was pretty sure her half-remembered mammal didn't have fur, but Galgrin certainly did. Most of it was concealed by his environmental suit, but his clear helmet revealed long braids of gray-white hair coming down from his head, and an enormous mustache which looked very much like the tusks the mammal had sported.

His modifications allowed him to exist in environments which were very cold and with not much air. But even the Frecendi could not survive in the place they were now. Regina, her guide, and several of her technicians were standing on a sheet of ice near the north pole of the fourth planet, 'Shangi-Lo', as the Frecendi called it. It was very cold here; Regina could feel it even though the heaters in her suit were going full-blast. And the air was too thin even for Frecendi lungs.

"I think so," she said in answer to Galgrin's question, gesturing to the probe. "At least some; the ice caps are thicker here than initial tests had indicated. That's a good thing. More ice — and a good bit of it is frozen carbon dioxide — will mean more water and more air when we melt it."

"So mebee we won't need these?" he asked, tapping his helmet. "Sure be niceta walka round without 'em. Least I think it would — never did it, ya know."

Regina pursed her lips. "Well, I don't know if that will ever be possible, Galgrin. Atmospheric pressure is only about three percent of standard and your people can tolerate about a minimum of ten percent. Melting the ice caps might bring it up to around five. There's some oxygen locked up in the rocks and soil too, and with some special bacteria we have we might be able to release some of that, but it would still only be another couple of percent. Maybe in some deep valleys the air might get thick enough, but it would be iffy."

"Howabout the cold? Damn chilly hereabouts."

"At the equator the temperature should go up five or six degrees on average."

Galgrin's mustaches seemed to droop. "Hardly worth all the work," he grumbled. Regina did not comment that her people would be the ones doing all the work.

"Well, the only other thing we can really do is try to tap the magma pockets, but we've already warned you about the problems with that."

"Yeah! Blowin' us all to bitsy-bits! Nothankya!"

"Actually, we have located two pockets which might be safely tapped, but your ruling council isn't convinced to let us try. If we could do those, we'd be looking at another percent or two to the air pressure and a couple of degrees of temperature. You might be able to walk around without a helmet then."

"Hmm, might be wortha shot. Thinkya will?"

"Not up to us, Galgrin. But I think we're done here. Time to get back to Hijanstan, if you don't mind."

"Don mind atall! Freezin' me buns off out here!"

The technicians had all the equipment packed into the shuttle now and Regina and Galgrin climbed aboard. She gave the go-ahead to the pilot and the small spacecraft's engines roared to life. A minute of medium thrust pushed them into a sub-orbital trajectory that would deposit them back at the city of Hijanstan in about thirty minutes. Galgrin quickly fell asleep and Regina spent the time looking at the planet rolling past. The ice cap was quickly left behind and the gray and dun plains and mountains stretched away to the sharply curved horizon. Regina sighed. Given a free hand and time she could make this planet bloom. The dust and hard rock could turn to green with blue lakes and rivers flowing. She'd done it elsewhere (or at least it would someday be like that—even with these methods the deed took time) and she could do it here.

But not without killing most of the planet's inhabitants. There were at least thirty sizable magma pockets which could be tapped, but nearly all of them were too close to the Frecendi domes. Between the shock waves from the nukes, the blasts from the suddenly released magma, and the inevitable earthquakes that would follow, scarcely a single dome would be left intact. And with over a million people here, relocating or evacuating just wasn't an option. Oh well. It irked her professional pride to only do half a job, but if she could make this place even a bit more friendly to the people here, she would have to be satisfied. There were other planets on this side of the Rift—a great many planets—which she could do a proper job on.

She pulled out her computer and began reviewing the current version of the Thermal Enhancement Plan. She supposed almost anyone other than a terraformer would call it the *bombardment* plan since it involved showering a planet with nearly a thousand very large thermonuclear devices, but her profession avoided that sort of terminology. She'd been over the plan a half-dozen times in the two weeks she'd been here, and she always found her thoughts wandering back to Charles Crawford. She missed him. And she was worried about him. Right now the fleet was making frantic preparations to meet the coming Venanci squadron, and when the fight came, Charles would be right in the thick of it. She wished she could be there beside him when it was time—better yet, she wished that *he* would be *here* with her when the time came!

A sudden thought struck and she nearly laughed out loud: suppose there were no Venanci coming? What if they'd set Citrone on her murderous mission and then had second thoughts and canceled the rest of the operation? Or what if there'd been technical problems that had forced them to call it off? Everyone here would be in a panic over nothing! The idea appealed to her very much, but, of course, there was no way to know for sure and they could only prepare for the worst.

The shuttle's descent engines activated with a muted roar that startled her out of her pleasant fantasy. They were coming in to land. Hijanstan was a cluster of connected habitation domes, a few were transparent, but most were opaque. She saw one dome which had collapsed; it looked to have happened a long time ago and never been rebuilt. In the short time she had spent dirtside, she'd gotten the impression things were not going too well for the Frecendi. Facilities seemed to be run down and technicians either poorly trained or poorly motivated. The place felt... shabby.

They landed on a pad of cracked and crumbling ceracrete and Regina went inside the dome for a few minutes to talk with the local officials and say good-bye to Galgrin. They asked her the same questions Galgrin had and she had to give them the same answers. "We'd hoped ya could do more, but anythin' atall would be welcome," said one of them.

"We'll do what we can, sir," said Regina. She shook hands with them and headed back to the shuttle. *They've lost hope, that's what the problem is.* The history she'd learned about the clans told her that the original colony ship had only brought about a thousand of each of the different types of Terraformers, and there was not a great deal of equipment to spare. When they'd arrived here, the Frecendi had chosen to colonize the planet instead of remaining in space with the others. So they'd been dumped here with enough equipment to build a few domes and not much else. The planet did not have much in the way of resources, so trade with the other clans had been limited. To a certain extent, Regina was impressed that the Frecendi had been able to grow as much as they had, although nearly all of their settlements were small mining communities scattered across the globe in search of what metal deposits there were. But it was clear to her that the growth had stopped a long time ago and the Frecendi were in a long, slow decline to extinction if something did not change.

It was a well-documented pattern, actually, which had happened many times before, back in the Orion Arm. Any society exclusively based in space or restricted to domes on a hostile planet had to devote so much of its resources to life-support, that real growth was extremely difficult. After a while, the growth stopped and the people became satisfied with just maintaining the status quo. And then after a while longer, they couldn't even do that anymore and the long retreat began. Most people who lived on hospitable worlds never appreciated just what a treasure free life support really was. The space-faring clans in this system were doing better, probably because there was enough out-system trade to maintain a spark of hope. But even they clearly weren't growing at any great rate. Their low numbers and lack of technical progress were proof. And the Frecendi were cut off from nearly all of whatever progress the others did make.

Perhaps I can change it. Do something to give them their hope back.

She studied the TEP all the way back to Bastet, looking for any trick she might have missed. It would only take the relocation of three very small mining outposts to give an adequate safety margin to tap those two magma pockets. *And if these other four could be evacuated, we could tap two more!* She was still excitedly working out alternate plans when the shuttle drifted into Bastet's docking bay. She walked through the ship's corridors to her office, nose nearly pressed to her computer tablet, oblivious to the people scurrying around her.

"Reggie! There you are!" She looked up with a start. Jeanine was standing there, looking peeved. "Where have you been? Your shuttle docked ten minutes ago!"

"Oh, just walking and thinking. I've got some new ideas for the TEP that I want to... what's wrong?" The look on Jeanine's face brought her up short.

"We just got word from the fleet. Long range sensors have picked up a dozen ships dropping out of hyper.

"They're here."

Chapter Twenty-one

Squadronlord Guilbert Dardas stared at the sensor display and frowned deeply. What it showed made no sense. Or rather, what it showed was completely at odds with what his briefings had led him to expect. If all had gone according to plan, there should have been some faint emissions from the Anderan super-ship, plus a homing beacon set up by the agent aboard. In that case, his orders called for him to rendezvous with the super-ship, debark the security troops, and turn the gate building operation over to Commissioner Hadronal. After that he merely had to provide back-up security to make sure the new serfs stayed in line. A two-year wait until the gate was completed and then a swift trip home to a hero's welcome by the Queen herself. His genetic code would be given priority and he, himself, could expect another set of enhancements.

In the event that the agent failed in its mission and the Anderans were fully awake and carrying out their tasks, then his orders were equally clear: deny everything. If the gate could not be seized — or destroyed beyond any hope of repair — then the squadron was to claim that it was merely an exploration expedition which had come, quite by chance, to this star system. It would be an absurd claim considering the millions of other likely stars on the edge of the Rift to which they might have gone, but in all probability the Anderans would be just as eager to avoid a war and the explanation would be accepted, if not believed. In that case, the squadron was to use its modest refining capacity to refuel and then come home again, the way it had come. Dardas did not like the prospect of spending yet another ten years in cold-sleep, but orders were orders and they would be obeyed.

Except none of his orders seemed to cover the current situation.

Sensors had quickly picked up a large cluster of contacts which must surely be the Anderans, about two hundred million kilometers away. The level of the readings clearly indicated activity and the expected beacon was missing, so Dardas's initial conclusion was that the agent's mission had failed. But in addition there were a great many other things — literally thousands of them — showing up on the sensors spread all over the star system. What did this mean? They were surely not all the Anderans; there were far too many and intercepted radio messages were in codes and languages totally unfamiliar. Was there someone else present here? It was a great puzzle, and Guilbert Dardas had never liked puzzles. Nearly an hour had passed since the squadron emerged from hyperspace and he had sat immobile, pondering in his command chair while his officers cast nervous glances at him. That in itself was annoying, but his flag bridge officers only had level two enhancements and required firm leadership in uncertain situations. He castigated himself for this passive show of weakness.

"What are your orders, Squadronlord?" said a voice at his elbow. It took every bit of control given him by his level three enhancements to keep from flinching. Purifier Kolstar had come up silently behind him, as he loved to do, and Dardas, deep in thought, had failed to notice. He very slowly rotated his chair to face the squadron's official conscience.

"It would appear that the agent has failed. I do not know what all of these other contacts are, but the Anderans clearly are not still in cold-sleep. That being the case, my orders seem… clear."

"Thus, after so much time and so much effort to reach here, we shall merely turn our tails and run for home?" The purifier's voice was pleasant, almost musical, but Dardas had heard him use that same voice when ordering some erring crewman to the re-education room—or the re-cycling vats.

"My orders come from the Queen herself, Purifier," said Dardas stiffly. "Only total success can justify a new war with Andera. If we could seize the gate, then we would do so. Such a coup would be worth the price of a war, especially since it would take the Anderans years to even real-ize what we had done. Failing that, if we could destroy the gate, then we should do that. It would be a hard blow against the Anderans and it would take at least ten more years before they found out about it. But unless ei-ther action has an absolute chance of success, I am ordered to make no attempt."

"Obedience is commendable, but boldness and initiative are some-times needed, as well, Squadronlord. Are you so sure that victory is impos-sible? Superior beings should be capable of superior efforts."

Dardas fought hard to keep the irritation out of his reply. He pulled a scented linen handkerchief out of the sleeve of his uniform coat and dabbed it under his nose for a moment. Kolstar's statement could be taken to mean the Venanci superiority over the Anderans, but he knew full-well that it really was a reminder that the purifier had level four en-hancements. And while Dardas fully belonged to the Queen, Kolstar was a creature of Minister Florat—who had power enough to disagree with the Queen at times. "That is certainly true," said Dardas carefully. "Man for man and ship for ship we are superior and were the odds even close to equal I would not hesitate to go ahead. But our information on the Ander-an forces is quite precise: two battleships, four battlecruisers, four heavy cruisers, five light cruisers, and thirteen destroyers. The Queen, in her per-fect wisdom, assigned only three battlecruisers, two heavy cruisers, and six destroyers, plus the two transports, to this mission. And considering that we have lost one of the destroyers…"

"Rather careless, that, losing a whole destroyer."

"I have a junior officer reviewing the sensor logs to discover what happened to Wichr," snapped Dardas. "But with ten years of records to re-view, it may take a while. I'll be sure you are informed as soon as anything is found, Purifier."

"Thank you, that's most kind."

"Yes. But as I was saying: the Anderans have us outgunned by a factor of four or better. Despite our superior personnel and equipment, we could not hope to win in a..."

"Lord! Great One!"

Dardas twisted his chair around, furious at this interruption. Who had dared...? A white-faced officer goggled at him. "I-I beg to report a signal, Lord! A signal for us!"

"What? Explain yourself."

"The signal is very faint, Lord, it appears to be coming from a great distance, but it is addressed to this squadron."

"Have you decoded it?"

"It is in the clear, Lord."

"Indeed? Play it."

"At once, Lord!" The man pressed a switch and voice came from the bridge speakers:

"*This is Carlina Citrone, welcoming my bothers and sisters of the Venanci squadron. Where the roots are deep, the seed is strong. I regret that I cannot welcome you in person, but my capture is imminent. However, you must know that I have completed the majority of my mission...*" The voice went on, outlining the specifics of her actions and then the message repeated. Dardas signaled to cut it off and then turned to face Kolstar.

"This changes the situation."

"So it would seem. Providing it is not a trick."

"The agent used the proper coded recognition phrase. I would judge the message to be genuine."

"They could have wrung that out of it after it was captured. Rather careless, that, allowing itself to be captured."

"Possible, but doubtful. Purifier, a moment ago you were urging me to attack against impossible odds, now you recommend caution when the odds shift in our favor. Which is it to be?"

For the first time, the purifier looked nonplussed, and Dardas suppressed a smile. "You are in command of the squadron," said Kolstar after a moment.

"So I am." He pressed a button on the arm of his chair. "Tech-chief Jubert."

"Yes, Lord," came the immediate reply.

"Come to my briefing room."

"At once, Lord."

Dardas stood up and his two servants sprang from their niches to attend him. The mechanical one snatched his sword from its holder beside the chair and deftly attached it to his belt. The biological one offered a cup of wine which he deigned to drink from. He turned and strode past Kolstar toward the hatch leading to the briefing room. The hatch slid open at his approach. Inside, he went and stood before his chair and the servant removed his sword and placed it in its holder. Both servants swept back the long tails of his uniform coat as he sat down and then retreated to their niches. A moment later the tech-chief entered through another hatch. He looked barely winded, although he had come from the engine room, over a hundred meters away. He bowed deeply and stood at the far end of the briefing table. Kolstar hovered off to the side, hands tucked into the voluminous sleeves of his robe.

"Be seated, Jubert."

"Thank you, Lord," said the man as he plunked into a chair.

"Attend." Dardas touched a control on his panel and the message from the agent played itself again. "What would you estimate to be the readiness of the Anderans, assuming this message is accurate?"

Jubert's face went blank. "Should I assume the Anderans will devote resources to gate construction?"

Dardas glanced at Kolstar. "If they captured the agent, they will know we are coming," said the purifier with a shrug. "Even if it did not survive capture, they will suspect that someone is coming."

"But they cannot risk missing their gate window. Assume fifty percent of their resources will be devoted to the gate, tech-chief."

"Yes, Lord." Jubert's eyes closed. The tech-chief also had third level enhancements, but of an entirely different type than Dardas. Half a minute passed and then his eyes opened. "Given these conditions, the Anderans will have a readiness level of between five and ten percent, Lord."

Kolstar smiled. "You gave the Anderans a four-to-one advantage, Squadronlord. Reduce their strength by ninety percent and suddenly the advantage is over two-to-one in our favor."

"Indeed." Dardas touched another button. "Communications, signal to squadron: prepare to attack."

* * * * *

Squadron Commander Charles Crawford watched the heavy cruiser *Shannin* dwindling in the rear-view monitor of his shuttle and then looked ahead to where his flagship, the battlecruiser *Indomitable*, was growing larger. "One more to go," he sighed, "but the biggest of the lot."

"I'm sure your personal inspection of the squadron is having a very positive effect, Sir Charles," said his flag lieutenant, Harvey Lindquist.

"Yeah, sure. At the least they can have a laugh at the sight of me in this get-up." He gestured to the uniform he was wearing.

"You look splendid, sir."

Crawford snorted. Governor Shiffeld and Petre Frichette had ordered that all officers in the Rift Fleet were to be properly uniformed. They claimed it was beneficial to the maintenance of discipline and proper respect. Much to his embarrassment and chagrin, they had produced a uniform tailored to fit his bulky, high-gravity dimensions. He'd been hoping he'd have an excuse to avoid this charade, but it was not to be. Hell, they'd not only produced a duty uniform, which wasn't that bad, but this ridiculous full-dress monstrosity he was wearing now. He wondered where they had gotten it. Nearly all the other new officers were wearing uniforms salvaged from the belongings of those killed by Citrone, but as far as he knew there were no high-gravity natives among the fleet's senior officers. And this was far too good a fit. They must have made it special...

"Harvey, just what exactly does a 'flag lieutenant' do — aside from butter up his commanding officer?"

"Uh, well, sir, I looked it up," said the young man. "In ancient times — really ancient times. I mean — the flag lieutenant was literally in charge of the signal flags a commander used to transmit orders. After they stopped using signal flags, they were in charge of whatever means of communications then in use. These days, with communications so easy and immediate, the flag lieutenants are used as aides, secretaries, assistants, or whatever the commander needs."

"Don't forget 'butter-upperers'."

"That, too, sir," nodded Lindquist with a grin.

He eyed Lindquist. Until recently, he'd been an officers' steward on one of the transports. Crawford wasn't sure how he'd been assigned to him, but he was proving useful, and he was certainly eager to please. Another thought struck him. "Harvey, what's the mood of the crews? You have a lot closer contact with them than I do. This inspection may be good for their morale, but with everyone all lined up in ranks with their swashes buckled and their spit polished, it doesn't give me any feel for what's really going on."

Lindquist took a moment before answering. "They're worried, sir. With the Venanci here and the battle in a day or two, it's all seeming very real now."

"Yeah, it sure is. Very real." It certainly was, and getting more real by the minute. The Venanci squadron had arrived, and after only a little over an hour, it had begun accelerating toward the fleet. They had spent one day burning at about one and a half gravities and then coasted — confirming Petre's assertions about their lack of reaction mass. Assuming they intended to slow to engage, they ought to begin their deceleration burn in the next few hours. Then another day and it would begin.

"But they have confidence, too, sir," continued Lindquist. "There aren't all that many of the Venanci and no capital ships at all, and we have the clans helping us and Lord Frichette really seems like he knows what he's doing."

"Unlike the rest of us?"

"I didn't mean that, sir. And it's not true anyway."

"A lot more true than anyone would like, Harvey. But there's nothing to do but make the best of what we've got." As he spoke, his shuttle approached *Indomitable* and turned to slide along its length for the exterior inspection. The battlecruiser was an elongated egg-shape about two-hundred meters long and seventy across at its widest point. Eight large half-globes studded the circumference near the widest point in two rings of four. These were the primary, thirty-four centimeter laser turrets; powerful weapons, but probably useless on manual control unless the clans were able to do their stuff against the Venanci. A dozen smaller turrets held the secondary weapons, each as powerful as *Felicity*'s main battery, and twenty smaller point-defense turrets were distributed all over the hull. At least the point-defense turrets worked. A hell of a lot of effort had gone into getting them ready, but they *were* ready and they, along with the ones on *Felicity*, would be providing the anti-torpedo defense for the whole squadron.

Crawford studied what he was seeing, comparing it with the drawings and diagrams of the ship, which he'd committed to memory. At least the engineer in him was good for something now—plans and specifications he could deal with. After a few days of study, he knew the layouts and theoretical capabilities of every ship in his squadron: the heavy cruiser *Shannin*, the light cruiser *Kensington*, three destroyers, *Avon*, *Lightning* and the good old *Felicity*, and his flagship. "Huh," he said, spotting something, "those sensor clusters, there, are shown as forward of 'C' turret on the drawings."

"Must have been modified at some point, sir," said Lindquist.

"You'd think they would have updated their drawings. How the hell do they do maintenance and repairs if they aren't where they're shown on the plans?"

"Uh, from what I observed on my old ship, the engineering types just know where everything is, sir. After spending years on a ship, they just know."

"Hmmph, I suppose they would. I'm used to building things, not maintaining them after they're built. But this doesn't make it any easier for new people trying to take over for them."

"They probably weren't expecting a situation like this, sir."

"No, I suppose not," said Crawford with a shrug. "All right, I've seen enough out here. Take us inside and let's finish this up."

"Yes, sir." Lindquist relayed the order to the shuttle pilot, and a few minutes later they were docked inside the boat bay. He grimaced as he stepped out and saw the party waiting for him. *I only left here three hours ago! You'd think I'd been gone for a year!* Captain Harold Speirs and at least thirty other officers and crew were waiting to 'pipe him aboard'. He'd gone through the same ordeal on the other ships of his squadron, but he'd assumed that he'd be able to avoid it when he came back. No such luck. The new marine detachment snapped to attention and managed to present arms without skewering anyone on their bayonets, the officers saluted, and one crewman made strange noises with a strange device. Captain Speirs welcomed him aboard and asked if he would like to inspect the ship. Crawford lied and said that it would be his pleasure and they started off, trailed by a gaggle of people.

For the next hour they walked up and down corridors, went up and down ladders and lifts, and generally saw a lot of people lined up at attention. As on the other ships, he recognized a large number of the people. A few weeks ago they had been part of his construction teams. Now they helped fill out the crews of the ships of his squadron. He nodded to them, spoke their names when he could remember them; made encouraging comments and patted shoulders when appropriate. They seemed to appreciate it, but Crawford could not shake a growing sense of dread. *These are my people, and if I do something dumb I could get them all killed!* Of course, that wasn't an entirely novel situation: any sort of construction project was dangerous, and if he did something dumb there it could get people killed, too. *But not in job lots!* There were nearly three thousand of his people on the various ships and if the battle went badly wrong, every one of them could be killed. *How do the professionals deal with this? Well, at least I don't have to worry about...*

"Good God, will you look at that fop, Sheila? Where in hell did you find enough gold braid to go all the way round him?"

"Wasn't easy, Greg, had to scavenge it from about six other uniforms. But it turned out pretty damn well, so watch out who you call a fop, big guy!"

Two people were standing to one side and their comments left the entire inspection party speechless for a moment, but unfortunately Captain Speirs found his voice an instant before Crawford did.

"Silence there!" roared a livid Speirs. "What are your names?"

"Now *him*, on the other hand, you can call a fop if you want," said Sheila MacIntyrre.

"Damned impertinence! I'll have you both arrested!"

"Oh cripes, you got 'im mad, Sheil, and he's got near as much gold braid on him as old Chuck, there," said Greg VanVean.

"Captain! Captain, please!" said Crawford, interposing himself. "These are some old friends of mine and they're just having a little fun with me. No offense was meant."

"Like hell," muttered VanVean.

Speirs got himself under control but was still frowning ferociously. "If you say so, Sir Charles, but I've noticed this appalling lack of discipline throughout the ship and it must stop!"

"Captain, these aren't regular navy people. They're not even regular merchant service. You can't expect them to have the same sort of discipline."

"I can expect them to show proper courtesy to their betters, damn it!"

"Did you hear that, Sheil?" growled VanVean. "He thinks he's better than us. Maybe he'd like to step outside and prove it."

"No air outside, Greg, I think you'd both lose."

"Shut up, you two!" hissed Crawford over his shoulder.

"Title's gone to his head," said VanVean sadly. "Look at him: drunk with power already."

"Captain," said Crawford, "if you wouldn't mind taking the inspection party on ahead, I'll have a word with these two and then catch up."

"Very well, sir, if you insist," said Speirs stiffly. He collected the others and moved off down the corridor. Crawford then swung around to confront his friends.

"Just what in the hell are you doing here?" he demanded.

"DC party," said Sheila brightly. "That's one of those navy acronyms for 'damage control' y'know."

"Yup," said Greg. "Any damage sneaks aboard this ship, it's our job to control it. I got traps placed by all the airlocks."

"I thought I left you in charge of the gate construction." He glared at Sheila.

"We started the main induction ring pour a week ago, as you well know, and there's damn little else we can do now with three-quarters of the crew dragooned off for this nonsense. We left things in good hands, Chuck." Sheila looked at him innocently and batted her eyelashes.

"Besides," added VanVean, "we weren't going to let you go off and have all the fun."

"Fun! We're headed into a battle, you maniacs!"

"Yes, we are," said Sheila, all the mischief leaving her face. "And if you think we are going to stay behind while you are getting shot at, you have another think coming, Mister Crawford!"

"Wouldn't be proper," agreed VanVean, nodding his head. "Anyway, someone needs to be around to keep you out of trouble."

Crawford's annoyance melted away and he found that he was deeply touched. He reached out two large hands and grasped his friends' shoulders. "All right. And thanks, you two. Thanks a lot."

"Aw, I think he actually means it," said VanVean.

"I do. And did I hear correctly? Are you responsible for this get—I mean my new uniform, Sheila?"

"Yes, you like it?"

"It… it's wonderful. Thanks."

"You're welcome. And be sure to wear it for your new lady-friend. Us girls just can't resist a man in uniform."

His mouth dropped open and a number of strange sounds came out as he turned red. "I... uh... I mean... that is..."

Shelia stepped forward and took his chin in her hand and pushed his mouth closed. "It's okay, Chuck. Really. I had my chances and just didn't grab them. I'm happy for you. But you let her know that if she doesn't treat you right, she'll have to answer to me."

Crawford stared at her for a moment and then wrapped his thick arms around her and hugged her tight. She hugged him back and they held each other for a few moments. Over her shoulder he noticed VanVean staring at them. "What? No snide comments, ya big lunk?"

"Hell no. I'm glad for you, too. Even gladder for me, though. Once she stopped mooning after you, Sheila actually started paying some attention to me."

Crawford held Sheila away from him and quirked an eyebrow. "Oh really?"

Sheila blushed. "Well, once you get past his coarse, crude, nasty exterior there's a coarse, crude, but actually kind of nice interior."

"You're kidding." Now VanVean was blushing a bit.

"No, I'm not. But you better be going, Sir Charles. Ol' Cap'n Ironbritches there looks to be getting annoyed." She motioned down the corridor to where Speirs and the rest of the party were waiting.

"Yeah, I guess I better. But you guys take care of yourselves, you hear? And try not to tick off the captain any more than you have to."

"No more than we have to, we promise," said VanVean.

They all nodded to each other and then Crawford turned and walked away. As he resumed the inspection he reflected that by comparison, the coming battle didn't seem nearly as complicated as it had a while earlier.

* * * * *

The Venanci are decelerating now and appear to be coming straight in. That's a real good thing for us. Just hope they don't have any tricks up their sleeves. We should be engaging in a couple of hour, so this will be my last message until it's over. I miss you, girl, but try not to worry about what's going on. I'll send another message when I can. Take care of yourself. Charles.

"Try not to worry!" snorted Regina Nassau as she shut off the com-terminal. "Yeah, fat chance!" She leaned back in her chair and tugged at her braid until it hurt. *Don't worry! Right. A Venanci squadron is bearing down to kill a man I'm falling in love with and turn the rest of us into virtual slaves if they win. Nothing to worry about!* She'd be worried enough even if Charles had been out of harm's way, but with him in the thick of things it was far worse. She wished she was there with him.

"Enough self-pity, damn it!" she snarled. "You've got a job to do."

In spite of everything else that was happening, the terraforming project was going ahead. The Frecendi ruling council had agreed to evacuate the three mining outposts, which would allow tapping two of the magma pockets, and they were considering her suggestions about the others. The TEP had been revised and checked and approved, both by the Frecendi and by Governor Shiffeld. They were to begin deployment of the nuclear devices into their orbits just six hours from now. That would take three days and then, even though the battle would have been fought and this whole operation might be under new management, the devices would be sent down to start the process. Regina felt that they were rushing things a bit, but on some visceral level she actually had to agree with Shiffeld's defiant statement that they would get something started that the Venanci could not stop even if they won.

She pulled out her computer and went over the TEP once again, but she found that she was too nervous to really concentrate. It was pointless anyway: the plan wasn't going to be changed now. She got up and wandered through her quarters, resisting the urge to go to the main control room. She'd be spending many, many hours there as it was and it wouldn't do any good to have her looking over peoples' shoulders any sooner than necessary. She was tempted to find Jeanine, just to have someone to talk to, but her assistant had been acting strangely of late. She was afraid it was the stories about her relationship with Charles that had been circulating. She wasn't sure how the young woman was taking that news.

Finally, she couldn't stand being cooped up any longer and left her quarters to prowl through the ship. She did glance in the main control room, but Ramsey was in there and he glared at her so darkly when he spotted her that she just kept going. She would have enough contact with him when things got rolling, and he had been even more irritable lately than she had. Her feet led her aft, past the labs and microbe storage. With the addition of the two magma pockets to the plan, the microbe wranglers were getting the sulfur-eaters ready to go, although the low temperatures were going to reduce their effectiveness. She exchanged a few words with the lab manager but then continued her tour. Further aft she came to a heavy door with a guard standing next to it. She had to show him her ID before he would let her past, and he seemed reluctant even then. He handed her a radiation exposure tag and let her through.

On the other side of the door was bomb storage. That wasn't its official designation, of course, but everyone—even her—called it that. It was a series of large compartments containing over two thousand thermo-nuclear devices—enough to devastate an entire planet if misused, which was the reason for the security. As she expected, there was a great deal of activity here and technicians were everywhere. All the bombs to be used in the TEP were being checked out and serviced. The bombs themselves, their re-entry vehicles, and guidance systems all had to be working perfectly.

She wandered through the compartments, chatting with the technicians. They all seemed excited and eager to proceed, but the bomb jockeys were all a little nuts anyway. The bomb servicing areas required special protective suits, so she stayed out of them, but she did take a look into the sections with the penetrator vehicles. These would be used for tapping the magma pockets. Each one was about ten meters long and a little over a meter thick. Their noses were sharply pointed, constructed of the hardest and most durable alloys that could be devised. About halfway down the length was the compartment for the actual bomb, and then the rest of vehicle was taken up by fuel tanks and a powerful thruster. After the de-orbit burn, the penetrators would come screaming down and then be boosted up to an impact velocity of about thirty kilometers per second. The special nose would punch through a couple of kilometers of rock before the nuke detonated. Hopefully this would excavate a crater four or five kilometers deep. Before the first explosion even subsided, another penetrator would flash through the fireball, punch another few kilometers, and then blow an even deeper crater. By carefully timing the impacts and throwing out a few flanking bombs to keep the crater from collapsing too soon, they could blast clear through to the magma pocket. The enormous pressure in the pocket would do the rest. Once the crust above it had been sufficiently fractured, the gas and molten rock would find its own way out.

The blast resulting from *that* would make the nukes look like firecrackers. She was very glad she would be observing from a high orbit.

They were planning to use twenty of the penetrators on each of the two magma pockets to be tapped, so she was somewhat surprised to see that the technicians had a regular assembly line servicing the vehicles. At least a hundred had their access panels off and it was evident that many more had either already been serviced or were waiting their turn. Regina searched out the chief technician.

"What's going on here, Jake?" she asked. "Looks like you are servicing all of the penetrators."

The man smiled and shrugged. "Doctor Ramsey's orders, ma'am. He said that these have all been sitting here for ten years and that we should service all of them."

"Which ones are going to be used for the upcoming operation?"

"Not sure. Doctor Ramsey said he'd be sending people to get the ones he wanted."

"Uh huh," she nodded abstractly. There was nothing really unusual in what Ramsey had ordered, but it did seem an odd allocation of their limited personnel, considering the circumstances. She'd have to ask him about it later. She finished her tour and headed back toward her quarters. On the way, she encountered Jeanine.

"Hey, kiddo, how's it going?" The younger woman seemed startled to see her.

"Uh, okay, Reggie. How are you?"

"Worried. Damn worried. What about you?"

"Worried."

"Yeah, I guess everyone is. But how is everything going from your end?"

"All the reports are green. We are good to go on schedule."

"Great. Well, I'm going to try and catch a nap. I have a feeling we'll all be pretty short on sleep for the next few days. You ought to try to get one, too. You look tired."

"I'm okay, Reggie, but I need to get this report to Doctor Ramsey. See you later." She turned and walked away. Regina looked after her for a moment, shrugged, and then headed for her quarters.

* * * * *

Tad Farsvar tried to remember what it had been like to just be a simple asteroid prospector. Had it only been three months ago that the Newcomers had dropped into his lap and changed everything? It seemed like years. And here, once again, he was sitting on the bridge of a powerful warship heading into battle. The other two times it had been a matter of chance, but this time he'd been specifically invited by Lord Frichette. He'd said that Tad was a good luck charm and he wanted him along. He had laughed and smiled as he said it, so Tad wasn't sure how serious he had been; but serious or not, here he was.

Agamemnon's bridge—flag bridge, rather—was five times as large as *Felicity*'s bridge, and the range of instrumentation and displays available was simply breathtaking. Tad had sat quietly for several hours just taking it all in. But his two previous battles—Life, he felt like some hardened warrior now—had allowed him to learn how the Newcomers' tactical displays worked and he was able to follow what was going on pretty well. And the displays were telling him that the battle was about to begin.

A wedge of red icons was slowly approaching a somewhat larger group of blue icons. In between the two groups was a vast cloud of green specks—the clan strike ships. The predicted vector of the Venanci squadron would take it right through the center of the cloud. There were only ten red icons instead of twelve, two of the Venanci ships had lagged far behind. Lord Frichette had said that they were probably troop transports. There were twenty-four blue icons and that was somewhat comforting—except nearly all of the blue ones were crippled to some degree.

"Range is down to sixty-eight thousand kilometers, My Lord," said Frichette's flag lieutenant, a man named Jones. "They seem to have completed their deceleration, closing velocity is now at eighteen point four kilometers per second. They're coming right at us."

"Yes, and thank God for that," replied Frichette. "I've been chewing my fingernails for the last five hours worrying they'd veer off and come at us from another angle."

"Yes, sir, but there's no way they can avoid the clan ships now. And they'll be in extreme range for our main battery in about ten minutes."

"Very well." Tad saw Lord Frichette take a deep breath, hold it, and then let it slowly out. "Mr. Jones, signal to fleet: 'Prepare to engage'."

"Yes, sir."

"And add a 'good luck' and..." Frichette paused. "And tell them that the Protector and Andera expects every man to do his duty."

"Yes, sir!"

Jones went to send the message and Frichette got up from his chair and took a turn around his bridge. As he came past where Tad was sitting, he smiled and nodded. "How are you doing, Tad?"

"I'm fine, sir. Well, kind of scared, actually. It is about to begin?"

"Yes, very shortly. And I'll tell you a secret: I'm pretty scared, too."

"You don't look it."

"No? Oh, good. I wasn't sure. All the manuals say that a commander has to look confident and fearless. Easier said than done! But I wanted to apologize to you."

"To me? For what?"

"For dragging you along. It didn't seem all that important at the time, but I'm realizing now that I may end up getting you killed. Sorry about that."

"I chose to come, sir. And a lot of my people are out there, too," said Tad, gesturing at the display. "I'm not taking any more risk than they are."

"I'm glad you feel that way. Well, good luck to you. At least I don't have to warn you to keep your helmet close by. Unlike our first two battles, we could definitely end up with a few holes knocked in us."

"Yes, sir, I'll be careful."

"Lord Frichette," called Lieutenant Jones, "we're getting some tight-beam communications from clan ships. They are asking permission to close in around the enemy's projected course more rapidly."

Frichette went back to his command chair and studied the display for a moment. The cloud of clan ships had started out nearly ten thousand kilometers across, but as the enemy's course became more and more certain, the cloud had slowly contracted in around the most likely point of intersection. It was less than three thousand kilometers across now and would be even more compact by the time the enemy came into range. Finally, Frichette shook his head. "No, too much risk that they would be spotted if they used their thrusters. We can't chance that now. We'll just have to hope enough of them get a shot when the time comes. Send the coded response to 'hold course'."

"Yes, sir."

The compartment fell silent except for one sensor operator giving periodic—and completely unnecessary—updates on the enemy's course and velocity. Every eye that wasn't already occupied was staring at the display and watching the red icons approaching the blue line that designated *Agamemnon*'s maximum rage. The minutes dragged by, but eventually the red touched the blue.

"We are in range, sir," said Lieutenant Jones.

"Very well, tell Captain Sowell that he may commence firing."

Chapter Twenty-two

Squadronlord Dardas clutched the arms of his command chair when his flagship, the battlecruiser *Prince Ardagan*, suddenly shuddered from the enemy laser's impact.

"Incoming fire!" exclaimed one of the sensor technicians. "The enemy battleship has fired on us."

"Damage?" demanded Dardas.

"Armor hit only, Lord. No penetration."

"It would appear that your tech-chief was in error," said Purifier Kolstar from beside his elbow.

"Not necessarily. If the enemy put all his efforts into getting just a few ships ready for action, they might have been able to accomplish this. And surely they would have concentrated on their capital ships. Sensors, are any other enemy vessels firing?"

"No, Lord, only the battleship, and that is at extreme range."

"Just letting us know they aren't completely toothless," smiled Dardas. The ship twitched again from another hit. "But then neither are we. Weapons, how long until we can return fire?"

"Eight minutes for the battlecruisers to reach effective range, Lord."

"The enemy will continue to pound us all that time?" demanded Kolstar. "Is there nothing you can do?"

"Do not worry, Purifier. Despite the jolt, these hits they are inflicting are still trifles. At this range, the laser beams have spread to the point that all they can do is chew off a few centimeters of armor where they hit. It would take them hours to do significant damage, and our own weapons will be in range soon enough."

"I see. So the battle will become an extended pounding match? Slowly eroding each others' armor?"

"A normal battle often amounts to exactly that if the commanders are cautious. As the range drops, however, the beams' spread decreases and the power increases correspondingly. After a while, the lasers can begin to punch right through the armor and inflict real damage. I would prefer not to have a protracted duel with the enemy battleship; it is far better suited to that sort of thing than our ships."

"So we will close with them?"

"Probably." Dardas said nothing more to see if he could draw Kolstar out. After a moment he succeeded.

"Probably, Squadronlord?"

"In a few minutes we will be in range for the battlecruisers to open fire, both ours and theirs," he said with secret satisfaction. "The enemy has four battlecruisers, and if my tech-chief is correct, theirs will not open fire. Or if they do, it will only be with a few weapons. In that case, yes, we will close with the enemy. We will close so that we can bring all of our ships' weapons to bear and finish these scum." He gritted out these last words through clenched teeth as the ship lurched again.

"And if your tech-chief is not correct?"

"Then we still have time to break off and avoid a close engagement with a superior enemy."

"And time enough to select a new tech-chief, I presume?" Dardas glanced at Kolstar and saw that the purifier was smiling a thin smile and fingering his ceremonial termination rod.

"No doubt that, too." Dardas shrugged. Kolstar undoubtedly knew that the tech-chief was a genetic-sibling of Dardas's, but if he thought there was any sentimental connection, he was mistaken.

The purifier said no more and Dardas went back to studying the enemy dispositions. Twenty-four of their ships had come out to meet them, while six, including their other battleship, had remained in the rear near the gate construction site. That fact alone nearly convinced him that the tech-chief's analysis was correct. Surely if the other battleship was operational it would have come out, too.

He wished that the enemy had come out a little farther to meet them. The battle was taking place uncomfortably close to the gate. That worried him; not just because of the danger that some errant torpedo might destroy the prize, but because the area seemed extremely crowded. Swarms of vessels, large and small, clustered around the construction site. Three days of analysis had concluded that the majority of those vessels—along with all of those other mysterious contacts—belonged to a previously unsuspected indigenous race. It seemed clear that they were some brand of humanity, too, although doubtless hopelessly inferior. Well, that was a mystery that could wait for later; he had a battle to fight.

But it was not just the ships that bothered him. The Anderans clearly had a major ore-processing operation going on to support the gate construction, and they had disposed of the dross by simply ejecting it into space—a sloppy and dangerous procedure. There were clouds of dust, pebbles, and larger rocks littering his path. The sensor displays were filled with tiny returns. The danger of collision had forced him to reduce his velocity below what he would have wished. He half-suspected that the enemy had done this deliberately and perhaps an approach from another direction would have avoided the hazard, but his dangerously low fuel tanks didn't allow that in any case. So, it was straight in.

"We are in effective range, Lord," said the weapons officer.

"Excellent. Communications, signal the battlecruisers to open fire. Concentrate on the battleship."

"At once, Lord!"

"You will not demand their surrender first?" asked Kolstar.

"No. Not immediately anyway. You have heard the messages they have been beaming at us for the last four days: haughty demands that we vacate the system. No offers to negotiate, not a trace of the proper humility. Such arrogance needs to be punished. We shall bleed them a bit and then listen to their cries for mercy."

"Very wise. I am impressed, Squadronlord."

"*Princess Kars* and *Archduke Schtorm* acknowledge, Lord," said the communications officer.

"All three battlecruisers are scoring on the battleship, Lord," added the weapons officer.

"Their armor is thick. We won't do much at this distance: knock off a few sensor clusters here, jam a turret there. We'll keep their damage control teams scrambling, but not much else until we close the range."

"There is no additional incoming fire, Lord," reported the sensor technician after a few moments. "Only the enemy battleship is firing."

"Excellent. I'm glad I won't need a new tech-chief, this one has served well." He looked at Kolstar who shrugged and smiled.

"Change in status," announced the sensor tech. "The enemy battleship has shifted its fire to the destroyer *Askold*."

"Cowardly scum!" snarled Dardas.

"Is this important?" asked Kolstar. "I would have thought you'd prefer to spare your flagship."

"We're built to take the damage," snapped Dardas. "A destroyer isn't. Even at this range, a battleship's main battery could turn a destroyer to scrap all too quickly."

"I see. They hope to do what damage they can before they are overwhelmed."

"Apparently. But I am not prepared to let them do it. It occurs to me that if the bulk of their ships are strictly on manual control, we can end this farce in a far quicker and easier manner."

"Oh? How?"

Dardas ignored the purifier and turned to one of his other officers. "Communications! Signal to squadron: 'pepare to launch torpedo salvo'."

* * * * *

"Oh crap," said Charles Crawford. "Are those what I think they are?"

"Yes, sir," said Lieutenant Lindquist. "The enemy is launching torpedoes."

A cluster of small red blips had broken away from the enemy force and was heading toward the fleet. The range was just under fifty thousand kilometers, and at the scale the main tactical display was set for, the torpedoes pulled away from the launching ships slowly, but began closing on their targets with increasing speed. Crawford had learned that the torpe-does possessed three separate engines; the first and largest could produce about a hundred Gs for two minutes and gave the weapon its initial boost. After that, a much less powerful engine would provide a couple of gravi-ties of acceleration on the trip to target. This was to allow modest evasive action to throw off any long-range fire from enemy vessels. When the tor-pedo had closed to point-defense range, about five thousand kilometers, the final approach engine would take over, delivering another hundred Gs until the torpedo reached the target and detonated. All of this meant that they had about eight minutes to wait for those red blips to arrive.

"Signal from flag," announced the communications tech. "Assume defense formation Delta."

"Acknowledge," said Crawford. He took a deep breath and then swallowed nervously. This would be his first real combat order. "Signal to squadron: execute Delta-two. Standby on point-defense." He tensed, but the ship didn't explode, and on the squadron status display he saw his command moving to obey the order he had just given. Wow. It worked. He relaxed slightly.

The fleet, and the squadrons that made up the fleet, realigned them-selves into a formation which would give the ships with working point-de-fense systems the best possible chance to protect those which did not.

"Seventy-two inbound, sir," said Lindquist. "They only launched a single salvo."

"Testing what we've got, I guess. Sure hope we've got enough."

"I'm sure we do, sir. *Indomitable* alone can handle over fifty torpe-does at a time. Uh, at least that's what it said in the manual."

"Right. Well, let's pray that our tech people got all the wires hooked up right."

"Yes, sir. And let's hope the clan ships hold their fire."

Crawford grunted agreement. There had been a major concern that if the Venanci used torpedoes this early that the clans, remembering what torpedoes had done to the Clorindans, might panic when they saw a salvo coming toward them and give the game away by firing their EMP cannons at them. He held his breath as the red dots passed through the cloud of green ones. No one fired. They were through the clan and coming on. The blips got closer and then closer yet. Crawford noticed that he was drum-ming his fingers nervously on the arm of his chair and forced himself to stop. He grasped the water bottle clipped to the chair and took a drink, trying to look as casual as he could.

"Targets are in range, point defense is engaging," announced the weapons officer.

Blips began winking out on the screen and in just a few seconds they were all gone. Crawford blinked in surprise and then snorted out a laugh. "Well, hell, that was easy!"

"Torpedoes are nearly useless against ships with intact defenses, sir," said Lindquist. "Or at least that's what it said in the tactical manuals."

"Yes, Lieutenant, I read those manuals, too, I'm just glad they were right. So, they can't hurt us with torpedoes right now. But the three enemy battlecruisers are all concentrating their fire on *Agamemnon*. How long can she last under that?"

"Quite a while, I would think, sir. A battleship is built to stand up under a long range pounding for hours."

"But unless the Venanci get closer, none of our other ships can do a damn thing."

"They are closing, sir."

"Yeah, but too damn slowly. And if they decide to veer off and not close, we are screwed."

* * * * *

"So, the enemy has some operational torpedo defenses," said Squadronlord Dardas. "Not unexpected, but irritating."

"The point-defense fire came from the battleship, two of the battlecruisers, a light cruiser, and one of the destroyers, Lord," reported the sensor tech.

"But those same two battlecruisers are not firing their main batteries?"

"No, Lord, only the battleship."

"The analysis of your tech-chief—and yourself, of course—seems to be accurate," said Kolstar. "So, we will continue this pounding match?"

"It is tempting. If we reduce speed and keep the range open, then eventually the combined fire of our battlecruisers will disable the enemy battleship and then we can stand off and smash the rest of them at our leisure. But that could take several more hours. Our current vector will bring us into range of the heavy cruisers in another twenty minutes and then the destroyers another ten minutes after that. The added fire of those ships would resolve things more quickly."

"Assuming none of the Anderan lighter ships have effective weapons."

"True."

"Lord, the destroyer *Askold* is reporting heavy damage to their armor," said the communications tech. "They request permission to drop out of formation and shelter themselves behind the larger ships."

"Blast. In another two hours our escort vessels could be gutted."

"A difficult tactical conundrum, is it not?" asked Kolstar. "We are fortunate to have one with your skills in command."

Dardas glared at the purifier but said nothing to him. "Signal to squadron: 'all ships hold formation and close with the enemy. Increase velocity on present heading by three KPS. Glory to the Queen!'."

* * * * *

Tad grabbed at his seat as the ship lurched again. The shaking was becoming more violent, it seemed to him. Or was it just his imagination? The ship had been under fire for over half an hour, although it felt like far longer. Lord Frichette and his officers were reacting very calmly as they carried out their duty, receiving reports and issuing orders. But Tad, with nothing to do, flinched each time the ship was struck. He'd been told that the battleship's thick armor was absorbing the punishment well, but he still kept expecting the bulkheads of the flag bridge to explode inward at each blow.

"Sir! The enemy is increasing speed! They're heading right at us!" The exclamation jerked Tad's attention back to the tactical display. New information had appeared next to the icons for the enemy ships. If he was reading it correctly, the Venanci were accelerating, adding to their current vector, closing the range faster...

...and heading right into the cloud of green specks which represented the clan strike ships.

"They've taken the bait, my Lord," said Lieutenant Jones excitedly. "Going after the destroyer to goad them in was a brilliant stroke, sir."

"Just something I read about somewhere," said Frichette distractedly. "Do we have a damage estimate on the ship?"

"Uh, still mostly armor impacts, sir. A half dozen sensor clusters are out, but DC is on them. Secondary turret six is jammed." Jones paused as the ship jerked again. "Lieutenant Himmens thinks we have another half-hour at this rate before we'll start taking serious damage—unless the range drops significantly."

"What about the Venanci destroyer?"

Jones turned to look at another display and it was a moment before he answered. "We are starting to read some debris and escaping air, My Lord. Looks like we're hurting them."

"Good, shift fire to another destroyer. Let's hurt someone else for a while."

"Yes, sir." Jones relayed the order. Meanwhile, Frichette touched some controls at his station and the main display zoomed in on the Venanci squadron. Their icons were only a very small distance from the edge of the clan formation. 'Small' on this display, of course, much farther in reality, but still very close relatively speaking.

"Just a few more minutes," muttered Frichette so quietly that Tad could barely hear. "It all depends on the clan ships holding their fire."

"And the Venanci not looking too closely at their sensor read-outs," said Jones. "Surely, they must be getting some returns from the closest strike ships. Look, they'll pass within a few dozen kilometers of the closest ones."

"Hopefully, they'll think they're just more of the junk we scattered out there. But if any of those people start to power up their weapons too soon, it will be a disaster."

Tad certainly wouldn't blame any of the warriors out there for going early. If he was out there, himself, he doubted he could force himself to sit there, helpless, watching the Venanci behemoths bearing down on him. It would take an incredible amount of nerve.

But the red icons neared the first of the green specks and nothing happened. This was the critical moment, just another minute and they would be right in the midst of them.

"Optimal firing position in thirty-five seconds, My Lord," said Jones. "We should be able to hit them with about..."

"Communications," snapped Frichette, interrupting Jones. "Give the execution signal: all clan ships in range may fire at will."

* * * * *

"*Askold* is reporting moderate damage, Lord, but they can maintain position. The enemy has shifted fire to *Kagoul*."

"Estimates of damage to the enemy battleship?"

"Still no air or significant debris reading on the scans, Lord. Their rate of fire is constant."

"That will change very shortly," said Dardas with satisfaction. "The cruisers will be in range soon and the battlecruiser's fire will become more effective."

"But it seems to me that we are going to get very close to the enemy in about a half hour, Squadronlord," said Kolstar. "Won't their weapons, even on manual control, be able to hurt us?"

"We will have to be within a few thousand kilometers for them to have any chance of hitting us, Purifier. And before we reach that range, we will have torn the heart out of these mongrels. I don't imagine I need to explain the inverse-square law to you, do I?"

Kolstar frowned. "Not the principle, no, but perhaps how it relates to our tactical situation."

"The laser beams from our weapons spread as they get farther from us," said Dardas, enjoying the opportunity to lecture Kolstar. "That is what restricts our range. We could easily hit the enemy at five or even ten times the ranges we do, but the beams will have spread so much that they will do no damage, merely heat up a section of the target's skin."

"I understand this," said Kolstar stiffly.

"Well, the principle works in reverse, too. The main battery of our battlecruisers can start to do real damage at a range of about fifty thousand kilometers. So, if we halve the range, we will increase the concentration of the beams by a factor of four. At twenty-five thousand kilometers, the beams will be able to punch through far more armor. Halve the range again and the beams are sixteen times as concentrated. So at twelve thousand five hundred kilometers, our weapons will be able to blast through the battleship's armor and savage their lighter ships. The process does not continue indefinitely, but once we are under ten thousand kilometers, the end will come very quickly—and the enemy still won't even be able to fire back. Sometime before then, however, I'll allow them to surrender…perhaps."

"I see. But will not their battleship, with its even larger weapons, do us some serious damage, too?"

"We will probably have a few minutes where it will be able to hurt us, but our massed fire will quickly overwhelm it and it will pose no more…" Dardas paused when he saw one of his techs staring at him, wide-eyed, nervous, obviously wanting to say something, but not daring to interrupt. The punishment he had meted out on the communications tech a few days ago had clearly made its point. "Yes? What is it?"

"Lord, we are detecting multiple energy sources. Very strong and very close by!"

"What? Put them on the display." The man swung his chair around to comply, and a moment later a swarm of yellow specks appeared on the tactical display. There were several hundred, at least, and they were all within five hundred kilometers. A few were only a dozen kilometers away! "What are they? Where did they come from? Why weren't they detected before?"

"I… I don't know, Lord! They just appeared! And the readings are getting stronger by the second!"

"A minefield of some sort…?" said Kolstar.

"No, they are too far away and too thinly scattered to do harm, even for a very large nuke," said Dardas distractedly. What were these things?

"Maker!" blasphemed the tech. "Lord the readings are…"

"Signal to squadron!" cried Dardas. "All point defense to en…!"

Before he could get the command out of his mouth, there were a dozen bright flashes of light from all over his command bridge and several loud cracks and bangs. The main display dissolved in a sizzle of static and the overhead lighting dimmed to half intensity. Shouts and cries came from all his people. An instant later, his senses told him that the drive had shut down and the artificial gravity was off.

"All stations report!" shouted Dardas into the bedlam.

* * * * *

"The clan ships are attacking, Sir Charles," said Lieutenant Lind-quist. "EMP cannons are firing... hell, a *lot* of EMP cannons are firing."

"But are they doing anything?" demanded Crawford.

"Uh, reports coming in now... two of the battlecruisers have stopped firing on *Agamemnon*... drive shut downs on five of the ships... active sensor emissions are way down...they're doing it, sir! They're doing it!"

"Thank God," gasped Crawford. The little white flecks, which indicated EMP bursts, were flickering all over the display as the clan ships fired their weapons. At the same time, the thousands of other green squares on the display were becoming green triangles—changing from ships drifting, to ships under power. The strike ships outside the fight were trying to close the range.

But after just a few moments, some of the green icons began to disappear.

"Well, they didn't take out all the Venanci," said Crawford grimly. "Damn, this could get ugly."

"Signal from Flag," announced the communications officer. "Execute Plan Gamma."

"Acknowledge," said Crawford. "Signal to squadron: 'execute Gamma-two'." He scarcely needed to think about this one, he'd been contemplating it for twenty minutes. A few seconds later, the acceleration alarm sounded and Crawford snapped at Lindquist: "Get in your couch, Lieutenant."

"Oh! Yes, sir!" The young man seemed to suddenly realize he was still standing next to Crawford's command chair instead of in his own. He quickly rectified the situation. Plan Gamma was intended to quickly close to engagement range to draw fire away from the clan strike ships. This would mean four minutes at maximum acceleration toward the Venanci and then eight minutes at maximum *deceleration* to avoid whipping past the enemy too fast to engage. At six gravities, even with the buffering effects of the artificial gravity system, it was going to be a rough twelve minutes for almost everyone except Crawford—and none too comfortable even for him.

"Hang on everyone, this is going to get a little rough."

* * * * *

"Any news?" asked Regina anxiously.

"Sorry, ma'am," said the com-tech. "Just that last word that the fleets have engaged. And with a twenty-minute com-lag, anything we get will be old news, anyway."

"I see. Thank you." Regina walked away, tapping her fingers nervously on her thighs. Damn this was frustrating! Three hundred and fifty million kilometers away a desperate battle was being fought. People she cared about were in mortal danger. One person she cared very much about was right in the thick of it.

And she was here, utterly unable to do a stinking thing.

If she'd had some work to do to distract her, it might not be so bad, but there wasn't really anything. *Bastet* was in the process of placing the bombardment 'devices' into their proper orbits. It was an exacting job, but one for pilots and astrogators, not her. And it would take nearly another fifty hours to complete. They could have done it a lot faster using the ship's six large cargo shuttles, but Doctor Ramsey had insisted that using the ship was safer and more accurate, and Regina had not fought him on the issue. So, as a result, she had nothing to do but fret and nag the communications people for news.

Well, that wasn't entirely true, she had paperwork to do. Quite a lot, actually. Jeanine had been bringing her basket-loads all day. She claimed that it was stuff that had piled up while she was away, but most of it was so routine — things Jeanine usually handled herself — that Regina suspected Jeanine was simply trying to keep her so busy she didn't have time to worry. Fat chance of that.

Jeanine had been so persistent in forcing paperwork on her that Regina had finally sent her off on some errand and then escaped — to go bug the communications people again. She was probably waiting impatiently back at the office right now — good reason not to go back there. But she had to go somewhere and she was so full of nervous energy, she didn't want to sit down. Another tour of the ship? Why not? She headed aft.

She wandered through the living quarters, stopped briefly to chat with some people in one of the recreation lounges, and then continued toward the rear of the ship. The main corridor passed between the two huge boat bays on either side of the ship and Regina was surprised to see the hatch leading to it closed and with a security man posted there. She walked up to him, but he did not open the door.

"I need to get through, please," she said politely. The man looked uneasy.

"Uh, the way is closed, ma'am. Authorized personnel only."

"Why?"

"Not sure, ma'am, just that those are my orders."

"Orders? Whose orders?"

"Uh, Lieutenant Hotchkiss, ma'am, he posted me here."

She started to ask who had given Hotchkiss his orders, but she realized the man wouldn't know that. She was tempted just to forget about it and take her walk elsewhere, but what was going on behind that door? "You can let me through, I have authorization."

"I... don't know, ma'am..."

"I'm Dame Regina Nassau, you know that. I outrank everyone on this ship except for the captain. Whatever orders you were given, I'm countermanding them. Now open the hatch and stand aside."

The man looked really uncomfortable, but Regina crowded him back against the bulkhead and eventually he relented. The hatch slid open and she went through. It took her about ten seconds to realize what was going on.

The shuttles were gone.

The central corridor had large gallery windows overlooking the two boat bays, and one glance told her that all six of the large cargo shuttles were missing. The smaller shuttles and personnel pods were still there, but the big ones weren't. However what was there instantly confirmed the suspicion which had taken shape inside her. Rows of stacked penetrator vehicles waited for the shuttles' return.

"Oh my God," hissed Regina. "I'm an idiot!" All the clues she had seen and ignored for the past weeks clicked into place and she knew what was happening.

But there was still time to stop this. She turned and...stopped.

The hatch she had just come through was now blocked by four security men. Just behind them was Doctor Ramsey, and behind him was Jeanine.

"Is there a problem, Dame Regina?" asked Ramsey with a slight smile.

"You know damn well there's a problem! You will recall the shuttles immediately! Any penetrators they've deployed beyond those called for in the TEP will be recovered and returned to the armory! Once that's done, you are relieved of any further involvement in this project."

"Oh, I don't think so. Here's what I think is going to happen: you are going to be confined and the TEP—my TEP—will be carried out. Just as the Protector directed."

Regina looked at Ramsey and then looked at the four security men. Unlike Shiffeld's newly recruited colonial police, these were professionals and she could see in their faces that they would carry out Ramsey's orders.

"Jeanine! Get a message to Sir Charles! To Lord Frichette! Run!"

But Jeanine didn't move. She looked away and wouldn't meet her eyes. Ramsey's smile grew larger. "Miss Sorvall doesn't work for you anymore, do you, Miss Sorvall?" Jeanine twitched her head but still wouldn't look at her.

"Jeanine, this is insane! Ramsey'll kill a million people!"

"Me?" said Ramsey in mock surprise. "Why Dame Regina, I'm not going to kill anyone—you are."

"What?" exclaimed Regina. Jeanine's head came up.

"It's really quite shocking, actually," continued Ramsey. "Despite the governor's explicit orders and contrary to the Protector's wishes, you decided, on your own, to radically terraform this planet. The records—and many witnesses—will prove that you secretly substituted your own plan for the officially approved one. Such arrogance! But then your contempt for authority, your impatience with anything interfering with your plans, is well known. No one will have any trouble believing that you did this. How sad that you destroyed your career like this. How tragic that your madness cost so many lives. No doubt the locals will want justice and the governor will—reluctantly—have to turn you over to them to maintain our good relations. Perhaps he'll be able to get the Citrone woman in exchange."

Regina just stared with her mouth open. Her anger gave way to fear. She couldn't say anything she was so shocked.

But Jeanine could. "Wait a minute! You never said anything about this! You said it was just a modified TEP, not a full one! You said no one would get hurt! I never agreed to frame Reggie!"

"Oh dear, did I misjudge you, Miss Sorvall? Are you going to have to be confined as well as a participant of Dame Regina's terrible conspiracy?"

Now Jeanine was frozen in place, but Regina wasn't any longer. As the security men glanced back at Jeanine, she launched herself down the corridor and plowed into them full force. She, the security men, and Doctor Ramsey all went down in a flailing heap.

"Jeanine! Run!"

Within seconds, the security men had her on her feet and her arms pinned. Ramsey got up, dusted himself off, and looked around angrily. Jeanine was gone.

"Put this one in detention," he said, indicating Regina. "And find the other one. Put her there, too."

Chapter Twenty-three

"**Y**ou will reestablish communication *now*, or I'll have your head!" snarled Squadronlord Dardas. The ship lurched from another hit and the frantic technicians were sent sprawling. One pulled himself upright and assured him that they were doing their best.

Dardas nearly drew his sword and carried through with his threat, but the ship was shaking so frequently he doubted he'd be able to cross the short distance without falling and disgracing himself. This was impossible, simply impossible. Everything had been going so smoothly, the enemy was nearly helpless and would soon be forced to surrender — and now this! It was he and his ship — possibly all of his ships — which were helpless. Somehow those… things — he still didn't know what they were — had crippled his ship, shorted out most of the electrical gear, shut down the drive, and left him blind and deaf.

Twenty or thirty minutes had gone by since that first, unexpected attack. Despite his frustration with them, his damage repair teams had actually responded brilliantly in the face of this totally unexpected situation. They had the auxiliary reactor online, the artificial gravity was operating, along with the lights and life support. Unless they could get the communications, sensors, and weapons running again, this was going to become a disaster. They had been pulling out and replacing circuit modules at a tremendous pace, but things were still not working.

In the wake of the first attack, nothing else noticeable had happened. Apparently those things had no other weapons than the ones they'd use to disable him. But now his ship was being hit, hit badly. Their motion had carried them into range of the Anderan ships and, even under manual control, their weapons were pounding them. The ship shook and groaned with each blow.

"This is unacceptable," said Kolstar, breaking a long silence. "You will correct this immediately."

"We are attempting to do just that, Purifier."

"I can assure you that this gross… *incompetence* will be reported when we get home, Squardonlord."

Dardas's hand instinctively found the hilt of his sword. To accuse one of the Selected of incompetence was the direst of insults. He very nearly killed the purifier in that instant. "If you don't stop distracting me, we will never get home so you can make your report," he grated instead.

"Lord!" exclaimed one of the techs, cutting off any reply Kolstar might have had. "We have contacted Shiplord Siiracc on *Princess Kars*!" An instant later one of the monitors flickered back to life and he was staring at his subordinate. The man looked harried, but relieved.

"Siiracc, report," he commanded.

"Lord, thank the Maker you still live! I had feared…"

"Save the gratitude for later, Siiracc! I am blind here, what is the situation?"

"Not good, Lord. The enemy's cowardly ambush has disabled most of our ships to one degree or another. I have lost most of my sensors and only a third of my weapons are still operational. *Schtorm, Mandjur, Kagoul, Axard,* and your flagship are completely out of action. Only the cruiser *Anadyr* and the destroyer *Koreitz* escaped serious injury, but the enemy battleship concentrated its fire on them during our approach. *Koreitz* is a wreck and *Anadyr* badly damaged. And now that we have entered manual range of the enemy, all the rest of us are being hurt." His remark was punctuated by a hard impact on his ship which shook the image. A moment later, Dardas was rocked in turn as *Prince Ardagan* was hit again. "I-I could have veered off with my ship and the others, but I couldn't leave you to face the Anderans alone and helpless."

"Your loyalty is noted and appreciated. What have we done to the enemy in return?"

"We concentrated what fire we had left at the battleship, per your last order, Lord, although as we closed we found that one of the enemy's light cruisers and one destroyer had operational long-range weapons. The battleship is badly damaged and has only one of its main turrets left in action. We hurt the other two ships as much as we could with secondary fire. But now all their ships are in action…"

"Lord," said one of the technicians. "We have the main display working again and we've tied into a sensor feed from *Princess Kars*." Without waiting for further instruction, the man activated the display, and Dardas could look on the ruin of the Queen's plans and his ambitions with his own eyes.

Of his ten ships, three of them, the battlecruiser, *Archduke Schtorm*, the cruiser, *Duke Mandjur*, and the destroyer, *Koreitz*, were listed as total losses; savaged beyond hope of repair under these circumstances. All the rest were damaged to a greater or lesser degree. Siiracc's battlecruiser was mangled worse than he'd admitted if this readout was correct and the cruiser, *Count Anadyr*, wasn't in much better shape. Of the four other destroyers, only one was still fighting back effectively. Disaster. What was he going to do?

As he sought frantically for an answer, several other displays came back on. One showed the status of his own ship, and while large portions of it were blank, he could see that the damage did not appear too severe and that some of the weapons were firing under manual control. A moment later, his tech-chief called to announce they had restored the drive and could produce a modest thrust with the auxiliary reactor. They weren't finished yet, but what to do?

The display showed him that their initial vector was carrying them right through the enemy formation. The Anderan ships—and whatever those other things were—would soon be falling behind. Out of manual weapons ranges...

"Siiracc, pass my command to the squadron: any ship with a functioning drive is to proceed at maximum thrust. Open the range as quickly as they can."

"Yes, Lord, but that will leave most of our ships behind..."

"There is no choice. All fire is to be concentrated on the battleship, cruiser, and destroyer with long-range weapons; we must knock them out."

"Yes, Lord."

Dardas paused and looked at the display, looked at where their course was taking them. "We have lost this battle, Siiracc. We cannot hope to seize the gate now—so we shall destroy it instead."

* * * * *

"Looks like *Felicity* has had it, Sir Charles," said Lieutenant Lindquist. "She's falling out of formation and can't keep up at this acceleration. Captain Chapman is reporting very heavy damage and heavy casualties."

"Damn, I was pretty fond of that little ship," said Crawford, trying not to think of the men and women he knew among the crew.

"The Venanci saw that she was a major threat and did their best to take her out."

"Yeah. How's *New Umbria* doing?"

"A little better, but still pretty bad, sir. She's falling behind, too."

"So, it's up to *Agamemnon* and the rest of us."

"Yes, sir."

Indomitable shuddered as something tore into them and Crawford cursed. "Where did that come from?"

"Uh, that heavy cruiser, number two, sir."

"Hell, I thought we'd finished that one."

"Apparently not, sir. I hate to admit it, but the Venanci damage control seems to be a whole lot faster than ours."

"Yeah, that's not surprising. But damn it, let's finish that cruiser now while we're still in range. Signal to squadron: concentrate fire on heavy cruiser two." The order was passed and his ships focused their fire on the crippled Venanci ship. Shortly, there was no more fire coming from it.

"Signal from Flag, sir," said the com-officer. "All ships, maximum thrust. Overtake and engage."

"About time," said Crawford. Three of the Venanci ships, two battlecruisers, and one destroyer had pulled out of range of the weapons under manual control and were heading straight for the gate site. Crawford didn't have the slightest doubt about what their intentions were. The fact that the fleet had already destroyed, or was in the process of destroying, the other seven enemy ships didn't satisfy him at all. That was his gate and a hell of a lot of his people who were at risk. He looked at the tactical display and cursed again. "Why the hell hasn't Briggs started to move? Frichette ordered him out ten minutes ago!" The icons for Tosh Briggs's squadron was still sitting by the construction site, although the clan support ships were starting to move.

The acceleration alarm sounded and Crawford was pressed back in his couch as the battlecruiser leapt ahead with every gram of thrust it could muster. It was even worse than the first dash to close the range and engage the Venanci. That had been harrowing enough. They had lunged toward the enemy and then reversed thrust to keep from flashing past them. Fortunately, most of the enemy ships had lost their drives to the clan attacks and could do nothing to avoid the Anderan ships bearing down on them. Still, the difference in vectors pulled them past the Venanci after five very frightening minutes of close range fire. Those five minutes had seen massive damage dealt out and received for both fleets, but the large numerical superiority of the Anderans had tipped the balance. Each of the four squadrons had picked a target and just smothered it until it stopped firing, and then shifted fire to another ship. They had not destroyed all of their targets on the first pass, but now they had caught up to the crippled ones again and would soon leave them behind. Crawford did not think another pass would be needed. And in any case, the clan strike ships would be catching up to the cripples pretty soon and make sure they were finished.

Thankfully, the clans had not paid too heavily for the priceless edge they had given them. Several hundred of the closest ships had been destroyed by the Venanci, but the Anderans had soon given them enough other things to worry about that they'd left the other ones alone.

"The formation is starting to come apart, sir," said Lindquist. "*Shannin* and *Lighting* have both taken drive damage and can't keep up."

Crawford nodded. A heavy cruiser and a destroyer lost from his squadron, along with poor *Felicity*. All he had left now was *Indomitable*, the light cruiser, *Kensington*, and the destroyer, *Avon*; all of them damaged. But they, along with the other ships in the other squadrons who could still stand the pace, should have been more than enough to take care of the three remaining Venanci.

If they could just catch them in time.

It was going to be close. The Venanci were burning directly away from them, toward the gate; and with nearly empty tanks, they were lighter and could accelerate faster. But fortunately, one of the battlecruisers seemed to be damaged badly and was only making a little over two gravities, and the other two ships were staying with her. If that didn't change, they should get back into range about ten thousand kilometers short of the gate. It should be enough.

It had to be.

* * * * *

Tad was very sure the impacts were worse now than before. It was not his imagination. That last one had thrown him against his restraining harness so hard, stars were floating in front of his eyes. He was going to be black and blue all over in the morning — assuming he survived until morning. The last hour had been amazing, thrilling, and utterly terrifying, but he was still alive.

"My Lord, the enemy destroyer is pulling ahead of the others," said Lieutenant Jones to Lord Frichette. "It's doing better than six Gs now."

"Communications, connect me with Sir Tosh," said Frichette. A moment later a monitor lit up showing the face of the commander of Frichette's fifth squadron. At this distance, the time-delay was scarcely noticeable.

"Y-yes, My Lord?"

"Sir Tosh, why haven't you advanced on the enemy? You received my orders over ten minutes ago."

"Uh, yes, I know, My Lord, but there's been an unavoidable delay getting the ships ready to move. I'm sure we'll be ready very soon now…"

"There is a single enemy destroyer closing on the construction site," said Frichette sharply. "You will engage and destroy it immediately. Is that clear? *Immediately.*"

"Of course, My Lord, but… but is it wise for me to leave all these transport ships unguarded? Perhaps I should send the rest of my ships out and remain here to…"

"Sir Tosh, you are relieved of command." Frichette touched a button on his console and Briggs's astonished face vanished. "Get me Captain Harris." The screen lit up again with the face of another man, someone Tad had never met.

"My Lord?"

"Captain, I've relieved Mr. Briggs of command. You are now the squadron commander. You will advance and engage the enemy at once. Get cracking, Captain!"

"Yes, sir! Right away!" The man was already giving orders to get under way before Frichette broke the connection.

"Well done, sir," said Lieutenant Jones with a grin.

"Long overdue, Lieutenant. But damn satisfying nonetheless."

"Harris should be able to handle that tin can without any trouble, sir."

"Yes, but we need to handle these two battlecruisers. They're still..." A sudden hammer-blow slammed into the ship. The bulkhead to Tad's right shuddered and an elaborate crest with the ship's name broke loose and crashed to the deck. Some of the overhead lights flickered and went out. Tad looked over at the damage control display and saw a new red light glaring on it. The display was covered with them now.

"As I was saying," said Frichette, "we need to deal with those last two BCs. Please tell the captain that he's got a clear shot at their sterns and I'd really appreciate it if he could take advantage of that. *Agamemnon's* the only ship left with long range weapons and she has to do the job."

"Right away, sir. But we do only have the one turret in action."

Tad sat and watched the battle continue as he had for hours now. The ship shuddered and lurched from time to time and the display told them that the battleship was also scoring on the enemy. But so far they had not managed to hit their vulnerable sterns. Apparently the exposed drives were hard to armor and much more susceptible to damage than the heavily armored bows. Of course, nearly all of *Agamemnon's* armor had already been stripped away...

"The crippled BC isn't even firing at us, sir, and only doing two Gs," noted Jones after a while. "But that's allowing the other one to weave back and forth to bring its own weapons to bear on us."

"Yes. And the rest of the time it's firing at Captain Harris's squadron and they can't reply at all yet."

"That will change pretty soon. They're almost in range of the destroyer."

"Status change!" cried one of the officers. "The BC's drive has shut off! We got it, sir!" A cheer went up on the bridge. Tad looked and saw that the icon for one of the enemy battlecruisers, the one which had been firing on them, had changed from a triangle to a square and was falling behind the other.

"Well done," said Frichette. "That one will be in range of the fleet in a few minutes. All we have to worry about is that last BC now and it can only do two Gs." The man cracked a small smile. "Let's go get it gentlemen."

* * * * *

"I am sorry, Lord, but the damage is severe." said Shiplord Siiracc. "There is no hope of repairing it any time soon. I regret to fail you, but we will cover you from your pursuers as long as we can."

"You have done your best, Siiracc," said Dardas. "If any of us live to bring the tale home, the Queen shall hear of your valor."

"My thanks, My Lord, from me and from my crew."

"The Maker watch over you." Dardas cut the connection.

"Just two of us left now," said Kolstar. The usually musical tone in his voice was completely absent.

"And soon to be only one. The complete inactivity of the six enemy warships near the construction site led me to hope that they were inoperable. That is why I sent Bogatyr on ahead. It could start the destruction while we held off the pursuers. But now I see those other enemy ships moving out to meet them. It won't last long."

"Then what shall we do?"

"Our primary mission has failed. I will send orders to the troop transports to escape and return home as best they can. As for us... we shall do our duty."

* * * * *

"Kill the bastard, dammit!" snarled Crawford as the ship shuddered from a hit.

"We're trying, Sir Charles," said Lindquist, his voice strained with the acceleration. "The Venanci fight well."

Yes they did, Crawford had to admit that. Not one of the enemy ships had even tried to surrender. Not even the totally helpless ones. This one, the crippled battlecruiser, was not helpless. Its drive was out, but it still had weapons, and it was using them to the last. As the pursuing Anderans swept down on it, it had concentrated its long-range fire on *Agamemnon*, but now it was just firing at anything it could hit. The fact that it was receiving ten-times as much fire as it was putting out did not seem to matter to them. But not even the greatest courage could prevail in the face of this sort of firepower. The fleet's massed lasers tore and gouged and shredded. Armor and bulkheads flashed to vapor and exploded under the hellish concentration of photons. Second by second, the ship was smashed to junk. After two minutes of this, there was no more fire coming from the Venanci, but the pounding went on for another sixty seconds until the range grew too long and the madly accelerating Anderans left it behind. Crawford doubted that there was anyone left alive on board.

"Damn fools," muttered Crawford. "Just what the hell did that prove?"

Lindquist didn't answer, but he indicated the tactical display with a twitch of his finger—all that could be managed with these Gs. "Captain Harris's squadron has taken out the destroyer, sir."

"Good," grunted Crawford in relief. "Just one more to go and we'll be catching up with them in plenty of time. Plenty of time."

* * * * *

"Contact lost with *Princess Kars*, Lord," announced the com-tech. "Nothing from *Bogatyr*, either."

"Lord, the enemy fleet will be in manual range in eight minutes," said the sensor-tech. "The enemy battleship is no longer firing."

"Siiracc didn't die for nothing, it seems," said Dardas. "He pulled their last long-range fang."

"Little good it will do us," said Kolstar. "The rest of them will be in range long before we can close on the gate site. You must give this up and escape, Squadronlord."

Dardas snorted a laugh. "There is no escape, Purifier. Our tanks are nearly dry. Even if we veer off, they will still run us down."

"But... but then there is only one alternative..."

"Indeed there is, Purifier!" snapped Dardas, surging to his feet. His servants were instantly at his side, the droid buckled on his sword. "Communications! Transmit our log and sensor records to the transports and confirm the order to escape. Helmsman, you will transfer operations to auxiliary control and accompany me there." He turned and strode from his bridge, trailed by the servants, the helmsman, and the sputtering purifier.

"What is your plan, Dardas?" demanded Kolstar as they walked. He ignored him. Auxiliary control was only a hundred meters away and, fortunately, none of the damage to the ship had pierced the main access corridor, so the trip took less than a minute with Dardas's long strides. As he entered, his first officer vacated the command chair with a bow, but he did not sit down. The prime helmsman swapped places with his own number two. Just as on the main bridge, access panels were open and circuit modules littered the deck. Technicians were still at work. But a quick glance told him that all essential systems—at least those essential for his needs—were operational.

At least he hoped so. There was one he needed to check.

He walked over to a blank section of the bulkhead and placed his hand flat against it. Hidden scanners confirmed his palm print and then disassembled a DNA string in a randomly chosen skin cell to confirm his identity. Satisfied, a portion of the panel slid away revealing a simple set of controls. He repeated the identification procedure and sighed in relief as the controls came to life.

"What is that?" said Kolstar, coming close.

"The controls for the ship's scuttling charge. I am glad to see it is still operational."

"Scuttling charge...?"

"To prevent capture. Some commanders are satisfied with just a small charge, but I've always favored a large one. Twenty megatons."

"You intend to blow us up?"

"Us—and as many of the enemy as can be arranged. They'll be on us in just a few minutes. Helm, I want the enemy battleship. You know what to do?"

"Yes, Lord, you can count on me."

"But this is insane!" cried Kolstar. "We must surrender!"

"You would have us fall alive into the enemy's hands, Purifier? Even now the Queen can deny knowledge of our actions to the Anderans. She can claim we were a rogue operation and avoid a pointless war if that be her wish. But if we are captured and questioned... No, our duty to the Queen is clear."

"The Queen!" spat Kolstar. "Minister Florat warned against this expedition, but she would not listen! Dardas, I am ordering you to surrender this ship! In the name of Florat and the Council of Purity!"

"I take my orders from the Queen. Not from Florat, not from the Council, and certainly not from you. Go make your peace with the Maker, Kolstar, and bother me no more."

"Lord, the enemy is nearly in range," said his executive officer.

"Cut the drive and bring us about. Helm, standby for my order."

"Yes, Lord."

"No! I forbid it!" shouted Kolstar. "All of you, do nothing! Communications, signal the Anderans and tell them we surrender!"

No one in auxiliary control moved, except for the helmsman who was carrying out his last order.

"Fools, I'll not have my bloodline sacrificed for nothing!" Kolstar's termination rod was suddenly in his hands and he lunged at Dardas. His fourth level enhancements gave him great speed that even Dardas was caught by surprise.

But his two servants were not. The biological one only had second level enhancements, but they were devoted entirely to his service and protection. The mechanical one had been similarly programmed. The blow meant for Dardas found the biological servant instead. The servant jerked as the lethal energy surged through it and it fell to the deck dead. Kolstar tried to thrust past the falling corpse to get at Dardas, but the droid was now in the way and he had to waste an instant to dispatch that one with another deadly charge.

The sacrifice gave Dardas time to draw his sword and stand ready. His sword, a family heirloom which no living man but him was permitted to touch, was a relic from before the Collapse. It was over two thousand years old, but still as deadly as ever. At his touch, the blade was wreathed in blue fire. The fire met Kolstar's rod and sliced through it like a twig. Dardas, prepared, looked away as the rod's power cells discharged with a great flash, but Kolstar was dazzled. In that instant, Dardar took a step forward and swept off Kolstar's head with the backstroke. The purifier tumbled to the deck in two pieces.

Dardas sheathed his sword and stared at his crew. None of them had moved. A moment later, the ship shuddered as the first of the enemy fire reached it. "Helm, are you ready?"

"Ready at your command, Lord. Intercept course is plotted."

"Range to the battleship is one thousand nine hundred kilometers, Lord, closing velocity is twenty-two KPS."

His ship had eighty-six seconds to live. Hardly enough time to say farewell properly. Still, the transports would see what had happened. They would carry the tale home. His genetic code and those of his crew would be honored and passed on. Sadly, there was no time to send word of Kolstar's failure at the end, so it was likely that his would be as well. *It is the nature of things that imperfections will slip through. But we do what we can.* He put his hand on the scuttling control. The ship was shaking more violently.

"All stations, standby! Duty calls us! Glory to the Queen! Helm, *execute!*"

* * * * *

"Sir, they're coming right at us!" exclaimed Lieutenant Jones. Tad's eyes flicked to the navigation display and saw that there was a red flashing line drawn between the enemy ship and *Agamemnon*. A collision warning blinked next to it.

"Trying to ram," snarled Frichette. "Inform the captain and advise maximum evasive action."

But the captain had already seen the danger and responded. The thrust, which had eased off as they neared weapons range, came back full force, only a fraction of a second after the acceleration alarm sounded. Tad was slammed back in his couch and his vision tinged red.

There was nothing anyone could do. Weapons from the fleet flayed the Venanci ship, but with its drive turned away from them, there was little hope of a death-blow in time. It was all in the hands of the two helmsmen; one, apparently determined to die, and the other desperate to live. Tad gripped the arms of his chair, watching the icons on the display get nearer and nearer, and wished he'd stayed home.

If everything had been equal there was no telling which helmsman would have prevailed, but fortunately, everything was not equal. *Agamemnon*, battered though she was, could still make nearly five Gs, while the Venanci battlecruiser could do little better than two. Even though the relative vectors would bring the ships right by each other, *Agamemnon* could zig faster than the Venanci could possibly zag. Still, it was going to be close, very close...

"I think we're clear, sir!" squeaked Jones. "They should pass a couple of kilometers astern of us and they can't possibly..." The icon representing the Venanci ship suddenly turned into a white circle.

A moment later, the hardest blow of all slammed into Tad and his vision went from red to black.

The Venanci scuttling charge detonated when it was five kilometers away from *Agamemnon*. A nuclear bomb, by itself, out in space, will not do a great deal of damage. With no air to transmit the blast effects, it must be very close to its target. Much closer than five kilometers, even for a twenty megaton bomb.

Unless the bomb happens to have a major warship wrapped around it.

The battecruiser was blown to bits and those bits flung away at high speed. One bit, perhaps something especially solid, like part of the reactor, collided with *Agamemnon* just slightly aft of her midpoint. Several thousand tons of semi-molten junk crashed through the ship at over twenty kilometers per second, shearing through armor, bulkheads, and her keel frame like they were paper. Had she been coasting it might not have been a fatal blow, but her engines were still putting out five gravities and that doomed her. With half her supporting structure sheared away, the remainder could not handle the strain and it buckled and gave way before anyone could kill the drive. The ship broke in two, the engineering sections zipping crazily away for a few second before the thrust died, the bow section tumbling slowly amidst a cloud of debris.

Tad groaned as he slowly regained his senses. He hurt in a lot of places and the flag bridge seemed to be sideways. After a while he realized that it was he who was sideways, halfway torn out of his chair by whatever had happened. He pulled himself upright and then realized that the gravity was off, so 'upright' actually meant nothing. Other people were starting to move and there were a few cries of pain. Nearly all of the displays were blank.

After a moment, Lord Frichette was issuing orders and demanding information. A few moments later, medics were tending to the injured. Tad's head hurt so much he could barely concentrate on what was going on, but it was evident that things were not good.

"Looks like we've had it," Lieutenant Jones was saying. "You need to transfer your flag, sir."

"Yes. Contact Sir Charles and have him rendezvous with us. We'll shift all the staff, Mr. Farsvar here, and, oh, bring our two 'guests' — assuming they're both still alive — we can't let them out of our sight."

"Right away, sir."

After a moment, Frichette drifted over to him. "Are you all right, Tad?"

"I-I think so, sir. A bit shaken up."

"I would imagine you are. Well, the battle is over and we're still alive. Guess neither of has anything to complain about, eh?"

"No, sir. Is it really all over?"

"I sure hope so. Just one more trip to make. Once we're with Sir Charles we can look things over and make certain."

* * * * *

Despite five years in the navy, Carlina had never been in a battle. After all of this, she was very glad she had not. Of course, being in a battle, shut up in the brig, with no clue what was happening, would have to be the worst way of experiencing one. The ship had been shaking and groaning, twisting and lurching for hours. Add in long stretches at very high accelerations, and there was no part of her that had not been bruised. And that last impact! She didn't know what the hell was going on, but it sure seemed like the Anderans were losing. Perhaps she would die in battle – or even be rescued – rather than be executed.

From the moment she and Brannon had been turned over to the Anderans, 'for safe-keeping' the Seyotahs had claimed, she was convinced she was going to be executed. Brannon had made protests and demands, all to no avail. But now, what was happening?

"Are you all right, Carlina?" In the dim glow of the emergency lights she could just see Brannon in the adjoining cell.

"Battered, but okay. How about you?"

"I'm all right. What has happened?"

"Not sure, but the drive is off and the gravity with it."

"Perhaps your friends are winning the battle. If so, a great many of the clan must be dead. Oh, how I had hoped to avoid this."

"There's no telling what has happened or who is winning. This ship may be badly damaged, but the Anderans had many ships. We shall just have to wait."

But they did not wait very long before a party of Anderans came and took them away.

"Where are we going?"

"To another ship," said one of them, almost cheerily. "This one's broken."

"But not near as bad your friends'," added another.

* * * * *

"Lord Frichette's party will be coming aboard in a few minutes, sir," said Lieutenant Lindquist.

"Good," said Crawford. "As soon as they're here, we can start transferring the rest of the crew."

"Yes, sir, there's no hope of salvaging the ship, what with its size and current vector."

Crawford nodded. *Agamemnon* was heading out of the solar system and there was no hope of diverting her. All they could do was rescue the crew and let the rest of it go. Waste of good material, but there was nothing for it.

"What about the other cripples—ours and the Venanci?"

"We've got ships rendezvousing with all of them. Any that can be towed will be. Doesn't look like they'll be many Venanci survivors, though."

"Damn fanatics."

"Yes, sir."

Crawford leaned back in his chair and let out a long sigh. "So it's over. And we won."

"Yes, sir, a great victory."

"Any word on our casualties?" A sudden fear for Greg and Sheila went through him.

"Very little so far. Little word, I mean. Some of the ships will have taken a lot, I'm afraid, but it will take a while to get numbers."

"What about here, on *Indomitable*?"

"I can check, sir. Probably not too bad, though. Our damage wasn't bad at all."

He was tempted to have Lindquist specifically ask about his friends, but no, it wouldn't change anything—except his anxiety—and he'd learned to live with that. Speaking of anxiety, he needed to get a message off to Regina as soon as he could decently...

"Incoming message for Sir Charles," announced the communications officer.

"From who?"

"Uh, no identifier, but it's coming from the direction of the fourth planet, probably *Bastet*, but it doesn't have the right... oh, it's from one of *Bastet*'s shuttles. That would explain why it's so faint. Trying to boost, but it's not a good signal."

"Let me hear it."

"Yes, sir. On speaker."

It was faint and it was filled with static, but it was a woman's voice. Crawford's smile faded when he realized it wasn't Regina.

"...get this to Sir Charles... need help... the Governor... Doctor Ramsey... betrayed us... Reggie is locked up... going to destroy the whole planet... please, we need help!"

Crawford looked at Lindquist who appeared as puzzled as he felt.

"What the hell...?"

Chapter Twenty-four

"There's been nothing more since that message asking for help?" asked Petre Frichette.

"No," said Crawford. "I think it was Regina's assistant Jeanine. She must have been in a shuttle—probably still inside the boat bay, the signal was so badly degraded—but there's been nothing since then."

"You tried contacting *Bastet*?"

"There's a forty-minute com-delay, but yes, I did immediately. Just got the reply a few minutes ago. They say everything's fine and that the first message was a mistake."

"Have you talked to the governor?"

"No, I was waiting to talk to you. With that stuff about 'betrayal' in the message, I wasn't sure who I could trust."

"It's not terribly clear who is doing the betrayal, Ramsey, the governor, or both." Frichette sighed. "Y'know, I was really hoping to take a nap once the battle was over..." Crawford looked at the young man and saw the dark circles under his eyes, the fatigue on his face. Considering how wrung-out Crawford felt, Petre must be exhausted.

"I could try to contact Regina directly, but if something really is wrong, they could drag it out for hours."

"And if that 'destroying the whole planet' part of the message means some sort of sabotage of the Thermal Enhancement Plan then we don't have any time to waste: it's scheduled to begin in less than forty-eight hours."

"So what do we do? I've already checked with the astrogator and by draining the tanks we could just make it—at five Gs the whole way. But only if we left right now."

"Ouch. That would be hell on the crew—not to mention me." They both glanced at the milling throng of celebrating officers on the bridge. They were tired, too, but they all thought the job was done. Could he ask them for more?

"I want to go, but dammit, I don't know what to do!"

Frichette rubbed at his eyes. "All right, let's try to look at this logically. The Venanci are beaten. Their two transports are no threat and I can send our least damaged ships to keep a close watch on them or catch them if they can. If we do make a high-speed run to rendezvous with Bastet, is there anything to be lost? Other than sleep and tempers, I mean?"

"Uh, I can't think of anything..."

"Neither can I. If it's a false alarm we lose nothing. And if it's not... Let's get cracking."

* * * * *

"Reggie, I'm so sorry. This is all my fault!" Jeanine was sobbing and Regina couldn't resist holding her and stroking her hair as she rocked her.

"Hush, little one, hush. Ramsey and Shiffeld must have had this planned from the start. There's no way you could have stopped them."

"I could have warned you! I could! B-but I didn't."

"When did you find out?"

"A few weeks ago. Just before you got back here." Jeanine sniffled, but stayed leaning against her. "I noticed the same things you did, I guess: the servicing on the penetrators, then I found flight plans for the shuttles that could have only one purpose."

"What did you do?"

"I went to Ramsey."

"And what did he do?"

"Bribed me. Threatened me, too, but mostly bribed. Told me how grateful the governor and the Protector would be. Made some big promises."

"So you agreed to do what he wanted?"

"Y-yes. He just wanted me to distract you. Keep you from finding out what was happening until it was too late. B-but he told me that there were only going to be a few more magma pockets tapped—not all of them! He said you were being too conservative in your safety estimates. He said that no one would get hurt. I didn't really believe him—oh, maybe I wanted to believe him. I was so confused I didn't know what I was doing! But he never said anything about framing you for it! I swear! Oh, Reggie, I didn't know! I'm sorry! I'm sorry!"

"I believe you, I really do. And while you were busy keeping me busy, you wouldn't see the scope of what he had planned. He's damn clever. But why'd you accept the bribe?" Regina thought she knew, but she wanted to hear it from Jeanine. It took a while before she answered.

"I was angry. And hurt."

"You'd heard about me and Charles?"

"Yes. It drove me crazy. I was so angry."

"I'm sorry I hurt you, Jeanine. I never meant to. I suppose I never should have encouraged you at all, but... but I do love you, little one—just not like that."

"I know. I always knew. But I just built up a fantasy in my mind and let it get too real. I love you, too, Reggie."

She gave the young woman a hug and then held her away. Her face was covered with tears, but she smiled a little. "Friends again?"

She nodded vigorously. "Yes. But, oh, what a mess I've made! What are we going to do? If Ramsey isn't stopped he'll kill all those people and you'll be blamed!"

"We'll both be blamed. He won't let you off, either. Not now."

"But why is he doing this?"

"Shiffeld bribed him, I suppose. Our dear governor is in terror of what the Protector is going to think about the sabotage and all this other mess. I think Shiffeld wants to carry out his mission as completely as he possibly can—and the locals be damned. And Ramsey has always resented my position here. He'd jump at a chance to take charge—and get rid of me at the same time."

"What are we going to do?"

Regina looked around at the detention cell. It seemed quite sturdy. "Only a handful of people know what's really going on and they're in Ramsey's pocket. He's told everyone else that I've had a nervous collapse and I'm confined to my quarters to rest. No one's going to get suspicious until it's too late. So, there's no hope of help from aboard Bastet. Did you really get a message off to Sir Charles?"

"I don't know," Jeanine started crying again. "I broadcast a message for as long as I could, until the guards caught me. But there wasn't enough time to get any reply. I don't know if I got through."

"Well, you did your best. All we can do now is wait... and hope someone's coming to the rescue."

* * * * *

The thrust eased off until Tad was under what he knew was normal gravity. After two hours at what felt like three Gs (but was really five) normal gravity felt very light. He had ten minutes to attend to bodily needs before the high acceleration would return. He flung himself into the washroom, stripping off his clothes as he went. A minute for the toilet, five minutes in the shower, two minutes to dry and dress, grab a few bites of food and something to drink, and then back to his couch just as the acceleration alarm was sounding. He settled into the cushions and didn't have to wait long for the crushing weight to return.

This had been the routine for the last eighteen hours: two hours of high gravity with ten-minute breaks. He'd tried to sleep as much as he could, but it was very hard. He'd doze off and then wake a few minutes later, gasping for breath. His sleeping body didn't seem to realize what it had to do to keep breathing properly. And from what he'd been told, he had to endure another thirty hours of this torture.

He just wished he knew what was going on.

Some sort of crisis on the Newcomers' terraforming ship, Sir Charles and Lord Frichette had said. No details, but they had to get there as quickly as possible. They'd offered to put Tad off the ship, but he'd foolishly said he wanted to come along. If he'd only known! Too late now, he was stuck here.

Something was digging into his back. Very, very carefully he lifted himself up and smoothed out a wrinkle in the back of his shirt. It was amazing that something as small as that could feel like a boulder under these circumstances. Even more carefully, he lowered himself back down, his arms quivering with the effort. Safely down, he lay there gasping. After a while, he activated the display screen with the controls by his side. There were an incredible number of entertainment tapes available, not that any of them made much sense, but they did help pass the time.

Thirty hours to go.

* * * * *

"Brannon, are you all right?" asked Carlina. Her husband was slumped in his couch, looking very gray and scarcely seeming to breathe.

"I will survive," he gasped. "I think. I have never experienced anything like this—nor do I want to again."

"I had some high-G training when I first went in the navy, but never anything as long as this. I wonder what the hell is going on. Those crewmen said the battle was over."

"Yes, it is a great mystery. But somehow I doubt any of these people are going to enlighten us."

"No. But just hang on. They can't possibly have the fuel to keep this up much longer."

"I do hope you are right."

Me, too.

* * * * *

"Reducing thrust to zero-point-two Gs," announced the helmsman. "Matching course with *Bastet* in… three minutes."

"Thank God!" gasped about a dozen different people around the flag bridge. Charles Crawford heartily agreed. He was exhausted. The acceleration had not bothered him as much as it had the others, but he, along with a few other high-gravity natives among the crew, had spent the last forty hours tending to those who needed assistance. The sick bay was full of them by this time.

"*Bastet* is signaling again, sir," said the communications officer. "They want to know what our intentions are?"

Crawford looked over to where Petre was sitting. The last two days had seen a strange and puzzling set of messages going back and forth across the solar system. Naturally enough, Governor Shiffeld had wanted to know where they were going once he became aware of *Indomitable*'s departure. They had sent back a vaguely worded reply stating that they were investigating a rumor of sabotage on the terraforming ship. Surprisingly, there had been no further word from Shiffeld, no request for more information and no orders, either. Very strange. Once they were under way, Crawford had tried to get in touch with Regina, but unsurprisingly, he'd been told that she was 'temporarily unavailable'. Clearly, something was wrong, but any meaningful communications was impossible with the long com-delay. Finally, for the last ten hours, as *Bastet* noted *Indomitable*'s approach, there had been a steady stream of requests for information on why they were coming. Afraid to tip their hand too soon, they had concocted a story about a Venanci ship slipping off in this direction, but it was obvious the people on *Bastet* didn't believe it.

"Sir, the last of those big shuttles is docking with *Bastet* now," said the sensor officer. Yes, they'd been watching those shuttles for hours. They, and their mother ship, had been busily shifting orbits, presumably placing bombs for the TEP. Had they finished?

"What about the bombs?"

"I'm still reading the transponder codes from one thousand and ninety-two of them, sir, and they all match the ones on the TEP. But I've been plotting the courses on those shuttles, and even though it sure looked like they had to be placing bombs into orbits, I'm not seeing any transponders at all from the places they had been."

"Can you pick up any radar returns from anything they might have placed?" asked Petre.

"Uh, picking up a lot of junk in various orbits. Sir. Hard to really get a good reading from way out here." *Bastet* had taken up a very high orbit in the last hour and *Indomitable* had matched it. They'd launched a recon drone to get a look at the other side of the planet, but it was still just as far out.

"This isn't getting us anywhere," said Crawford. "Let's get Ramsey on the line and demand to talk with Regina."

"Yes, I think you're right. Communications, get us Doctor Ramsey. Don't take no for an answer."

"Yes, sir."

It only took a few minutes, but Crawford was fuming by the time Ramsey appeared on the screen. He looked tired—and worried. "Ah, Sir Charles, oh, Lord Frichette, I wasn't expecting…what can I do for you?"

"I would like to speak with Dame Regina," said Crawford, trying hard to keep the worry and impatience out of his voice.

"Uh, ah, I'm afraid that's not possible. The poor woman has been working so hard she's had a bit of a collapse. She's in sick bay under sedation and needs rest. I'm sure you can understand."

"We're coming over to see her. Immediately."

"Ah, no, I'm afraid I can't allow that. We'll be initiating the Thermal Enhancement Plan in just a few minutes. All the orbits are set and we cannot delay. Nor can we afford the distraction of an official visit. I'm sure you understand. Perhaps tomorrow…"

"We are coming over. *Now.*"

"*Tomorrow*, gentlemen," said Ramsey, and now there was steel in his voice. "My orders come direct from the governor. For the moment, our locks are closed to you and you will not be permitted aboard. Until tomorrow, then." The connection broke and the screen went blank.

"Damnation!" snarled Crawford. "Who the hell does he think is?"

"The Man in Charge, apparently," said Petre. "This could get a bit awkward."

"It'll be damn awkward for *him* when we get aboard! Come on, I'll rustle up a few marines and we'll go pay the good doctor a visit."

"It's not quite as simple as…"

"Sir Charles! Lord Frichette!" exclaimed the sensor officer. "I'm reading multiple thrusters firing in orbit around the planet!"

"The bombs?"

"Yes, sir! But not just the thousand and ninety-two bombs with transponders. I'm reading nearly a thousand others!"

"Good God. Can you plot their courses? Their impact points?"

"Working on that now, sir." The tactical display lit up and a steady stream of icons began to appear. Icons and lines connecting them to spots on the planet. After only a few seconds it became clear what was going on.

"The magma pockets. Ramsey's going after all the magma pockets!"

"Going to blow up the whole planet, just like Jeanine said."

"We've got to stop them!"

"Not from here," said Petre, shaking his head. "We're well out of point defense range and you have no long-range weapons on this ship. And from what I know about those penetrators, they're damn-near indestructible anyway."

"They're controlled from *Bastet*. If we went aboard we could abort them from there. Come on! Let's go!" Crawford grabbed at Petre's sleeve, but the young man didn't move. "What's wrong?"

"Have you looked at *Bastet*'s specs, Charles?"

"No, why the hell should I have? And what does that have to do with anything? We're running out of time!"

"I have, and it will be very difficult to board if Doctor Ramsey doesn't want us to."

"What do you mean?"

"With all the bombs she carries, *Bastet* is far better protected than any normal merchant ship. She's got point defense, Charles! Only a half-dozen turrets, but more than enough to blast any shuttles trying to board."

"Working point defenses?" asked Crawford in amazement.

"Yes, I noticed that when I was analyzing the fleet's capabilities. If we hadn't been able to get a few of the other ships up and running, I was going to see about drafting *Bastet* for the battle. Of course, I suppose we could try blasting their turrets..."

Crawford cringed at the thought of firing at the ship with Regina aboard. "Surely Ramsey would never dare fire on a shuttle!"

"Maybe not, but he might not have to. The internal security on the ship is impressive. Remember how much work it was to get on board *Exeter* when we went after Citrone? It could be worse here."

"Damn! We haven't got much time!"

"About twenty minutes until the first impacts, sir," said the sensor officer.

"I'm not sure what we could do with so little time," said Petre. "If Ramsey just activated the anti-boarding routines, they could hold us off for far longer than twenty minutes. And even just blasting every com antenna from here wouldn't do any good: the bombs are on their way, we need the facilities on *Bastet* to stop them."

Crawford tried to hold down the panic that was building in him. Regina would never have let this happen if she'd known about it. But apparently she had found out about it and that led to the desperate message from Jeanine. Would Ramsey have dared hurt her? But what could he do? If Petre was right about the security programs, then the ship would be as secure as any of the warships...

The warships...

The engineer in him instinctively looked for the flaw in any plan, the mistake in any train of logic. Now it found one. "That ship would be as hijack-proof as any of the warships, wouldn't it?"

"Yes. Maybe more, so."

Crawford looked straight at Frichette. "So how did Citrone get aboard to reset the cold-sleep capsules' timers?"

Petre blinked in surprise. "I don't know..." He hesitated one second longer and then turned. "Security! Get the prisoners up here! Now! This is an emergency!"

* * * * *

The terrible crushing weight was finally gone. Brannon Gillard breathed easily and thanked the Lifegiver for this merciful moment. He turned his head slightly and saw Carlina beside him, changing the air bottle for his breathing mask. He smiled at her and she smiled back, reached out a hand to touch his cheek. He was very glad she was here with him.

"Feeling better?" she asked.

"Much. I guess we have arrived at wherever we were going?"

"Yes, the drive has shut down, this isn't just a rest period. Do you want to sit up?"

"Thank you, that would be good." She put an arm under his shoulders and helped him upright. He'd already noticed how strong she was. "Where do you suppose we are?"

"Well, since they didn't bother to provide this cell with a window, I really can't..."

She stopped talking when they heard the cell door sliding open. Before either could react, a crowd of Anderans swarmed into the cell and seized both of them. Handcuffs were slapped onto wrists and they were hustled out.

"What is this?" demanded Carlina. "What are you doing?"

"Shut up, traitor!" growled one of them. "You're wanted on the bridge—now!"

Apparently they were wanted pretty urgently because they were half-dragged, half-carried to the huge control room of the ship. A crowd of people were waiting for them, but the only ones Brannon recognized were Lord Frichette, the Newcomers' military commander, and Sir Charles Crawford, the man who slew Caspari's son. They were taken right to Lord Frichette.

"Miss Citrone, that's the terraforming ship, *Bastet*," he said, pointing to an image in one of the monitors. "We know you have the security codes to her computer. We need them urgently and you are going to give them to us." The intensity on the young man's face was frightening. He could see that even Carlina was shaken, but she still looked defiant.

"Yes, I have them. They came along with my orders. I have no idea how they were acquired, but it was considered important to secure the terraforming operation intact. Why should I help you?"

"Because if you don't, in about nineteen minutes, a million people—a million of your husband's people—are going to die!"

"What?" cried Brannon.

"What are you talking about?" demanded Carlina.

"Some... misguided individuals have initiated a radical terraforming program on the fourth planet. About two thousand very big nukes are going to blow the whole place to hell unless we stop them. We have to get aboard that ship quickly, and you are the only one who can let us do that."

Carlina looked as startled as he felt, but she did not quail. "Such... such an act would have serious consequences for your relations with the clans. I don't see why I should help."

"Carlina!" cried Brannon, aghast.

"Yes, Miss Citrone, this goes far beyond any political or military issues. A lot of innocent lives are at stake. With your help we can save them. Are you going to let them all die?"

"Carlina! Give them what they need!" She looked at him, but through her uncertainty and indecision, he could see *those* eyes looking at him. The eyes that appeared whenever she talked about the Protector. Would she sacrifice all those people just to strike one final blow against the man she had never met but hated so?

"We're almost out of time, damn you!" spat Crawford. He took a step forward, his huge fists looked like hammers. Still, she didn't flinch—until Brannon grabbed her arm.

"Carlina! Don't do this! Your family died not just because bad people acted. *They died because good people did nothing to save them!* Don't become one of them! Please!"

That got through to her, he could see it. Her mouth opened and closed and then opened again.

"One condition," she whispered.

"What?" cried Frichette and Crawford in unison.

"My husband goes free."

"Done!"

He flinched in surprise. "And you, too!"

She just smiled and shook her head. "We'll leave that to your Life-giver, priest. All right, the overide code is GCQ-897-D34..."

* * * * *

"Sure hope this works." Crawford looked nervously through the viewport of the shuttle at the point-defense turret on *Bastet*, which had been tracking them all through their approach. "How much time left?"

"Thirteen minutes," said Petre distractedly. Among his seemingly endless store of talents, the young man appeared to know computers very well. He was hunched over a terminal, getting ready to access *Bastet's* computer and shut down the security system using the code Citrone had given them. Crawford glanced over his shoulder at the 'marines' crowding the shuttle. The order had been given to assemble them and get the shuttle ready even before Citrone had reached the bridge, so no time had been lost once they had the code. He noticed Citrone and Gillard stuffed into one corner, looking glum. Frichette had brought them along insisting that if they were aboard, then Citrone was less likely to give them a fake access code since she and her husband might end up blasted, too, if things went wrong. It was a rather dubious comfort in Crawford's opinion.

"Attention approaching shuttle. You will not be permitted to dock. Please back off..." The same message had been coming over the com for three minutes now. At least there had been no threats to fire—so far.

"All right, I'm ready," said Petre. "Here goes... Okay, the code works, and I've got access. Shutting down point defense... now." Crawford looked out the viewport again and almost cheered when the turret froze in place and did not continue to follow them as they moved in toward the emergency air lock where they planned to dock.

"It's working, Petre!"

"Good. Opening air lock outer door." The hatch set in the side of the ship began to slide open.

"Take us in—quick," said Crawford to the pilot.

"Yes, sir."

The man took him at his word and a few seconds later the shuttle banged against the hull with a considerable jolt. "Hard docked, sir."

"You're not kidding. Get the hatch open!"

"It's open, sir," shouted one of the marines. "Air lock's empty, and the inner door is closed."

"Opening air lock inner door," said Petre. "And all interior locks and bulkheads, too. Done! Shutting system down; it should take them a good while to figure this out. Let's go!"

The marines were already moving into the ship and Crawford and Frichette joined them. Crawford had a small computer pad with the ship's layout, although he nearly had it committed to memory. "The detention area is to the right and down two decks."

"You sure you want to get Regina first, Charles?" asked Petre. "We've barely got ten minutes."

"She'll know how to abort the bombs in case Ramsey won't cooperate. Can you do that?"

"No..."

"So we get Regina."

"Okay, lead on."

He tried to, but there were two marines, bulky in their combat armor, in front of him who refused to let him by. So, he was obliged to just tell them which way to go from behind. They all hurried, and with every hatch and bulkhead door standing wide open, it took them less than a minute to reach the detention area.

Unfortunately, there were a half-dozen security men there waiting for them.

They turned a corner and the two leading marines halted instantly, there were shouts and the buzz of stunners. The marine in front of Crawford grunted and fell back a step, bumping into Crawford, who didn't budge. More shouts and more stunner bolts and then both marines stepped back, together out-massing Crawford and forcing him to retreat.

"I got one of 'em, sir, but the rest are under cover," gasped one of the marines. "Damn, those stunners still hurt like hell even through this armor."

"All they've got are stunners," said the other marine. "We could rush them, sir—if we had to."

"Wait!" said Frichette, pushing his way through. He went to the corner and stopped. "You men over there! Hold your fire! I'm coming out to talk." He unbuckled his belt and dropped his stunner to the deck. Without waiting for an answer, he stepped out. Crawford gasped, but there was no fire.

"You men, take a look! You know who I am?"

"Shit, it's Lord Frichette!" came a startled voice.

"That's right, and I'm telling you to put up your weapons. Whatever orders you've been given are invalid. I'm here to claim Dame Regina Nassau, who's been improperly detained." Frichette glanced in his direction, made a 'stay put' motion with his hand, and then moved forward, out of sight. Crawford pushed up to the corner and looked around it. Petre was boldly walking right past the startled security men. An instant later, Regina and Jeanine appeared. Crawford nearly dashed forward, but he had the sense not to. They didn't need to tempt any itchy trigger-fingers out there! Petre collected the two women and escorted them back in his direction. "Sergeant, I assume your commander is on the bridge?"

"Uh, the main control room, sir. With Doctor Ramsey."

"Good. Contact him and tell him I am on the way up there. Tell him I have direct orders from Governor Shiffeld and he is not to offer any resistance. Understand?"

"Yessir!"

Without another word, Petre moved on. An instant later, Crawford had Regina in his arms. "Thank God you're safe!"

"Thank God you're here!" countered Regina. "Are we in time?"

"We've got about eight minutes," said Petre. "So we'd better hurry."

"Blessed excrement, let's move!"

They moved. Bastet was a large ship, but like most, it had the majority of its inhabited spaces concentrated forward, so it was a thirty-second jog to the main control room. Several security men were in the corridor outside and Crawford tensed, but their stunners were holstered and they stepped back as the party approached. From inside came angry voices.

"He's lying, I tell you!" shouted someone who sounded like Doctor Ramsey. "I have my orders from the governor and I'm telling you to keep them away!"

"Too late, we're here," said Petre as they trotted in the door. Everyone turned to face the new arrivals. The commander of the security detachment was there with several more men, but none of them made any move. Petre stepped out in front. "And now that we are all here, there are stories to tell. Doctor Ramsey, you first: what are you doing and why?"

"What are you talking about, Petre?" cried Regina. "We've got no time for stories! Let me at those controls!" She started to move forward, but Petre put out a hand.

"Sorry, but stories first. Keep it short, Doctor."

"There's nothing to tell. I am carrying out Governor Shiffeld's orders." Ramsey drew himself up and glared at pretty much everyone in the room.

"Which are?"

"To carry out the Protector's mandate to terraform the habitable planet in this star system! What else?"

"What else indeed? Dame Regina?"

She looked as confused and dazed as Crawford felt. What the hell was Petre doing? Suddenly Regina was furious. "Petre! If we don't stop those bombs a million people will die! I am going to stop them! Right now!" She boldly moved toward the main control console.

An instant before she got there, the back of the chair she was reaching for exploded in a spray of fragments. Crawford shouted and Regina stumbled back in shock. Frichette had left his stunner lying on the deck in the detention area, but he now held a small, very lethal-looking, slug-thrower of some sort—and it was pointed right at Regina. "Don't," he said. "And I mean it, Regina. You would not be the first person I've killed."

"Petre, what are you doing?" she moaned. Crawford's hand went to his stunner, but Petre had positioned himself to cover both of them, and a stern glance in his direction warned him not to move. He felt so stunned, he wasn't sure he *could* move.

"My duty. Now, I want to know what you are doing? You sent a message implying that treasonous activities were going on here. I was forced to investigate. Doctor Ramsey appears to be acting within his authority. Convince me to let you intervene."

"All those people will die!"

"Yes. So?"

Regina's mouth hung open and she couldn't seem to get any sound to come out.

"The...the Frecendi are our allies!" said Crawford. It was the first thing he could think of.

"A point, although they are contributing nothing to the Gate Project," conceded Petre. "Any more?"

"The Protector's orders are ten years old!" said Regina, apparently regaining her wits. "They were written without knowing about these people!"

"Another point. Not necessarily relevant, but proceed."

"If we kill them, it wrecks the trade agreement and jeopardize the gate construction!" cried Crawford.

"Better. But I'm still not convinced. The clans are not a unified entity and the trade agreement could survive this."

Crawford looked at Regina and she looked back frantically, her eyes wide.

"Uh..."

"Uh…"

"Time's running out…"

"It… it will only be two years until the gate's done!" blurted Regina. "The terraforming project will take decades! If the Protector wants to massacre these people then, he's got plenty of time later, damn it!"

"An interesting observation. There would appear to be more slack in the time-table than the present activities might account for." Frichette looked thoughtful, but his gun was still trained on Regina. Crawford tried to think to something else to say. Frichette had talked of his duty… duty to who? The Protector?

"If… if we begin our relations with the clans like this — with mass murder — it will taint all future dealings! The Protector wants to expand throughout this whole arm. With the clans as enemies, it will make that vastly harder. It's in the Protector's best interest to spare these people!"

"A dangerous thing it is to make assumptions about what the Protector would want," said Frichette. But then he nodded and seemed to relax. "And yet I am convinced." He motioned at Regina with his pistol. "Go."

Regina flung herself into the mangled chair and began pushing buttons. Crawford glanced at Frichette and went to stand beside her. Ramsey was sputtering a protest, but Frichette now had his pistol pointed in his direction.

"Can you do it? There's no code lock-out?"

"No, not for this! If an abort became necessary, we couldn't risk any delay. I can render all the bombs inert, but that would ruin the whole TEP. If I can just figure out how to deactivate the extra bombs and leave the original plan intact…" While she spoke, her hands were flying over the controls.

"We've got about ninety seconds until first detonation," said someone.

"We noticed that none of the extra bombs had transponders, Regina."

"Really? That's great! I can segregate them that way." Her fingers continued to dance. "Shit!"

"What?"

"Nothing! Stop distracting me!"

"Okay! Okay!"

"Sixty seconds," said that person again.

"Shut up!" snapped Crawford and Regina in unison.

Lights were flashing all over the control screen as Regina worked faster than Crawford could follow. Suddenly he was pushed aside and Jeanine was working right alongside her. "The G-19 interface, Reggie."

"Right! That's it! Isolating all penetrators from the original TEP… deactivating the rest…*Now!*"

Crawford looked up at the main display. It showed several thousand red icons moving down toward the surface of the planet. Suddenly about half of them flashed briefly and then changed color from red to green. "We did it!" cried Jeanine. Regina touched a few more controls and then leaned back with an outrush of breath. The display changed from the diagram to an actual view of the planet. The brown and gray sphere hung there with one ice cap almost completely in shadow. Then there was a flash. Almost instantly there were more—and then a *lot* more. The whole ice cap was bathed in a dazzling radiance.

"Came the dawn," whispered Crawford. It was the only sound in the whole room.

The glow persisted as more and more bombs came down, adding their heat to what the others had already provided, bathing the frigid place in a nurturing warmth. Then there was another flash, well away from the ice cap, in the barren lands off to the side. *One of the authorized magma pockets.* It was followed a few seconds later by another in the same spot. Flash, flash, flash… But each flash was dimmer than the one before it. The penetrators were going deeper and deeper. Finally they could not be seen at all.

"What happened?" asked Crawford. "Didn't it work?"

"Keep watching," said Regina with a smile. After perhaps a minute, a red glow could be seen in the spot where the flashes had been. By this time, the glare around the ice cap had diminished almost completely, making the red light all the more noticeable. Slowly, very slowly, it seemed from this distance, a boiling red cloud rose up from the surface. Higher and higher, broader and broader, the cloud grew and grew. Brighter flecks were flung well beyond the cloud's edges.

"God, some of that stuff's getting thrown above the atmosphere!"

"Why do you think we're in such a high orbit? All traffic has been cleared out of the low orbitals today."

"I'd sure hate to be down there close to that."

"Anyone would." Regina turned and fixed a withering stare on Doctor Ramsey, who obstinately refused to be withered.

"What about the bombs you deactivated?" said Crawford following her stare. "They're all down there right? Could they survive the impact and be detonated later?"

"They were built to survive, but since their final penetration thrusters didn't fire, and by not detonating in sequence, they are all just piled up close to the surface. If they were detonated now they would make a hell of a bang, but they'd never break through to the magma pockets."

"They could still kill a bunch of people."

"Yes, I am going to lock them out with a personal code right now, but I'll give some thought to a permanent solution later." She did some more typing and then stood up and stretched. He smiled at her and she smiled back.

"Good to see you."

"Yes."

* * * * *

Carlina waited until the shuttle pilot turned away and then she shifted over until she was very close to Brannon. It was hard to move with her hands shackled together in front of her and a strong chain linking them to more restraints on her ankles. "You can breathe this air for a while, can't you?" she whispered.

"Yes. Why…?" He flinched when she used her shoulder to dislodge his breathing mask.

"Pretend to be unconscious." He stared at her for a moment and then nodded and closed his eyes. The stink of chlorine assaulted her, and she had to turn away. But she endured it and didn't say anything. It wouldn't take long for the gas to spread in the small, enclosed shuttle…

"God! What the hell is that?" cried the Anderan after less than a minute.

Carlina gave in to a loud cough. "Chlorine!" she gasped. "His breath mask is loose! Help him!"

"Shit! The hell with him, help the rest of us!" snarled the man. He came over to Brannon as Carlina curled up into a ball, coughing horribly.

As soon as the man was within reach, she uncurled — very rapidly.

Her feet caught him right in the solar plexus and he was flung backward to slam into the bulkhead. He slumped to the deck and didn't move. Carlina lurched to her feet and turned to face Brannon. He hunched over so she could use her hands to put his mask back into place.

"Did… did you kill him?"

"I don't think so. See if he has a key for these shackles on him will you?"

Without waiting to see if he would obey, Carlina hobbled forward, into the small control cockpit. She thanked the Maker when she saw that all the systems were still activated. She cursed when she couldn't quite reach the controls because of the chain. "Have you found the keys?" she shouted over her shoulder.

"Not yet."

"Does he have a weapon?"

"Yes, but it looks like a stunner."

Which would not cut through a chain. Still cursing, she hopped up in the pilot's chair and by squatting there and resting her knees on the edge of the control panel, she could just reach the controls. She hit one switch and then called back to Brannon: "Are the airlock doors closing?"

"Yes, they are."

"Okay, I'm detaching us from the hull. Get back into one of the chairs, there could be some high accelerations soon."

"All right."

She deactivated the magnetic grapples and the shuttle was free from the hull of the ship. She studied the sensor read-out for a moment and then gingerly activated the maneuvering thrusters. The Anderan battlecruiser was hanging out there, only a kilometer away, and would notice if she went zipping off into the black. All right, she would have to block their view. She piloted the shuttle slowly around the curved hull of the terraforming ship until the warship was not in direct view. *Okay, now a vector to keep us out of sight for a while.*

"Damn!" she snarled when the chain pulled her hands up short. "Have you found that key yet?"

"Uh, you told me to get in a seat."

"Never mind, he was the pilot, the guards probably took the keys with them. Just get ready." Awkwardly she typed in the course she wanted and the shuttle turned to match it. She checked over all the readings, silently thanked the small-craft instructor she'd had during her training, scrunched herself down in her seat, and then hit the main thruster controls.

A powerful force pressed her back against the padding as the shuttle leapt away toward freedom.

* * * * *

Regina snuggled against Charles as they stared out the large viewport at the planet below. There was an enormous swirling storm of white clouds growing out from the one pole that they could see from here. A similar storm existed at the other pole, invisible behind the curve of the planet. A smaller, orangeish cloud was spreading from another point to meet the white one. At the edges they were already merging in a pink smear. Preliminary reports were good and there had been almost no damage among the Frecendi. They didn't seem to have any clue how close they'd come to extinction.

"Y'know, I always thought I did big projects," said Charles. "But they all pale in comparison to this. It must be very satisfying work."

"It is. Very. It's a shame we can't do a better job of this here."

"I think you've already done a very good job."

"We all have. But I think I'm going to need some serious help keeping the nightmares away tonight. Damn, that was too close!"

"I'd be glad to help. Want to get a head start?"

"That sounds like a very good..." She stopped short when she saw Petre Frichette and Jeanine approaching. A chill went through her. She'd actually *liked* Frichette! Thought of him as a friend! How could she have been so completely wrong about him?

"Hello," he said as if he were passing the time of day. They all stared at each other for a long moment.

"You would really have done it, wouldn't you?" said Regina, at last. "You'd have let all those people die."

"If you had not convinced me otherwise, I might have," he admitted. He didn't seem the least bit embarrassed.

"So, all of that 'a million people will die' stuff you threw at Citrone to get the code was just an act?" demanded Charles.

"Putting the subject into a highly emotional state is an effective interrogation technique," said Frichette with a shrug, neither confirming nor denying Charles's statement.

Another silence followed until both she and Charles asked simultaneously: "Just who the hell are you? Really?"

A tiny smile played over his face. "My name really is Petre Frichette, and I really am from those Frichettes. But I'm not seventeen, I'm thirty-five standards. My youthful appearance is part natural and part cosmetic surgery. People don't tend to be suspicious of kids—a very useful thing in my line of work."

"Just what is your line of work?" asked Regina icily.

"I'm a captain in the Protector's Special Security Forces."

Regina gasped. The SSF had a reputation for efficiency and... ruthlessness. She could understand how they'd gotten the reputation if Petre Frichette was a typical example.

"I joined the navy at fourteen," Frichette explained. "Made it to lieutenant commander by twenty-five, got tapped by the SFF, and I've been with them ever since."

"That would explain... a great deal," said Charles slowly.

Frichette nodded. "I was one of an eight-man team the Protector sent along to keep an eye on things. But when Citrone killed off all the rest of the team—including my boss—I had to... improvise."

"Well, you did a pretty good job—up until about an hour ago."

"I serve the Protector and his interests. I won't apologize for that."

"I don't think I like you much anymore, Petre," said Regina.

He shrugged. "One of the more common hazards in my business. But if it will help you think less badly of me, I have been rather thoroughly trained to act in the Protector's best interests. To unilaterally decide to nullify one of his orders because of a changing situation was... difficult. We're trained to use our initiative, but still... I'm not sure I could have done so without your help. Simply being 'the right thing to do' isn't usually good enough. Thank you for finding additional reasons. I have enough blood on my hands as it is, I don't need any more." He looked at her and she looked back. After a moment they both dropped their eyes.

"So what do you want now?"

"Oh, I was chatting a bit with Jeanine, here, and she mentioned that Doctor Ramsey had threatened to place the 'blame' for killing the Frecendi on you and turning you over to the locals. Is that true?"

"That's what he said, yes."

"And he implied that Governor Shiffeld was fully aware of those activities?"

"Yes, but why the concern? If you were willing to let a million people die, what do you care about what happens to me?"

"It's a matter of... jurisdiction, I guess you could say. The Frecendi aren't Protectorate citizens and not really my concern—until you convinced me otherwise. But you, Dame Regina, are a peer. Granted that you were made a peer by the governor, but even so, a plot to wrongly accuse you of a very serious action—and possibly subject you to some very serious consequences—is something I have to take notice of." He stared out the viewport for a moment before continuing.

"I think I shall have to pay a little visit to our dear governor. I'd like you to all attend and..." He paused when his communicator buzzed. He pulled out the device and held it to his ear. After a moment he frowned. "I'll be right there."

"Trouble?" asked Charles.

"Yes. It seems that the shuttle we came here in is gone."

"Gone?" said Regina. "But what could have..." She stopped when she saw Charles's face.

"Citrone was on board that shuttle, Regina."

Chapter Twenty-five

"**Y**ou all ready for this?" Charles Crawford looked to where Regina, Jeanine, and Petre were waiting. The two women nodded nervously. Petre just nodded. All during the voyage back to the fleet, Crawford had been studying Frichette. It seemed like he was acting differently: older, more confident, and in-charge. Or was it his imagination? Had he really been acting that way all along, and it was only the revelation of his true identity that was coloring Crawford's observations?

The voyage back had been at a much more sedate pace than the voyage out had been. It had taken a week and that was rather nice. Having Regina there was even nicer. Not that the week had been free from work — or worries. A steady stream of reports had come in that had to be read and answered; mainly reports from the construction site and damage reports from his squadron. Casualty reports. Casualties from the battle had been, well, Petre said they were gratifyingly light, but Crawford found them pretty shocking. Nearly a thousand dead, mostly from *Felicity*, *New Umbria*, and *Agamemnon*, and another thousand wounded. Petre said it was the usual ratio in space combat where the vacuum contributed to make survivable wounds fatal. He'd been relieved that Greg and Sheila were unharmed, but over a hundred of his own people were dead, including Beshar Hannah. He could not help but think if he'd just let Beshar escape with the family ships he'd still be alive. But if he'd let that happen, how many others would be dead now as a result? Sometimes there weren't any right answers.

The ships of the Rift Fleet were battered to a greater or lesser degree. Temporary repairs had been made where possible, but there was no sense of urgency. With the Venanci taken care of, there were no other threats on the horizon. The two Venanci transport ships had fled the system, and the other warships were either destroyed or captured. The odds of anyone else arriving were almost nil, and the only other possible source of danger would be the clans and — at least for now — they were still friends. Their losses had been relatively light, too, although any losses at all were very shocking for them. Overall, the feeling in the fleet and among the clans was one of relief. The crisis was over and everyone could get back to their real business.

That, in fact, was the most urgent task. They needed to get people back to work. The construction on the gate had fallen dangerously behind schedule and everyone was going to have to work like mad to catch up. The main induction ring pour was proceeding on schedule, but the assembly of the supporting equipment was over a month behind. He had to get the workers transferred from the warships back to where they really belonged. And that included himself: he'd been playing hooky far too long.

Unfortunately, there was still one, very unpleasant task to do.

"Dame Regina, Sir Charles, Jeanine," said Petre, "I'd strongly urge you to let me do the talking here. We cannot just go barging into the governor's office and accuse him of conspiracy."

"But that's what he's guilty of!" said Regina.

"That's what we *think* he's guilty of. The only evidence we have is Doctor Ramsey's claims."

"Then why are we even doing this?" demanded Crawford.

"I'm starting to have second thoughts about it, I'll admit. But I do want to see what we can shake out of Shiffeld while the incident is fresh. But please don't go flying off the handle in there, okay?"

Before anyone could answer, Shiffeld's receptionist appeared and directed them into the governor's private office. Shiffeld certainly did not look like a man worried about being accused of a serious crime: he smiled and stood up from his chair when they entered. "Ah, Lord Frichette—I suppose I should say: Lord Admiral Captain Frichette, shouldn't I? I must say you had me completely fooled! Although I suppose I should have wondered how someone so young and supposedly inexperienced could have done all the things you did. In any case, congratulations on your victory! And congratulations to you, too, Sir Charles, and to you, Dame Regina."

"Congratulations?" said Regina suspiciously, "for what?"

"Why for saving the Frecendi from annihilation! I'll tell you that I was stunned to learn of Doctor Ramsey's madness. I had talked with him a few times and I could see how jealous he was of your abilities, but I never dreamed it would drive him to something like this! Thank God you were able to stop him."

Regina's mouth was hanging open, but before she could say anything, Frichette stepped in. "Uh, yes, it was a near run thing, for sure. Before we left *Bastet*, I was going through Ramsey's records in search of evidence. You know, trying to find out who else was involved. He certainly could not have done it alone."

Shiffeld's face didn't even twitch. "Oh, no doubt he had a lot of unwitting help, like poor Miss Sorvall here who thought they were carrying out lawful orders. I don't think they should be treated too harshly, do you? I mean all's well that ends well. But as for the involvement of others, I'm quite certain all the evidence you'll find will prove that Ramsey acted entirely on his own."

"Uh… yes. I imagine you are quite right, Governor."

Regina twitched and Crawford seized her hand. She fixed an angry glare at him, but said nothing.

"Now, I've gone over your report from the battle and I must say it was a brilliant victory! Absolutely brilliant! I will insist that the Protector properly reward you—you and all of our commanders." He glanced at Crawford and smiled. "Our losses were low, the threat has been completely eliminated, and there is now nothing to prevent us from completing the gate and finishing our mission, correct?"

"I would say that was accurate," said Frichette.

"So it would seem," said Crawford. Regina said nothing.

"In fact," continued Shiffeld, "the only thing that disappoints me is the fact that the traitor, Citrone, managed to escape. When I arranged with the Seyotahs to have her transferred to your ship for security reasons, I assumed you'd take better care of her. I read your report, but I'm still rather amazed that you let this happen—considering how well you handled everything else."

"I take full responsibility, sir," said Frichette. "In my eagerness to see to the situation on Bastet, I did not think to leave a larger guard with Citrone. She overpowered the shuttle pilot and got away."

"And no one noticed?"

"She carefully kept *Bastet* between her and *Indomitable* during her boost. The people on *Indomitable* would have realized immediately that something was wrong if they'd seen the shuttle, but they couldn't spot it. The people on *Bastet*'s bridge did spot it, of course, but they didn't know what was going on and saw no reason to report it. It was over an hour before anyone realized what had happened and Citrone was gone by then."

"And you could not track her?"

"She shut down her systems after her initial boost and then waited until she was around the planet and beyond the sensor drone we'd launched earlier. Then she made a random course change. We looked, of course, but could not find anything. Four days later, a clan ship reported finding the shuttle and the pilot, but Citrone and Gillard were not aboard. They obviously transferred to some other ship. Finding them now will be difficult."

"Well, in light of your other successes, I don't think there's any need to put too much emphasis on this in any reports to the Protector, do you, My Lord?"

"I'll be making my own reports, sir, and I won't leave *anything* out."

Shiffeld frowned slightly. "I see."

"But, since the need for me as a fleet commander seems to have passed, I can revert to my original function. Or at least one of my original functions. With your permission, I'll begin work on tracking down Citrone. There's still a chance of finding her."

"Certainly. An excellent idea. It would be wonderful to see her brought to justice."

"It would be wonderful to see *someone* brought to justice," growled Regina, very quietly. Shiffeld did not appear to hear.

"But now, while I realize that we need to get everyone back to work, I think that a modest celebration of our victory is in order..."

An hour later they emerged from Shiffeld's office. Nothing at all was said until they were well out of earshot of any of his people. In fact, they didn't say anything until they were aboard a shuttle heading for *Neshaminy*. Finally, Regina could not hold it in any longer. "So, Shiffeld gets off Tosc-free?"

"For now," said Frichette. "The man is an expert at this sort of thing, and I'm quite certain he is right: I won't find any hard evidence implicating anyone but Ramsey. Shiffeld's far too clever to leave anything incriminating lying around."

Crawford nodded. "That's why there were no messages from him during our dash to reach *Bastet*. He realized what we were doing, but he could not tell us to cease and desist without revealing his role in it. He was willing to just stand aside and see how things went."

"And Ramsey probably told him we could not get there in time to stop him," said Regina bitterly.

"Ramsey was a fool to trust Shiffeld," said Crawford. "Now he'll take the fall for both of them."

"No less than he deserves!" spat Jeanine.

"I will, of course, be making a full report to the Protector when contact is re-established," said Frichette. "And my reports don't have to follow court-law; I can include all of my suspicions even if I don't have hard data to back them up. As for what action the Protector might take…"

"He'll probably give the bastard a medal!" snorted Regina.

"Quite possibly. All the bad guys don't always get their comeuppance in the end, Regina. And the Protector will be far more interested in having a batch of heroes than in a messy conspiracy case."

"I noticed Shiffeld's little bribe-threat to you by offering not to make a stink over Citrone's escape," said Crawford. "You going to take it?"

Frichette stared at him coldly. "As I said: I will be reporting everything. Maybe I could gloss it over in the report to the Protector himself, but the head of my department would catch it for sure. No, I'll have to face the music over that screw-up — unless I can catch Citrone in the next two years, of course."

"Not much chance of that."

"No, probably not," he sighed. "I have almost no contacts or resources here, and if Citrone has any brains, and I think she does, she'll leave the system as soon as she can. Oh well, I don't think she'll prove any further threat to Andera."

"I must say you don't seem all that upset about her escape, I'd almost think that you admire her."

"On a strictly emotional level and as a loyal Anderan, I'm appalled by what she did, of course. But I have to admit that it was a brilliant scheme. If you had not woken up early, Charles, it would have worked. On a pro-

- 330 -

fessional level, I do admire the operation, if not her, personally."

"But all those people died!" protested Regina.

"They were all military or civil administrators, legitimate targets in war time."

"But there isn't any war!"

"You mean there *wasn't* any war when we left, ten years ago. For all we know, the Venanci declared war six months ago. If so, then Citrone's actions were a legitimate ruse of war. Everyone takes advantage of that sort of communications lag—including us."

"So she gets away with her crime, too?" said Regina. "She murders nine thousand people and gets away with it and you say 'oh well, it was a brilliant operation'? Your sense of justice is a bit warped for my tastes, Petre."

"She also was instrumental in saving a million Frecendi. If it wasn't for her, they would be dead now. So count it a bargain exchange. I had a bit of a talk with her husband when they were aboard *Agamemnon*. He insists that Citrone was just a pawn working for the Venanci, and I tend to agree."

"Well, what's done is done," said Crawford. "Hopefully, we'll never see her again."

"Amen to that."

* * * * *

"I hate to impose on you again, Andra. But we won't be staying long. We just need you to hide us until we can arrange passage on a starship," said Brannon Gillard to his priestess friend.

Andra Roualet frowned. "You are really going to leave the system?"

"Yes, I think it is the only practical choice. Carlina is convinced that the Anderans will hunt her down and kill her if she remains here." Brannon glanced over at where his wife was reading a book from Andra's collection. "That's why I'm asking you for refuge instead of going home: we'll be harder to find here."

"But you had diplomatic safe passage, why did she insist on 'escaping' like that?"

"She did not trust the Anderans. And considering how badly they managed to get the Seyotah to stretch the rules, I have to agree with her. She's certain they will expend every effort to track her down and assassinate her."

"Would that be such a bad thing?" whispered Andra. "I understand that she murdered thousands of people!"

"She was just a tool in other peoples' hands, Andra. I... would not want to see her killed."

Andra looked at him very closely. "You care for her, don't you? This marriage wasn't just a diplomatic ploy, was it? Why Brannon, are you actually in love with her?"

"I think that perhaps I am. I used the same technique on her as I did the Seyotah boy—only a much deeper probing."

"Brannon! That was very dangerous!"

"I know. But I think it has done us both some good. I looked inside her, Andra, and I did not find an evil person. She's hurt, confused, and desperately in need of healing. But I think that, perhaps, I do love her."

"Perhaps you can heal each other." Brannon looked at Andra sharply. She was clearly referring to his dead wife—his first wife, he corrected. Had his sorrow and loneliness really been that obvious?

"In any case, we are asking for refuge. Will you grant it to us?"

"Of course I will. But I still can't believe the things I let you talk me into, Brannon!"

* * * * *

The celebration was... dull. Shiffeld had gone all-out to prepare a proper celebration aboard *Starsong*, but despite the excellent food and drinks and music, it was still dull. Crawford wasn't sure why, it just was.

"Our governor could have taken a few lessons from the Seyotah on how to throw a party," said Regina.

"Yes!" laughed Crawford. "I was just thinking the same thing."

"Not even any gardens to slip off to." She slid her arm around his waist, well, halfway around his waist; that was as far as she could reach.

"Well, there have to be a few empty cabins on this ship. Maybe we could..."

"Not likely. Shiffeld has spies everywhere. If he got word we had slipped off together, he'd suddenly decide he needed us for another round of toasts just to spite us. The bastard. Of course, we could go back to your quarters on *Neshaminy*..."

Crawford snorted. "They've got their own party going on over there. To celebrate the victory and Greg and Sheila's engagement. I don't think they'd be any likelier to leave us alone than Shiffeld. On the other hand, it would probably be a lot better party..."

"Except you don't like parties."

"Who told you that?"

"A few people. And my own astute observations."

"I guess it's true. I never felt comfortable at parties. Everyone was supposed to be having a good time and I never would, which only made me more uncomfortable. A feedback loop of sorts. After a little while I'd feel like the walls were closing in on me and I'd have to get out."

"You didn't seem that uncomfortable on Panmunaptra."

"No, that's true. Guess maybe it was the company." He gave her a squeeze.

"I'm flattered."

"No, I'm serious. I was so happy being with you, I just didn't notice what was going on around me. And while this party might be dull, I'm not uncomfortable at all."

"Well, that's good. But I think I'd like to see that party on Neshaminy, later."

"Knowing them, it will probably go on for hours yet. We'll have plenty of time."

They stood there for quite a while, letting the other celebrants flow around them. Holding Regina, he didn't feel the least bit uneasy. Yes, definitely the company.

Tad Farsvar came by and they exchanged a few words. The young man seemed about as comfortable as Crawford used to feel at parties, but it was far more understandable in this case. "So what will you do now, Tad?" asked Regina.

"Assuming my leaders don't need me for any more diplomatic duties, I think I shall go home."

"And do what?"

"Well, our family's commission from the trade agreement is already making us rather absurdly wealthy and I will be due a fair portion of that, personally, for being the first ones to spot you. I might even have enough to buy my own ship after a while. Then I could think about starting a family..."

"Really? Do you have anyone in mind?"

"Well, there is this girl."

"A good first step," said Crawford. "I recommend girls very highly." He squeezed Regina tightly until she hit him. "But what sort of ship? You were a prospector before."

"I might do that, although I'm thinking that trading might be more interesting—especially once your gate is finished. Will clan ships really be allowed through?"

"I would imagine. Although I could not begin to imagine what sort of licenses and fees would be involved."

"Well, that is some time in the future," said Tad. "For right now I will start with going home. You Newcomers certainly lead exciting lives, but I'm exhausted!"

They both laughed and Tad moved on. Crawford went back to pleasantly hanging on to Regina until he spotted Petre. He was surprised to see him standing next to Jeanine. Rather closely next to her, in fact. "Say, are they...?"

"Maybe," said Regina, with a lopsided smile. "She hasn't confided in me, but I think she was rather smitten by the brave, handsome young man who rescued her from a dark, dank dungeon."

"Uh, that would make sense, but I thought she … er, that her tastes were…"

"She's still finding herself, I think. However, I can't say I'm all that thrilled with her knight in armor."

"Hmmm, I was about to say that Petre's a good kid, but I have to remind myself that I really don't know a damn thing about who he really is. The Petre Frichette I thought I knew is just a facade."

"Well, if he hurts her, he'll have to answer to… to you."

"Me?"

"Well, you are a lot bigger and stronger. He won't be afraid of me."

"On the contrary, I think he'd be a lot more afraid of you. When you get charged up, you are damn scary."

"All right, we'll take him together."

"Sounds good. Or at least the together part does."

"Yes. Together does sound nice. I like you, Charles Crawford. I've told you that before."

"And I like you, Regina Nassau. But I'm not sure how much time together we're going to have for the next few years."

She nodded and squeezed him. "Yes, I have a planet to terraform."

He looked out through one of the huge viewports. In spite of the celebration, dozens of bright specks moved around the spot where an enormous ring was taking shape.

"And I have a gate to build."

Epilogue

Brannon Gillard, underpriest of the Lifegiver and Assistant Crèchemaster of the Hidran-Clorinda Clan, slowly walked down the row of gestators, carefully noting the readouts with the easy assurance of long familiarity. His practiced eye checked each of a dozen different indicators and verified them satisfactory, as much by instinct as by actually reading the numerical data. When he reached the last one and there had not been a single problem, he paused and gave thanks to the Lifegiver. This was a well-run facility, nearly as well-run as the one he had once administered, and problems were few.

He completed his shift without incident and then returned to the modest quarters which he shared with his wife. It had a small airlock where he changed out of his work clothes, put on his respirator, and let a strong blast of compressed air and suction pull away the chlorine. It had been decided that for safety's sake their home would be suited to Carlina's needs and he would wear a respirator, rather than vice-versa. A mishap with this arrangement would merely make him ill, while under the opposite conditions, Carlina could die in a matter of minutes. It was not a small sacrifice for him, but one he was glad to make. They had been together now for over two years and he had come to love her very much.

She met him on the other side of the airlock and embraced him warmly. She kissed him on the neck and he nuzzled her hair with his mask. As she pulled away, a tear dripped from one eye. At first he thought that something was wrong, but no, it was just some lingering trace of chlorine. It had happened a hundred times before, but it fooled him every time. In spite of every precaution, chlorine got loose in their home all too often. It must have been very irritating for her, but she never complained.

"How was your day?" she asked with a smile.

"Oh, nothing unusual. Archpriest Neerlam does things differently than I'm used to, but we get along."

"I'm sorry you had to take a subordinate position when we came here."

"I was lucky to find any position at all. Our arrival here was not exactly a common event. I might have had to become some wandering preacher, living off the kindness of strangers."

"Like I do?"

"We are hardly strangers anymore, my love. And you more than earn your keep."

"How?" she snorted. "By keeping the apartment tidy? Still, an ex-saboteur and mass-murderer should be grateful for any job she can get."

"I wish you would not refer to yourself that way."

"It is what I was, Brannon. You can forgive me for it, you can even try to get me to forgive myself, but nothing can change what I did."

"But it does no good to dwell on it. Think instead on the good things you have done."

"Like what?"

"Like the million lives you saved. Like the happiness you have brought me."

"Are you happy?"

"Yes, as a matter of fact, I am. I just wish I could make your life more fulfilling."

"I am fine. I spend my days on the information network learning more of your people. The time will come when I find a place where I can be useful." Her eyes fell and she looked troubled. "But I discovered something... interesting today."

"Oh? What?"

"It was a news item brought by a starship last week. You know that the Anderans have been sending out scouting ships from their base in Refuge?"

"Yes."

"Well, there has been a little contact between them and some of the nearest clan colonies—still a long way from here, thank the Maker."

"There's nothing new about that, it's been going on for a year or more."

"Yes, but this bit of news was about contact with a strange ship that was from beyond the Rift—but not Anderan."

"What? Who?"

"They weren't sure. But it was close enough to this area that it probably isn't Petrunan or Hebyrnan, so the only thing I can think of is that it was one of the Venanci transport ships."

"But I thought they went back across the Rift?"

"We assumed they did, but it's possible that one ship went back to take the news of what happened and the other stayed here. Maybe they are trying to find a habitable world to set up a colony. The Venanci troops have a nearly equal sex-ratio, so it would be possible if they found a suitable planet."

"That's...interesting. Where did this encounter take place?"

"No exact location was mentioned in the article, but I gather that it is several hundred light years from Refuge."

"They are trying to put some distance between themselves and the Anderans."

"Yes, that is what I thought. Oh well, it's all academic anyway. I have no interest in contacting them even if I could. My warrior days are over."

"I am glad of that. I think my fight may be over, too. I keep warning the people I meet about the threat of the World Stealers, but few are willing to listen."

"The threat probably seems very abstract and remote. You may get more converts when the Anderan gate is finished and their colonizers come swarming through."

"It may be too late then."

"Perhaps, but the Perseus Arm is huge. I hope they will leave your people in peace."

"So I keep praying." He paused and looked at her a little shyly. "I... uh... I have been doing some research myself."

"Oh? What about?"

"I was... I was looking at the possibility of adapting one of our gestators so that it could handle your genome." He looked at her nervously, unsure of her reaction. Her eyebrows shot up.

"Brannon, are you talking about *children*?"

"Well...yes. If you wanted one, of course."

"I... I'm not sure what I want. Whose child would it be? I mean I can donate the egg, but how...?"

"That would be the big question. There is no possibility of using my unaltered DNA, the result would be totally unviable. But there could be ways to introduce certain aspects of my genome into your own. The result would be... ours."

"You can do this?"

"There have been some experiments in the past with cross-clan pregnancies. A few have worked out. I would have to do a great deal of additional research and some experimentation. But only if you agree." He looked at her, trying to gauge her reaction. With great care, they had found ways that they could safely make love, but this was something different. He tried to find some memory from those he'd borrowed from her to give a clue to what she might be feeling, but could not.

"I'm going to have to think about this, Brannon," she said at last.

"Of course. As long as you like. We have all the time in the universe."

* * * * *

Tad Farsvar touched the controls on his ship and the bow thrusters nulled out the last of its motion relative to the Newcomers' gate. *His* ship! He could still hardly believe it. She was small, but brand new and even had the new artificial gravity devices. Her cargo capacity was modest, as was her drive and fuel bunkerage, but she would do very well as a free trader. It was not as though he actually had to turn a profit with her. He had money in the bank. No, he wasn't planning on making a big profit, but it would be nice if his... hobby could at least pay for itself.

"Life! It certainly is big, isn't it?" He turned and smiled as Sasha came into the control room. She was staring, wide-eyed, at the enormous structure hanging a few dozen kilometers away. "I mean, I've seen asteroids that were much bigger, but they built this all from scratch!"

"Yes, it is amazing. And they did this in just two years." Sasha sat down next to him and he took her hand. They had been formally betrothed a few weeks ago and they were now in their pre-marriage, cohabitation trial. So far it had been going very well. Tad had thought that this little trip might be a nice getaway, and so it had proved.

"Is it working?" she asked. "The news reports said that was, but I don't see anything except the gate—and a lot of ships."

"I gather that the hyperspatial 'carrier wave' is invisible. You can only see anything when a ship actually passes through. But it is working. Several test ships have gone through in each direction in the last few days."

"But today is the official 'grand opening'?"

"Yes, some big delegation of Anderan leaders will be coming through today. There will be all sorts of ceremonies and celebrations."

"And we're invited?"

"Yes. But we don't have to go if..." He stopped when he saw Sasha go all starry-eyed. Tad found the Newcomers' ceremonies boring, their parties stuffy, and not much fun. But Sasha clearly was thrilled at the idea of being included. Oh well, it would probably be a lot nicer having her along. He'd survive.

"And after the ceremonies... are we really going to go through the gate?" Her eager expression faded into apprehension.

"If we are allowed. There's still been no official word on clan ships using the gate. But a lot of people want to." He glanced at the sensor display; several hundred hopeful clan ships had gathered, although none had been allowed to approach as closely as Tad—there were advantages in knowing the right people. But he wasn't sure what would happen next. He had a nice cargo of fissionables to trade if he was allowed through.

"It's hard to believe we could just go through there and be in another whole star system," whispered Sasha. "It's kind of scary, too. What if we can't get back?"

"I don't think the Newcomers would spend all this time and effort on a one-way gate, Love. Of course if your drive should fail..."

"The drive is just fine, thank you very much! It's your navigation we should be worried about." Tad smiled. Sasha was a very good engineer, despite her youth and relative inexperience. Not that he was any older or much more experienced as a ship's captain...

"If they do let us through, how far were you planning to go?"

His immediate reaction was to answer: 'as far as I can', but he knew that would not sit well with her. But in truth, that was what he wanted to do. He'd always wanted to get out among the stars and see new places. But even his newfound wealth wasn't enough to buy a starship, and positions in the crews of the few starships that the clan did own were highly prized and hard to get.

But with the gates you didn't need starships!

Apparently, on the other side of the Rift there were gates like this one (well, smaller gates) linking nearly every inhabited star system. You could get almost anywhere worth going in a normal ship. The prospect was dazzling. Tad wanted to just go and go and go. But Sasha wasn't quite so daring (reckless, she would say). So, something a little more modest for the first trip.

"Oh, I think just to the other side of the Rift and back." He paused and then laughed. "Just to the other side of the Rift! I can't believe I said that. A thousand parsecs and back again! Incredible!"

Sasha laughed, too. She was amazingly pretty when she laughed and Tad leaned over and kissed her. She kissed him back and they became so involved in that they almost missed what they had come here to see.

"Oh! Look! Something's happening!" cried Sasha.

Tad disentangled himself and looked where she was pointing. The empty area inside the ring of the gate was shimmering. Stars and vessels on the opposite side began to blur and ripple as if viewed through a sheet of falling water. As he watched, the ripples were tinged with a wildly shifting spectrum of colors. Then the colors combined into a dazzling white flash, and for a moment he was looking through into *somewhere else*. A large vessel was suddenly there, where an instant before there had been nothing. The ship moved out from the gate and then the ripples were back again.

The newly arrived ship maneuvered clear and then the process repeated itself and another ship was here, flung across the Rift in an instant. Ship after ship passed through the gate and Sasha was gaping in astonishment. "Wow!" she gasped. "That's incredible!"

It was incredible, but Tad was hardly paying attention to the ships. During the instant that each ship made the jump, he could see through, to the other side of the gate. There were stars on the other side. And the stars were beckoning to him.

* * * * *

"My God, is he bringing the whole bloody fleet with him?" grumbled Sir Charles Crawford. "We've been watching this parade for an hour already and the Protector's ship hasn't even come through yet!"

"We've only been waiting twenty minutes, dear," said Regina, patting his arm. "But I agree: he is overdoing this. On the other hand, it is certainly a spectacular opening for your gate."

"It's not mine anymore. Once the construction is done and the operations staff formally takes charge it's not mine anymore."

"That might be true for some normal gate, Chuck," said Sheila Van-Vean from a few meters away, "but not this one. The big wigs might name it after some other big wig, but for anyone who ever worked on this project, it will always be 'Crawford's Gate'."

"Damn right," said Greg VanVean. "Without you riding all of our asses it never would have been done in time. Hell, without you, the stinking thing would be hooked up to some Venanci gate right now."

"The main thing is that you all did it," said Regina. "It was the thing you came here to do and you did it."

"Well now," said Greg, "that must be his High, Grand Imperial Muckety-Muckedness now." He pointed to the ship coming through the gate. It was the biggest one they had seen by far.

"Yes, that's *Invincible*," said Crawford. "Congratulations, folks, the Protector is here and this is now officially Anderan territory."

"Whether the clans like it or not," snorted Regina.

"Hey, the march of progress," said Greg. "You can either get in step or get trampled. That's the way it's always been."

"Unfortunately."

"Well," said Crawford to change the subject, "we have to be over on *Invincible* for all the hoopla in less than two hours, Regina. We better get changed. I can't believe I'm going to have to wear that ridiculous... er, I mean that marvelous uniform again." He glanced at Sheila, who laughed.

"You look wonderful in your uniform, Chuck."

"Yes, he does," agreed Regina.

"And I'm sure you'll come back with a chestful of medals to hang on it, Boss," said Greg. "And your knight's sash and sword. You will really look the fop then!"

"I suppose. Assuming the Protector confirms the knighthood."

"He will," said Regina. Then she grimaced. "And mine, too, I imagine. He's had a week since the first test ship went through and brought him all the news. It's like Petre said: he'll want heroes, not scapegoats."

"So, Sir Charles," said Greg, "when are you starting your own firm, and when can we sign up?"

"Oh, that will take some time. It will take a lot of negotiations with the baron and then I have to find financing..."

"You may have more money than just twelve years back pay," said Regina. "I'm sure there will be rewards and grants coming your way. I understand you'll get a share of any prize money for the captured Venanci ships, and any ransom gotten for their crews, too."

"Huh. Hadn't even thought about that. Well, it will still take some time. Have to go back and do some thinking and planning."

"What about you, Regina?" asked Sheila.

She stared out the viewport and shook her head. "I'm not going back," she said quietly.

"What?"

"I'm not going back to Andera. I didn't like what was happening there before we left and I doubt I'm going to like what I'll find there now. It's becoming filled with people like Petre Frichette. Oh sure, he's a nice young man, but he'd have let a million people die if he thought it was in the Protector's best interest. I can't deal with that sort of thinking. I'm not going back."

A chill went through Crawford. He'd become very fond of Regina and he didn't want to lose her now. "But... but what will you do?"

"Well, there will be a need for terraformers on this side of the Rift, too. Probably a big need. Heck, I could probably find work among the clans if I had to."

Crawford stood there in confusion, uncertain what to say, until Sheila nudged him. "Hey, big guy, seems to me there will be a need for construction firms on this side of the Rift, too. A zillion new gates to build."

"And who says that a construction outfit can't have a terraforming department?" added Greg.

Crawford looked at Greg, then at Sheila, finally at Regina. "Crawford & Nassau Construction?"

"Crawford & Nassau Construction & Terraforming."

"C&N Construction & Terraforming?"

"C&N *Worldbuilders*," said Regina firmly.

"Not bad," said Greg.

"I like that," said Sheila.

Crawford looked out the viewport and put his arm around Regina. He looked out, past the assembled ships, to where the stars were beckoning.

"Yeah, so do I."

The End

Look for more books from Winged Hussar Publishing, LLC – E-books, paperbacks and Limited Edition hardcovers. The best in history, science fiction and fantasy at:

https://www. wingedhussarpublishing.com
or follow us on Facebook at:

Winged Hussar Publishing LLC
Or on twitter at:

WingHusPubLLC
For information and upcoming publications